## ARMY JAILS HER

In a stunning exa~~mple~~ ~~of military~~ bungling, the Army jailed Private Charles Connolly for desertion.

Connolly, whom Lieutenant Colonel Van Klomp of the 1st HAR Airborne said "should be considered for as many medals as he can wear and still stand up under the weight," was listed as dead when a Magh' advance overran his position.

Buried alive in a cave-in, Connolly survived, dug himself out and fought courageously on behind enemy lines. Battling million-to-one odds with a group of loyal Military Animals, he succeeded in rescuing the daughter of our late Chairman, Virginia Shaw.

Against all probability and with suicidal courage he and his companions then managed to destroy the force-field generator, allowing our heroic 5th Infantry Brigade to make their dramatic advance in Sector Delta 355. Private Connolly, described by Virginia Shaw in her interview on her release as "the finest soldier," was liberated during Major Fitzhugh's successful push forward.

However, when he returned to his base, Colonel G. Brown, CO of Camp Marmian, promptly had Connolly arrested for desertion because the record listed him as "died in action."

When questioned later by reporters, Colonel Brown placed the blame on the camp's clerk, whom he said would be severely punished.

## Baen Books by Eric Flint

### Ring of Fire series:
*1632* by Eric Flint
*1633* by Eric Flint & David Weber
*Ring of Fire* ed. by Eric Flint
*1634: The Galileo Affair* by Eric Flint & Andrew Dennis
*Grantville Gazette* ed. by Eric Flint
*Grantville Gazette II* ed. by Eric Flint
*1634: The Ram Rebellion* by Eric Flint with Virginia DeMarce et al.
*1635: Cannon Law* with Andrew Dennis (forthcoming)

### Joe's World series:
*The Philosophical Strangler*
*Forward the Mage* (with Richard Roach)

*Mother of Demons*

*Crown of Slaves* (with David Weber)

*The Course of Empire* (with K.D. Wentworth)

### With Mercedes Lackey & Dave Freer:
*The Shadow of the Lion*
*This Rough Magic*

### With Dave Freer:
*Rats, Bats & Vats*
*The Rats, The Bats & The Ugly*

*Pyramid Scheme*

### With David Drake:
*The Tyrant*

### The Belisarius Series
*An Oblique Approach*
*In the Heart of Darkness*
*Destiny's Shield*
*Fortune's Stroke*
*The Tide of Victory*
*The Dance of Time*

### Edited with David Drake & Jim Baen
*The World Turned Upside Down*

### With Ryk E. Spoor:
*Mountain Magic* (with David Drake & Henry Kuttner)
*Boundary*

# R<sup>THE</sup>ATS, B<sup>THE</sup>ATS & <sub>THE</sub>UGLY

# ERIC FLINT
# DAVE FREER

THE RATS, THE BATS & THE UGLY

A Baen Books Original

Baen Publishing Enterprises
P.O. Box 1403
Riverdale, NY 10471
www.baen.com

ISBN 10: 1-4165-2078-3
ISBN 13: 0-978-4165-2078-8

Cover art by Bob Eggleton

First paperback printing, August 2006

Distributed by Simon & Schuster
1230 Avenue of the Americas
New York, NY 10020

Library of Congress Cataloging-in-Publication Data:
2004014347

Printed in the United States of America

# To the world's beasts

**HARMONY & REASON**

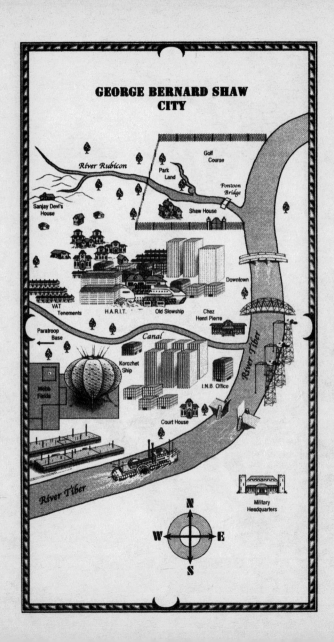

## DRAMATIS PERSONAE

### Hominidae

Chip: A vat-grown conscript. A thing of rags and tatters.
Ginny: A damsel of high degree-o.
Fitz: The very model of a modern Major.
Van Klomp: A large parachute officer.
Sanjay Devi: Hecate.
John Needford: A schemer, well-dressed.
Len Liepsich: A schemer, hitching up his pants.
Mike Capra: A legal beagle.
Ogata: A legal eagle.
Talbot Cartup: A villain in the first degree.
General Cartup-Kreutzler: His brother-in-law; and accomplice.
Tana Gainor: the original asp in Cleopatra's bosom; with bosom.

### Rattae

Fal: Great of stomach and small of martial vigor.
Doll: A rattess of considerably negotiable virtue.
Melene: A rat damsel of acumen and a very attractive tail.
Pistol: One-eyed rat-at-arms.
Nym: A veritable giant among rats; with a mechanical bent.
Doc: Rat philosopher and medic.
Ariel: A rattess of fell repute; and always with Fitz.
Pooh-Bah: A rat of many parts.

### Battae

Bronstein: She-bat who must be obeyed.
O'Niel: A somewhat plump bat, fond of drink.
Eamon: A large and dangerous bat.

### Et Alia

Fluff: Alias Kong
Yetteth: Jampad; a prisoner on the Korozhet ship.
Darleth: Jampad; head of the Ratafia

Various Korozhet villains.

And a large supporting cast, numbering in millions for the greatest production off Earth!

# Prologue

❧

*The planet Harmony and Reason, a human colony;*
*a starship, both vast and alien, in the middle of*
*George Bernard Shaw City, the colony's capital.*
*At center stage: five Korozhet conspirators,*
*all members of the inner-high,*
*in their adjoining waterbaths.*

"The un-implanted human, the one that was reported to the spawnship as being involved in this disaster, must certainly die—and as soon as possible. He will have seen too much when he rescued the juvenile Shaw creature."

So spoke the Ruling Five-high, with the certainty that always characterized her while in female form.

The Purple Seventh-instar clattered its spines in

1

vigorous agreement. "While he is a low-status creature, we cannot overestimate the importance of this human's immediate death. It was from just such neglect that the campaign against the Jampad suffered. Serious steps must be taken with the human military. Fortunately, we have virtually complete control of their command structure. We will of course not be betrayed by the implanted human or the uplifted creatures. Nonetheless, I agree it is wise to have the implanted human taken into custody as their social structure makes her death undesirable. Difficult, for a certainty."

"Do you think that this 'Cartup' will understand the implications of the device he has been provided with for securing her compliance?" asked the High Five-spike. "There are certain inherent dangers involved. We do not want the trigger phrases to be discovered."

"The calculators indicate a very low probability. He is unaware that the device would affect anyone except this 'Virginia Shaw.' He is quite unaware of what it actually does. It contains the standard self-destruct booby traps, after all."

In the diffuse green light, cringing figures moved hastily between the spiky shadows reclining in their waterbaths. The slaves were careful not to make any noise that might disturb their masters. To do so was to invite certain pain, if not death, and even the most wretched slaves still clung to life. The air was full of hissing sighs. The squat, blue-furred, four-armed slave carrying the bucket of live baby Nerba, the master species' favorite snack, almost gagged at the thickness of the naphthalene reek.

"Still. One of the Overphyle is dead at the hands of a human. We cannot allow subject races to think that this is even possible—let alone something that will go unpunished. Is there any chance that word could spread back among the Magh' nests or the human hives?"

The Nerba-carrier did not allow the faintest change in his posture or manner to betray his pleasure. The implant in his head said that the death of one of the Overphyle was an awful thing—but the Nerba-carrier's hatred of the Overphyle, and all their works, was almost as intrinsic to him as the programming not to attack a Korozhet was in his implanted soft-cyber chip.

He walked closer to one of the inner-high, and placed the Nerba cub on the floor. The soft-furred little creature creeled weakly and hungrily. A dart hissed out of one of the Korozhet killing spines, and impaled it. The little thing screamed as the neurotoxins were pumped into it. The Purple Seventh-instar heaved itself out of the bath, humped over the prey, and began to evert its stomach into the snack. Nerba died slowly, and this one was still pleading weakly as the digestive enzymes liquefied its flesh.

Controlling his revulsion, the slave walked on to the next inner-high of the Pentarch. This one was speaking, so he waited, respectfully. "They are still putative subjects. I hold, despite their dexterity, that these humans will make poor slaves."

The Purple Seventh-instar that was busy feeding clattered its spines again. "Those we have captured and implanted have proved more than adequate."

"But their ability to resist our Magh' client-species is better than predicted. And if the confused reports coming

from their media are to be believed, there is a possibility
that our plans and works might be uncovered."

As always, that being its principal function, the High
Five-spike was the voice of caution. The Ruling Five-high
shifted in her waterbath.

"It is a low probability, considering the level of influence we have on their leadership structure. But
nonetheless we must send in a clean-up squad. And
perhaps step up supplies of materiel from the spawnship
to our client-species. See that the Magh' are contacted
on the closed beam, and given such information as the
clean-up team can gather. As a final alternative there is
always direct action. We have a large slave army, potentially, at our disposal."

The youngest of the inner-high flicked his spines in
respectful assent. The slave had learned to read the clat-
ters as clearly and easily as the soft-cyber implant had
taught him the Overphyle's speech. The youngest of the
inner-high was still diffident in his suggestions. He was
only a sixth instar, after all. "Perhaps some chemical
agents, Highest? And some more sophisticated delivery
mechanisms, for the client-species?"

"Yes. And bring my snack, slave. Before I dine on you."

The slave did. Then moved cautiously away, as hastily
as he dared. He was just in earshot when he heard one of
them say something that made him nearly drop his bucket.
"Do you think that there is any substance in the report
that a Jampad was freed in this debacle?"

The slave desperately wanted to stay and listen. But
he dared not. There were slaves of some seven different
species on this ship. But he was the only one of his kind,
and he had not believed there could be others, so many

light-years from home. Had one of his people succeeded in breaking free?

*Elsewhere in George Bernard Shaw City,
in a space more cavernous but no less dark.
At center stage: other conspirators.*

The third of the plotters, as usual, arrived late for the meeting.

"Where the hell have you been?" demanded one of those already there. "How can somebody with a reputation for being a genius not read a clock? You know—those gadgets that have two hands, one long, one short."

"Save that tone for those who intimidate easily. You ought to know by now it's wasted on me. Besides, I've been productively occupied."

The conspirators, from long years working together, knew each other's tastes. One of them smiled evilly at the tardy one. "Killing swine, eh?"

"Not yet. Just sharpening the blades."

When the meeting was over, the old tastes resurfaced.

"When shall we three meet again?"

The other two laughed. "When the hurlyburly's done, of course," chuckled one of them.

"And the battle's lost and won," added the other, in a grimmer tone of voice. "Assuming you don't show up late again."

# Chapter 1

Ꮟ

*The colony world of Harmony and Reason.*
*Enter a military vehicle, returning from the front.*
*Its motley inhabitants, each in their own fashion,*
*celebrating the first victory of humankind and*
*its allies against the alien Magh' invaders.*

"Hic!"

Private Chip Connolly looked up into the terrifying upside-down gargoyle-face. The long white canine teeth gleamed against the twisted, folded blackness of that face. The batwings briefly unfolded, as the jeep hit some severe corrugations.

"Hic!" said the plump bat again, dangling from the metal struts that held the canvas cover.

"Why are you making that funny noise, O'Niel?" asked

Virginia, snuggling into Chip and blinking myopically at the bat.

The bat blinked back at her. "Why Ginny, 'tis traditional when you're drunk as drunk can be. And it is feeling I am as if the drunk is turning into a hangover, indade. So in the interest o' prolonging the drunk, I'm after stickin' to the tradition."

Chip grinned. There was something reassuring about the fact that after all they'd been through, the bats still stuck to their phony Irish accent, right down to the detail of saying "indade" instead of "indeed."

"The normal method," he explained considerately, "is to drink some more." Bats were new to strong drink. It was only in the interests of trans-species friendship that they'd ventured on it at all.

The cyber-uplifted bat's genome had been spliced heavily with the leaf-nosed Rhinolophidae. It wasn't possible for the evil black crinkled face to turn pale. But the bat shuddered. "Indade . . . no. I . . . I couldn't, Chip." Somehow the voice managed to carry the very essence of a green pallor.

A long nose twitched up from underneath the seat. It was the front part of a ratlike creature the size of a small Siamese cat, which, with a stoatlike lithe sinuosity flowed up onto the seat. The ratty thing had an eye-patch, a bottle of grog and a suitably piratical expression to go with these accouterments. He waved the bottle at O'Niel in a friendly fashion. "Here, you fat swasher, take some sack."

The bat shuddered, shook his head so vigorously that his large ears flapped. By the pained grimace that followed, he plainly regretted that action. "No . . ." he said, weakly.

The elephant shrew wrinkled its long nose, and with a red-toothed snigger waved the bottle under the bat's nose. "I'faith, methinks 'tis a fine brew, and here we are back on wheels. 'Twas the best way to travel you said. You had to choose between drinking and flying, and, as you had a vehicle, you gave up the flying."

"To be sure, I am fond o' vehicles, Pistol," said the bat. He looked disdainfully at the truck. "Though, indade, this one is no patch on a foine noble beastie loike the tractor, but I'm after wondering if they can arrest the motion o' this one for a while. 'Tis vilely ill I think I am about to be." O'Niel descended in a sprawl of wings onto the seat.

Pistol winked at Chip and Virginia. "I will not say 'greasy egg,' O'Niel—or what of a fine fatty slab of cold Maggot?"

Chip was always amazed at the range of expression that the soft-cyber-uplifted creatures could coax out of their voice-synthesizers. Rats didn't have a lot of spare sympathy for anyone at the best of times, and, on the subject of hangovers, even less. But O'Niel, who could normally give as good as he got, looked distinctly unwell. Best keep the peace . . .

Before he could intervene, however, the bat lurched erect and launched for the open back of the truck. He didn't quite make it and landed clumsily on the last seat, retching.

A gargantuan ear-shattering bellow of outrage erupted. "Santa Maria, San' Marco . . . San' Cristophoro . . . you *conjone*less flying mouse! Watch where you are up-a-bringing!"

The owner of the vast voice stood up and shook a furious fist at the hapless bat. The creature was considerably smaller than his voice—and smaller than the bat. Except for his tail, the little lemurlike galago would have fitted into a soup mug. He wore the remains of a frogged red velvet waistcoat, and made up for his size with volume and attitude.

The huge-eyed miniature primate-caballero twitched his tail angrily. Flicked at a spot on his waistcoat. "My honor she is impinged upon! To say nothing of my precious waistcoat! I challenge you, you . . . *fledermaus*. I demand a duel!"

"Name your seconds, sir!" he bellowed at the hapless bat. The bat was at least twice the soft-furred galago's size, but was certainly in no condition to respond.

O'Niel groaned and clung to the tailgate of the truck with his wing claws. "If it is killing me you wish, Don Fluff, could you not be after doin' it quietly? It's something of the headache I have."

"Indade. Will you all be shutting up?" demanded another sleeper, in the Irish accent of the bat-voice synthesizers.

Then the vehicle veered wildly. It overcorrected and skidded, tossing them all about. With a squeal of brakes, it bounced, nearly rolled. Righted . . . and then came to a stop at about a forty-five degree angle.

Chip picked himself up off the floor, off Ginny. She was smiling worriedly up at him. "Is your arm all right?" she asked.

"I'm fine," he said, feeling at the laser wound on his shoulder. The infantry doctor had said it should recover more easily than a knife wound would have. "Everybody else okay?"

The bats had taken to the wing when the crash occurred. They were all fine. The fierce caballero had flung himself into Virginia's arms, and clung as tightly as only a small primate can. "I had to protect you, *señorita*," he said, shakily.

Meanwhile Chip was doing a quick roll-call of rats.

They were all unhurt, barring Pistol, who was nursing a cut paw-hand and lamenting over the loss of his looted bottle of over-proof brandy.

And Nym. The gigantic rat of mechanical inclination was missing. For an awful moment, Chip thought he must have been flung out of the vehicle, and be lying broken at the roadside.

Then the horrible truth dawned. Obviously, to judge by the vile language issuing from Bronstein, Fat Fal and even Doc, the same thing had dawned on all of them.

"Who let that shogging mad bastard whoreson drive?!" demanded Fal.

It proved to be true enough. Chip crawled backwards, out into the ditch full of glutinous mud, and then around to the cab. The trooper who had been driving was still sitting there, staring in shock at the ditch . . . and the stone wall they'd missed. Barely. And Nym was still clutching the wheel, his eyes manic and his snout still contorted in a wild grin, making *brrm-brmmm* noises.

Chip shook his head and sat down in the mud and started laughing.

Three minutes later, they had hauled the shocked driver out of the vehicle, even if it was apparent that the vehicle was not coming out of the ditch.

The trooper shook his head. "He said he could drive . . . So I thought it would do no harm to have him stand on my lap and let him hold the wheel . . ."

"Here," said Nym waving a bottle at him. "Some griefs are med'cinable. 'Twas not a patch on the tractor, but not a bad vehicle to drive."

"Drive? Drive! You mad animal—" The driver coughed as he took an unwary swallow of the proffered drink. It was raw, uncolored, high-test brandy looted from an abandoned wine-farm. It would have made great lighter fluid.

They all pushed. The rats and bats didn't have much push to offer, given their mass, but they tried. They bounced, heaved at the truck. Piled rocks in the ditch. Became covered in mud . . . and the vehicle stayed embedded in the mud-churned ditch.

"Well, at least we're stuck in the mud on this side of our lines," said Chip, digging for a jack behind the seat of the jeep. "And I'm not in that much of hurry to rejoin the army, anyway."

"Yes. Things could be worse," said Doc cheerfully, offering Melene some of the brandy. "One has to view this in Neoplatonistic terms, I think."

"Adversity's sweet milk, philosophy," said Fal sourly. "Spare me. So what do we do now? Send the bats to fetch a rescue?"

"Indade, no. I think we hang tight. A vehicle will be along presently and they can pull us out." O'Niel was one of nature's laziest fliers.

"Methinks 'tis goodly advice," said Pistol, stealing Fal's bottle. "If they're going to hang us for this, that is. If I have any choice I'll not hang sober."

" 'Twas not what I meant," said the bat. "I meant a comfortable dangle by our feet."

Standing in the soft rain, looking at the truck in the

ditch, listening to the rats and bats bicker amicably, with a mutual lack of understanding—despite a common tongue, Virginia Shaw had to think about her own implant. An alien-built, lentil-sized chip of imprinted semiconducting plastic that had given back her life . . . only it wasn't quite her old life. Without the soft-cyber implant between the hemispheres of her brain, she'd been a child in an adult body, with a damaged speech center and uncontrollable tantrums born out of confusion and an inability to communicate. With the implant, her parents had found their brain-damaged child a far more socially acceptable mechanical doll, no longer able to shame the colony's first family with her condition.

They'd never realized that she wasn't a doll. She had become a person. She was shaped, perhaps, by the material downloaded into her soft-cyber's memory chips. In her case, Brontë had had a large effect. But, just as the rats remained ratlike despite Shakespeare and Gilbert and Sullivan, and the bats remained bats, despite Wobbly songs and Irish folk music, she remained human despite the implant. Not a doll, but someone who could think, reason and love.

She looked fondly at Chip. Private Charles Connolly . . .

Now attempting to put a jack under a vehicle that was chassis-deep in mud. He was neither Heathcliffe nor Edward Rochester. He was just himself: a Vat-born human, born in poverty, raised to servitude, indebted for life to the company of which her father had been the majority shareholder. A company whose founding purpose, in theory, had been to build a new utopia based on the ideals of Fabian Socialism.

Like the truck, the ideal had lost its course, got stuck

in the ditch and was now axle deep in the mud. It had become trapped in entrenched privilege. It had betrayed the trust that the clone-fathers of such men as Chip had put in the dream. And now, with the Magh' invasion, the new Utopian dream had become bogged down in worse: Enslaving two new-created species, the rats and the bats— on the assumption that they were biomechanical cannon fodder, not creatures of reason who should be accorded the same rights as any sentient being.

Like getting the jeep out of the ditch, it wasn't going to be easy to change the status quo. It had taken betrayal, capture and living side-by-side with them, having her own implant, and then falling in love, to do it for her.

As if he'd been aware of her gaze, Chip turned and looked at her. He dropped the jack, walked over, and took her in his arms. "Chin up, Ginny. It's not that bad."

She smiled at him. She couldn't wait for new glasses, to see him clearly again. Not, she admitted to herself, that he was the nobly born, handsome-faced, swallow-tail-coat clad hero that she'd once dreamed of. He was short, stocky, spiky-haired, and full of combat-scars. The battered remains of his uniform bore not even the vaguest resemblance to an elegant coat of superfine. He was, as the bats put it, as common as vatmuck. But he was a hero, her hero, and worth ten of any noble from between the covers of a Regency romance. She kissed him, treasuring what she'd found.

"I am surprised it's not a full-on debauch you'd be indulging in," said a disapproving Bronstein.

Chip was good at ignoring Bronstein, at least while he was kissing Virginia. Well, if by "ignoring" he meant not standing to attention and doing what Senior BombardierBat Michaela Bronstein said. The bat was one of nature's organizers. But kissing Ginny was a powerful distraction. He'd wasted a lot of time thinking her one of the vile Shareholder class. Someone better put up against the wall and shot, than kissed. It had taken everything the war and treachery could throw at him to change his mind.

Fat Falstaff, the paunchiest of the rats, snorted. Chip watched him with one eye while continuing his lip-and-tongue gymnastics. Fal turned to his henchman, Pistol, who was sampling the canvas cover of the jeep for flavor. Knowing the rats had engaged in rampant gluttony less than an hour ago, and, in the way of field soldiers on this or any other world, had packs bulging with looted food, Chip wasn't too worried. Otherwise—given the rats' metabolic rate—once they started to eat the furniture, it was usually a sign that you might be next on the menu. For all that the alien cybernetics had uplifted the cloned creatures they remained essentially shrewlike. Their morality was not that of humans. Actually, they only had any morals at all, if and when it suited them.

"Well, Auncient Pistol? What think you? Methinks 'tis fine talk from a set of cozening flyboys who have mass orgies."

Pistol shook his head mournfully and spat out a piece of canvas. "No texture this stuff has. I say for a good long-lasting well-flavored chew you can't beat Maggot-hide, and a few little kickshaws on the side—like a fresh Maggot. But," he added, composing his villainous face into his best effort of injured sanctimoniousness, "if you refer to the amorous peck of our companions, and the self-righteous 'plaint of the bats . . . You have the right of it. To think of all of them indulging in the slipping of the muddy conger in concert, in a public place like that. Shocking, I call it."

The bats rose to the bait. Bats, Chip had long since concluded, were a trifle dim that way. They thought deeply about things, which rats never did. Politics was meat and drink to them, and argument about it was as intrinsic as breathing. Humor and sarcasm, natural to the rats, came only with effort to the bats—if it came at all.

"Indade, 'tis not like that!" protested Eamon. "We're a social species, and live together. Estrus just occurs simultaneously. We're faithful to our spouses."

Doll Tearsheet, reputed to be the naughtiest rat-girl in the army, lowered her eyelashes and said thoughtfully: "I'faith, 't must be true they're full. To think of waiting a year before having to do it again."

"You mean, to think of being able to wait a year," grinned Melene, the littlest rat-girl. Her tail was firmly entwined around her chosen partner, the philosopher Doc. "Mayhap after such a public orgy they know not how to look their fellows in the face again, until the level of passion doth again become too much."

"Begorra! It's not like that, I tell you!" The bat O'Niel was now plainly feeling better, having cast up the cause of his afflictions. He turned to his friend and chief drink-purveyor, the rat philosopher. Doc—or Georg Friedrich Hegel, or, as he had lately renamed himself, Pararattus—was an experiment in the download tolerance of the soft-cyber implant. They'd put the whole of Hegel's *Phenomenology of the Spirit* and *Science of Logic* into the chip's memory.

The chip hadn't cracked, but one had to be less certain

about the philosophical rat's sanity. Still, given the dire state of the war effort, even experiments such as he had been drafted into the line. He was—as an aside from being a bad philosopher—a very good medic.

"Doc, explain to her, 'tis not wanton slaves to constant lust that we be, like rats or humans. 'Tis . . . 'tis . . ."

Doc nodded. "Merely biologically different, with each species considering theirs the only right and proper way to do things," he supplied, wrapping his tail around his love's in turn. "And you bats should, by now, comprehend that it is not disgust, but envy, that motivates the mockery of such as Pistol."

The bats blinked at the idea. Michaela Bronstein was, as usual, the quickest on the uptake "You mean . . . ?" She looked in horror at the one-eyed rat, who was winking lewdly at her.

Pistol nodded cheerfully. "We'd love an invitation next time, you saucy winged jade."

Bronstein shook her head. "Rats!"

"That's us," said Fat Falstaff cheerfully. "Mind you, I am not so sure about doing it upside down. There is a great deal of me to hang by the feet, while distracted." He hauled a small bottle of the looted brandy out of his pack. "Methinks I'll quaff a stoup of this sack. At least we can drink in public, even if our girls prefer some privacy for other pastimes."

He looked at the others. "What? Do I drink alone?" he jeered. "What paltry rogues!"

"I might as well join you," said Chip with a grin, taking the bottle from Fal. "We humans don't feel the same as the bats do about sex in public either. So, although heaven knows when I'll get to see Ginny again, after this, and I'd rather be doing other things, I might as well drink. We're bound to be stuck here for ages."

It was obviously an inspired decision, because a ten-ton truck immediately came around the bend. It drove straight past, showering muddy water at them as they tried to flag it down.

Chip was just working up to a good swear . . . when the truck stopped, and began reversing cautiously. The rain, the muddy road, and poor light all made good reasons to reverse cautiously. But when the truck got closer it was apparent the real reason was Bronstein. She was cling-ing to the little sill above the driver's side window. By her wing-claws. She had the trigger bar of a bat-limpet mine between her feet.

When the truck drew level with them, they saw that the limpet mine was attached to the glass just in front of the driver's wide-eyed face.

"Nice of you to offer to help," said Chip evenly.

Once a little misunderstanding got cleared up, the driver had been very cooperative.

The misunderstanding had been that they couldn't do this to him.

They drove on, all squashed into the cab, through the rain and the gathering darkness, showering a convoy of motorcyclists in mud.

"Wonder why they were out here? This road doesn't really lead anywhere except to Divisional headquarters and the Front. Those looked like civilian police," said the driver.

"They're probably looking for Ginny," said Chip, giving her a squeeze.

Ginny shook her head. "For all of you. You're important people, too. Major Van Klomp said so."

"Huh," said Chip, with a conscript's natural suspicion of any officer coming to the fore. "Van Klomp should stick to parade jumps. That's not how the army works. They're looking for *you*."

"But that's not right," said Ginny, determinedly. "After all, you are all heroes. If it hadn't been for the rats, bats, Fluff and the Jampad, we'd have died, and the army would never have captured the scorpiary. You'll surely get promoted and be used to train the army. Every general must just be dying to talk to you. To shake your hand. Or paw," she said, after the briefest of pauses.

Chip laughed. "Not in this man's army! You watch, Ginny. We're more likely to be charged with desertion, negligent loss of equipment, and failure to salute an officer."

Chip was quite wrong.

That wasn't more than a quarter of the charge sheet.

# Chapter 2

ᏽ

*An odd but unpretentious house perched above a small ravine and waterfall, on the wooded outskirts of George Bernard Shaw City.*

Sanjay Devi was an unlikely conspirator. She was the colony's Chief Scientist, and the "mother" of the rats and bats that now fought beside humans against the Magh' invaders of Harmony and Reason. Their genetic engineering was in no small part her work, and the choice of material downloaded into their soft-cyber brain implants all her own.

In her choice of download material, as with everything she did, Devi had her reasons, not all of them obvious. Perhaps it was just that she was fond of Shakespeare, and nothing more sinister. After all, she was one of the founding patrons of the New Globe Thespian Society, and a devoted amateur dramatist. One of her favorite statements, in fact, was that life tended to imitate the Scottish Play.

Right now she was attempting to decide whether to clutch the dagger that she saw before her.

It was an odd-shaped dagger, and made entirely of paper. Part of it was a pile of news-reports. Part of it was a printout of several confidential biographical snoops prepared by the HAR Special Branch. Part of it was a history book—a rare thing on HAR. She'd been carefully reading up the details of the trial and fate of an obscure artillery captain.

His name had been Alfred Dreyfus.

She took a deep breath, then muttered: "If you can look into the seeds of time and say which grain will grow, and which will not . . ."

If only it were that simple. She needed to select and promote an evil grain. It had to be both evil and weak, if it was to work as she planned it to. There were three possibilities—and each of them would kill innocents, and destroy lives. She'd cultivated all of them carefully.

Finally, she made up her mind and reached for the telephone. She'd grown up using a bonephone-implant and vis-vid. But, chasing the dream, Sanjay had left the technological advances of Earth behind. Here, on Harmony and Reason, there had been none of the vast interlocking support systems a technological society required to support itself. They'd had to step backwards to technology that didn't require such an interfacing of support-systems. Back to carbon-granule telephones, for one thing.

At least no one saw your face while you spoke to them. That sometimes had advantages.

"Talbot," she said, when the phone was picked up on the other end. "Fascinating news about this Major Fitzhugh."

She waited for the explosion from the man who was in charge of the colony's Security portfolio to subside.

"The general is a fool, Talbot. Even if he did marry your sister. That was probably the one and only intelligent thing he ever did. You'll have to lead him. He's not exactly mentally capable."

She shook her head sympathetically at Talbot Cartup's pungent reply.

"The answer seems obvious," she said calmly. "Treason, Talbot. You have the means to arrange the evidence. He may not be a Vat, but he's plainly a Vat-sympathizer. He not only trained with them, he *volunteered* to train with them. That's as good as an admission of guilt to me. Why would any man who was not some sort of fanatic do that?"

As it happened, she had a very a good idea why Fitzhugh had done it. But Sanjay Devi always played her cards close to her chest.

Apparently, Talbot Cartup found himself in bitter and complete agreement with her. And found her suggestion remarkably attractive.

After she put the telephone down, Sanjay sat for a long time looking at the odd-shaped dagger. At last she sighed.

That hurt, as usual. Deep breaths always did, but there was nothing that could be done about it other than to take painkillers. And she couldn't afford to take those. She needed her mind sharp for the time she had left.

Finally, the pain eased. She muttered "by the pricking of my thumbs, something wicked this way comes," and reached for the telephone again. But this time she clipped a little piece of solid-state circuitry onto it. It was a relic of old Earth, a piece of technology this colony could not dream of mastering for another two centuries. The scrambler-recorder was singularly useful to a conspirator.

"Major General Needford, please."

The JAG switchboard system was slow. But she got hold of Needford eventually.

He listened to her in silence. He was unnerving in that way, as well as in others. John Needford had a mind like a razor, and Devi knew that he was neck deep in the "young Turks" in the Army. He asked incisive questions—as always.

She was surprised to find that his special investigator had encountered Fitzhugh before . . . but she shouldn't have been. Their paths had been bound to cross, given the nature of the men.

When the conspirator put the phone down, she muttered "eye of newt" with some satisfaction. None of the other three calls would be as stressful as the one to the man she privately called "the Spanish Inquisition." It was almost a pity his ancestry was Liberian instead of Iberian.

She saved the most enjoyable of the calls for last.

She answered the sour grunt from the other end of the line with a carefully planned insult. "Liepsich, you stink. And HARIT's physics is at grade school level."

A smile twitched across Sanjay Devi's face at his pungent reply.

"And the same to you. With brass knobs on. Now, how goes the slowshield research?"

＊　　＊　　＊

She put down the phone for the last time, detached the device she'd used, murmuring "and toe of frog." She bit her lip, thoughtfully.

"I still need some more ingredients. Wool of bat . . . and although it is part of the witch's role . . . the rat without a tail."

# Chapter 3

ᴏᴏ

*A mock-chateau on the edge of HAR wineland-country.*
*Now the Divisional Military Headquarters of the Fifth*
*Brigade.*

No one had explained to the Vat driver about the wisdom
of avoiding the rats' stolen booze. In fact it was a good
thing that Chip had restrained him after the first unwary
swallow or he might have had more, and they'd have ended
up in the second ditch . . . if they were lucky.

But even that one fiery chug had been enough to relax
him. He joined them in some rowdy songs and was quite
cheerfully willing to drive up to the front porte-cochere
of the huge fake chateau that had been expropriated as
Divisional Headquarters, instead of around to the vehicle
park.

A number of brass in full-dress uniform were standing on the steps, looking anxiously out into the dark. There were a fair number of television cameras and reporters too. When the ten-tonner blundered towards them a couple of frantic lieutenants and a sergeant major tried to stop it. The two lieutenants had to dive out of the way. But the sergeant major was made of sterner stuff. The truck had slowed slightly to avoid actually killing the two lieutenants, and he managed to leap onto the running board.

"You stupid bastard!" he bellowed through the inch of open window. "Get out of here! There is a reception for a really important person. The outriders should be here at any minute. Get this vehicle out of here before I have you mucking priv—*aaaagh*!"

"Indade, I cannot stand this being yelled at," muttered Eamon, licking blood off his fangs with a long red tongue.

No one really heard him. The others were all too busy singing. As O'Niel and Bronstein were singing "Casey Jones" and the rats were singing a bawdy version of the same, which involved a conger, the noise in the cab was pretty horrendous.

They screeched to halt—a belated halt, as the truck mounted the first step. The reception party showed its mettle and fell over each other in their haste to get out of the way.

Chip opened the cab door, and they all piled out.

As the singing died away, the enormity of the sea of brass they'd nearly driven into dawned on Private Chip Connolly. There was an awful silence. The kind of silence that presages serious repercussions.

And then one of the stunned cameramen said: "That's her! That's her! That's Virginia Shaw!"

*          *          *

When she'd been trapped in the scorpiary, walled into a tiny cell, Virginia had dreamed of being free. Of getting back home. As their madcap adventure through the scorpiary had continued, being with her new-found comrades had become more important to her than anything else. She'd never had actual friends before. And finding love had made escape—while certainly desirable—not really something she had thought about much.

Now she realized she hadn't thought about dealing with the reality at all.

The camera-flashes, the barrage of questions. The people crowding around. She found herself desperately wishing that she was merely facing certain death at Chip's side on a little vineyard tractor without any brakes. She was suddenly aware that both her skirt and blouse had been partially torn up for rags and were now very skimpy indeed. She was muddy. She had a bandage around her head.

However, she was Virginia Shaw, and these were the heroes who had rescued her. They deserved recognition. But how to get a word in edgeways?

"*Santa Maria! San Cristoforo!*" bellowed a sergeant major voice. "This asking of questions all at once, she is too much!" roared Fluff. He rose to his full height, perched on her left shoulder.

"One at a time, and the Señorita Shaw will do her best. One question each. No more!" He pointed to one of the thrusting microphones. "You. You with the mustachios of the most inadequate. Ask."

The startled reporter—who would shortly be clean shaven—took his cue. "Abe Telermann of Interweb here,

Ms. Shaw. Were you present when your parents were murdered?"

She felt Chip's hand on her other shoulder and found her voice. "No. But my kidnapper told me that they had been killed."

"Who kidnapped . . ."

"Enough!" bellowed Fluff. "You with the hair of the color of my jacket. Ask."

"Er. Sandy Degan here. IPN. Who kidnapped you?"

Virginia knew the terrible compulsion provided by her soft-cyber chip's inbuilt bias. "My tutor. He drugged me and took me behind Magh' lines." They would find out who her tutor had been soon enough. But for now she'd beaten the compulsion to believe the best of the murderous Korozhet "professor."

"Miz Shaw, we've heard that the army rescued you from the Magh'. Is this true?"

Ginny nodded. "Yes. I was rescued from a Magh' cell by these brave soldiers here." She pointed to the bats that hung above her, and the rats that twitched noses around her legs. "I'd like to thank all of them from the bottom of my heart. The uplifted rats and bats are finest soldiers . . . no, the finest *people* I've ever met." Her voice cracked slightly. "Three of them died to keep me alive. They died for me and for all of us humans. The people of Harmony and Reason, Shareholders and Vats alike, owe these soldiers a debt. They—"

"Ahem. Ms. Shaw will answer further questions later," said a red-faced man in a beautifully tailored uniform, pushing through the crowd. "Brigadier Charlesworth, Divisional Officer Commanding, ma'am. Welcome. We've been informed that you were injured, Ms. Shaw. We have your personal physician here from the Shaw Estate. If you could accompany me . . ."

"My friends must come with me," Ginny said firmly.

The brigadier looked doubtfully at the rats and bats. "These?" asked uneasily. "We don't normally allow animals into the building."

"These," said Ginny, firmly. "I won't go without them. They're my bodyguards."

"Er. I have detailed some of my men to take on this duty . . ."

"Ah, Virginia!" A white-coated man with a stethoscope around his neck and a face full of sculpted features cut through the crowd. "Allow me to offer my condolences. Now, if you will all excuse us. I see Ms. Shaw needs medical attention. I'm sorry but you will all have to wait."

Virginia found herself somehow unable to resist, or even able to speak.

The doctor was speaking English, but he was also saying something else, something far more important, in a whispered voice—in a language she'd never learned, yet that she understood perfectly. She realized suddenly that it wasn't Doctor Thom giving orders in the language that the implanted chip in her head said must be obeyed, but his lapel badge. As she gathered her resistance, she felt the prick of a needle.

"She's been through a terrific amount for a young, delicately reared girl," said the doctor. "But she's in safe hands now. Thank you all."

As if from a great distance she heard Chip ask the brigadier, "What do you want us to do now, sir?"

The brigadier sniffed. "Get back to your unit, soldier.

As quickly as possible. And get your platoon sergeant to put you on a charge for the state of your uniform and that half-beard of yours. Just because we're at war doesn't mean you have an excuse to ignore dress and appearance codes! Now, get these scruffy military animals back to their units, before I have them put down."

Chip's "Sir" was the last thing she remembered hearing.

Private Chip Connolly stood there, looking at the departing pack following Ginny. He'd said that the army would reward him with a kick in the pants—but somehow he'd always thought that there would be *some* recognition. And he'd never thought that Virginia would just turn her back on him like that. He'd thought . . .

But then, when it came right down to it, she was a Shareholder. *The* Shareholder, in fact, the wealthiest in the colony. And he was just a Vat-conscript, after all. The lowest of the low.

"Excuse me, Private." It was one of the interviewers and his cameraman. "Tim Fuentes, INB. Am I right in saying that you were actually part of the Special Services force that rescued Ms. Virginia Shaw? Can you tell us about it?"

Chip snorted. He knew that there was no point in feeling hard done by. It was the way of the army and the way of the damned Shareholder class. But he was still furious and hurt about it. "Oh, yes. That's us. Me and these scruffy military animals. But we're not Special Services. We're just a bunch of grunts. We were in the wrong place at the right time."

"I quite understand that the details of your unit and the finer details of your operations must remain secret,

Private, but . . . can you tell us your name? Or is that confidential too?"

"Private Charles Connolly, 21011232334000. That's what captured soldiers are allowed to tell you. And if you excuse me, I've got get back to my unit as quickly as possible. Then I need to find a medium to help me to tell my platoon sergeant that he's to put me on a charge for my appearance."

The reporter and cameraman pursued him as he tried to walk. "Just a few questions, Private Connolly. Did you take part in freeing her? Did the kidnappers put up a fight?"

"Her kidnapper is dead. It was that thing she called her tutor. You could say it put up a fight. It tried to kill her. That's where I got this hole in my shoulder."

"Did you capture the kidnapper?"

"I told you. It got killed."

"And Ms. Shaw, during this ordeal, how did she take it? Was she terribly traumatized?"

Images of Ginny filled his mind: clinging to him after she'd killed her first Maggot; after Behan's death; hanging on to the back of the tractor as it plunged through the Magh'-filled corridors. He turned on the heel-yapping media jackal: "She wasn't 'traumatized' and she fought beside us. She fought," he said slowly, "like a lioness. And now, leave me alone or I will kill you."

By the way they backed off, they obviously believed him . . . even though Chip didn't really want them to.

"Ahem." Bronstein cleared her throat. "What are you going to do now, Connolly?"

"Go back to my unit as quickly as possible like a good little soldier," said Chip, savagely. "Didn't you hear that nice Shareholder officer? You scruffy military animals had better do the same."

He walked off, blindly.

They followed.

Fluttering along behind Connolly, Michaela Bronstein tried to formulate strategy. Revolution! Throwing off the cruel yoke of human oppression! Liberty, equality and belfry! These were the dreams and ideals that Michaela Bronstein had always lived by, ideals that had governed her, and indeed, all batdom.

Of course, bats, by their very nature, had always chittered and argued about how liberation should be achieved. Eamon Dzhugashvilli was one of the notorious Bat Bund who had advocated straight and bloody murder, blowing every non-bat to kingdom come with as much high explosive as they could lay their claws on, and allying batdom with humankind's foes. Michaela came from another faction, who were considerably more moderate in their approach. Of course, it still involved sending everyone except the bat-people to perdition, but letting them get there on their own, without using high explosive to speed their passage. Well, without using high explosive just for the sake of it, anyway.

Now, with the knowledge that they themselves had been cruelly betrayed by the Korozhet, Eamon had changed his tune. The bats had all been through a Damascene conversion, realizing that the humans and even those feckless rats were their allies in a far greater struggle. Realizing that humans, especially the Vat-class, were victims too, entrapped in debt servitude, and that there was honor, nobility and comradeship in them—

and even in those drunken, lecherous rats.

The nascent union and common revolutionary front was just that. Barely new-born. Without care, it would be still-born. She, O'Niel and Eamon had only accepted the facts by having the very unpalatable truth thrust in front of their faces. Now they faced a far harder task than a mere revolution. They must unite batdom with their historical enemy against an unimaginably evil foe.

It was literally impossible for those with soft-cyber chips in their head to imagine evil of the Korozhet. The soft-cyber implants had an inbuilt bias which told them—forced them to accept—that the Korozhet were good, wonderful and to be obeyed at all costs.

Only . . . English, unlike the Korozhet language, was a slippery thing. Its semantics—the slang, poetical allusions, the spelling quirks—enabled the thinker with a Korozhet soft-cyber implant to work around the Korozhet bias. The "Crotchets," not the Korozhet, were despicable genocidal slavers.

Now they had to convince the rest of the bats.

"We should stick together," said Eamon. "I have no liking for that bunch that have taken Virginia under their wing. No liking or trust at all. I swear I heard someone speak in . . . Crotchet before she went with them." He bared his long fangs and stretched his new-stitched wing.

"Don't do that." Bronstein swatted the wing down. "It won't be healing properly if you don't rest it."

"Resting is not in my nature," grumbled the big bat. "And I say we should fly after her."

Bronstein shook her head. "No. They'll not stop Ginny. That's true steel there, Eamon. Or do you forget that she, and she alone, could go against the compulsion that the

Crotchets have set in our intelligence?"

"Would I ever forget that? That's why we must stand by her, wing to shoulder!" Eamon, as he was wont to do, assumed what he thought of as a noble stance. Bronstein thought it just made him look constipated.

She shook her head. "No. We must bring all of batdom to stand with her. And that is the harder task. Needs must the three of us should go back to the belfries and raise the new revolution."

Eamon blinked. "I had not yet thought of it that way. You are the better strategist, Michaela Bronstein. Force is more my forte."

That was true enough, thought Bronstein. Eamon was a positive genius at mayhem, especially with explosives. But all she said was: "The time for force will come."

"Soon, I hope," said Eamon, stretching the wing again and getting another swat from Bronstein.

"And what of the rats?" asked O'Niel. The plump bat had crossed more boundaries in the field of interspecies friendship than the others. He liked rats, and was becoming positively ratly in his attitudes to good bat virtues. It was a bit shameful, really. The other bats would drink with the rats out of solidarity, because that was how rats expressed it. O'Niel would drink because he liked it.

Bronstein shrugged. "Indade. And what of you, rats?" she asked. "Well, Fal? Melene? Doll? Doc? Nym? Pistol? What of ratdom? Will you be able to call all ratdom to rise beside us?"

"*If, when all a vigil keep, the rats' asleep, then well may freedom weep,*" intoned O'Niel.

"Whoreson," Fat Fal shook his head. "You bats really don't understand rats at all, do you? We're not like you bats. There is no such thing as 'ratdom.' 'Tis every rat for himself and the devil take the hindmost."

"You mean, you're not with us?" snarled Eamon.

Fal yawned. "Well, not if it doth mean hanging by my feet and only indulging in tail-twisting once a year. I would not say 'no' to being invited on that occasion, mind. But if it is a common front against the Crotchet, I'm with you. They're set to destroy the humans, and without humans we would be helpless against our worst foe."

He struggled with the top of his nip-size bottle. "See? This! This evil and fiendish invention, the screw-top! Fain would I have someone with opposable thumbs to open screwtops, or what will the use in looting be?"

O' Neil chuckled. *"Then a voice like thunder spake. 'Cry no hurrahs but let the Crotchets quake, we'll fight to the death for looting's sake.'"*

"That, and a little touch of Harry in the night," said Pistol, with an agreeing nod.

"We need humankind," said Melene. "They make chocolate."

Doc scratched his long nose thoughtfully. "I think ours is the easier task, Bronstein. You see, one simply has to understand the philosophy of rats. We are individuals, and live principally for ourselves. You bats are social and altruistic creatures, so maybe it is less than obvious to you. What the Korozhet have done is to make sure that *we* are the hindmost. There is no rat that can ever accept that. We need to save humanity, even if only to assure ourselves that there will always be someone else to be hindmost. And, of course, to open screwtops and make chocolate."

Doc was the only uplifted creature who could accuse

the Crotchets by name. The rat-philosopher claimed that he could do so by using Plato's forms—the first good use Bronstein had ever come across for paper. Despite his obviously dented sanity, the rat had her respect because of this ability. "So what do you advise us all to do at this point?"

"Why, go back to our units. Go and spread the word," said the rat, waving his arms and tail messianically.

"Just like that?"

"Well, no. Not quite," said Melene. "We must gild the philosophical pill."

Bronstein looked puzzled. "And how do you plan to do that? Paint Doc gold?"

"Why, methinks I shall just tell one or two rats. In the strictest confidence, of course." Melene smiled mischievously. "Or doesn't bat society work like that?"

Bronstein fluttered thoughtfully. "There is truth in what you say."

"Aye," said O'Niel, snagging Fal's bottle. "Indade we must go to be the sea in which the fish of revolution swim. Or something like that, anyway."

"Where has Chip gotten to?"

# Chapter 4

♋

*A large room, decorated with horsy prints and*
*expensive leather tack, in a crenellated and*
*imposing den of iniquity, otherwise known as*
*Military Headquarters.*

General Cartup-Kreutzler looked around the room at the grim faces of those of the General Staff that he'd summoned to his office. The small standing army that the colony of Harmony and Reason had had through twenty-seven peaceful years had expanded a thousandfold to deal with the Magh' invasion. But the people in this room all had twenty-seven years of service behind them. In their opinion, this made them the only competent people for the job. Korozhet advisors helped, of course.

"Gentlemen. We're going to have to do some very

major damage control here. What with Shaw's daughter also being involved, there are major political ramifications."

"To say nothing of us having egg on our faces," said Brigadier Charlesworth bitterly. He'd arrived barely minutes before from his Sector HQ. He had a pile of newspapers with him.

"The papers and newscasts are praising this blasted Fitzhugh fellow to the skies, and calling us incompetent!" Charlesworth's plump red face was positively choleric at the idea. Major Fitzhugh had—much against the inertia of the General Staff—managed to see to it that the HAR army had had its first victory.

The general nodded. "We need to rectify the situation with the media. I've already gotten onto John Carsey, just before this meeting. He's pulled the plug on the live television coverage with HBC. In the interest of maintaining security. Allen, you've got contacts with Allied Press?"

The balding-bulldog-faced man tugged at his jowled chin. "My cousin. He's managing editor."

"He has editorial control?"

Bulldog-face grimaced. "I suppose he could have," he said. "He usually leaves most of the day-to-day running to his staff."

"Leave it to me," said the only civilian present at the meeting. All of General Cartup-Kreutzler's lackeys—who, to a man, regarded those who were not in the army as nonentities—treated this man with wary deference. Talbot Cartup controlled the Special Branch of the HAR police force. That made the general's brother-in-law a man to be feared.

"I play golf with Erwin. He'll be amenable to my

suggestions. What did you have in mind, Henry?"

"A blanket ban on coverage of this incident!"

Talbot laughed. "Not a chance. Even I can't do that . . . yet. The anticensorship laws of the colony are rigid, Henry. The best I could arrange would be to plant a story about this military operation having been planned by yourselves, but kept a secret as you found that communications were being intercepted by the Magh'. I'll have them mention that the hoo-ha about this in the press has prejudiced further operations. That should provide me with a good reason to push the Board of Shareholders to legislate some limitations on freedom of speech clauses."

The general nodded, grudgingly. "That'll have to do. But you won't get the Freedom of Speech stuff modified. I spoke to Aloysius Shaw about it, er . . . just after that unfortunate incident at the ballet, when the media had a field day about you. It would require a constitutional amendment and that would require a full sixty-seven percent of the vote. Even with Shaw's thirty-four percent block he'd didn't think it could be swung. With the vote passing to his daughter Virginia, now that she's still alive and rescued, thanks to this victory, there's no chance."

Talbot Cartup's eyes glinted. "She's already been dealt with. Believe me, I have that matter in hand."

Brigadier Charlesworth was slow on the uptake of anything except for whiskey. But he'd finally caught onto the idea of a planted story about the capture of the Magh' scorpiary. Major Fitzhugh had almost single-handedly directed and stage-managed this victory, despite the refusal of Military Headquarters in general, and General Cartup-Kreutzler in particular, to take any action. Fitzhugh—in charge of the pitiful HAR army intelligence unit—had spotted a situation created by some stray HAR troops inside the enemy's force field. The general had refused to act on the information, so Major Conrad Fitzhugh had gone right ahead and done it anyway, taking the law—and the chain of command—into his own hands. That had included having the brigadier arrested in his own comfortable chateau-headquarters!

Charlesworth was not the forgiving kind. "I say! If you plant this story . . . then that blasted upstart bounder, Fitzhugh, will get away with it all."

General Cartup-Kreutzler and his brother-in-law pinned the brigadier in spotlight glares. "Not a chance in hell," hissed the general through clenched teeth.

Talbot Cartup rubbed his meaty hands together. "Fitzhugh has been a thorn in my flesh. We've already decided. He will be court-martialed and shot."

General Cartup-Kreutzler nodded. "I had given orders for him to be arrested and brought for trial. I've changed those to orders for a field court-martial and summary justice, if possible. The MPs hadn't succeeded, and anyway, they're inclined to do things by the book. I've dispatched Lieutenant Colonel Jeebol from Divisional HQ. He'll deal with the matter immediately and personally. A good man. Expeditious. The sooner Fitzhugh is out of the picture, the easier the clearing up of this mess is going to be."

"I think we might just put all the blame on him," said Talbot Cartup. "He was the leak. And when he discovered the Special Branch were onto him, he attempted to cover himself by doing some glory-grabbing."

Brigadier Charlesworth nodded. "Let me know what witnesses you need. I'll see to that."

Talbot Cartup smiled on him. "We also have some

photographic morphing machinery from old Earth. I'll need some old confidential battle plans, Henry."

The door of the room swung open. The guilty-looking group of conspirators tried hastily to look as if they'd been discussing football scores. A red-purple spiky beach-ball shape ambulated through the doorway on jointed flexing spines.

"Ah," said General Cartup-Kreutzler, seeing the alien. "Advisor Tirritit. What brings you here?"

"Good day, General." The Korozhet military attaché dipped his spines respectfully. "I have been dispatched by my commander to ask a favor of you. We would find it of great value to go and inspect this front your bold troops have opened up. A daring initiative! I gather you have captured some enemy territory. I should like to take a party of military advisors from my strategy group into the area."

Cartup-Kreutzler was somewhat taken aback at this request. "Well, I suppose so, Tirritit. But what you'd want to see there I don't know. Battlefields have very little to do with military strategy. And you chaps know everything there is to know about the Magh'."

Advisor Tirritit hissed a naphthalene reek at them. "True. But we'd like to gather fresh material. And to confirm certain things. I hadn't wanted to broach this with you yet, General, but, strategically speaking, this attack could have catastrophic side effects on the whole war effort. Really, you should not undertake such exercises without first consulting us."

"It wasn't exactly our plan, Tirritit," said Brigadier Charlesworth sourly. "And we didn't know about it until it had happened."

The Korozhet advisor gave a sort of hissing sigh. "You are Brigadier Charlesworth? This did happen in the sector of the front under your control, where, if I remember correctly, a planned strategic retreat was in progress. Most unwise!"

Charlesworth looked sullen. "I told you. This wasn't our idea. Some blasted intelligence major did it off his own bat. We were just discussing how best to deal with him."

The Korozhet military advisor spined forward into the ornately wood-panelled room. "Perhaps you should tell us more. This sort of individual could prevent you from winning the war if he continues this sort of interference. By the way, the request we put in for this . . . Private Charles Connolly. How is that proceeding?"

"Ah. I am happy to say that he appears to be dead," said General Visse. "Our records show this clearly."

Tirritit clacked his spines. "Most satisfactory. I mean, we did want to debrief him and question him about the death of the Korozhet tutor assigned to Virginia Shaw. But his death removes the necessity."

# Chapter 5

☊

*A grim and debatable land: a captured Magh'
corpiary, newly conquered and still smoldering.*

"What in hell are we going to do with them, Fitzy?" asked
Parachute Major Van Klomp, looking down over the red
spiral walls of the Magh' scorpiary. His paratroopers had
blown a hole in the roof to gain access to the brood-heart.
Now Van Klomp had come up here to escape the chaos
within. What was happening down there wasn't fighting.
Not really. More like the butchery of rather nasty but stupid insects. The Magh' brains seemed to have died with
their brood-heart. "We can't talk to the *befokte* things to
persuade them to surrender, and we may just die of
exhaustion killing them. I'm sick of it. I am almost missing parades by now."

Major Conrad Fitzhugh, head of HAR Army Intelligence—at least until the MPs caught up with him—grinned tiredly. "You've always got something to bitch about, Bobby. Last time you wanted action, not display jumps. I get you action, now you want back to display jumps. There's no pleasing you!"

Van Klomp exhaled gustily. "It's because you cheated me, boykie. You promised we could rescue some commando-heroes from certain death. And what do I find when we get in there? A bunch of drunken rats and bats having a Maggot barbeque. And a solitary troepie making whoopee with Shaw's bloody daughter."

A sleek rat with ragged ears and a few new scars stuck her head out of the capacious magazine pocket of Fitz's BDUs. "You might have scrounged some of their drink, Van Klomp. Do you know how dry I am, and how irritable I get when I'm dry?"

Van Klomp blew the most dangerous she-rat in the army a raspberry. But, to prove that, despite being big, he wasn't entirely stupid, he also produced a hip-flask. "You and Fitzy stole all my port. You stole my Christmas bottle. You even drank the cooking sherry. But Meilin got me some rum from somewhere. You don't like rum, do you, Ariel?"

"It's at the bottom of my list of human drinks," said the rat, reaching for it. "As for your sack, 'twas terrible stuff. I was doing you a favor drinking it." Because Ariel had spent so much time in human company, her speech was less Shakespearean than that of most rats. But every now and then bits slipped out, especially when she was thirsty.

Van Klomp poured some of the contents of the hip flask into the small silver lid-cup. "Here. And be happy.

The stuff those rats were drinking made rum look like cola. A mouthful of the stuff nearly killed me."

"And you let them take it away!" said Ariel, downing the small cup and shaking her head.

Van Klomp shrugged. "I'd have liked to keep them all here so Fitzy could debrief them when he got through with playing chase-the-Maggot. But I wanted our late Chairman's daughter out of danger. Shaw wasn't going anywhere without them. And they weren't going anywhere without that grog of theirs. They'd kept her alive right through attacking this patch of hell with a fire bucket, so I reckon they must make a fairly good bodyguard. I'd have choppered them out except for this weather." The cold front was lifting now, but rain and mist had followed the army into the area. Not that it had made much difference. Most of the fighting had been in the labyrinthine tunnels of the scorpiary.

Fitz stood up and yawned. "Well, aside from missing out on their booze, I'd have liked to talk to them myself. They know more first hand about Magh' than anyone else. And we owe our victory here to their efforts. I'd have liked an explanation of all of it—that dead Korozhet, and that other alien critter, to say nothing of all the dead Magh'—those huge bloated ones they said were the brains behind the whole nest. But realistically speaking, I won't be dealing with that intelligence. I've got to go back and face the music. I just came looking for you, to say goodbye."

Van Klomp sighed. "I know you too damn well to think I'm going to change your mind, Fitzy. So." He reached out a large hand and took the cup from Ariel's paws. Topped it up. Handed it to the scar-faced intelligence major. "A last drink together, boykie. Bottoms up."

Fitz took it. "To the living and the dead," he said, and drained it. "Pfeh. That's vile stuff. My God . . . it's strong . . . Ariel . . ."

Van Klomp caught him as he fell, and lowered him gently to the ground. The silver cup was less lucky. It bounced and clattered away, rolling down the seven hundred foot slope of the scorpiary arms. "Sorry, boykie," said Van Klomp, quietly. "But you won't look after yourself, so your mates have to. Here, Ariel. Loosen his collar. And then go and give Cunningham and Garcia a call. They're waiting just inside the first gallery with the ropes and stuff."

Ariel was already at her major's throat. "You're sure he'll be all right, Van Klomp? I'll kill you if he isn't." There was no hyperbole at all in that statement.

"You can kill me right after I kill that damned doctor, if he isn't," said Van Klomp, heavily. "I never thought he'd swallow that bit about me drinking rum."

"And I thought he'd notice for sure that I hadn't actually drunk any of it," said Ariel, feeling for the carotid pulse. "That's steady enough, anyway. You go and call your goons. I'll stay with him."

Van Klomp shook his head. "If he stirs you won't be able to stop him rolling. I'll take care of him, Ariel." He gave the unconscious man a wry look. "I always have," he said quietly, "since we were kids."

With no more than a disapproving sniff, Ariel left and ran to the hole that the attacking paratroopers had left in the Magh' adobe dome. In a few minutes she was back with two paratroopers, ropes, a field stretcher and the doctor. The doctor checked Fitz's breathing and pulse hastily. "I don't approve of this, Major," he said stiffly.

"*Ja.* I know, Captain. You've said so maybe six times already. But short of me hitting him and maybe making an error of judgment—which could have been even more dangerous—how else are we supposed to deal with this? We've been leading that useless *bliksem* of a lieutenant colonel up the garden path for about as long as we can. He's met up with Colonel Nygen now and between them they would have found Fitzy soon."

The doctor sighed. "Are you sure—"

Van Klomp turned to the medical officer, his face grim. "I took the radio message myself, from General Cartup-Kreutzler. Fitz is to be arrested, by force if need be. To be captured dead or alive. Preferably, according to the general, dead. He is to face summary battlefield court-martial. You served under Major Fitzhugh in this campaign. He's determined to plead guilty. But it wouldn't make any damn difference. This Lieutenant Colonel Jeebol who is to chair the court-martial is Cartup-Kreutzler's hatchet man. He's already tried and sentenced Fitz. You know what the maximum penalty is, in a battlefield court-martial. All we're asking is that you see to it that he stays alive long enough to get a fair, open general court-martial, not a kangaroo court and summary execution."

"I was *trying* to ask whether you were absolutely sure he had no preexisting medical conditions," said the doctor irritably. "It's something we normally try to establish before administering anesthetics. I'm well aware of what high command are up to. And they're not going to succeed. I'm a doctor because I want to keep men alive. He might have to face trial, although they'd be wiser to give him a chest full of medals. But no one, and I mean no one, is going to kill him while he is in my care."

Van Klomp bit his lip. "Sorry, Doc. I spoke too damn hastily. Made a fool of myself, again. I know he had many anesthetics after his face got ripped up like that. I never heard of any problems. Look, along with Major Del'annancio of A company, I've arranged some extra stretcher bearers for you."

"I don't need any. We've only got a few casualties, for a change. A pleasant change."

Van Klomp smiled. "Doc. You've got the legal authority over any patient in your care. But your medics are—medics. They're unarmed. Lieutenant Colonel Jeebol has a number of armed men with him. If anything unpleasant happens . . . just remember these men are there, under your command."

The doctor blinked. "It won't come to that, surely?"

"It already has," the big paratrooper replied.

"And always remember, I'll be right next to him," said Ariel. "Human throats are a lot softer than pseudochitin, and I haven't sworn any oaths to keep anyone alive." The rat left no one in any doubt that she meant every word, and that she'd be able to do it, too.

The medics had put together a makeshift ward in one of the now-empty scorpiary chambers. The upper levels were seldom disturbed by wandering Magh'—the leaderless creatures seemed to want to burrow down into the lower chambers. Nonetheless, there were two platoons in position behind the barbed wire and broken masonry fortifications. There were several other badly wounded soldiers in the other cots in the ward. At least, they all looked to be. They were heavily bandaged, anyway.

Ariel lay just under the edge of Fitz's blanket and waited. She didn't have to wait long. Fitz was still in the whirly stage of semi-consciousness when they came.

"Lieutenant Colonel Jeebol, 3rd Motorized Division," said the voice crisply from the next chamber. "I believe you've got Major Conrad Fitzhugh here. Number 24950101803371."

"Yes," answered the doctor. "He's out of theater and recuperating in the ward. And where do you think you're going?"

"I have to place him under arrest. He's to be taken for court-martial immediately. Now get out of my way before I have you arrested and charged as well."

Ariel peeked. She couldn't resist it. The medic captain was standing four-square in the doorway. "No," he said, calmly. "He's recovering from an anesthetic. I must forbid it."

"Sergeant," snapped the lieutenant colonel. "Arrest this man."

"If you even attempt that, Sergeant," said Van Klomp's gravel-crusher voice. "I'll be obliged to arrest you."

Ariel blinked. Van Klomp wasn't supposed to be here! He was going to keep his nose clean, in case he needed to stick it in later. Still, she'd been none-too-sure that the doc was going to be able to manage this. Van Klomp would.

"I am entirely capable of dealing with this myself, Major," said the doctor, in a tone that explained very clearly that he might only be unit MO now, but he'd been a hospital senior surgeon before the war. "Understand this very clearly, Lieutenant Colonel Whoozit. This area is a field hospital. I am the ranking officer in charge of it. As such I have ultimate medical responsibility for the welfare of all the patients in my care. I am also the final authority on the conduct of military matters inside this area, as it may affect my patients. On medical grounds. I have given a clear instruction. Attempt to countermand it, and I'll have you thrown off the premises. And I will see you charged for it. It is a clear breach of military law. Do you understand me?"

"You can't stop me! I've got orders from General Cartup-Kreutzler himself! Now out of my way!" yelled the lieutenant colonel.

The small medic captain stood his ground. His voice was frosty enough to chill liquid nitrogen, now, never mind mere lieutenant colonels. "I've made it very clear to you, sir, that I don't care if you have orders from God. Unless they're from the Army Surgeon General and in writing, Major Fitzhugh stays here in my care until I deem him medically fit to leave. And I warn you, Lieutenant Colonel, if you shout again and disturb these critically ill men, I'll have you removed by force and give orders to the guards that you are not to be permitted into this area again."

The lieutenant colonel was plainly unused to this. He gaped like a new-caught fish. "Don't be a fool! Fitzhugh is a dangerous criminal who is due for battlefield court-martial and summary execution!"

"Then you can court-martial and execute him, once he is discharged from my care as fit and well," said the captain. "Now, I have work to do. And where are *you* going, Samuelson?"

Ariel saw that one of the genuine patients was

staggering towards the doorway occupied by the doctor.

"Call of nature, sir," said the man, saluting weakly. "Needs must when the devil drives, sir."

The doctor sighed. "Orderly. Go with this man."

"I'll be fine on my own, sir."

"If you're not back in two minutes we'll come looking for you," said the doctor irritably. "Go."

The man went. But the interruption had eased some of the heat in the situation. The lieutenant colonel had had a chance to think. "Look. We'll get clearance from the Army Surgeon General's office immediately, Captain. I've got orders to apprehend and try this man ASAP."

"And that will be after he is discharged from our care, sir. Now will you please leave. It's not visiting hours."

"Ahem," Van Klomp cleared his throat. "If I can suggest something, Doctor. Let's just resolve this peacefully. While the colonel gets clearance to move the patient, why doesn't he just leave Major Fitzhugh under guard?"

"So long as the guard remains outside until the patient has fully come around from the anesthetic. After that you can put a guard at his bedside."

"He must be manacled!" snapped the lieutenant colonel, determined to seize whatever small victory he could.

The doctor shrugged. "He's in plaster and in traction. He's not going anywhere. But if you insist. So long as we hold the key and the patient's comfort and well-being is not affected."

This was not exactly what the lieutenant colonel had had in mind. But any further protest on his part was stymied by the arrival of a large party of soldiers. Armed and hardbitten veterans, filling the passage as far back as the eye could see. They'd arrived carrying the patient who had said that he was off to answer a call of nature. The man lolled limply between them.

The corporal who was supporting one side of the patient managed a salute. "He walked into our platoon a few minutes ago, sir. Said it was an emergency, sir. Said some jackass was here trying to pull a field court-martial and execute Major Fitz, sir. Is it true, sir?"

It was said loudly and clearly. It was also said in a tone that suggested that if it was true, the aforementioned "jackass" was a dead man walking.

The doctor gave his attention to the collapsed Samuelson. "Ask the lieutenant colonel," he said shortly. "While I deal with this idiot. I hope the damned young fool hasn't killed himself."

The lieutenant colonel's face was, thought Ariel, quite a study. But the corporal wasn't letting the doctor off the hook yet. "He also told us Major Fitz was injured, sir. Is he going to be all right, sir?"

"He almost certainly has multiple fractures. I don't have X-ray facilities here, of course. But he should recover. I'm less than certain about this man. Come. Help me to lift him. I'll want him back in bed and I need to get IV fluids into him. And then I want this ward clear of all nonmedical personnel. Before I count to three! That includes *all* of you. Go!"

Ariel had been amazed when they did. Mind you, she'd nearly scrambled out of the bed herself. And she didn't have the human disadvantage of a lifetime of conditioning to obey doctors. She lay there quietly, until the man himself came to check on Fitz, which was quite some time later. Fitz was distinctly restless. He'd already made two half-hearted efforts to sit up.

"Is that soldier going to live? And is this really going to work?" whispered the rat.

"He's put himself in hospital on antibiotics for another month," said the doctor quietly, checking Fitz's pulse. "But the boy should live. And as for your major here, it's a post-hypnotic, rat. So long as we stick to the story he'll believe it."

He sighed. "Though why the hell I'm doing this I'll never know. I could be struck off for malpractice."

Ariel shook her head at him. " 'Tis not what I meant. I meant with that base phrygian Turk who wanted to kill Fitz out of hand. We've made it so Fitz cannot even defend himself. And he certainly can't run, even if I could persuade him to. He has but to get an order from your Surgeon General. You humans have a depressing habit of following orders, even when they're really stupid. Then there'll be nothing for it but for me to kill that Jeebol."

The medic officer laughed softly. "I suppose you've only seen this war from a rat's point of view, and in the ordinary army. Let me explain. Most of the army command has its origin in the prewar force. To understand what's happening here, you have to understand who those people were. The colony needed an army like a man needs an extra left leg. No enemies. No reason to exist. It's had twenty-seven years of getting more and more ornamental and useless. The officer corps lost everyone with even the smallest vestige of real ability or ambition. Apparently it was not uncommon back on Earth in the late nineteenth and early twentieth centuries for the same to thing to occur between wars. That's parallel to the industrial and in many ways the social period we're going through here."

"Oh, I know they're useless," said Ariel. "Fitz and I

were at military headquarters, you know. But what does that have to do with this situation?"

"Everything, actually. You see, back on Earth, when they had a war, even if they had this sort of loser still in the military, you always had a few that weren't. And good officers who'd left came flocking back. But, because of the age and fitness constraints on the cryopreservation, only people under the age of thirty-five came to HAR from Earth. Wealthy under-thirty-fives. Not senior officers. So, twenty-seven years on, when we finally had a military emergency—we only had these jerks."

Ariel scratched the stump of her tail, thoughtfully. "I see. But I still don't see what that has to do with your Surgeon General?"

The doctor smiled beatifically. "Everything, as I said. Before the war there was no Medical Corps. The Surgeon General must be a medical doctor. So: Surgeon General Paul DiMillio is a fine physician, as well as my ex-medical superintendent. Lord! I'd give anything to see his reaction when he gets General Cartup-Kreutzler on the line, demanding he order me, of all people, to release a patient."

"Ah. So you mean the senior medical officers are not such fools as the rest of them?" inquired Ariel. Her tone was skeptical, almost caustic.

Doctor Scott could exchange sarcasm with the best. "I wouldn't go that far. But almost all the officers were simply doctors before the war, not part of this military system. The same thing applies to the Judge Advocate's department. Most of the officers were attorneys. The quartermaster, technical and mechanical support are mostly part of the old slowship crew, so they're also fairly good at what they do, too."

Fitz opened his eyes. Tried to move. "What the hell . . . ?"

"Just lie still. You're fine, Major."

"Ariel?" he croaked, trying to focus.

"I'm right here, Fitzy. Lie still, dearest."

Fitz blinked. "I can't move anyway."

"Correct, Major," said the doctor. "You're in hospital in traction. You have a possible fracture of the left femur, an almost certain fracture of the right radius and ulna, a possible concussion and a possible spinal fracture. A lot of nasty possibilities."

"What happened . . . ? All I remember was having a last drink with Bobby."

Ariel, standing on his chest, said solemnly, "You triggered a Magh' archway deadfall, which collapsed through to the next level. You're lucky to be alive."

"I wish I wasn't," said Fitz. "It would solve a few problems. God . . . I feel sick."

"It's the anesthetic," said the doctor. "Don't worry. It'll wear off."

Fitz attempted to move. With the skin-traction on his leg and strapped to a fracture board, he failed. "Not as sore as last time."

"You're full of painkillers, and the bones have been set and immobilized. You're due for a long bedrest, but you won't feel much pain. They'll have you on electronic muscle stimulus so you won't even lose muscle tone. Six to eight weeks and you'll be as good as new. We can't take a chance on moving you yet."

But Fitz had lapsed back into sleep.

The doctor stood up. "Work on your story. You're not very convincing," he said to Ariel, as he turned to leave.

# Chapter 6

∽

*George Bernard Shaw City, an elegant, wood-panelled coffeehouse with Art deco styled frosted windows and the buzz of expensive clientele in the background.*

"You're losing the media war, you know, Talbot," said Sanjay Devi. "You've done well on the other fronts. But you should have done more there. INB has been showing live coverage of the troops running down the Magh' and countless interviews of the soldiers in that section. I won't say I suspect anything, but those interviews have all been with junior officers, or even Vats. INB has got a big Vat viewership, don't forget."

She took a forkful of the Dobos torte from the beautiful hand-painted gilt-edged plate. "This is all stoking unrest among the lower classes. And we don't want that, do we?"

The Cafe Gerbeaud used these beautiful fine china plates, despite the fact that it meant that every one had to be washed by hand. But then, before the war, labor had been cheap and plentiful. It was strange to think that there had been a time, back when the colony was new, that this had not been so. When the Shareholders had been all the labor there was. After the first Vat-bred kids had come onto the labor market, however, the tide had turned. The colony had had ten years of going from shortage to glut—and then the war had come.

Sanjay wondered, sometimes, if the war could have been engineered. Or was it just fortuitous for the Shareholders? It gave her something to think about while Talbot fulminated at length about the vileness of Vats. Something other than the pain in her chest.

"Naturally I have to agree with you, Talbot. But what are you going to do about it?" she asked.

He snorted cake crumbs and threw his hands up. "What does one do about Vat ingratitude? I proposed that indoctrination in suitable patriotism be part of their school curriculum, but that was blocked by some bleeding heart. I mean we raised, educated and cared for them. They owe us . . . Oh, you mean about the media. Well, I've dealt with the two main ones. And nobody pays much attention to the rats and mice like INB."

She raised her eyebrows. "I've heard rumors—and you know I am very good at hearing those—that HBC is going to start on covering the campaign again."

Talbot hoped that his dismay didn't show. HBC! Sanjay Devi took very little part in public life. She was head of the HAR Scientific Council, and a powerful woman in her own right. She also obviously had her sources, in among people he struggled to touch. The top Shareholders all had a greater or lesser security compliment, and his men had infiltrated most of those. But she had contacts in the business community—often minor Shareholders, but wealthy people despite this. Private wealth outside of the Share-dividend was something Talbot held in distrust. Nonetheless it was a reality.

Sanjay obviously saw herself as a kingmaker, bridging the growing Shareholder/money divide. By the way she had sought him out and advised him, she was grooming him. Well, he certainly didn't mind. But HBC! HBC was the largest network, and he'd been sure that their disinterest would lead the public and the minor media players away from the story. It came as a bit of a shock to discover that he might be wrong.

"Why?"

"The board of HBC has demanded an emergency meeting to get editorial control removed from Carsey." She smiled, maliciously. "I'm a shareholder in that company and I got a call from Marcus Sidaropolis. You can't rely on him, you know."

Marcus! Marcus was an ally. You couldn't trust anyone these days. "I'll get on top of it," he promised, his eyes narrowing.

"Better deal with INB first."

"Oh, I plan to. A move to have their license rescinded is already underway. That should shut them up. Their finances aren't great, according to my agents." He laughed. "If all else fails, we'll blow up their offices and blame it on the Vats."

Sanjay Devi murmured something which Talbot couldn't quite hear. "What?"

She shook her head. "Nothing. Just thinking aloud. If I were you, I'd try threats first. The licensing board could be tricky. And open to legal challenge."

She was probably right. But he'd brushed against Independent News Broadcasting before . . . He'd have to think about it. He would go and lean on John Carsey first.

# Chapter 7

☾

*Later: back at the mock-chateau on the edge of HAR*
*wineland-country. Now the Divisional Military*
*Headquarters of the Fifth Brigade.*

"Get out of his office before he called pest control, indade!" Eamon was dangerously close to exploding.

Nym suppressed a chuckle. Even he didn't laugh at Eamon in this mood. The bat had a habit of translating explosive temper into explosive substance. The transport officer had been more than tempting his luck, making that statement. He was just lucky that Bronstein had restrained Eamon from taking a bite out of his throat or pushing a bat-mine where it fitted best. Still, thought Nym, they did have a genuine and serious problem.

Breakfast.

The lack of breakfast was not an unsurvivable problem to other species. But the rats were built on elephant-shrew metabolism. They had to eat—often, a lot, and regularly. And the army had introduced a grog-ration too. Missing it was not something rats did voluntarily.

They'd all had a fair amount of looted grog and pieces of Maggot in their packs. Rats had nothing much against eating dead friends. Worrying about eating dead enemies was definitely an idea only something as daft as a human could find disturbing. Nym liked humans nearly as much as he liked mechanical things, especially vehicles, but they were odd in their foibles. However, the food supplies were getting low. They really needed to get back into the human supply chain before morning, or there'd be trouble. Like someone eating someone else. And most of them looked stringy, or else he was becoming positively human in his own foibles.

"So, how do we get back to our units?" asked Melene. By the look in her eyes, she'd also started thinking ahead to breakfast. A rare rattess, that. Her current lover, Doc, might have more deep philosophical thought rattling around in his skull than was good for him, but she had the edge when it came to that rarest of rat intellectual jewels, forethought.

"Methinks we could help ourselves to a vehicle," Nym said, without any real hope that the others might go along with it. O'Niel loved vehicular travel. But for some reason not even the fat bat wanted Nym to drive.

The chorus of "No!" was unanimous. Unfair, it was. All he needed was a vehicle that was a bit more his own size.

"We," said O'Niel, pointing with his wing-tips to the

other two bats, "could fly, to be sure, although Eamon should not be flying far, yet. But what o' the rats? We cannot abandon our comrades."

That was bats for you. A social species. There was some comfort in it though. Nym found himself, against his better nature, wondering what a furry flier would taste like.

The thought was a bit ghastly, and galvanized him into action. "We need some goodly vittles. And soon! Otherwise . . . I cannot even think of mechanical things. We need to get back to camp now."

Doc nodded. "This matter belongs in the sphere of objective spirit. We need to assimilate that which has been created by the state. If one is at the source of that, why go to the tributary?"

"Huh?" asked Pistol, scratching his privates.

"Full of sound and fury, signifying nothing," said Fal, disgustedly. "As usual. Philosophy. Why study it? You cannot eat it, much less drink it."

Melene looked thoughtful. "Methinks he means that this is the supply depot for the camps."

"A remarkable understanding, my dear. We need to get into the storehouse."

Doll Tearsheet sauntered around the corner with studied carefulness. She had a box of chocolates in her paws. "You poxy lot could have waited for me," she said. "You left me behind, rifling his desk. I had to wait until he was called out to escape."

"Chocolate!" squealed Melene. "Remember what good friends we are, Doll."

" 'Tis amazing what good friends a girl hath when she holds all the chocolates," said Doll. "Now, I think we should make haste. Without actually running . . . yet."

"Why?" asked Eamon, suspiciously.

"Because I have set a-fire to his wastepaper basket." Doll moved along to the nearest corner at not quite a run. "Methinks he will discover it soon."

Eamon fluttered down, and bowed to her. " 'In truth, ma'am. I've not appreciated your finer qualities enough before."

There was a yell from behind them. "You can buss me later, my sweet rogue," said Doll, pushing him aside. "Now we need more haste and far more speed!"

Later, while sharing the chocolates and looking at the stores depot, the rats and bats considered strategy. "That fence looks to be electrified," said Nym. He was getting a grip on electricity. It had bitten him. And not one bit of good had come of biting it back.

Pistol and Fal, having eaten their chocolates, paused in the act of converting complex rat strategy into action. "You mean we cannot just go though the wire?"

"Not without dying," said Bronstein, dryly. "Not with your waistline, Fal. We'll have to fly over and take what we can. And the place is busy, even though dawn is a few hours off yet."

Nym found himself studying the vehicles. The chocolate wasn't much, but it had sent his mind back onto its normal channels. Men were loading the trucks with small-wheeled things with a sort of fork in front. Nym eyed them with interest. They were a bit smaller than most vehicles. Nym had an eye for vehicles and for detail. "Methinks," he said slowly, "we can have our trip home and eat it too."

It was a good idea. The only thing he didn't like about

it was that he wouldn't have an opportunity to steal one of those little vehicles with the fork.

"What do you mean, Nym?" asked Bronstein.

"That truck being loaded. 'Tis the one used to bring rations to our old camp. We can board it, and ride back. 'Tis full of food, too."

# Chapter 8

♋

*Amid the red Magh' adobe tunnels and galleries of
the conquered scorpiary.*

"I thought my life was complicated enough!" grumbled
Major Van Klomp, looking at the two civilians that a patrol
had brought to him. Van Klomp was *de jure* not in charge
of the infantrymen. Officially, Colonel Nygen was in
charge. Except that he had not yet made it past the old
front lines, apparently.

Oddly enough, lines of communication back to there
were terrible. Lieutenant Colonel Burkoff was supposed
to be Nygen's second in command, and he had been sent
forward by the colonel to assume control. It appeared he
hadn't been seen for the last day or so. Van Klomp had
very little doubt that the man was at the bottom of a
Maggot pit somewhere, definitely not stabbed with a

bangstick. There were several surviving majors from Brigadier Charlesworth's hijacked brigade. Fitz had sent them to the various edges of the scorpiary, to set up defenses. Such chaos was reigning that, while Military Headquarters had sent a number of messages that Major Fitzhugh was to be summarily arrested and tried . . . no one there had got around to giving orders as to the deployment of the troops, yet.

And no one had given Van Klomp orders to pull out yet, either. As the orders for him and his paratroopers to be here were fakes, made by Fitz's clerk, that was hardly surprising. So: by virtue of being smack bang in the middle of the scorpiary, and having a powerful personality and an overwhelming voice, Fitz's illegally assumed mantle of command had fallen on Van Klomp. He'd been quietly taking advantage of it to ship out as much of the captured materiel as possible.

He was a realist. The HAR army was going to lose this huge hunk of territory by sheer stupidity and inertia. But he was going to make sure that every untrashed piece of equipment from the brood-heart chamber, and as many of the Magh' artillery pieces as could be transported, went back to human-held territory. In the meanwhile, he had men making maps, taking photographs and generally scouring the territory to try to fill in the dreadfully thin human supply of knowledge about their enemy. So far he had established that most of the information the Korozhet advisors had provided for humanity was startlingly inaccurate.

Actually, the word "garbage" sprang to mind.

And now they'd brought him these. "Parachute Major Van Klomp?" asked the one without the camcorder.

"*Ja.*" With a large hand, he redirected the camcorder to point at the floor. "And who are you gentlefolk, and what are you doing here? This is a combat zone. Not a good place for civilians."

The woman smiled, obviously a practiced-for-camera smile. "Sally Borodin, Independent News. Mind if we ask you a few questions, Major?"

Van Klomp's face, he hoped, revealed none of his real feelings. Or the fact that he had suddenly realized that these people could be very powerful weapons in what was bound to be an ugly fight. "Do *you* mind if I ask if you're officially accredited war journalists?" he asked in reply.

"The public is hungry for first-hand news about this campaign, Major," she said, avoiding a direct answer as smoothly as any politician. "Especially the role that the paratroopers have played in it."

Ah. Excellent. So she wasn't one of the sanitized journos the War Office normally gave permits to.

"No reason I can't tell you what happened," said Van Klomp. "Although the main man behind this campaign was an intelligence major by the name of Fitzhugh."

"We've been trying to track him down."

Van Klomp put on a suitably mournful expression, and tried to ignore the camera. "Major Fitzhugh was unfortunately caught in a Magh' deadfall, when he was bravely leading the troops in deadly chamber-to-chamber, hand-to-hand combat. He's been severely injured."

"Are his injuries life-threatening, Major?"

"Fortunately not. The medics assure me he has an absolute one hundred percent chance of recovery." That should stop General Cartup-Kreutzler attempting to have someone silence Fitz.

For the next hour and a half Van Klomp hammered it up, as large as life and twice as natural. He gave them a graphic—if fictitious—version of "the commandos' " heroic capture of the brood-heart, and their rescue of none other than the late chairman's daughter. He told of the race to rescue these heroes. He had some of his men reenact the final assault on the brood-heart. He let them photograph the dead alien. And he got them a few interviews with troops who had seen action with Fitz. They had had a number of those already. And just to make doubly sure it all got out, he had them escorted onto a captured hover-artillery piece and flown out of the combat zone. In the interests of their safety, of course.

He was just getting up to go and see Fitz when a patrol brought in another couple of reporters. This pair had sneaked in past the patrols by coming through the minefields, proving reporters to be entirely crazy.

"They must be as thick as flies around the old front lines," muttered Van Klomp. "You'll just have to wait," he said to the pair from Interweb. "I'm going to see someone in the field hospital."

He went down to see Fitz in the makeshift field hospital.

By Fitz's expression, it looked as if it was a good thing the major was immobilized. A terrified-looking MP lieutenant was standing against the far wall, doing his best to pretend that he wasn't there at all. "*Ja* boykie? Lazing in bed while the rest of us work, eh?"

"Bobby, tell this lot they're to stop terrorizing the kid," said Fitz, jerking a thumb at the MP, not bothering to rise to the bait Van Klomp trailed.

"Don't you think I have done enough?" asked the paratrooper cheerfully, making the makeshift bed groan as he sat on it. "I had to save the Lieutenant Colonel Jeebol from a lynch mob. Sent him sneaking home in a plain coat with his hair shaved off, and his tail between his legs."

Fitz was not to be distracted. "It's not fair on the boy. I was planning to go and hand myself over."

"I know," Van Klomp said cheerfully. "So, that was why, when you got injured, I sent some of my men back to fetch you an MP. Seeing as you couldn't go to them, they've come to you. My boys found several of them ornamenting the old front line. So: the record reads that you surrendered to them, to the best of your ability, and I assisted the MP." Van Klomp beamed broadly at the idea.

The young MP had finally had enough. "Your men brought us here by force, Major Van Klomp. They held a bangstick to my head!"

"My men *forced* you?" Butter would have frozen solid in Van Klomp's mouth. "But you had orders to arrest Major Fitzhugh, didn't you? What did they do but to bring you to him? He's in no fit state to come to you. The way it looks, you were being derelict in your duty."

"We . . . we don't have slowshields," protested the MP. "We're not supposed to be front-line soldiers."

"Ah!" exclaimed Van Klomp, beaming. "Now I understand, Lieutenant. There's been a misunderstanding. My men weren't abducting you. They were protecting you. If you find it irksome, they won't do so on the way out."

"Lot of Maggots still on the loose out there, aren't there, Major?" said one of the patients with a nasty smile. "I wonder if the loo-tenant knows what a 'scorp-sting does to a man?"

"It's an awful way to die," said another. He issued a truly histrionic moan. "Excruciating agony. I've seen a soldier snap his own spine with the pain."

"And those aren't the worst—" said Ariel.

"That's enough, Ariel," said Fitz, "or I'll ration your chocolate, no matter how many times you protest that I don't love you any more." He turned on the others, ignoring her outraged sniff. "Stop winding him up, you lot. Lieutenant. Pay no attention. I'll see you get a safe escort out of here. With me."

Van Klomp laughed. "Mind you, I'm not sure who is guarding who. The doc tells me he has had to quarter the other MPs in the spare ward. The troops outside were rather nasty to them."

The MP shifted, his expression angry. "I don't want to be here, and I certainly don't want to arrest the major. I'm just obeying orders."

"Major Van Klomp!" A runner panted from the door. "There is some kind of alien skycraft setting down on the roof of the scorpiary dome."

"Shit!" Van Klomp was up and running.

They were met in the upper corridors by another of Van Klomp's men. "It's Korozhet, sir. They say they're military advisors. They got some major general and a couple of brigadiers from headquarters with them. They came in a Korozhet landing craft because of the weather. Those babes have real all-weather flying ability."

"Hmm. Well, I suppose I had better go up and meet them." Van Klomp straightened his uniform. He lacked Fitz's patience and tact. Fitz had put up with months of being sidelined and ignored at Military Headquarters. Bobby Van Klomp had a shorter fuse. To deal with this lot he wished he had some of Fitz's patience. He was glad he didn't suffer from Fitz's honesty!

The official party of observers and brass were still on the roof in the gentle rain that had set in again. They were looking at the small, jagged-edged hole in the scorpiary roof, and the rope ladder going down.

"Good day, gentleman, ma'am. Alien friends," said Van Klomp as he hauled himself up it.

The major general and his team of factotums in their dress uniforms surveyed the major. "Who are you, Major?"

"Major Robert Van Klomp. First HAR airborne."

"Airborne? I thought you chaps only did display jumps at parades," said the female brigadier. She had a very credible sneer, Van Klomp thought, for someone whose makeup was running in the rain.

"We are supposed to be the army's elite assault troops, ma'am. Which I assume is why General Cartup-Kreutzler decided to use us in his attempt to get the commando forces out. We didn't expect them to be so successful."

"The general wasn't even involved in this fiasco!" snapped the brigadier. "It was all that blasted intelligence officer. The one who always had a rat in his pocket. Fitzhugh."

"The orders were signed by the general. I don't know which of his staff planned it, ma'am, but it was a brilliant operation on the general's part, if I may say so." Van Klomp was one of those people who enjoyed rubbing salt into the wounds of people he detested. He was finding this whole situation a little on the cheery side, actually, for all his tenseness. "The most—in fact, the only—successful recapture of territory from the Magh'."

"Strategically a very poor idea," said one of the Korozhet.

"Exactly," said the major general. "No matter what it looks like to you junior officers. This operation had absolutely nothing to do with General Cartup-Kreutzler. It's a complete botch. Now, we and the Korozhet need to get down to the Magh' command room. The area must be sealed."

"Certainly, sir," said Van Klomp doing his best to restrain a grin. He had, he suspected, been quite right to order everything in the chamber loaded up and sent off to HARIT's Alien research unit. "My men have secured the area. If you'll follow me down the ladder, I'll lead you there."

The major general, who was as round as a grease spot, looked at the ladder swaying down into the lumifungus-green-tinged darkness. He was fifty-five if he was a day old, and looked as if he hadn't done any exercise more violent than riding a golf cart for the last twenty years. He blanched. "There must be another way. Our Korozhet friends can't manage that."

"Oh, I have it on good authority that they're very agile on their spikes, sir," said Van Klomp, with a face that would have won him any game of poker he ever played in. By what Private Connolly and the others had said, the Korozhet who had kidnapped Virginia Shaw had definitely been hand in glove with the Magh', not humanity. Young Chip Connolly had shown a remarkable degree of good sense about that part of their story. He'd said that he didn't think it was going to be popular with the powers-that-be.

Van Klomp was ready to bet large sums of money that it wasn't going to be. The scary part, to him, had been the information that there was a built-in pro-Korozhet bias in the soft-cyber implants in the heads of mankind's warriors, the rats and the bats. Connolly had explained the linguistic dodges which the rats and bats had been using to circumvent the bias, but it all sounded awfully dicey to Van Klomp.

"Pish-tosh, man! Anyone can see they're too round for climbing," said the circular major general. "And what good authority was this, eh?"

"Ms. Virginia Shaw, sir," replied Van Klomp smoothly. "She had a Korozhet tutor. His remains are below, sir."

There was an agitated clattering from the spines of the assembled Korozhet. The air was thick with a sudden smell of naphthalene. The major noticed that at least two of them had raised slightly thicker spines to point at him. What was it that Private Connolly had said? Harpoonlike darts, and gas secretion? The Pricklepusses gave out that they were peaceful vegetarians, but he'd put the testimony of Connolly, and the rats and bats, above the veracity of the aliens.

"Her remains . . . they have been left in public for the Underphyle to gawp at!" huffed one rather vermillion-spined Korozhet. "Outrage! Disrespect! Punishment!"

Another one of the prickly ones clattered spines, hastily. The clatterer was larger and a purpler shade of red than the one who had made the furious outburst. The smaller one lowered its spines.

"My apologies, if we've caused affront," said major general. "I'll see that the appropriate censure is given, Advisor Tirritit." He turned back to Van Klomp. "Now, Major, the sooner we can get the Korozhet down to their dead, the better. We need an alternate route."

"Certainly, sir. We've opened up a track from the front lines. It is rather rough, sir. But we've been able to get specialized ATVs through in about three to four hours. If you would like to fly back there, I'll have vehicles waiting for you. I'll get men to prepare a mine-free landing area, and put down some beacons."

"What? But that's miles, man!" snapped the general. "And I'm not having our VIP guests bounced around for three hours. There must be a closer way. If there isn't, make one!"

Van Klomp nodded. "I believe a request for engineers has been put in to HQ, sir. I'll happily set my men to blowing a more accessible passage. But our experience with this Magh' adobe hasn't been good, sir. We certainly can't guarantee your safety. We're soldiers, not structural engineers. The stuff tends to collapse, sometimes immediately, sometimes for no apparent reason, later. We've had a couple of nasty accidents with it. If we tried to cut you an access we might end up killing you, sir."

Van Klomp paused thoughtfully. "We could always get a cargo net and lower you down. That would be the quickest and easiest." And it would be most tempting to cut the rope, he thought, but did not add.

"Hmph. Would it be safe?"

"Safe as an elevator, sir. I'd let them lower me first," said Van Klomp earnestly.

"Set it up then," ordered the general. "As quickly as possible. An elevator would be acceptable."

"Right away, sir. Excuse me."

Van Klomp went down into the smelly belly of the Magh' mound. It still stank less than up on top. A ten-ton truck with a winch and a cargo net brought along as close as possible did the trick. Van Klomp's paratroopers scurried about attaching anchors and setting up a tripod with a pulley in it. A plank, Van Klomp knew, would have made it more comfortable, but he wasn't feeling generous.

"Uh, Major," interrupted a private, tentatively. "Those two reporters. They're still sitting in your 'office.'"

Van Klomp smiled nastily. "Bring 'em here, boy. Let them interview some top brass."

The private looked at the arrangement and the careful measuring of rope. "Major . . . you're not giving them the whoah-belly, are you?" he asked suspiciously.

Van Klomp's expression of saintliness should have gotten him instant canonization. "Me, Private? You know as well as I do that the winch only winds in. That you have to pull cable out. The brake does stop it being entirely unwound and perhaps damaging the cable or drum. I do promise I'll tell them that it is a bit jerky at times."

The private struggled to run and fetch the journos, he was laughing so much.

It was a two-hundred-foot drop, straight down, to the level where the ruined bridge led to the brood-heart chamber. The "moat" that protected the chamber meant that there was still another drop of five hundred feet below that. By swinging the rope ladders in and attaching them to a stick-out bastion, it was a forty-five-foot climb. Not un-strenuous, but not that long, either. But, if they wanted an elevator, by all means let the brass have one. In comparison to the whoah-belly Van Klomp had set up for training the recruits, this was a lollapalooza. He couldn't wait to try it out himself.

But then, he was an adrenaline junkie with a long-established habit.

°          °          °

Van Klomp stood rigidly to attention as the hysterical major general shrieked at him. "You said that it was *safe*! I'll have you court-martialed! Reduced to the ranks!"

"It's as safe as houses, sir. You were warned that it was jerky and I did offer to arrange transport around. You refused and insisted on doing it this way, sir. I explained that the cable winch only wound in, but used a speed-governed brake to prevent sudden jerk stresses from damaging the cable or drum. I've been up and down it twice now, and I can't say I found it unsafe. I'm sorry you found it distressing."

He was interrupted by a terrible shriek from above. The brigadier, hurtling down in the free-fall stage, obviously also found it distressing. No sense of adventure, these brass-hats.

The brake slowed the net bag's descent, and then began allowing it to accelerate again. The brigadier whizzed past them, the pitch of her shriek beautifully displaying the Doppler effect. At the next braking the winch operator hit the retrieve button, and gently winched the gibbering wreck back to level with the platform. A paratrooper leaned out with a crudely made boathook and hauled her in. The winch operator cut the power providing the final undignified drop into the arms of Sergeant Harris. Two troopers cut the net loose from the cross brace at the top. The brigadier, released from the support of the net and Harris' arms, fell to her knees and was sick.

"General, do you want me continue bringing your staff down with the hoist?" asked Van Klomp calmly. "They seem to find it rather alarming. Colonel Pumbrey has come around from his faint, by the way." The major felt rather well disposed toward the colonel. If he'd yelled instead of being silently paralyzed with terror when he and Van Klomp had done the first descent together, the general would never have dared come down. "I don't see why they should suffer unnecessarily."

"If I had to do it, they will," snarled the general.

"Very well, sir. However, I'll send a man up to tell them they've no need to worry, but that your aides have found it slightly alarming. I want a volunteer, men. Raise a hand, someone who is willing to go up. Tell them part of the descent is rather worrying, but the general says they are to come down. And warn the Korozhet too. I'm not sure how their physiology would stand up to it. If they feel that there is any danger they'd better not try this."

Every soldier present shot his hand up—even those who Van Klomp knew were not fond of the whoah-belly. Obviously a lot of enlisted men were eager to show the brass that they didn't scream or lose their lunch. The major picked on one of the smaller men—one of the most acrobatic and steel-nerved of his troops—and sent him up. "In the meanwhile one of you go and see if you can find the general some new trousers," he added cheerfully.

"Major General Fredricks?" asked the reporter, stepping forward out of the shadows. "Mike Sherry from Interweb. Can we ask you a few questions for our viewers?"

It was a great psychological moment to interview someone.

Van Klomp knew that giving the general and his staff the whoah-belly ride was a rather childish and ultimately self-defeating pastime. But it had been very sweet.

It was also nearly terminal. Private Oliver had reported

back, saying that the Korozhet had said that they were capable of surviving far greater physiological stress than endoskeletal species, and were certainly not frightened. By the private's description, it was the smaller, redder one who had gotten very upset by the thought of the dead Korozhet being looked at by what, if Van Klomp understood it right, amounted to "lesser species."

The smaller, vermillion-spined Korozhet came down next. The Korozhet did not scream. But as the paratrooper swung it in with the boathook, it pointed those thickened spines at him through the net. If Van Klomp had not been primed by Connolly's description of this event, the young trooper would have been dead. As it was, Van Klomp hit the spine with a bangstick, and hauled the youngster aside. The edge of the dart gashed across the young paratrooper's arm, before striking the Magh' adobe, sending a spray of fluid across the ground.

The net bag swung wildly back into space as the vermillion Korozhet fired its second dart. It missed completely as a result. The winch operator had a moment of genius and hit the power switch. The Korozhet rose steadily, swinging wildly, hissing like a kettle that was about to explode.

"Stay away from that stuff," snapped Van Klomp, pointing to the liquid that had spilled out of the protoplasm-hosed harpoon. He was hastily tying a tourniquet onto the trooper's arm. "With any luck you won't have the poison in you, son. But let's keep it to the arm. Winch! Stop that bastard about halfway. Let him dangle until we can deal with this." He'd never forgive himself if his practical joke on the brass cost this kid his life or even his arm. "Let's get this soldier to the medics."

"It's just a gash, sir," said the paratrooper.

"It could be poisoned, Private. That liquid definitely is." He poured perfectly good booze into the wound, washing it thoroughly. He turned to look for the major general.

By all reports, Fredricks had joined the army twenty years ago, on the clear understanding that it was a nice secure job with no heavy lifting, requiring, principally, the ability to march in step. Lately, it had required the ability to play politics and golf, drink whiskey and kiss butts. It had obviously ill-prepared him for this sort of action. He cringed nervously next to a wall, surveying the nearest thing he'd seen to actual combat.

"Major General Fredricks." Van Klomp beckoned to a radio-op. "The corporal here will get a radio-link with my men at the top. You will inquire whether the dart the Korozhet fired has any toxicity on the outside, or whether it is just the liquid pumped down it. If the thing is toxic we need to know exactly what sort of toxin it is. Make it very clear that we're holding them responsible for this incident."

By the timid look, the major general did not find it at all odd to find their roles reversed, and the major giving him orders. In fact he looked relieved, if somewhat terrified by the Jekyll-and-Hyde transformation of the formerly respectful major. He did as he was told.

" . . . Yes, Tirritit. Fired darts at a soldier. Cut his arm quite badly. We hold you responsible for this injury. We need to know if there are toxins on that barb."

The odd breathy speech of the advisor carried some reassurance. "A defense mechanism. Advisor Shurrit must have been frightened. There is a lytic haemotoxic protease

in the toxin pumped down the center of the spine-
harpoon, but there will be very little on the outside of it,
Major General. The miscreant will be dealt with. Our
apologies."

"Er. Accepted . . . out."

Van Klomp nodded to the radio-op. "Get the MO. He
has a radio down there. Give him that information. Tell
him what has been done so far. And then we'd better
decide what to do with that one." He pointed at the dangling alien, some hundred and twenty feet above their
heads.

The general had recovered his wind as well as his wits.
"Major. How dare you give orders to me like that! I'm
your superior officer, you know!"

"My apologies, sir. Decisive action was called for. A
man's life might have hung in the balance. Would you
have preferred it if I had wasted time on flowery polite-
ness? Did you—as a result—do anything that you wouldn't
have done to assist our soldiers?"

The general noticed just what Van Klomp was looking
at. Realized he was about to make a fool of himself on
camera. "Er. Quite. I was merely rather taken aback at
your telling me to do exactly what I was just about to do."

"I apologize again," said Van Klomp, knowing he
sounded anything but contrite. He turned to the two
reporters. "Isn't it strange that the slowshields are set to
only stop something moving faster than the Korozhet's
darts?"

The general looked at the two reporters. "Have you
two got clearance to be here? Sensitive military matters
are being dealt with. I don't think you should be filming."

Sherry shrugged. "Tell you what, General. I just sent

through the pics of you coming down the hoist on the satellite-link." The reporter had one of the now incredibly valuable and rare Earth-built satellite phones. GBS City had cell coverage, but otherwise you had to rely on land-lines . . . unless you had one of those. "I'll ask my editor to consider holding them back if you don't give me any more trouble about filming."

The general did a very good imitation of a turkey-cock. "You . . . you can't hold me to ransom! Get these journalists out of here, Major. You tell that editor of yours if he releases those pictures I'll sue. Major, confiscate those cameras!"

The kind of reporter who picks his way through a mine field to get a story isn't that easy to get rid of. "I wouldn't do that, Major Van Klomp. General Fredricks, this is now going out live. You do know the law, don't you, as far as censorship, damage to equipment of reportage, and the withholding of information which is in the public interest?"

Van Klomp smiled pacifically. "I've had a direct order from a superior officer. I can't disobey."

"Leave them," said Fredericks sourly. "But you aren't allowed into combat zones without permits, which I am sure you haven't got. So you'd better get out of here. Major, see these men removed from the front."

Van Klomp saluted. "Sir. Sergeant Daniels. See to it."

"Look, Major!" said the sergeant.

The Korozhet were descending with magnificent slowness on a gleaming metal platelike craft. The device appeared to have no visible means of support.

"Another little toy they somehow neglected to mention," said Van Klomp dryly.

The reporters were ardently filming, as their escort was busy watching the descent. The strange plate stopped beside the dangling Korozhet. A brief bright lance of light flickered. The net bag fell. Now there was no cable brake to slow its passage to the distant bottom.

"They've killed him . . . My God. They've just killed him!" said the shocked reporter.

The plate continued to descend until it got to their level. By now the soldiers had begun to hustle the protesting reporters away. Van Klomp felt that it was just as well. He didn't know quite how to handle this himself.

The alien did. He inclined his spines to the major general and asked: "I trust that the matter is now resolved to your satisfaction?"

"Uh." General Fredricks swallowed. "We . . . um, didn't mean that you had to kill him."

"But how else do you chastise an underling who has failed?" asked the Korozhet. "I will send two of my staff down to deal with the remains as is respectful. Now, if we can proceed to the brood-heart chamber?"

The brood-heart chamber was scarred by the explosive damage from the shorting of the power cables that had run the force-field generator. The walls, once hung with rich fabrics, were now firescarred and stripped.

The general and his aides still seemed very impressed by the vast dimensions of the brood-heart chamber.

The alien Korozhet, however, looked at the chamber with different eyes, and not just in the sense that they were ocelli on the end of some of their spines. "What has happened to all the equipment?" demanded the purple-red spined one Van Klomp had come to recognize as Advisor Tirritit.

"How did you know that there was equipment here, sir?" asked Van Klomp.

The creature clattered its spines. "I am in my female-phase, Major. And naturally we have seen captured scorpiaries before."

"Ah," said Van Klomp. "It was just that, based on what we found here, the information the Korozhet advisors have provided to the army seems to have been very inaccurate."

More spine clattering. Van Klomp was getting the idea that it probably signified irritation. "Most of the scorpiaries captured have only been taken after tremendous fighting and structural damage. This is in better repair than is usually the case. We hoped to update our data. That is why we are here, Major. So where is the equipment that should be here?"

"Yes, Major, where is it?" demanded Major General Fredricks. "You assured me you'd secured the area. This doesn't look secured to me . . ." He kicked at the remains of coals and ashes from the Maggot-barbeque that the rats and bats had enjoyed, with a highly polished shoe. As a gesture this was all very well, but was ill-advised in his new trousers. The only pair of BDU trousers that the paratrooper sergeant had been able to find with a large enough waistline for the general had belonged to a far taller man. The huge bulge of extra leg snagged on a half-burned piece of priceless Terran antique gateleg table that must have been among the loot with which the Magh' had furnished their once-plush nest. The general landed, with a crunch and a billow of ash, on the remains of the dead fire.

"Of course we secured the area, sir," said Van Klomp,

as the general's aides helped him to his feet. "And in accordance with standing instruction amendment 202-b, subsection iii, all captured alien material has been sent back to the Alien equipment research section, at the HAR Institute of Technology, as quickly as possible. We've been very busy, sir. Normally, as you know, the Magh' fighters don't have any equipment for us to capture. But we've sent five truckloads of stuff off under guard already. There has been no looting."

The Korozhet seemed very displeased, if the clattering of spines was anything to judge by. "We must always be the first to examine this sort of material. It is entirely possible it is booby-trapped."

Van Klomp shrugged. "I'm sure the general can arrange something, sir . . . I mean ma'am. It's out of my hands, I'm afraid." Hopefully, it was already in Dr. Liepsich's hands. And heaven preserve anyone who tried to get the physicist to part with his new toys. He was renowned for his rudeness.

Plainly, General Fredricks had had a previous encounter with the infamous Liepsich. He tried hastily for a distraction. "What about that alien you told my friend Major General Visse you'd captured, Major? Perhaps our Korozhet friends would like to interrogate him."

"He wasn't exactly captured, General. He was liberated. He was also a Magh' prisoner, and apparently played quite a role in the final fight for the Magh' brood-heart. Unfortunately, he speaks no English. He's been sent back too, under escort."

"What sort of captive alien was this?" asked Advisor Tirritit. "This is the first we have heard of it."

The general blinked. "Oh. I am sorry, Tirritit. Visse

mentioned it to me, and I hadn't brought it to your attention yet. We didn't think it was important enough to trouble you. It was just one alien."

"Describe the alien."

Van Klomp obliged. "Short. Blue furred. And it had four arms . . ."

"A Jampad!" fluted the advisor squeakily. "A Jampad here! Doubtless in league with the Magh'. It must be killed as soon as possible. Jampad are telepathic and can control lesser races! Fortunately we Korozhet are resistant, or they would have exterminated half the species in the galaxy."

"We'll see something gets done about it at once," said the general. "I'll get onto Visse immediately. Major Van Klomp. Get me a radio operator."

"Sir, these mobile units wouldn't have the range. There is a more powerful unit over at my temporary headquarters. Sergeant Daniels. Accompany the general."

"It is unnecessary," said the Korozhet. "The matter has already been communicated to our lander, and the news will be sent to the ship. I must however caution you to silence on this matter. We, in conjunction with your headquarters, will deal with it in the utmost secrecy."

# Chapter 9

☞

*1st HAR Airborne base, just outside George Bernard Shaw City. George Bernard Shaw City: various media offices, both rich and poor.*

**FITZHUGH ACCUSED OF TREASON!**

*Major Conrad Fitzhugh, the intelligence officer who has been credited with the successful capture of the scorpiary adjacent to Sector Delta 355 has been placed under arrest. He has been accused of spying for the Magh'.*

Nobody looking at Parachute-Major Van Klomp's impassive face could have guessed at just how pleased he was to see this news article. The idiots. The brass obviously had no idea how the psychology of someone like Fitzy worked. On squirmers like themselves, this would have been an effective stitch-up. They'd have rolled over and died. Tried plea-bargains. Given in.

Fitzy . . .

This would make Fitzy fight. Charging him with what he was prepared to accept he had done wrong would have been a lot wiser. It was a good thing they'd decided to draw, quarter, and crucify Conrad Fitzhugh instead. That, he assumed, was what this pack of nonsense was all about.

"It's not that I don't want to oblige you, Talbot. It's just that you're costing us. Both money and market leadership."

The rich mellow tones of John Carsey hid none of the fact that he was rich. He was not mellow.

"HBC used to dominate the news broadcasting market," he continued harshly. "We had about eighty-three percent of the viewership. Since we stopped live coverage of the captured scorpiary, and events on the front—at your brother-in-law's request, mind you—we've lost market-share. A *lot* of market-share. Our ratings are on a one-way skid to nowhere. INB has just taken up the slack. My company's shareholders have called for an emergency meeting tomorrow morning. If I don't go back to covering what the public wants to see—right now, today—I am out of a job tomorrow. And even if I was in a position to tell our shareholders to sod off, it wouldn't help you at all. Because soon HBC would disappear. Our viewers are pulling the plug, and so will our advertisers. Unless you leverage INB, you're wasting your time and our money. You already have. And if you leverage INB, no doubt viewers would turn to Interweb. You've obviously muzzled the Allied Press' papers. Interweb and the Sun Group must be ready to kiss you. The public wants to know what's happening. They like the story of our troops winning, for a change. They like it a lot."

Carsey sighed. "We're also being shredded over our reportage about Fitzhugh. We're getting a few hundred letters and calls a day. INB is giving them air-time. So are Interweb and the Sun Group. You've got protest growing out there."

"Tabloid trash," snapped Cartup.

"Tabloid trash, seeing their market-share increase, Talbot," said Carsey grimly. He hung up the phone.

So Talbot Cartup, one of the most powerful men on HAR, went around to see Lynne Stark, something he'd never imagined he'd ever be doing. Stark was one of those women whom Talbot Cartup truly detested. Lynne Stark was an upstart. She had, still, one solitary share in the HAR colony. She'd battered her way up from apartments on Clarges Street, one step above the Vat tenements, to owning her own company.

The INB offices were the sort of places he truly disliked also. They were too small, too crowded, with not one cent spent on decor or plushness. And, right now, they were frantic. Looking through the open door and into the next room, he could see an array of screens. Across one of those screens leapt live coverage of a bunch of Magh' warriors and three rats, playing tag with them. The rats were darting in and slashing at the deadly creatures in some vast red-walled cavern.

Another screen had an interviewer talking to a wounded soldier. " . . . yeah. I was with Major Fitzhugh when we went in. Not more than ten yards from the great man himself." There was naked hero-worship in the soldier's voice.

"Can I help you, sir?" asked a harried receptionist.

"Talbot Cartup," he said, irritably. "I've come to see Ms. Stark."

She shook her head at him. "Sorry. Lynne's not seeing anyone without appointments, Mr. Cartup. Things are too busy right now."

Cartup examined her coldly, for a moment. The receptionist was a young woman, obviously a Vat, and just the right age to be serving in the army.

"I *said* my name was Talbot Cartup, young lady. I'm the Security portfolio of the HAR Company. If you don't get her for me in ten seconds, I'll have the Special Branch track down your name and have your draft exemption canceled. Your name will be on the top of the conscription list by tomorrow morning. And I'll have this subversive dump raided."

The young woman looked considerately at him. Then she pushed her chair back from the desk. Belatedly, Cartup realized it was a wheelchair.

"Tell you what, Talbot Cartup, I'll save the Special Branch some trouble. My name is Janice Younna. You just get my name on that list. Please. Then I'll happily arrange you an interview, with Lynne or God in person, if you like. However, I will tell Lynne you are here. Let her decide whether she wants to talk to you or not."

Three minutes later, the girl in the wheelchair came back. "Follow me, please," she said coolly. He walked along behind the wheelchair, with his bodyguards trailing, to an office in the back.

The owner of INB sat at a tubular steel and glass desk, on a tubular steel chair. The steel was softer than the woman sitting on it. Talbot Cartup knew from her dossier that Lynne Stark was nearly his own age. But she was slim, unlined, and could have been anywhere between thirty and sixty. Her hair was undressed, merely long, thick and dark. She wore steel-rimmed glasses, too.

"Talbot Cartup. And your goons. How nice. What brings you to Independent News Broadcasting?"

Talbot Cartup gritted his teeth. "Stark, I need some cooperation from you. And I am going to get it. You can make it easy or hard for yourself."

She raised her eyebrows at him. "What cooperation could the head of HAR's Internal Security require of me? And should I be calling my lawyers before I talk to you any further?"

"I don't think you should, Stark. You want to play hardball with me, I'll play hardball right back. I want this live coverage of that piece on the front off your channel. I want this praise of Major Fitzhugh scrubbed. He had nothing to do with that attack. It was planned and coordinated by Lieutenant General Cartup-Kreutzler and his staff. I'm sure you've seen the article in the GBH Times. Fitzhugh is a traitor who took advantage of a long established secret project to try and cover his own treachery."

She sat back in her chair. "I also saw the article in the Post tearing that press release to shreds. Most entertaining that while the general was supposed to be directing the most successful campaign of the war he was in fact in detention, having been arrested as drunk, disorderly and indecent."

"That's a blatant lie! Those charges have been squa . . . dropped!"

"Yes. A lot of people are asking questions about that," said Stark, dryly.

He pushed himself forward, leaning over her desk. It was a good way of intimidating people. "Look, Stark. I'm not here to bandy words with you. Are you going to stop this reporting?"

She didn't appear to even be slightly intimidated. "Let's imagine the answer was 'no.' What are you going to do about it?"

"Shut you down." He thumped his meaty fist on the table. "By fair means or foul, Stark. See how well you can operate with only cripples for staff. The rest of them will be getting letters from the conscription board. And we'll be going into your finances, too. Let's see how well you can manage without advertising revenue."

"Talbot Cartup, your attitude towards the handicapped doesn't sit too well with me, or the people of Harmony and Reason. And neither does your attitude to the freedom of the press." She stood up and glanced at a corner of the room. "Thank you for appearing live on our program, Talbot Cartup. And the answer is 'No.' INB will not be intimidated out of giving the people of HAR the coverage they want. And don't come back here without a warrant."

"This media circus certainly hasn't been helped by your making an idiot of yourself on TV, Talbot," said General Cartup-Kreutzler. "Now you've got to keep your hands off."

"It's the kind of dirty trick I'm not going to forget and forgive in a hurry," snapped Talbot. He did not need his idiot brother-in-law telling him he'd botched it. He was painfully aware of the fact.

"She's put the brakes, temporarily, on direct action. I'll get my men to work on the indirect harassment. Bug their phones, slow their mail, break into their apartments and cars and see what we can find. We'll plant something if we need to. But we're still going to get at her advertisers. The new upstart money may stick to her, here and there, but I wield a lot of influence with shareholders in a lot of the larger traditional companies. INB is pretty fragile, financially. And yes, HBC is going back to covering the sector, but I had a long and fruitful discussion with their editors. The public needs some kind of hero figure to lionize. So we agreed to have them shift attention to the parachute major who led his troops into the middle of the scorpiary. "

"Van Klomp?" inquired the general.

Talbot nodded. "I think that was the name, yes."

"He's the man who got Lieutenant Colonel Jeebol out of trouble, and I believe he arranged for the MPs to actually capture that son of a bitch Fitzhugh."

"Sounds like a good man," said Talbot, approvingly. "I think the army should make a fuss of him. Promotion. Medals. And then he can go back to doing display jumps at parades. Heaven knows how he got involved in the first place."

"Fitzhugh called the paratroopers in," said General Cartup-Kreutzler. "I have no idea why. Probably just because the man's an idiot romantic. The paratroopers are purely a ceremonial unit. A volunteer unit. No conscripts. They've never been used in combat before, as they're mostly the sons of Shareholders. Some of the first families have kids in that unit. It's glamorous, without being dangerous."

Talbot Cartup leaned back in the very comfortable arm-chair, trying to keep from sneering openly. His brother-in-law was about as dense as a man could get and still be a basically functional adult.

"For Chr— Um. That's the reason right there. Romanticism had nothing to do with it. Fitzhugh's an anarchist. Vicious. He called them in thinking they'd mostly be killed."

Talbot rose to his feet. "I'll get my staff onto drafting the paperwork. And let Van Klomp have some conscripts, enough to make into a second unit that can actually do some fighting. If we're going to build up his reputation, we'll have to keep some paratroopers in the fighting."

"That should do," agreed Cartup-Kreutzler. "Seeing as it looks as if we'll only get our hands on Fitzhugh when he comes out of the hospital. That means he'll be a facing general court-martial, which will be open to the public. But if we've built up another hero by then . . . The public's attention span isn't very long anyway."

# Chapter 10

එ

*George Bernard Shaw City, HAR Institute of Technology, in the skeletal remains of the great slowship that brought humans to Harmony and Reason.*

There was a realistic possibility that if someone stood behind this human, to provide the extra pair of hands, and it had slightly longer fur, and dyed it blue, that it could pass for a giant Jampad. Darleth found that faintly reassuring.

Or, perhaps not. She'd been away from the People too long, when one of these aliens started looking comforting! She knew that by the standards of his people, she was already insane. That was all right. Madness helped her cope with the aching pain of losing her clan-sibs. Jampad were not solitary creatures and kin-bonds were life-bonds.

By her talk to the Korozhet-speaking aliens, it was not so with the little sharpnosed ones, or to a great degree with the ones like this two-legged tailless hairy one. The little fliers seemed to have some measure of it.

But they were all alien . . . and she was alone on an alien world, twenty-eight light years from home, with the only interstellar FTL craft here belonging to the murderers of her kin.

She had been a captive, live-food-to-be for the Magh' young. She'd been given a weapon by the alien enemies of the Korozhet, and had helped the small party gain its freedom by killing one of her clan-sibs' murderers. She was at least not live food any more, but she was still unsure as to what her status actually was. None of the species that called itself, if she had the pronunciation right, "Human," spoke any Korozhet. They certainly didn't speak Jampad!

The room she'd been taken to was palatial, compared to the bare Magh' adobe feeding cell she'd been rescued from. It had running water. Their faucet concept, though rather different from Jampad systems, was ingenious. There was a soft covering on the floor. There were soft things which she assumed were for night nests . . . standing on the floor! It was, of course, too warm, but the furry alien had taken a long look at her and had adjusted a device on the wall that sent a delicious stream of cold air spilling into the room.

But the entry portal was undoubtedly sealed. She was still a prisoner. A prisoner on a world where her people's most deadly foe roamed free, believed to be allies.

True, it was a feeble prison for an arboreal species. The skylight was only fifteen feet up. Hardly a hop.

Still . . .

The hairy one and several assistants were plainly trying to establish her diet and initiate communication. And if she got out, she had nowhere to go. The purpose of the Jampad expedition had been to alert this species to the danger of the species that farmed the Magh'. She might as well try to do that.

Besides, she had not eaten for nearly two weeks. She was going to have to try alien food or die, soon. None of it smelled quite right, though.

"The protein analysis we've done from tissue off the wound covering suggests it has a very similar biochemistry to mammals. But it won't eat what we are certain are safe compounds like glucose. We're offering it exotic things now, to see if it'll give us some behavioral cue as to diet. If we can't feed it, it'll die."

Dr. Liepsich shook his head at Mary-Lou Evans. "I do love your habit of stating the obvious, Mary-Lou. So Shakespearian." He drank more of his ubiquitous coffee. Liepsich's one human frailty was his addiction to caffeine.

Mary-Lou didn't rise to the bait. If you worked with Len Liepsich, you had to get used to ignoring the physicist's gratuitous insults. That was just the way he was. He preferred it, of course, if you fought back, like Sanjay did. But that wasn't her nature.

She also knew that he'd not slept for the last two days. It showed in his overbright eyes and even-more-abrasive-than-usual manner. "I'm worried, Len."

"That is fairly obvious. So am I, but for an entirely different reason. I've had more alien technology to examine in the last two days than I have got my greasy little paws on in the last two years. It's giving me enough headaches, without worrying whether a potentially inimical alien eats din-dins."

She knew him well enough to know that he certainly didn't mind having several tons of alien technology to examine. "So what is wrong with it?"

"You're too clever for a biologist," he muttered. "It's wrong. It's . . . it's not alien enough. Same booby traps. Same metallurgical analyses."

"It was looted from a captured Magh' scorpiary."

"You know, you have a real *gift* for stating the obvious," he said, with a feigned look of amazement. "And that means it shouldn't be what it is. I wish I could talk to this alien, or examine some of its technology as well, to get a handle on all of this."

"Well, according to this report—I must say this Van Klomp is very efficient for a soldier—the alien speaks Korozhet. We could ask them to translate. Or at least what it eats."

"That's precisely what I don't want to do. Not in light of the technology of all this equipment that Van Klomp has sent us. I'm stashing a lot of bits where the prickles and the army won't find it, hopefully."

It was fairly plain that he wasn't planning to explain why.

*In the bowels of the Korozhet ship,*
*in the slave quarters.*

Yetteth huddled on the metal rack that was his assigned sleeping nest in the slave quarters. It was at least high up, even if it had none of the other features that made a good nest. Right now he hugged himself in a vain quest for comfort. If he closed his eyes he could almost imagine himself in the tall-tree swamps of the Norheth clans. But there was no escaping from the smells.

To a lifeform with as keen a sense of smell as the Jampad had, this was close to hell. He could close his nose but not cover the scent tendrils. And right now he needed to imagine the tall-tree swamps and their green-blue water. The Overphyle had confirmed that another Jampad was out there, on this, their latest farm. He had overheard them planning to kill it.

The Overphyle liked having one of the Jampad as a slave, feeding them, cleaning their fecal pools. It ministered to their vanity. That was one of the reasons they'd not mindscrubbed him before the implant. The Overphyle felt that it asserted their dominance over the one species that had successfully resisted. Mind you, not all the slaves were mindscrubbed before being implanted. It was a good way of questioning them. And once they were implanted, the information could not be withheld.

The siren clanged. Food ration. A slave was always hungry, and he dared not miss the revolting block of decaying slush that they gave him. He was weak enough as it was. And he would need every last bit of strength he could muster if he was to find any way to escape, although the thing they had put in his head said that that was impossible and wrong. But he couldn't stand by when the Overphyle were planning to murder one of the People.

He climbed down the bunk stack. On the bottom tier a human female moaned weakly.

"What is wrong?" he asked, in the language of the masters.

The other woman, who sat stroking the moaning one's head, answered. "She was given the nerve-lash for making errors in the production line. She was going to spawn, and now the offspring is dead. It is poisoning her."

Yetteth knew that "spawn" was the wrong word. The humans were live-bearers, as the People were. But Overphyle had no words for the biology of lesser creatures. And slaves were forbidden to speak other languages. "Is there anything I can do?"

The human female who had been moaning began tossing about frantically, her alien eyes wide, seeing nothing, totally unaware of the other human's efforts to calm her. Her helper shook her head, a gesture that Yetteth had learned—oddly enough—that this species used to indicate the negative.

Yetteth left. The door to the narrow chamber had opened and the meal-slot would disgorge his food soon. If he didn't collect it, it would be trodden underfoot by others fetching theirs. There seemed to be nothing else he could do for the woman, anyway. She was dying, if he was any judge of alien physiology. The Overphyle did not medicate or assist sick slaves. They either lived or died. If the disease appeared infectious, they just killed and burned the slave, and dumped the ash.

It was the only way out of this huge metal prison, with the bars they had put into the prisoner's minds. You couldn't even think . . . easily, how much you hated them. Creatures of a low-order intelligence before they were implanted didn't appear to be able to think around it at all. The Nerba, for example, fawned on the Overphyle.

# Chapter 11

♋

*General Cartup-Kreutzler's horsily decorated office,*
*Military Headquarters.*

Considering that Major Tana Gainor was a mere lowly
major in the presence of the colony's Security Chief and
a general, you would have thought she'd look at least
slightly ill at ease. But despite the non-regulation pur-
plish lipstick, she remained perfectly poised. General
Cartup-Kreutzler found that disturbing.

She was a remarkably beautiful woman, even in uniform. The general might have been more interested,
except for that poise. Self-confident, self-assured women
made Cartup-Kreutzler uneasy.

"Most of these charges are very close to the laugh-out-
loud level, General."

"I was told you could make anything stick, Major Gainor."

She looked coolly at him. "For a fee, General, things can usually be arranged." She looked at the charge list again. "And it's going to be a high fee, General." She lowered her sooty eyelashes and looked at him speculatively. "Very high, indeed."

"Cut the sales pitch, Tana," said Talbot. "And forget using him. He's my brother-in-law, and you don't want to get on the wrong side of me."

"I've done my homework too, Talbot," she sniffed. "The general likes dim-witted and buxom blondes, of which I am the second and third but not the first."

Talbot ignored his brother-in-law's squawk of outrage. "Let's talk business, Tana. How much do you need for a war chest? Fitzhugh is to go down like a lead brick. You dot every 'i' and cross every 't' on this one."

"For this, I'll need plenty," she said. "Call it half a million up front and the same again when he's sentenced. And I might need the services of a few of your operatives, Talbot."

General Cartup-Kreutzler choked. But Talbot took it in his stride. "Done. The money will be in your usual account."

"Before I start working," she said, coolly. "I won't lift a finger otherwise."

"Let's not forget who holds the whip hand here, Tana," said Talbot Cartup, heavily. "I've got you. I've got you pinned like a butterfly."

She smiled. "But you need me for this. And you'll need me again. The JAG's department is getting more and more sticky by the day. But I can still work the system."

"What are you going to do?"

"If you must know, manipulate the roster of military judges and defense attorneys. I have . . . leverage. I'll handle the prosecution myself."

When the heavy outer door had swung shut behind the major, General Cartup-Kreutzler exhaled in a long shudder. "Just what have you got on her, Talbot?"

His brother-in-law laughed. "You name it. She's pretty and comes from a wealthy family. You'd think we'd struggle to pin anything on her. But right from cheating on her bar exams, by sleeping with several of her oral examiners, to dealing in drugs . . . she's been there. And stay away from that body of hers. She uses it well, but never for nothing. You know the old chestnut about the whore with the soul of a high-born lady and a heart of gold? Well, this is high-born lady who is a hooker at heart, and would sell her soul for the gold. I nicked through Thom. She was one of his prime dealers. That woman is pure poison."

"So long as she poisons Fitzhugh," said the general vindictively.

"Oh, she will. Literally, if need be."

# Chapter 12

୭

*Camp Marmian, some thirty miles from GBS City:*
*a small and choice piece of barb-wire fenced hell,*
*otherwise known as a transit camp.*

The camp's commanding officer looked at Chip; blinked. "But, according the records, Private Connolly, you are dead."

"Does that mean I get to go home, sir?" Chip paused. "Or just that I can't collect my pay?"

"I don't need your insolence, Connolly! Any more and I'll put you on a charge. I'm trying to work out what to do with you. The remainder of your unit has been disbanded and reassigned. You should have been reassigned with them, but you're listed as dead." The colonel looked most affronted at this. "If you're not dead, then you've been AWOL for more than a week."

"I was trapped behind enemy lines when the enemy advance came through, sir. Myself and a handful of rats and bats were the only survivors in our bunker."

The colonel snorted. "A likely story. And you fought your way out, and then found your way back here."

Chip could see where this was heading. So he thought he might as well do it properly. "Yes, sir. That's right, sir. But to get out we had to destroy the Magh' force-field generator. So we did. We killed a couple of hundred thousand Maggots, rescued Ms. Virginia Shaw, liberated a scorpiary for the army, and here I am. I knew you'd be pleased to see me here at good ol' Camp Marmian again, sir."

The company clerk poured her coffee onto her keyboard. Chip nearly killed his first officer by giving him apoplexy. It was fascinating. To get a lobster to go that color you had to boil them.

The colonel, it appeared, was too incoherent to talk properly. But he did have Private Chip Connolly dragged off to the stockade in record time.

An hour later the company clerk came over to the cells. "Private, I need some details for the charge sheets. The computer system has locked up most of your data as you're still being captured as dead."

"Best time to capture someone, when they're dead," said Chip cheerfully. He was still lost in that heady area of lightheartedness which comes out of not being dead, when you expected to be. Somehow, being listed as dead brought it all back.

She was not amused. "The colonel is already going to

throw the book at you at the court-martial, Connolly. Don't make things worse for yourself."

"Oh, good. I've always wanted a book," said Chip giggling. "I could use something to read in here." He went and sat down on the bunk, still laughing.

"This isn't a laughing matter," she snapped. "Be afraid, Private Connolly. You're in dire shit!"

Chip got up and walked over to the bars. "Listen, Corp. I've been in dire shit for so long that I've kind of run out of 'being afraid.' I've survived nearly six months as a front-line soldier. I've seen Maggots kill most of my squad. My girlfriend bought it in that attack. We got buried alive and over-run. We dug ourselves out inside the frigging scorpiary. We spent days on the run from the Maggots. At one stage I had a choice of starving to death or being eaten by the rats. We decided that as we going to die there, we were gonna take a lot of Maggots along with us. And in the end of it, me and a handful of crazy bats and drunken rats blew the crap out of the whole scorpiary. We took on ten-million-to-one odds, on a junky old tractor without any brakes. And some of us died, Corp. But I didn't. Between us we cracked the force field and killed the Maggot colony's brains. When the paratroopers got there, I was getting lucky with a really fantastic girl, who also happens to be rich and beautiful. My mates were getting drunk and having Maggot barbeque. Major Van Klomp told us that we're an invaluable military asset, and a bunch of useless drunks."

Chip rubbed the stubble on his chin. "So when I come back to my unit like a good little soldier . . . The colonel craps me out for not having shaved and puts me in the brig, because I'm dead." He shook his head at the corporal.

"And you tell me it's no laughing matter. Well, if I didn't laugh, I'd have to cry. And I'm too happy to be alive to cry."

The colonel's clerk looked at Chip as if actually seeing him for the first time. "You're either completely crazy . . . or you're not joking." She turned to the sergeant who was in charge of the cells. "What do you think, Ngui?"

The sergeant scratched his chin. "Well. Like you say, he's either crazy or telling the truth. I'd say crazy—if it wasn't for the fact that it's been on the news last night. The scorpiary being captured. Shaw's daughter being rescued. Only they said it was some Special Services commando that did it."

Chip's shoulders shook. "Commandos, my ass. We told them we were just a bunch of grunts in the wrong place at the right time. The reporters wouldn't believe us. That's all there was to it, Sarge. The Maggots didn't know how the hell to deal with us, once we were inside their nest. We got lucky, and we got out alive. And now I've come back."

The both stared at him. Finally the corporal spoke. "But . . . did they just send you here without any travel instructions?" The colonel's clerk plainly lived by paperwork. It was obviously hard for her to accept that anything could be true without it.

"Who's 'they,' to write it in the first place?" asked Chip, shrugging. "Lieutenant Rosetski isn't writing anything without an Ouija board. He died the first hour of the Magh' assault. And the next officer I saw was Major Van Klomp. He was told by some major general at HQ to send Ginny Shaw back at once with an armed escort. Ginny told him that she wanted us for an escort. So he radioed the general and said he was sending her back with us."

Chip had to grin at the memory. Van Klomp had described the rats and bats as "the toughest commando group in the HAR army. Really special Special Services soldiers." Which, as Van Klomp had said afterwards, was a fine description so long as the major general didn't actually see them.

"Major Van Klomp organized an escort back to line three," he continued, "and a driver and transport to take us to divisional headquarters. Weather was really down and the choppers couldn't fly."

"But . . . didn't he get his clerk to cut you any orders?" demanded the colonel's clerk.

Chip looked pityingly at her. She was a slight young woman with a pale face, and she walked with a pronounced limp. He would wager a guess that she was probably stationed in the camp because she was medically unfit for combat duty. That was hardly her fault, even if a lot of women would like to swap places with her. She obviously knew very little about front-line conditions. "Things were kind of confused, Corp. There were a lot of Maggots still around, and not one hell of a lot of paper. We had an escort from the major with us back through to the vehicle. There was supposed to be an escort waiting there for us, but it got delayed, and we didn't wait."

She thrust her head forward inquisitorially. "Then how did you get back here from division headquarters?"

"I asked some brigadier . . . Charlesworth. Yeah, that was his name, where we should go now. He was kind of taken up with fawning over Ginny and was in a flap because somebody had locked him up in his own head-quarters. You can't believe the chaos there. I thought the captured scorpiary was a mess, but that camp was more like a disturbed ants' nest than a camp. He said we should get to our units as soon as possible. I asked around and they told me that the remains of my unit were sent back to Camp Marmian. I tried the transport officer. He didn't know or care who some grubby Vat was, but he told me that I could go on next Vat redeployment trucks in a week or two, if I could find space. Or make my own plan. He said much the same but worse about the rats and bats. He was too busy trying to please explain why they'd cooperated with Major Fitzhugh and would I bugger off. So I did. I cadged a lift with one of the trucks transporting the captured Magh' stuff back to the university research unit. Got the driver to drop me at the turn-off and walked to the gates. Made the guard commander take me to the colonel and told him I was reporting for duty. He told me I needed a shave and threw me in the brig."

The corporal looked at the sergeant. Looked at Chip. Then back at the sergeant.

The sergeant reached for his keys. "Nobody could actually make up such a stupid story, Corporal. Nobody, but nobody, is quite that dumb. So he's probably telling the truth, you know."

The corporal put her hands around her head. "What a mess. I'm sorry, Private."

"What are you doing?" demanded Chip, as the sergeant began unlocking the cell.

"Letting you out," said the sergeant tersely. "It's not procedure, but I'm damned if I'm going leave you in the cells for a minute longer. I was a front-line soldier myself, before I was invalided out, and this isn't right. We'll go and explain to the colonel now."

Chip reached through the bars and caught his hand. "Oh no you don't, Sarge. I'm staying right here. I'm happy here." He grinned. "I'm dead. Dead people need lots of rest. You guys just leave it, and me, alone."

"I think he *is* crazy," said the corporal, warily.

"Nope, Corp. Well, not more than most of the front-line troops, hey Sarge," said Chip cheerfully. "But if I go out there, ten to one the bastards will have me doing drill. Or your colonel, who sounds like a real *champion* at handling things well, will post me back to the front. Now. I don't like drill. I sure as hell don't need to get back to the front in a hurry. Here I can sleep, and the sarge'll see I get three squares a day. I'll probably even get a shower and a quiet mooch in the exercise yard. Carrying rocks and the other delights of Detention Barracks don't start until you've been court-martialed and sentenced, do they?"

"Uh. No."

"If you get me out of here, do you see your colonel giving me a week's pass?" asked Chip.

"Uh." The corporal shook her head. "To be honest, no. The colonel will probably feel you made a fool of him, and he's a vindictive son-of-a-bitch."

"Yeah. That's about what I figured," said Chip. "I also reckon I owe him the chance to make a proper fool of himself. So, have I actually done anything wrong? I mean, when they get to the court-martial can they actually do anything to me?"

"You got witnesses for the brigadier giving you the order?" asked the sergeant.

Chip started to giggle. "I got one better. The guys who were filming Ginny filmed that bit. One of them came and tried to interview me, afterwards. Thinking about it now, I reckon Charlesworth hadn't figured out that we were the bunch that had rescued her. He thought we were just part of the escort. He told me to tell my platoon sergeant to give me a demerit for my uniform and not having shaved. Got maybe fifty witnesses. About half of them civilians—Shareholders, no less."

"So long as we can find some of those people, it should be open and shut. You were given a legitimate order from the senior ranking officer, and you obeyed it."

Chip shrugged. "Piece of cake. Tim Fuentes, INB. There were the rest of the bats and rats too. You should have seen that brigadier's face when Ginny said we must come along."

"Well, rat testimony has been used in a few cases," said the sergeant. "So that's got precedent. And tracking down this INB guy should be easy."

The corporal nodded, serious faced, just the edge of an unpracticed dimple in her cheek showing. "And you reported for duty to the colonel. He accused you of going AWOL . . ."

"He's a prat. It should have been desertion under fire," interrupted the sergeant. "AWOL is for back here, out of the combat zone."

"AWOL," continued the corporal smoothly. "You told him exactly where you'd been. I heard every word. He decided to throw you in the brig." She smiled, transforming her face. "We'll get you a shave, shower, clean uniform and a defense attorney from the JAG's office. You're entitled to that, even for a regimental court-martial, which is what you're up for. You just tell your story with a nice straight face and you should actually get a public crow-eating, and, if you play your cards right you'll probably get some leave, too. They owe you."

"The Army owes you," said the sergeant, heavily. "But, speaking as someone who has been through the system, it doesn't usually pay, Corporal. It collects. Look, son. I still reckon we should go and talk to the colonel. But it's up to you. You do it the way you want to. You can stay in my cells just as long as you like. But anytime you change your mind I'll take you up to the colonel. Should take 'em a while to get to the court-martial. They might even work out what is going on and come looking for you before that."

Chip yawned. "They might. And it's fine if they do. But I reckon this lot couldn't find their own ass without both hands. And I haven't slept on a mattress for a long time," he said, longingly.

The corporal looked at the inch-thick strip of gray foam. "Uh. Sergeant. Couldn't he get a better one?"

Chip yawned again. "Don't bother, Sarge. It's not mud, it's not rocks, and it's probably going to stay dry. Sounds great to me."

Chip heard them talk as they walked away, and he snuggled down on the mattress and pulled the thin gray blanket over him. Just snatches . . .

"Combat veteran all right . . ."

"Pictures in the newscast. I thought the face looked familiar . . ."

"It's not right . . ."

"Post traumatic stress . . ."

"What he wants, Corporal."

They weren't quite right. What he *really* wanted was Virginia. Well. Maybe he wanted to sleep first. He was too screwed up about the way she'd turned her back on him to feel up to handling the question of Ginny right now. But a veteran learns to sleep when he can. And where he can.

# Chapter 13

⊙

*Ward 11 (officers, male), First Military Hospital,*
*George Bernard Shaw City.*

Fitz made the trip back from the front in an ATV army ambulance. It gave him more insight into why it was best to drug patients. He was accompanied by Lieutenant Pringle, and two other MPs. Once through the front lines an MP escort joined them. Fitz would be going to the military hospital for examination, and thence, if pronounced fit enough, to the hospital wing of the military prison, and thence to trial. Having been in a great hurry to field court-martial and summarily execute him, it now appeared that they were in no hurry to send him for trial. Fitz was. He was sharing his stretcher with Ariel, and taking her into a military prison could tax his ingenuity.

* * *

CHARGE I, Violation of the Military Code, Article 90 (Assault on a Commissioned Officer)

SPECIFICATION: In that Major Conrad Fitzhugh, Military Intelligence, Southern Front Headquarters, Army of Harmony and Reason, did, in time of war, strike Brigadier General Winchester Charlesworth, his superior commissioned officer, then known by Major Conrad Fitzhugh to be his superior officer who was then in the execution of his office, in the stomach with a bangstick with intent to cause severe or deadly injury.

CHARGE II, Violation of the Military Code, Article 94 (Mutiny)

SPECIFICATION: In that Major Conrad Fitzhugh, Military Intelligence, Southern Front Headquarters, Army of Harmony and Reason, with intent to usurp and override lawful military authority, did seize command of the Fourth Division, Army of Harmony and Reason and unlawfully direct its operations with intent to lead their destruction.

CHARGE III, Violation of the Military Code, Article 95 (Flight from Arrest)

SPECIFICATION: In that Major Conrad Fitzhugh, Military Intelligence, Southern Front Headquarters, Army of Harmony and Reason, did flee apprehension by Military Police.

CHARGE IV, Violation of the Military Code, Article 104 (Aiding the Enemy)

SPECIFICATION 1: In that Major Conrad Fitzhugh, Military Intelligence, Southern Front Headquarters, Army of Harmony and Reason, did, without proper authority, knowingly attempt to aid the enemy by attempting to disrupt secret plans for offensive operations conducted by the Fourth Division, Army of Harmony and Reason, and did attempt to lead the Fourth Division to its destruction through enemy action.

CHARGE V, Violation of the Military Code, Article 104 (Aiding the Enemy)

SPECIFICATION 2: In that Major Conrad Fitzhugh, Military Intelligence, Southern Front Headquarters, Army of Harmony and Reason, did, at divers points in the Southern Front Area of Responsibility, without proper authority, knowingly give intelligence to the enemy by informing the enemy of the numbers, resources and operations of the Army of Harmony and Reason.

*CHARGE VI, Violation of the Military Code, Article 106 (Espionage)*

SPECIFICATION: In that Major Conrad Fitzhugh, Military Intelligence, Southern Front Headquarters, Army of Harmony and Reason, did, in time of war, at divers points within the Southern Front Area of Responsibility, act as a spy while purporting to serve as Military Intelligence Officer for the Southern Front Headquarters, Army of Harmony and Reason, for the purpose of collecting information regarding the numbers, resources and operations of the army of Harmony and Reason, with the intent to impart the same to the enemy.

*Signature of accused* _____

Conrad Fitzhugh looked incredulously at the list of charges. Then at the woman major with her pale mauve lipstick. Then at the list of charges again.

At least they hadn't tried to forge his signature. Fitz thought he'd taken everything this war could throw at him.

And now he realized that he hadn't even begun to catch it.

"Do you have a problem, Major Fitzhugh?" Major Gainor asked coolly. "You've had the charges read to you. You've now looked at them at some length. Unless you're prepared to sign it right now, which means confessing to the charges, I'll require some information. And I really doubt that you are prepared to sign it, because I'm sure that you're innocent. I just need to track down the witnesses to prove it. Can you help me?"

She ended by patting his thigh. Tana Gainor was the kind of woman who hadn't patted his thigh for a long time, not since well before his face had been so disfigured on the left-hand side. "You're with the JAG, aren't you?" he asked.

She nodded. "Yes, I am."

"I was prepared to plead guilty for what I did do." Fitz shook the sheaf of papers at her. "This however, is a pack of vicious lies. It's a load of rubbish, which, you must know as an attorney, has not a chance of getting a guilty verdict. I am not a traitor, or a spy. They don't have a chance of making this stick."

She fluttered her eyelashes at him. "I know. But if I have a list of witnesses, we can really sew it up." He realized that she'd slipped a hand inside the sheet and was kneading his biceps. Hard to think straight with this charmer . . .

She shrieked and pulled back her hand. "Get your hands off, you hussy!" Fitz heard Ariel hissing. "He's mine!"

The major backed off, clutching her fingers. "That's a rat! You've got a rat in there!"

"Hello. It's the stitcher," said a cheerful voice from the door. "Don't talk to her, Fitz. Not unless you've got two lawyers present, and an anti-shark fence."

It was Mike Capra, who had been a flamboyant young attorney and fellow skydiver. He used to favor exotic waistcoats. Now, instead, he was in uniform with a pair of pips on his shoulders. He'd seen Major Gainor clutching her fingers, seen Ariel's head popping up from under the sheets . . . and had obviously added things up.

Capra saluted. "Good afternoon, Major. Don't you return a fellow officer's salute?"

She ignored the question, preoccupied with trying to stop the bleeding. "What are you doing here?" she asked poisonously, her voice very different from the sweet tones she'd used moments before.

"The same as you, I imagine, but for the other side." Capra winked at Fitz. "I'll bet Tana didn't inform you of your rights either."

Fitz tried to get his head around all this. "You're prosecuting me, Mike?"

Lieutenant Mike Capra shook his head with mock regret. "No. For my sins, I've been ordered to offer my services as part of your defense team. You are, of course, entitled to ask for someone else, and I hardly think the prosecution could refuse to allow you a second attorney in a case of this size. They'd try, mind you." He pointed to the major who was now sucking her bitten finger. "This is the prosecution. Doubtless come to 'help' you. That's usually her line. Isn't it, Tana?"

With a look at him that could wither steel wire, she stormed out. Mike Capra exhaled, long and slow. "I hope you didn't tell her anything, Fitz?"

"No. Fortunately." He sighed. "How long am I likely to lie here, Mike? I can't get a straight answer out of these medics. I think that electrode-muscle stimulus should come under the heading of cruel and unusual punishments. Look, with nothing to do but lie on my damn back I've had nothing to do but think. And I need to talk to Bobby Van Klomp."

"I don't think that would be at all wise. He's got to keep his nose clean, Fitz. You need to say anything to Van Klomp, tell me."

"I need to discuss our supposed allies with him. Those 'treason' charges just crystallized some ideas in my head."

"You just go on letting them crystallize. I've been told that basically the medics can't find anything wrong with you and you're due to be discharged from here and into the tender care of the MPs. But don't worry. I'll still be around to hold your little hand, from time to time."

On getting back from the hospital, Mike Capra discovered that this was not indeed going to be the case, either. He'd been reassigned.

He went immediately to his chain of command. That took him as far Lieutenant Colonel Ogata.

"No. It has nothing to do with Major Gainor, or anything she's been able to fix, Lieutenant. It's a direct instruction from General Needford. I attempted to question the issue and he only said one word. And that was 'Dreyfus.' "

Ogata gave Capra a stony look. "You know Needford's reputation as a judge as well as I do. He believes in Justice, with a capital J, Lieutenant. Justice will be served. Do you believe Major Fitzhugh innocent or guilty?

"Guilty as hell, but not of what he's been charged with."

"Then I think you should always keep in the back of your mind the fact that General Cartup-Kreutzler's SJA is not a fool even if he is a drunk and scared of his boss," said Ogata.

On that cryptic note, Mike Capra was dismissed. He tried to figure out what Ogata meant, as he left. Like all top generals, Kreutzler had a legal advisor—Staff Judge Advocate, as they were called. He would be the one who actually drew up the charges against Fitzhugh.

*Oh.* Capra smiled thinly. A capable lawyer, after all, knew exactly how to draw up charges that would look good on paper but be full of holes—which a general was not likely to spot, before it was too late.

# Chapter 14

ᏽ

*A large third floor bedroom in Shaw House, a Palladian-style mansion, set in extensive gardens, with a park and private golf course.*

Virginia woke from a dream-tortured sleep in the strangest of places: Her own bedroom. The soft-toys that had always been arrayed on her bed had been neatly placed onto their night-shelf, and looked down at her. She felt . . . odd. Her thoughts seemed somehow fuzzy.

After a while, she realized that part of the oddness was that she was clean and wearing a nightdress. After what she'd been through, that no longer felt quite natural. She looked at the bookshelves full of antique Regency romances. They were all there. The room was as she remembered it, down to the details of the way it smelled.

So, was it all some sort of terrible—and wonderful—dream? She must ask Fluff . . .

She suddenly realized the small galago wasn't in his usual spot beside her.

Virginia Shaw knew fear, then. She felt her temple. There was a small, neat dressing—not the crude bandage that Doc had put on . . . and where was Chip? He wouldn't have left her, surely? He loved her. He'd said so.

Slowly she began to piece together her memories of how she'd got here.

A cold sweat of fear prickled at her.

She'd been rescued from the Magh'.

She'd fallen into the hands of something worse.

A maid came into the room. A familiar face, a normal part of the vast household staff of the Shaw mansion. "Good morning, Miss Virginia. Can I draw the curtains for you? Order you some coffee? Doctor has said you can get up for an hour today." She had two tablets on a saucer, and a glass of water. She handed it to Virginia. "Doctor said you were to take these, please, miss."

"How long have I been here?" asked Virginia, drinking the tablets and then leaning back against the pillows. She felt curiously weak.

"Since yesterday morning, miss. Now, can I order you something else to drink? Coffee? Chocolate? Tea?"

What she felt she needed right now was some of the rat's looted over-proof brandy. But she needed to establish just what was going on before she started to kick and scream.

"Coffee would be nice," she said.

"And perhaps some toast, miss?"

"Yes. Why not? Have you seen Fluff anywhere, by the way?"

"They haven't caught the nasty little creature yet, miss. But it is only a matter of time."

Virginia felt a mixture between elation and terror. Fluff was around. He hadn't deserted her, then. But obviously someone was trying to catch him.

She yawned. This woman was definitely part of the staff, but not one of the sullen maids who had taken "working for the dummy" as a form of punishment. She probably wouldn't know how attached Virginia and Fluff were to each other.

"Why bother," she said disinterestedly. "He'll come in when he's hungry."

"They've put bait out for him, Miss Virginia. But he hasn't come in for it yet."

Virginia shrugged. "He will, when he gets hungry enough. Why do they want to catch him anyway? He's harmless."

The maid looked shocked. "He bit Doctor Thom!"

"How sad," said Virginia, boredly. "While I can quite understand that the doctor would like Fluff captured, I will be very unhappy if he is hurt. Please tell everyone that. And I would like that coffee and toast, now."

The maid hurried away.

But, by the time coffee came, Virginia felt curiously lethargic, and somehow unable to care very much. She got up and sat in a chair in the sun. But she did not even bother to take a book down from the shelf. A curiously detached portion of herself said that this was very odd indeed. *Wrong! Wrong! Wrong!*

Later Dr. Thom came and examined her. He seemed very pleased with her. She did notice that one of his hands was bandaged, but she couldn't be bothered to ask why. It was all dreamy and oddly comfortable. She ate and then she slept again.

But something inside her head was still shrieking that none of this was right.

The next morning was a carbon copy of the first. Except . . . after the maid had brought the coffee, the glass of water and the tablets, she left to order a more substantial breakfast. A little skylight window opened, very cautiously.

Virginia froze, the cup halfway to her lips, hearing it creak. She looked up. There were a pair of huge soft eyes peering at her. It was an impossible climb to the overhanging balcony window.

But for Fluff, a climb like that was easy.

Virginia was about to give a glad cry when she noticed that he had his long black finger across his lips. Perhaps someone was listening, said the odd detached part inside her head.

Fluff was now mimicking her drinking. He wanted her to drink coffee? To pretend everything was normal, perhaps? Well, she really wanted that coffee anyway. But as she raised it to her lips, he shook his head frantically.

He *didn't* want her to drink that coffee? Virginia was puzzled. Fluff pointed to her bathroom. So, obedient, she got up and walked in there and opened the little clouded glass window. There was no point in that clouded glass, here, four floors up. Reaching this window to peek in would have taken an insane acrobat.

Fluff swung in. Galagos are small primates, but possibly one of the most acrobatic of them. They are normally nocturnal, so not many people get to appreciate their climbing skills. He did not jump for her reaching arms. Instead he leapt for the basin and turned on the tap. Then he leapt to her, and clung to her neck. "*Señorita*, they have the devices for listening everywhere," he whispered. "And do not drink the pills. She is the drug for tranquilizing."

No wonder she'd drifted through yesterday! She'd been drugged. And she would have been again today.

"What's happened?" Virginia whispered. "All I remember was Doctor Thom . . . I think he injected me. And he ordered me to come quietly, in Korozhet. I wasn't expecting it and I couldn't resist."

"He had the badge on his jacket. The badge she spoke, very quietly, in Crotchet. I too obeyed. I saw him inject you with a small thing. I clung to your neck, and they carried you to the helipad. Even in the rain, the helicopter she flew. I hid under the seat. The pilot he swore much about the instruments. They came to this place and I was seen running from the helicopter."

Fluff shivered. For all his Don Quixote antics, Fluff was still a very small and not naturally courageous primate. "They tried to shoot me, 'Ginia! They had guns. I jumped and ran and hid. Then I went looking for you."

"Oh, Fluff. You're so brave." Ginny hugged him, knowing that he enjoyed being told this, and knowing he really deserved it.

"What else is a true caballero to do?" whispered Fluff, his chest expanding a little. "Now, 'Ginia. I think you must go back into the room because I hear that pig-person spymaid. I wait outside. They cannot catch me there."

So Virginia went out again. But now she was not quite

as afraid as she had been that morning. Fluff was a very little galago, true. But he had brought Chip and the rats and bats to her rescue before. There was hope. And besides, there was strength in not being alone.

"I can't tell you how nice it is to have coffee again," she said, cheerfully.

The maid's bearing was stiff. "Doctor said I must make sure you drank your pills."

"Oh, I will. Now, I wanted to wear my jade chiffon today. I think I can get up a bit more today, don't you?"

"Doctor said so. Drink your pills, miss."

"I'm going to. But I couldn't find my jade chiffon dress. The last time something of mine went missing Daddy had two of the servants jailed . . . and then it turned up that it had been put into Mummy's closets. Imagine that. So you'd best go and look."

Ginny took the pills, and a mouthful of water. Unfortunately, the maid waited for her to swallow. So Virginia did.

"And now what is keeping you?" she asked crossly.

"Are you sure it isn't in these cupboards, miss?"

"Are you questioning me?" Virginia echoed her mother at her most unpleasantly haughty. "Off with you." She took another mouthful of coffee.

The woman turned and left. Virginia waited until she was sure the maid was gone, and then went into the bathroom and turned on the shower.

She tried sticking her finger down her throat. It took more effort than she'd thought it would—*yuck*—but eventually it worked. She got rid of some coffee and the pills. The pills had started to soften already, but she didn't think she'd ingested much of whatever was in them.

"Are you are all right, *mi* Virginia?" enquired Fluff anxiously.

She made a face. "Better than I would be if I kept that stuff in me," said Virginia. "But I think I am going to go on a crash diet. I'm not eating anything that could be doped. And I really would love some more coffee."

"Food it is no problem. I can steal that from the kitchens. Coffee . . . I will see."

"You'd better be careful, Fluff. That jail-warder maid of mine let on that they're putting out bait for you. It's probably poisoned."

Fluff laughed scornfully. "They are fools, Virginia. They think I am some dumb beast. And it is not only your maid who is a jail-warder. This place has been taken over by many I do not recognize. Only a few of the old faces are still here. This whole place she is now a prison. I have found out that Doctor Thom has taken over your father's old study. He has made it his office. He does not know that with the ivy it is a good place for me to hide. I have listened to them planning . . . *hist!*"

Standing on the edge of the basin, Fluff assumed a dramatic pose—his posture tense, one hand cupped to a huge ear. "Danger! Someone comes."

There was a knock on the bathroom door. "Miss Virginia? Are you all right?"

"Of course I am." She didn't have to work at all to put an irritated tone in her voice. That "Miss" was beginning to grate. "I'm just about to have a shower. I'll call for you if I need you." She motioned Fluff out of the window. Then, just in case, stripped off her nightgown and stepped into the shower.

     ◦      ◦      ◦

In the days that followed, Virginia cultivated a glazed look of vacant amiability. It did allow her to walk around a little and to find out that the Shaw mansion had been entirely taken over by someone her father had disliked and feared. It also allowed her to find out that she was most definitely the man's prisoner, in all but name. She took her meals—as far as possible—in solitary state, in her room. Fortunately, she had usually been made to do so, before the soft-cyber implant had enabled her to leave being an incoherent seven-year-old in an adult body. The remaining old staff of the mansion took that as the norm, and the new watchdogs therefore seemed to accept it also.

So, Fluff was able to steal food from the orchards, gardens, and the kitchens for her, and to meet her in secret. And she was allowed to wander around, though she was careful to make no effort to go where she was steered away from—places like the vehicle park, the kitchens and the gardens.

The other thing that was denied her, quietly but firmly, was news of the outside world. The news channels on the television in her room had been blocked. When she had the chance, she found out that this was the case for the large-screen TV in the Oriole Room too. And none of the newspapers, magazines and periodicals that used to be delivered to the library were there any more. When she asked, in a bored tone, why the TV in her room was skipping channels, she was told that it was for her peace of mind, on Dr. Thom's orders.

She and Fluff discussed, at some length, the galago's going for help. Fluff had three problems with the idea:

Firstly, perimeter security was tight. There was

everything from ten-foot-high electric fencing to flight-detectors in place.

Secondly, the galago's departure would leave Virginia without food.

And thirdly, the little creature, raised as a pampered ultra-rich girl's pet, had no idea where to go for help. The world outside was a strange, unfamiliar and terrifying place. Who did he approach? Where would he find Chip or the rats and bats that Ginny knew she could trust?

Doctor Thom hadn't quite moved in yet. But it was plain that he regarded the place very much as his own. It was also plain that his agents had infiltrated the staff far more thoroughly than Aloysius Shaw had ever dreamed. Obviously, the Shaws' personal physician had been his kingpin. Doctor Thom was now absolute lord here, except . . .

When his master arrived.


Virginia had the dubious pleasure of meeting the man some two days later.

"Miss, you have a visitor," said the chambermaid. There was distinct nervousness and awe in the woman's voice.

The maid's name had turned out to be Juliet. *Juliet the Jailor*, as Virginia privately thought of her. The "Miss" had got to the point where Virginia was wondering if it was a justification for homicide.

"Oh?" said Virginia languidly, doing her best to hide the quickening of interest. "Who?"

"It's Talbot Cartup, Miss. We'd better get you dressed quickly. The boss doesn't like to be kept waiting."

She yawned. "Who is he?"

"He's a very important man, Miss."

Virginia knew what Talbot Cartup's portfolio had been, and how her father Aloysius had been angry about it being given to him. *The man's completely unfit to be in charge of public security—for anyone, much less the Shareholders Council!* she remembered once hearing her father snarling to her mother.

At the time, Virginia hadn't really understood what her father had been concerned about. In retrospect, thinking over that old overheard conversation and some others, it was clear to her that whispers of a possible Vat insurrection had terrified enough influential Shareholders to push Cartup into the position of power he had held before the war. Her father had objected, but he'd been outvoted.

The war, of course, had increased the Cartup family's power vastly—and had driven Aloysius to employ his own security staff. It obviously hadn't helped. Not if Cartup was Jailor Juliet's boss.

Virginia allowed herself to be dressed. She shook off the escort downstairs, and walked down to the Webb Salon. Dr. Thom and Cartup were both there, sipping her father's Barbadillo Olorosa Seco Cuco sherry out of Waterford crystal glasses.

"Ah, Miss Shaw. May I say how pleased I am to see you up and about," said Talbot Cartup, standing up, and adjusting the window as he did so.

She smiled vacantly at him. She noticed he knew exactly where the electric window controls were, and how to use them. "You have the advantage of me, Sir." Ah, the Brönte words. So perfect for this setting.

"Talbot Cartup," he introduced himself. "I was a friend and admirer of your late father."

She had seen him a few times before, actually, in public

venues where Aloysius Shaw could not avoid him. But she was sure her reputation for brain damage would allay whatever suspicions Cartup might have.

"I don't remember you, I'm afraid, sir. My father didn't talk much to me." True. He had talked to others as if she wasn't there.

There was some slight relaxation in the set of Talbot Cartup's shoulders. "A great man, Miss Shaw. A great loss for us all! I miss him sorely."

Virginia couldn't say the same, not with a straight face. Again, in retrospect, she could now understand that her parents had been fairly moderate in their political views—certainly compared to such as Cartup. But that hadn't led them to treat her with any sympathy. She'd been a very good clockwork doll-model-of-a-daughter to her parents, once she'd gotten the implant, and nothing more than that. She was certain Talbot Cartup missed Aloysius Shaw as much as she did.

"It is sad, yes . . . And what can I do for you, sir?"

"Why, nothing, Miss Shaw. Rather, in my role as an executive member of the Council of Shareholders, I came to see if there was anything we could do for you."

"How good of you," she said, letting her tone sound vaguely pleased. "But Doctor Thom is looking after me very well."

"He was about to get me some records when you arrived," said Cartup, meaningfully.

The doctor started. "Er. I'll go and get you that file right now, shall I? Miss Virginia can look after you for a few moments, Mr. Cartup."

When he'd left, Talbot Cartup turned to her. "Is everything all right?" he asked in a whisper.

Ginny looked at him with what she hoped was an expression of vague puzzlement. "Why, fine. No problems . . . not a problem in the world."

"That doctor. Do you trust him?"

*More than I trust you, you snake, which is to say not at all. If I hadn't heard Daddy talking about you, and Fluff hadn't heard Thom reporting to you, and your Jailor Juliet-spy hadn't let the cat out of the bag, calling you "the boss," I might just have asked you for help.*

But she let none of that show. By now, Ginny had mastered the art of keeping her expression mindlessly vacant. It wasn't hard, really, since she had years of experience with brain damage to call on.

"Dr. Thom has been so kind," she said dreamily.

"So he's been helpful?"

"Very. But I'm so tired. I hope I'll feel better one day soon. Doctor said I was just to rest."

Cartup nodded, sympathetically. "Good advice, Miss Shaw. Good advice. I was just concerned. You know you can confide in me if you have any trouble."

"Why, thank you. You are too kind."

The doctor returned with a slim brown folder. "Miss Virginia, you're looking a little pale."

"I'm just tired," she said, "and a bit shaky." She didn't have to fake the tremor in her hand. The doctor wouldn't know that it was from fury.

"I'll call someone to take you back to your room, then."

"I'll be fine on my own, Doctor," she said with just a trace of her mother's hauteur. "But I will ask you to excuse me, Mister Catsup." She enjoyed that little twist on his name. "Very kind of you to call." She drifted toward the door, which the doctor hastily opened for her.

There were no servants in the hallway. Doubtless the spy-master didn't want anyone eavesdropping on him. Silently, and with no sign of the shaky footsteps she'd affected before, Ginny slipped into the adjoining Wedgewood room. Her mother had been a shrewish woman and had really disliked being excluded from some of Aloysius's private meetings—held so often in the Webb Salon. She'd had her own simple but effective way of dealing with the security measures Aloysius had taken. Virginia had seen her do it, twice, though she'd had no understanding at the time what her mother was doing—or why.

Mechanical snooping was impossible, but . . . Virginia searched her memory. She found the glass behind the leather-bound books, where she remembered her mother had hidden it. Then she pressed it against the wall and strained to listen.

She could make out the words. Barely, but enough.

" . . . unnecessary charade. I was worried she might know too much about me," said Cartup.

"I told you, Talbot," said Dr. Thom. "I have the matter entirely in hand. She's doped to the nines."

"I wish you'd stick to injecting her. I've been told that drug absorption varies with what they eat."

"Oral dosage is quite safe, Talbot," said the doctor. "Trust me. The stuff is quite addictive, anyway. She's already heading for the stage where she'd beg us for it, if we stopped."

"It's not going to make her raving stoned is it?" asked Cartup. "Because we need her up, about, and apparently *compos mentis*, Thom. We need control of those votes of hers."

"She'll be fine," reassured Dr. Thom. "Rather vague, but very willing. She'll do anything so long as we keep her well dosed."

"Good. Because she'll have to appear in public eventually. Possibly a few times. There is considerable public curiosity about all this, and I haven't been able to damp it all down."

"All the more reason for not injecting her, Talbot. These summer fashions would make finding hidden veins tricky. And intramuscular absorption really is erratic."

"We're going to have to get her to sign those proxy forms soon," said Cartup. "Will she do that?"

The doctor snorted sarcastically, loudly enough for Virginia to hear. "She'd lie down on her back and let you screw her if I told her to, Talbot. Besides we've got that device you got from the Korozhet. That'll make her do anything you fancy."

Talbot laughed. "Someone else might want a dummy, but I prefer a bit more spice in my bed partners."

"Someone did want this dummy," said the doctor lightly. "She's not a virgin any more, which she definitely was last time I examined her. I took reasonably fresh seminal fluid samples from her vagina when I examined her while she was unconscious."

"Good lord," said Cartup, plainly amused, by his tone. "Probably some hard-up soldier."

Ginny nearly dropped the glass. She didn't even bother to put it away in its hiding place. Some part of her mind told her to keep listening, but she was just too shaken with sheer fury.

She fled back to her room. *How dare they say that about her—and about Chip? And how dare that vile*

*Thom pry into her unconscious body?*

She was going to get out of here! Somehow, someway. And there would be a reckoning. She cast about for a means. Her first inclination was to use something to bludgeon that creep into a pulp when he next came to "examine" her.

Cold reflection said that wouldn't work, or be worth it, no matter how sweet the idea. She could dwell pleasantly on the thought, but Dr. Thom was a large and well-built man. To her own present disgust she'd once had something of a crush on him, and thus she knew that he was a martial-arts expert—or claimed to be, at least.

Whether he was or not, she knew he'd been practicing faithfully every day in the mansion's gym. Even if she managed to catch him unawares . . . she was not sure just how hard to hit, or if she could hit hard enough. For a moment, she wished savagely for her chainsaw, the one she'd used to slaughter Magh' in the tunnels. That would deal with him! Martial arts, be damned. *Riiiipppppppp. Arms and legs flying everywhere . . .*

She drove those thoughts forcefully from her mind, concentrating on what was feasible. Or at least might be.

So: escape. She couldn't drive. Well, she'd never driven anything but a golf cart. So stealing a vehicle and driving it through the fence wouldn't work. Besides, the fence was electrified. And also there were various hidden booby traps along its length. She knew where the plans for those were kept, but still, it was no little obstacle. The gates would stop a tank, she remembered her father saying, never mind a mere golf cart. Anyway, there were at least three burly guards between her and the motor pool.

And when she got out, where could she go, where they

wouldn't just bring her back to the disgusting doctor's "care?"

# Chapter 15

♋

*Military court C, southern suburbs of George Bernard Shaw City.*

"Not guilty to these charges, sir."

Fitz had known something was very seriously wrong when Mike Capra had been pulled off his case. The young lieutenant he had acting for him now would have had difficulty spelling her own name right.

The court too was empty, except for the defense, the trial attorney and the panel of gray-haired officers.

He'd never seen the first witness in his life before. Nonetheless, this Mervyn Paype claimed to know him well. Paype was a counterintelligence agent with Special Branch, it seemed, and he swore that Conrad Fitzhugh had received large sums of money from him. Paype even had a number of excellent photographs of Conrad

Fitzhugh handing over battle plans to himself.

The female witness who followed, claiming to be a typist in General Visse's office who had been seduced and misled by the despicable Fitzhugh, cried quite artistically. Fitz had never seen her before in his life, either. Odd, really, given the rather graphically intimate details the woman gave of their various trysts.

The young lieutenant defending him put up not one question, and raised not one objection. Fitz was not even called to the stand himself. Fitz had never been to a military court before. But there seemed a marked paucity of justice here.

The entire case took less than forty-five minutes. The panel didn't need more than thirty seconds to decide on his guilt. Major Gainor smiled seraphically at him as the judge pronounced it.

He was hardly surprised at the death sentence that the panel thought an appropriate punishment.

"I can have you out of here in ten minutes," said Ariel conversationally to Fitz, through the bars of the paddy wagon. She wasn't supposed to be here. But then Ariel never let that stop her.

Conrad Fitzhugh looked speculative. "Which would effectively be an admission of guilt, wouldn't it?"

Ariel shrugged. "Who cares?"

"I do, Ariel. I broke the law half a dozen ways to breakfast. I'll take the consequences. I've always said that. But I won't take a load of trumped-up rubbish. That was all I wanted to say. But obviously they didn't want the truth coming out, especially about the Korozhet."

"That's a part that not even I am sure about. They're

our allies. But I love you, even if you're wrong."

"Talk to Van Klomp about it. Actually, that's what I want you to do anyway. Can you get to the paratrooper's base on your own?"

"I think I could. It's a longish march, but at least I know the town. What do you want him to do? Prepare a hide-out?"

"No. I want him to feed you and provide you with chocolate while I'm inside. I sent messages to that effect while Mike was still my counsel. He was supposed to be here to pick you up."

"I'm staying with you," she said determinedly. "There isn't a prison on Harmony and Reason that can keep me out. They're all built to keep humans in. Methinks they fail on rats."

Fitz shook his head. "One of the few things I do know is that the right of appeal is automatic in cases of the death penalty given out by a general court-martial. There's no way they can get around that. I want you to get to Van Klomp. He'll get Mike. Between them, they can get the process going. I want my chance on that witness stand. I want you there too, to tell the people of Harmony and Reason just how their general was spending the evening while he was supposedly directing operations. I need you to do this, Ariel. I need you to stay out of trouble long enough to do it."

Reluctantly she nodded. Then, leaped up to the bars and whiffled her nose against his cheek. " 'Kay."

Fitz heard the MP drivers arrive. Ariel slipped away.

"Let's see. Is there any law that they didn't contravene?" asked General Needford, his fingers steepled.

"Off-hand, no," said Lieutenant Colonel Ogata. "The entire thing should be declared a mistrial. The time and the court in which the case was taking place were altered in the record. You have the press baying furiously at you about that. The clerk of the court says that the necessary pre-trial offer of an alternative defense simply wasn't issued. In fact Judge Jeffers made several dozen straight errors of law. You're going to have to take serious action there."

Ogata looked down at the file in his hands. "The defense . . . Well, to say the woman was out of her depth is the kindest interpretation." Flipped a few pages. "The panel . . . The phrase 'unlawfully influenced' comes to mind very easily. No Challenge was issued to any of them. General Cartup-Kreutzler must have gotten some advice from his SJA. He's a lush, but capable enough when he's sober. It must have been his idea that the charges were pressed by Major General Visse, so Lieutenant General Cartup-Kreutzler was the convening officer. Very convenient. The sooner you act, the less public outcry there will be."

General Needford raised an eyebrow. "Ah, but I don't really want to stifle public outcry just yet. *Dreyfus*, Ogata, Dreyfus. That's what we need to finally start cleaning up this political cesspool. There is a historical precedent for nearly everything. By the way, you'll be conducting the defense this time. And I suggest you have young Capra as your junior counsel."

"Capra cheeks too many judges, and thinks he's too clever to be caught out at it," Ogata said, sniffing. "But he's a bright boy, I admit."

Ogata still looked doubtful. "And so, you think this

parallels the Dreyfus case do you, sir? That might be a bit rough on Fitzhugh. If I recall correctly, Dreyfus went through several retrials over a good five years before he was pardoned."

Needford smiled wryly. "Communications and the media move a little faster now. They call it 'progress,' I believe. I anticipate Fitzhugh going for retrial in a week or two."

Fitz had expected things to take a rapid turn for the worse when he arrived back at the Central Detention Barracks.

This appeared to be incorrect. He was ushered into Colonel Trevor's office.

The officer looked more than a little uncomfortable. "Major Fitzhugh."

Fitz felt that there was no longer any particular need or justification to giving any recognition or respect to senior ranks. "I thought I had been stripped of my rank," he said curtly.

"Well . . . ah. I've just had a call from General Needford, advising me that this is not going to be the case, and advising me . . . Well. It seems the JAG is not entirely satisfied with your trial."

"It wasn't a trial. It was kangaroo court. I'm hoping my appeal will be slightly better. Based on what I have experienced so far that's unlikely. But I'll give it a try. So: how do I appeal?"

Colonel Trevor looked at his desk. "The judge ought to have dealt with that. As a death-sentence prisoner, you do have the automatic right to appeal."

"Well, the judge didn't deal with it," said Fitz curtly.

"I know," admitted the colonel. "General Needford pointed that out to me."

"Who is this General Needford?" asked Fitz. "I worked in Military HQ. I thought I knew all the idiots available."

"General John Needford is the Judge Advocate General, Major," said the colonel stiffly. "And he certainly is no idiot. He's advised me that your trial will, in the next few days, be declared as requiring retrial on the basis of substantive errors of law. Of course, it will take some time for the paperwork . . ."

Trevor cleared his throat. "In the meantime, I have to treat you as if the previous trial is valid. However, I can advise you that you will be permitted visits from the attorneys that the JAG has delegated to defend you in the appeal: one Lieutenant Colonel Ōgata, and a Lieutenant Michael Capra. They'll be here in approximately an hour."

And he'd left Ariel out there, to walk. Fitz cursed himself silently. There were dangers out there.

# Chapter 16

♋

*George Bernard Shaw city, HAR Institute of Technology, Genetic Bio-research Section, and latterly on the rooftops of the city.*

Darleth waved her scent tendrils at the array of substances on the plates. The trouble was . . . they brought so many at once. She hadn't been able to get through to them that the odors from the other foodstuffs made it so hard to decide what could possibly be safe. Besides, right now starvation made all smells too intense, almost nauseatingly so.

Finally she decided that she had to try the least offensive one. It looked rather like a water-roach, but smelled slightly of iodine. She took a tentative bite.

Wasn't quite sick. Swallowed. It was salty.

Took a second bite.

.        .        .

"It's eating!" Mari-Lou held her breath and clutched the lab-coat sleeve of her assistant, causing him a great deal of unnecessary worry about how to politely fend off your boss' advances.

"Did you see those teeth!" he exclaimed. "God help you, if that thing bites you. It looks cuddly enough, but those teeth. Like little tridents!"

Mari-Lou exhaled. "I should have thought of that. How stupid can anyone get? I wonder if I can examine the dentition properly without causing offense? But looking at it I was so sure it was arboreal!"

"Huh?" Not for the first time, Mari-Lou's assistant scrambled to catch up with her.

Mari-Lou Evans smiled and tapped her own teeth. "Its teeth. They're designed to catch slippery things. They're the same sort of teeth piscivorous mammals have. Which would fit in with what it chose to eat."

The intercom crackled. "Dr. Evans. We have a party of Korozhet here, insisting on seeing the alien. They say it's a Jampad. A Magh' ally and very dangerous. Better get out of there."

"It doesn't seem very dangerous. Oh, hell. Get me Dr. Liepsich. And make it fast, if the Korozhet are already on their way here. We'll run interference."

Liepsich's trousers were in grave danger of running interference themselves. They were a standing joke among the staff of HARIT, as the physicist's personal proof that gravity could be defied.

Right now, not even the fact that he'd had to stop and haul them up was cause for laughter. All that remained of

Mari-Lou Evans was too late for saving. Her assistant, Dr. Wei, was merely unconscious.

The door to the room where the blue-furred alien had been kept was splintered. And the room within was a smoking ruin.

Sanjay Devi was already there when Liepsich arrived. He could see the same grief and fury in her expression that he felt himself. But there was something else, too, which bordered on quiet elation.

"The cracks are spreading," she murmured. "Finally."

He shivered a little. There had never been any doubt in his mind which of the three witches, in the end, was the oldest, wisest—and the most cold-bloodedly ruthless.

"You're a little scary," he grumbled.

Her thin smile had no humor at all in it. "Big sisters are always a little scary."

Darleth heard the alien intercom. Only one word made any sense. The gray head-furred one rushed out with her assistant, the door locking behind them.

Something bad was coming, and Darleth wasn't planning to wait for it to get here. Even if she had to kill one of these aliens to escape . . . well, so be it. She was not going to fall into Korozhet hands again.

Darleth was already heading along the skeletal girders above the buildings, moving as fast as she could on three arms, when the explosion came.

Perhaps taking a handful of the alien food with her had not been logical. But she was beyond logic now. Beyond anything, really, except for blind flight.

Darleth had eaten the alien food slowly, over a number

of hours, waiting for ill effects. Then, had found fresh water to drink. That had been yesterday, and she had not died, been sick, or gotten caught.

They were certainly looking for her. She'd seen patrols of soldiers on the street. One of them had shot at an animal in a tree. The animal had plainly been someone's prized possession, because the human had come out of a house and screamed at the soldier and hit him with a heavy metal object.

Darleth stayed away from trees, after that. She was hidden, at the moment, on the roof of a partly ruined building. But she'd have to go out foraging sometime soon. Her stomach said that now that it had had food, even strange, salty, alien food, it wanted more. Darleth tasted the evening breeze. No hint of the alien food that hadn't killed her. Jampad sense of smell was superb, at the two molecules per million level. To Darleth there were entire stories written on the breeze.

Another thing she did not smell was the naphthalene reek of Korozhet. That pleased her more than not smelling food.

She went out into the darkness, swinging from roof to roof. There was no water near here, or she would have taken to that.

At length she picked up a trace of the distinctive odor of the alien food.

She moved stealthily towards it. The scent came from a well-lit building, with white pillars hung with some kind of leafy greenery, and oddly-blue tinted many-paned windows. Undoubtedly some kind of human eatery. She found her way up a building opposite and settled down to watch, hungrily, on an iron staircase on the outside of the building.

Smelly vehicles were discharging patrons, and it appeared business was brisk. Darleth picked up a trace of Korozhet, too. Not as if they were there in the building themselves, but as if the patrons had been with some of the enemy recently.

Eventually, Darleth became aware that she too was being watched. Black beady eyes were looking at her through the expanded metal landing above her.

She knew those eyes. And recognized the smell, now that she was thinking about it.

There was one thing about the soft-cyber chips that the Korozhet had sold humans so that they could uplift creatures to fight the Magh', that the Korozhet somehow forgot to mention: The default language is Korozhet. And obedience to orders in that language and bias towards it, is built into the programming. The Korozhet feared slave-revolts more than anything else . . . with good reason. They insured against it with the soft-cybers.

Darleth did not see mere uplifted rats, therefore. She didn't even see hungry runaway deserters. She saw tools, that could be seized from her enemies and turned against them.

"Come down here," she commanded, in a language that they could understand and would obey. It would be good to have something to talk to, even if she hadn't been planning on making them into her private army.

Pooh-Bah was at the moment a rat in search of a meal. But he had been a number of other things, from Minister of Defense to Chancellor of the Exchequer, not to mention Groom of the Back Stairs. So he'd been a bit doubtful about the meal-qualities of the blue hairy thing, even before it spoke.

Of course, the best way to experiment with meal-quality was to eat some, preferably after another rat. But dinner had just talked back—and in a language that Pooh-Bah understood, but had never heard before. Various parts of Pooh-Bah's multiple personalities recoiled in alarm. However, something else insisted that he obey. None of the personalities liked that much. But, looking at Gobbo, he saw the other rat was obeying too. Cautiously, reluctantly, but going down.

The creature was odd, Pooh-Bah thought. Blue fur was a little unusual except down at that club on Dellman street. And six limbs tended to go with delicacies like grasshopper or cockroach, which didn't usually have fur. This was also a little large. Not even the family-size roach was quite that big.

"You will find you can speak this language," said Blue-fur. "Are you two soldiers in this human army?"

"Not recently," said Gobbo warily.

"Good. They are trying to kill me."

"Well, I think they'd do that to us, too. We are . . . people from vast acreages of sand." Pooh-Bah was sure that wasn't quite what the word meant, but that was the best translation the soft-cyber could do.

"I am wanting to get some food from that place." Blue-fur pointed to the restaurant across the street.

"It's a dump," said Gobbo dismissively. "Doesn't even do curried tripe."

The creature peered at them from under the blue-fur fringe. Pooh-Bah realized that the English words puzzled it. He filed the information in his mind under the Archbishop, a devious thinker, for future reference.

"Still. I can smell a food-kind I can eat there," said Blue-fur. "I am hungry. I have eaten only one handful in many days."

*Days!* "Well, excuse us," said Gobbo, backing off. " 'Tis needful for us to eat every four hours. So: we're off foraging now. Bye."

Pooh-Bah realized that the soft-cyber had translated hours, a concept rats were rather vague about, into a measure of time he understood with precision. The more he dealt with this alien language, the less he liked it.

"I need you to help me raid that place," said Blue-fur, pointing.

"It's hard work," protested Gobbo. "It is quite rat-proof, too. There's places with better food and grog which are much easier to get into."

"Food for you, maybe," said Blue-fur. "But I have only found one kind of local food I can tolerate yet. And I am wary of using my body to experiment with."

Half an hour later, they were sitting in the rooftop nest the rats had assembled. Blue-fur, concluded Pooh-Bah, was a positive addition to burglary. It had thumbs—four of them, in fact, two better than humans—and that made burglary a lot simpler. It didn't want a share of the grog they'd stolen. A double bonus.

"Are there many of you people from vast acreages of sand here in this city?" it asked.

Gobbo yawned. He'd eaten, drunk and wanted to sleep. "Quite a few. Living is soft here. We came to see a human who owed us. Got lost. Been here ever since. We've cut out a nice piece of territory for ourselves. It's better than fighting in the front line, although we don't get a grog-issue. We nearly went back to the army until we found we could steal it for ourselves."

"I want to make a network of all of you in this town," said Blue-fur.

"Why?" asked Gobbo.

"Because something that wants us all dead or in slavery is here. I do not wish to be a slave."

Pooh-Bah considered, and found that all of the people that he was agreed with that. He was a bit worried about Blue-fur's enslavement designs himself, but the creature seemed content to thieve beside them, rather than sending them out to do it. And he had to admit that the alien creature was good at it too. Better than humans, anyway.

Military Animal regrouping centers— Camp Marmian for rats and bats.

The collection of body hair and B.O. that was the cook's assistant at Microsceledia Military Animal Regrouping and Holding Center 4 hefted cardboard boxes out of the ten-tonner. He then began hauling the boxes into a kitchen storeroom that was the kind of place even roaches tended to avoid. Of course, that could also have been because the rats ate them. Despite the name, the "rats" were primarily derived from an insectivorous genome.

One of the boxes the cook's assistant was carrying burped. Loud and long.

He dropped the box, which split. It disgorged the remains of twenty kilos of precooked curried tripe, third grade. And a very plump and irritated rat.

"Malmsey-nosed whoremaster! What sort of welcome is this, to be flung about as if by some angry flood?" demanded Fal. "Have you no respect for the dead, man?"

"Henry! There's a muckin' rat in the boxes!" squalled the cook's assistant.

The cook and two more assistants arrived at a run. "The thieving bastards get in everywhere," said the cook. He slammed the metal-clad outer door.

The next box popped open. "Some of us did think to sleep, perchance to dream of some rest," said Nym, irritably. "Canst not kill Fal quietly?"

"What the hell are you doing in the food boxes?" demanded the cook. "What do you want here, eh?"

"A cup of hot wine with not a drop of allaying Tiber in it," said Doll, sleepily.

"Half of this box has been emptied out! You—you— *rats!*"

"Tch. A beggarly account of empty boxes for returning heroes. Fie!" Loftily, Melene preened her tail.

"Lowe, get Captain Clewes. We'll make an example of these food-stealing devils. Why the hell did I have to end up cooking here? I'm beginning to think even front-line soldiers have a better deal."

"Ha," said Fat Fal rubbing his paunch. "Knowest nothing of the front, then."

And so it was that the rats returned in triumph to their unit, and were promptly put in the cage. Punishment, except for the death sentence, required no more than the whim of the camp's commander. They got three weeks of confinement on basic dry rations for their crime.

It was quite a good deal, Nym thought. In the front lines they'd get basic dry ration, and Maggots would try to kill you. Here they only got the basic dry ration.

They had explained they'd been on the front and been

told to come here. But then the rat-minders didn't really care where they had come from. Dealing with the rats was the lowest of all jobs in the human army, and tended to have the lowest caliber of humans.

Still, Nym thought, after two days gossip to passers-by, they were doing rather well at fulfilling their promise to the bats. The better part of the rats on the front, transferring in and out of here, knew their story by now. And also had heard a story that the soft-cyber chip in their heads left them forced to obey something called "the Crotchets." The rumor that "the Crotchets" were Korozhet was a separate one, also circulating. Sometimes the two met, with a bump.

If there was one thing that rats didn't believe in, it was being guaranteed to be Number Two. In every rat's mind, he or she is Number One. From what Bronstein had said, bats felt that this meant that they'd have to try harder. The rats knew it simply meant that you'd have to do in Number One.

Bronstein had to admit that when it came to a natural ability for ignoring the law, any one rat had the edge on all of batdom.

If it had been left to her, or O'Niel or Eamon, they'd still have been getting the fly-around from various human officials, trying to get a ride back to their units. Instead the rats had taken things into their own paws—driven, admittedly, by the need for food. She would never have thought of helping herself to a ride back. To the rats, once the vehicle had been identified, the thought was as natural as a scamper and leap up to the ropes securing the canvas cover, while the driver was being signed out by the stores depot's gate-guard.

The two Military Animal Regrouping Centers were close together, and it was simply a matter of flapping off the truck when the Bat Center came in sight. The rats had cheerfully assumed that there would be some horrendous penalty incurred by them for returning to base, having failed in the human expectation of dying to defend humans. They were rather like Connolly, in that way. Bats lost in the tide of war did flutter into Bat-Base from time to time. It was accepted. Bats owed no loyalty to humans, at least as far as the bats could see, but had a vast amount of loyalty to the other bats. Bats might lose their units, but they did not desert. If rumor was to be believed, there were quite a few rat-deserters, living out lives of quiet banditry on their own. There was no bat equivalent.

# Chapter 17

*Military Courtrooms.*

A lieutenant by the name of Capra had been appointed to act as Chip's "friend" at the regimental court-martial. What a stupid term, he thought. As if some Shareholder-officer was going to be the friend of a Vat-grunt. Why not just call the man "defense attorney" and be done with it?

Still, he'd been recommended by Corporal Dusannay, the colonel's clerk. She said he was the best, and she had reason to know, as all of Colonel Brown and Camp Marmian's business was handled through her. By her, in practical fact.

Now that he was standing here in shiny boots and a new uniform, Chip was a lot less certain that all of this had been a good idea. The charges were ridiculous, but when did that stop them from sticking? He hoped that the lieutenant from the JAG was good. He was a Shareholder, after all. You couldn't trust Shareholders . . . except maybe Ginny, and she'd deserted him.

"Not guilty to all the charges, sir."

Lieutenant Capra stood up and turned to the major who was serving as presiding officer. "Major Betelsman, I would like to move that this case be dismissed. Not one of these charges can stand. Not even with someone propping up either side of them."

The major was in charge of a neighboring supply depot and was an old friend of the colonel in charge of the camp. He had quite an impressive way of snorting. "Colonel Brown drew up those charges, Lieutenant Capra! Seems a pretty open-and-shut case to me. Private Connolly was AWOL. He told some stupid lie about it, from whence the charges of disrespect to a senior office stem."

The JAG lieutenant coughed. "Firstly, technically, the charges cannot stand, sir. The charge of AWOL is incorrect. It should be Desertion, sir, which is a capital crime and must be prosecuted by a general court-martial, and not by a regimental court-martial."

"Aha. More serious charges. Well, I suppose . . ."

Lieutenant Capra shook his head and sucked air in through his teeth. "That's not all, Major."

"That's quite enough for me!" snapped the major, standing up. "Colonel Brown can have the charges sent to the JAG department for their correction, and this private sent up for a general court-martial. Desertion and cowardice are problems that must be stamped out. Take this man back to his cell."

"Ah. You can't do that, Major. He can't be in pre-trial custody—"

"I'm going to, *Lieutenant*. Remember that you're a lieutenant and I am a major. And don't tell me what to do!"

"I'll consult with the JAG about it, sir," said the lieutenant stiffly.

*Great,* thought Chip. *My "friend" just got the charges upped to a capital case. With friends like this, who needs enemies?*


So at fifteen hundred hours, three days later, Chip Connolly found himself pleading not guilty yet again. He was a little more confident this time. Lieutenant Capra had been to see him.

"Your colonel is being sticky and bloody-minded. Somehow these charges of his got pencil-whipped through. We're overstretched, and this stuff about Fitzhugh is making waves. I'm sorry. At your regimental court-martial I was still furious about Fitz—and at least that's going for retrial."

Capra flipped through some papers. "But your case: I've gone all the way up to Lieutenant Colonel Ogata. He's arranged for the case to be set forward so that it can be cleared up quickly. The only problem is we couldn't find a military judge free for this session. You'll be up before a judicial panel of officers and enlisted men advised by trial attorney and myself from the JAG. I can, however, spring you from the brig. Colonel Brown has exceeded his authority already, and I've put in a recommendation that Major Betelsman be brought before a investigative commission for his conduct of the regimental court-martial. If this case goes as I foresee, he'll never serve on one again. In fact, he'll be lucky if he doesn't get demoted."

The lieutenant had been startled to hear that Chip preferred to remain in the brig, but he'd been quick enough to understand why. And Capra seemed to be the sort who could sniff out a silver lining in any cloud.

"If it's okay with you, Private, it's okay with me. It won't do your case any harm, that's for sure, when I list it as pre-trial punishment and point out that it was illegal."

And there was Tim Fuentes in the court—the fellow who had tried to interview him—and his cameraman . . . and dozens of other civilians, all watching. Mike Capra had said he was going to tell a few people in the media. Chip hadn't believed him, or hadn't believed they'd listen. He'd been wrong, obviously.

Their presence might have worried some prosecuting attorneys. But this trial counsel was a certain Captain Tesco, who had a reputation for being an arrogant ass. He also had a big caseload, and this was, after all, an open-and-shut case.

"His unit record shows Private Connolly as killed during the assault on Sector 355," stated Tesco. "He arrived back at Camp Marmian several days later. The survivors of that assault were sent on from Divisional headquarters to Camp Marmian to join units being posted again to the front. The only conclusion that this court can reasonably reach is that Private Connolly was not killed, but had in fact deserted his unit."

It did sound very unarguable, especially when Colonel Brown was called to the stand to testify about the time, date and manner of Chip's return. It was apparent that insolence was a question of perception.

Lieutenant Capra stood up to cross-examine. "Colonel Brown, could you tell the court exactly what Private Connolly said to you?"

"A lot of disrespectful rubbish and cheek!"

"His exact words, sir," said Capra. "To the best of your ability."

The colonel was unimpressed. "Hmph. Ask my clerk. I know you came and interviewed her."

"I will be calling her as a witness later," said Capra patiently. "I am asking you now, sir."

"I don't remember," grumbled the colonel.

Unlike Brown and Tesco, the presiding officer *had* finally noticed that the court had filled up alarmingly for the open-and-shut case of an insignificant Vat deserter. "Colonel Brown," he said firmly, "you will answer the question to the best of your ability."

The colonel puffed himself up like an irritated bullfrog. "Some nonsense about killing millions of Magh'. And whether he could go home if he was dead."

There was a titter from the audience. Capra waited for it to subside. "Anything else, Colonel? He didn't by any chance try to tell you where he'd been?"

"Ha. He said he had been trapped behind enemy lines and had fought his way back." The colonel plainly found this ludicrous claim quite funny.

"I believe he also claimed to have destroyed a Magh' force-field generator, and to have freed Ms. Virginia Shaw?" prompted Capra.

The colonel snorted. It was obviously his favorite noise. "Yes. He did. I suppose you're going to claim that the man was not of sound mind or something."

The lieutenant looked at him, as unblinkingly as a cat, and then slowly shook his head. "No, Colonel. I am not. I have no further questions for you."

Standing in front of them all in his polished boots and pressed BDUs, Chip felt as if he was naked. In uniform, dressed as if for a parade—but without a bangstick or a trench knife. Lieutenant Capra had just read the colonel's clerk's statement to the court. "Do you confirm this as substantially correct?"

Chip swallowed. It was the first time that he'd had to say anything but "Not guilty" and "I do." So he kept it to a monosyllable. "Yes."

You couldn't go too far wrong with that. He hoped. He didn't trust these Shareholder bastards not to stitch him up.

"Thank you, Private. I have no further questions for you at this point." Chip was relieved. He was sweating as it was.

"Now," said the defense attorney. "I'd like to call the court's attention to exhibit 1: dispatches from Divisional headquarters for that period. This is the period in which Charge 1 Specification 1 accuses Private Connolly of having deserted. I call your attention to Dispatch D3728. It states that the front line, having sustained heavy shelling, fell with the loss of all but four human survivors, at 1100 hours. Notice the date, please. The territory is also described as lost to the enemy advance. Private Connolly is among those listed as killed in action."

He paused. "We no longer have a category 'Missing in Action.' I asked the Bureau of Military Statistics why. They said that the nature of this particular war has made such a category virtually meaningless. I am here to present evidence that they are wrong, and that Private Connolly has been unjustly accused."

He cleared his throat. "I would like to call my next witness, Lieutenant Colonel Robert Van Klomp of the 1st HAR Airborne."

Chip's heart lifted at the sight of the huge man stumping down to the witness stand. They'd obviously promoted him, at least. Well, far be it from Chip to praise any officer, but this one was almost . . . sort of . . . possibly . . . okay.

"Lieutenant Colonel Van Klomp, do you recognize the private in the dock?"

Van Klomp nodded. "Connolly. He's cleaner, and has had a shave. And I presume his shoulder has healed."

"Could you tell the court just where you were when you encountered Private Connolly?"

"We had just assaulted the central hub of the Magh' scorpiary in the area now known as Delta 355 advanced. That's the center of the thirty-two odd miles of Magh' territory recaptured from the enemy. It's more or less seventeen miles from the point at which I believe Connolly was stationed when the Magh' launched their assault. When I and my men reached the brood-heart of the scorpiary, I found that Private Connolly had beaten us to it, sir. He, Virginia Shaw, and whole lot of rats and a few bats. They'd destroyed the power cables to the force-field generator and had killed the Magh' in the control center. We couldn't have captured all that territory without them."

The presiding officer had to quell a semi-riot, before Lieutenant Capra could continue. "In other words the statement that Private Connolly made to Colonel Brown was simply the truth?"

Van Klomp beamed. "*Ja*. Other than the fact that he grossly understated what they had achieved. I've put in a motivation that the *boykie* and those rats and bats should be considered for as many medals as they can wear and still stand up under the weight, Lieutenant. Ten or twelve of them managed to advance seventeen miles into enemy-held territory. At Carrack, a full division supported by three days of heavy artillery managed to advance less than half a mile, with horrendous human casualties, before being driven back. Now, between their efforts and Major Fitzhugh's advance, we've recaptured thirty-two miles of territory. They gave us our first major victory against the Magh'. When I got back to base, they told me the Airborne was being expanded to take conscripts, too. So. I put in a motivation that Private Connolly be transferred to the Airborne, with immediate effect. The Airborne is supposed to be Harmony and Reason's elite unit, and I want this man. His transfer has been okayed. I believe he's also in line for promotion."

Van Klomp bestowed a ferocious glare on no one in particular. "But the desk-jockeys at HQ told me they hadn't been able to find him. Idiots. When Private Connolly and his troops escorted Ms. Shaw out of the combat zone—she insisted on having her rescuers for an escort—I had radioed through to Divisional HQ and told them that these troops were on their way. I requested that they deal with their redeployment to somewhere they could be debriefed after their ordeal, but Divisional's staff claimed that they had never arrived. I was deeply shocked when the lieutenant told me Colonel Brown had put

Connolly here in the stockade at Camp Marmian for being AWOL. That's no way to treat a hero."

Looking at the deflating bullfrog of a colonel, pinned by the gazes of the media, Chip had his payback.

The trial counsel stood up slowly. Captain Tesco was plainly smarting too. He looked as mad as a chef discovering he only had powdered egg, and just about as nasty. "While I appreciate that the private plainly did not desert, he still hasn't accounted for the fact that he didn't arrive at Divisional headquarters, never mind remain there."

Mike Capra's eyes widened dramatically. "Let me see if I've got this straight. Despite the fact that the prisoner turns out to be a hero, innocent of the ridiculous charges heaped on him, a man who has been abominably treated, illegally kept in pre-trial custody—Captain Tesco still wants his blood. Well, fortunately I still have two witnesses, and other items of evidence. Lucky us. Oh, lucky us!"

"Cut out the theatricals, Lieutenant," growled the presiding officer. "Just present your evidence."

"Certainly, sir. Entered as our second item we have here a DVD disk. It is part of an interview shot by my witnesses, at Divisional headquarters. They can be called, if necessary, to confirm its veracity. There were a number of other witnesses present, who can also be called if the court deems it necessary. You will all excuse the fact that Private Connolly has been in combat for five days, out of reach of showers or razors. He'd been fighting for his country, not dressing for parade, ladies and gentlemen. If we can just show the clip on the rear screen."

Brigadier Charlesworth had his moment of glory, faithfully recorded:

"Get back to your unit, soldier. As quickly as possible. And get your platoon sergeant to put you on a charge for the state of your uniform and that half-beard of yours. Just because we're at war doesn't mean you have an excuse to ignore dress and appearance codes! Now, get these scruffy military animals back to their units, before I have them put down."

There was nothing like reminding the public that you were the man who told a war-hero and new idol of the press, that he should get back to his unit and get himself put on a charge, for not shaving, when he'd just rescued the colony's most prominent citizen and caused the greatest victory of the war. Even the most Vat-despising Shareholder would find the lack of recognition given to Private Connolly for his achievement hard to accept.

Lieutenant Capra cleared his throat in the stunned silence. "And then Private Connolly, like a good soldier, obeyed orders. He discovered that the remains of his unit had been sent to Camp Marmian. He arranged for transport there, and he reported to Colonel Brown. He told his story honestly and was imprisoned . . . for courageously fighting for his country, and obeying the orders of a superior officer."

The trial counsel knew when to abandon a sinking ship. Tesco turned to the presiding officer. "I'd like to move that all these charges be dismissed, sir. There are no grounds for them, and the army would be wrong to pursue the matter further. I should like to offer my apologies that I have had to act against this gallant soldier."

Chip happened to be looking at the lieutenant who had defended him at that moment. He could lipread the word "Asshole," but the rest he hoped he'd misunderstood.

The presiding officer nodded. "We'll have to withdraw so that the panel can consult. But I agree, I don't see any grounds for any of these charges. Not even the minor ones of disrespect."

Five minutes later Chip was carried shoulder high out of the court. Onlookers pressed in to try and shake his hand.

One of the first was the INB reporter. "You owe me an exclusive, Private. I want your story."

Outside were the cameras and questions. This time they were for him, not Virginia. After battling for a few minutes, he found a step that allowed him to look over their heads and address the crowd. He wasn't given to making speeches, but this had to be said. He knew Virginia had been planning to point out that it had been the efforts of the rats and the bats that had made it work, not just humans. And then, somehow, she hadn't been able to finish saying it. So it was up to him. He owed it to them. He wished now that he'd at least said a proper goodbye to them. He'd just been so upset and so mad at the time.

"I'd just like to say one thing. You're all clamoring around me. I'm just a Vat-grunt who was in the wrong place at the right time. And I'm only one of those who did this. We couldn't have done it without the rest of my buddies. My fellow soldiers, comrades, who were all fighting for us, for humans here on Harmony and Reason, were rats and bats." He swallowed. "Some of those . . . brave comrades didn't come back. Every one of us, from rat soldiers like Falstaff and Phylla, to the bats, and little Fluff, and . . . Virginia, fought to try to at least pay the Maggots back for killing so many of our people. My comrades, both the living and the dead, deserve the credit. Not me."

"You mean Ms. Shaw actually fought?" demanded a reporter eagerly.

Chip nodded. "Yes. I saw her cut a Maggot in half with a chainsaw, mister. No slowshield, no training, just pure guts."

"With a chainsaw! We've been trying to get to interview her. They say she's still too unwell for visitors. Was she badly injured? Sick?"

A bubble of uneasy fear pricked at Chip. "No. She had a slight concussion . . . but our medic—the Airborne's medic, too, and the doc with the infantry—all examined her. They all said she was fine. Ginny's no stinking Share—ah—fainting violet. She's tough as army boots."

There were a few more shouted questions, most of them having to do with the overall course of the war. Chip answered as best he could, doing his best—he truly believed this—not to heap undue sarcasm and ridicule on the army's high command. For some reason the crowd laughed a lot.

After people started drifting away, Lieutenant Capra tugged at his elbow and spoke softly, so only Chip could hear him. "I attempted to subpoena Ms. Shaw as a material witness. I thought she'd knock that son of a bitch Tesco out of the park. I got, um, an odd response."

Chip felt the hairs on the back of his neck prickle. "What?"

"None," said Lieutenant Capra.

"And that's odd?" Chip asked.

"It is indeed," replied Capra. "Harmony and Reason may have its flaws, Private. But it has the finest constitution, and a legal system derived from that, that the New

Fabian Society was able to devise. And that law extends through to the military code. Put simply: No one, not even Virginia Shaw, is above the law. Willfully neglecting or refusing to appear is a crime. And her legal advisors would know that. A written deposition could be taken if she was unfit to travel. But . . ."

He shrugged. "The case was due, and we really didn't need her. I didn't follow it up, as the news reports say that she is still very ill. And now you say she shouldn't be."

Chip took a deep breath and turned to Van Klomp. "Sir. You say I've been transferred to your unit. Do I have to go back to Camp Marmian?"

"I don't think you should have gone there in the first place. But according to the army, if you aren't dead, you're in the 1st HAR Airborne. And I'm your new commanding officer."

Chip saluted smartly. "Can I have a pass, please, sir?"

Van Klomp gave a wry smile. "Common sense tells me to say: 'no.' But I think you deserve it. Will two days do you . . . Lance Corporal? I think more than that might go to your head." From a pocket of his tunic he handed Chip a set of stripes, a beret badge with wings—and a pass-chit. He'd obviously been expecting this.

Chip looked at the pass. The form was made out to Lance Corporal Charles Connolly, 1st HAR Airborne. "Sir. I don't think I'm noncom material, sir."

"Privates don't think, Connolly. So if you do, that proves you're an NCO at heart already. This pass is made out to Lance Corporal Charles Connolly. Not Private Connolly. Do you want it?"

Chip gritted his teeth. He'd always been militant about

being a grunt. As a combat veteran, they'd tried to make him an NCO a couple of times. In the front lines that just meant you died sooner. But he put the pass and stripes in his shirt pocket, all the same.

"See that those stripes and the badge are on when you get back from pass," said Van Klomp. "I want to talk to you about rats and bats when you get back. And Lance Corporal . . ."

"Sir?"

"Stay out of trouble, will you?"

Chip saluted. "I'll do my best, sir."

"When you've finished your parachute course you'll be due for some more leave," said Van Klomp, with an absolutely straight face.

Chip could only stare at him in utter horror. "Me? Jump out of an airplane? You must be fu . . . mad . . . sir," he added, belatedly.

Van Klomp laughed. "I have a feeling you'll be up for disrespect again soon, Lance Corporal. That's what airborne do. And we don't need a company chef."

Chip realized that the big paratrooper had checked on his background. He also got the feeling that Van Klomp would cheerfully throw anyone out of the plane that wouldn't jump for themselves. He took a deep breath. "I'll see you in three days time, sir."

He saluted and turned, hastily, nearly bumping into his old jailor, Ngui. The sergeant beamed at him. "I have taken the liberty of bringing here certain personal items of your kit. If you would like to sign for them, Lance Corporal."

"And when you've done that," said the INB reporter who had stayed behind, "how would you like a lift into the City? I presume that's where you're going for your pass?"

My. He was going up in the world. A lift in a Shareholder's car. Mind you, he was sure that was just because the man wanted to pump him for the story. Well, he might as well make the best of it. In fact, he might as well grab as much cover as he could. The Shaw family were *not* going to like some scruffy little Vat-grunt showing up on their doorstep. A good soldier takes cover wherever he can get it, even if it meant hiding behind the press.

"Actually, I want to go and see if I can see Ginny . . . uh, Ms. Shaw. I'm, uh, concerned about the stories I'm hearing of her health." He felt his face glowing a dull red. They'd think he was going to ask for some sort of reward. Well, so what? What did he care what this bunch of pansy-Shareholders thought of him? They'd never believe him if he told them that the thought had never even crossed his mind. That he was going simply because he had a feeling that she was in trouble, and he was going to see for himself.

"Well," said the reporter, "you'll have to go in the morning, Priv— Corporal. That district has a curfew, unless you have a special resident's pass, or one of them to vouch for you." He hauled out a mobile. "You could try calling. But I hope you fail, because we want to film this, and they'll never give curfew-permission for all of us. But otherwise I'll take you to the gates of Shaw House, myself, in the morning. You tell us your story and we'll organize you a slap-up supper and a bed. Do we have a deal?"

Chip looked at the mobile. He'd never even held one before. They cost more money than a Vat could dream of affording. "I don't know the number," he mumbled, feeling his face go puce.

"123-SHAW," said one of the other media women, sourly, "and he wouldn't be offering if he didn't think you'd get the same runaround as we all did. We get the estate switchboard. And they say: 'Sorry, Miss Shaw is not taking any calls at the moment.' "

It was exactly the reply that he got.

"Uh. Well can you give her a message from me?"

The cool voice on the other end said she would see that Miss Shaw got the message.

"Just tell her Chip called. I'm going to come out there to see her tomorrow."

"Miss Shaw is not receiving visitors."

"Just tell her. Please."

He had to accept the receptionist's arctic assurance that all messages were delivered.

# Chapter 18

ᕤ

*A rat's-eye perspective of George Bernard Shaw City.*

Ariel had discovered that there was a huge difference—if you were a rat, anyway—to traversing a city by car, with a human who knew where they were going, and walking it. The paratrooper's base was somewhere outside town to the northeast of the city. And the court had been somewhere to the southeast.

There was an awful lot in between. If Ariel had been a crow, not a rat, it would have been about sixteen miles.

As a rat, it was much farther. There had even been a stupid cat or two on the way. Ariel had found that when she shouted at most dogs, they tended to become very confused. Cats usually needed to be bitten. And they were fast. But she'd noticed that in the middle of town they tended to steer around her.

The only problem she'd had, besides a need to forage and cross streets, was that when she'd gotten to the far side of town . . . she'd realized that she was in suburbia, a long way to the west of where she wanted to be. This was Shareholder suburbia—which seemed to mean pretentious houses, smallish yards and an awful lot of dogs. There were Vat tenements just further west, and maybe that explained the dogs.

It was a choice of crossing a wilderness of roads and gardens—or heading back into downtown, and going back to where she thought she'd gone wrong. Night was falling, and that should make keeping out of sight easier. And the sooner she got walking . . .

But it was an awfully long way and her paws were soft from being human-carried so much. She snuffled a bit. After all, there was no one around to see her missing Fitz.

"Misery me, lacadaydee. What have we here?" asked a voice from the shadow of some dustbins.

Instinctively, Ariel dropped into a crouch, and prepared herself to either attack or flee.

A noble ratly nose poked itself out of the heavy darkness. "Now, lass. There is no need to be so affrighted. It's not *trouble* I intended . . . Oh."

He'd plainly caught sight of her amputated stump of tail. For a rat that was a severe lack of physical attractiveness.

She, on the other hand, had identified him. "Gobbo! You cozening rogue! What are you doing here?"

"Ariel?" he asked incredulously.

" 'Tis none other, Gobbo." She bowed. Gobbo had been a rat in her section during Fitz's front-line stint. He'd been one of the rats in the "glorious rearguard," who had held off the Magh' when Divisional headquarters had refused to provide reinforcements. He was a drunkard, a thief and a lecher: in other words, as good a rat as you could find. "So: you answer my question. What are you doing here?"

"A little banditry," he said cheerfully. "A spot of conveying. Some drinking and wenching when we get the opportunity. 'Tis rich pickings on soft country."

"How long have you been here? Fitz tried to find you when he got out of hospital."

Gobbo nodded. "Indeed. We came to look for him. But as hayseed lads we got lost. And then, well, the living was good here in the city. We found that we hath no desire to go back to being soldiers. So: hath swapped soldieree for burglaree. 'Tis more rewarding."

"We? How many of you are there?"

"Well, some ten. In a manner of speaking."

"In what manner of speaking?" asked Ariel, suspiciously.

"Well, some of them are called Pooh-Bah," admitted Gobbo.

Ariel understood, then. Pooh-Bah was several people. Eight, if she remembered rightly. They all just happened to live in the same ratty soft-cyber, and, usually, worked together for profit.

"So. Where is Pooh-Bah? And who is the other one of your little band."

"Ol' Bluefur-bigteeth. Come and see him," said Gobbo, proprietarily. "We have prog, and not just that fishy stuff Ol' Bluefur-bigteeth eats, and fine grog."

The thought of food—and of course drink—were tempting to any rat. But Fitz came first. "Methinks I'd love to. But I need to get to the paratrooper's camp. 'Tis a weary walk."

Gobbo stared at her with his mouth open. "Walk!" He shook his head incredulously. "Hath not heard of busses?"

"And how would a kiss help me, Gobbo?"

"Nay, not proper busses," explained Gobbo. "Omnibuses. Vehicles for the transporting of Vat-labor. The number eighty-nine doth head out that way, if I have the right of it. In which case you've just missed it. There'll be another along in an hour from the Malham Street depot."

It was Ariel's turn to look at the streetwise rat in openmouthed amazement. "Doth catch this 'bus' to wherever you want to go?"

Gobbo nodded. " 'Tis a situation much to be desired. We city rats do not walk. Come, you can meet Ol' Bluefur-bigteeth, see the crowd that is Pooh-Bah, and find some victuals and a mouthful or two of as fine a sack as you've yet tasted. Then I shall set you upon the next 'bus with my own paws."

It was too good an offer to be refused.

Ol' Bluefur-bigteeth was indeed worth seeing. He would have been worth seeing even if she had not seen him before in the captured scorpiary.

All of Pooh-Bah was delighted to see her. "Methinks you are what we chiefly need." In a slightly shifted tone of voice he said: "And all of us are agreed. There are other rats in town. Bluefur wants to organize them."

Ariel had ideas of her own on that. She could use a squad of rats to rescue Fitz. Especially if he didn't want to be rescued. She'd been at a loss as to how to carry him, before meeting Gobbo and Pooh-Bah. "Methinks it hath merit. But why? And how many?"

" 'Tis thought twenty to fifty or so," answered Gobbo. "And Bluefur doth not say. No doubt he has his reasons. He is a capital rogue, even if he doth eat only fishy stuff."

"Tell you what. You take me to the 1st HAR Airborne and we have a deal. Needs must I should talk to a human there."

"Not about Ol' Bluefur-bigteeth?"

"Nay. Fitz. He is in durance vile and I must spring him."

"The captain! He is still here?" asked Gobbo eagerly.

"Aye. But a Major now. Or was. Methinks they have made him a private again."


So Ariel had eight escorts on her trip in the spare tire of the number 89 bus. It was not everyone who had a First Lord of the Treasury, Lord Chief Justice, Commander in Chief, Great Scientist, Master of the Buckhounds, Groom of the Backstairs and the Lord Mayor to accompany them. It was a good thing that they conveniently occupied one body or they would have had to travel on the roof, which was a great deal more breezy.


Van Klomp was fortunately still at his desk. "Where the hell have you been?" he demanded. "Fitzy has been worried stiff about you."

She leapt up onto his desk, knowing that Pooh-Bah was listening in. "Where is the strong drink then?"

Van Klomp raised his eyebrows. "You don't care much, do you?" he said irritably. "He's in jail, due to be hanged, and all he's doing is worrying about you."

She reached out and tweaked his nose. "Doth know where a suburb called Highbury is?"

He blinked. "Yes. It's a fair distance away."

"And doth know where the building used for the military court is?"

"Naturally. I seem to spend too much of my time there. It's a good three-quarter hour's drive each way, too," answered Van Klomp.

"Hath ever thought how far it is for a rat on foot . . . via Highbury?" asked Ariel.

Van Klomp had the grace to look discomforted, and got up and fetched a beer. "Uh. Well, have some beer. I've only got beer here. I hadn't thought of that. Why Highbury?"

"I got lost. I've never had to find my way on foot before. And beer doth go straight through me," she said grumpily, tilting the bottle and sneezing froth.

"Fitzy asked me to look after you. So you'll have transport again."

"Doth not need it anymore. But I do need to talk with Meilin." Meilin was Van Klomp's chief factotum and general bottlewasher. She was also a particular friend of Ariel's, and figured in Ariel's ratty plans for organizing the rats and freeing Fitz. "And then I could use a lift back to the Siradolalis Center."

"But that's in the middle of town!" protested Van Klomp. "Meilin can take care of you at my apartment."

"I am going to stay in the middle of town. And if they try to kill Fitzy, I will deal with it," said Ariel fiercely. "And the less that you know about it the better. Now take me to see Meilin. We will need a hedge."

"Hedge?"

"Ach. I mean fence."

# Chapter 19

ↄ

*The largest office in Military HQ. No Horsey Prints.*
*18th century Naval engagements instead.*


## ARMY JAILS HERO FOR NOT BEING DEAD!

In a stunning example of military bungling, the
Army jailed Private Charles Connolly for desertion.
Connolly, whom Lieutenant Colonel Van Klomp
of the 1st HAR Airborne said "should be considered
for as many medals as he can wear and still stand up
under the weight," was listed as dead when a Magh'
advance overran his position. Buried alive in a cave-
in, Connolly survived, dug himself out and fought
courageously on behind enemy lines. Battling million-
to-one odds with a group of loyal Military Animals,

*he succeeded in rescuing the daughter of our late Chairman, Virginia Shaw. Against all probability and with suicidal courage he and his companions then managed to destroy the force-field generator, allowing our heroic 5th Infantry Brigade to make their dramatic advance in Sector Delta 355.*

*Private Connolly, described by Virginia Shaw in her interview on her release as "the finest soldier," was liberated during Major Fitzhugh's successful push forward. However, when he returned to his base, Colonel G. Brown, CO of Camp Marmian, promptly had Connolly arrested for desertion because the record listed him as "died in action."*

*When questioned later by reporters, Colonel Brown placed the blame on the camp's clerk, whom he said would be severely punished. Connolly spent eight days in the cells awaiting trial, before being completely acquitted.*

General Blutin put the newspaper down and sighed. Another article on the front page had been about Conrad Fitzhugh. The editorial had been by a military history buff. The army—more precisely, the high command—was now being shredded almost daily in the papers, on radio and on television screens. The media, having slavishly quoted the military press releases for the past year and a half, had suddenly discovered the army brass could be wrong. They were still one hundred percent behind the men and women on the front lines. It was just the crenalated Military HQ that was becoming the place everyone loved to hate.

He'd liked being a general, back in the peaceful pre-war days. There had been just three enlisted men for each officer, and, other than a liking for spit-'n-polish, there had been no vast military demands made on the army. At first, the huge increase in power and influence that had come with the Magh' invasion had been heady, if frightening. The Korozhet advisors had helped them to cope with the unknown, and Lieutenant General Cartup-Kreutzler had expanded like a peony to take control of the now burgeoning army.

Blutin had been content to let him. Cartup-Kreutzler had always intimidated him, to tell the truth. The booming, powerful personality of his subordinate was stronger than his own.

Too late, he was beginning to wish that he had reined the man in. Or that he'd listened to that terrifying half-Halloween-mask-faced intelligence officer, Fitzhugh. Blutin hadn't liked the man. Disliked him intensely, in fact. But at least the intelligence major had made the army look good for a change. It was only since that Delta 355 victory—and the idiotic subsequent arrest of Fitzhugh—that media attention had suddenly focused on the way the army was run by the General Staff, almost as if they were waking up to the idea that it could be done differently. For the first time, the media had cameramen right up there on the front. The people of Harmony and Reason were getting the war right in their living rooms. And they wanted to know why it couldn't be like old DVDs. At the moment they seemed ready to blame the General Staff for losing . . . now that they'd seen that they could win.

And then had come Fitzhugh's trial: General Cartup-Kreutzler had assured him it would all be over and forgotten in a day. "Best done quickly," he'd said.

Only it hadn't worked like that at all. The media were

calling it a kangaroo court. There were daily demands for a retrial. There were scathing editorials. More and more evidence was emerging about Fitzhugh's role. And none of it made the high command look good.

General Blutin wasn't enjoying suddenly becoming a social outcast. The vendetta that Cartup-Kreutzler and his brother-in-law Talbot had pursued against Fitzhugh had certainly not worked out the way that they'd planned. This latest story about some blasted private—as if the army couldn't make an innocent error about one stupid Vat!— just made things worse.

He needed to do something about it. Blutin scratched his jowls. There, as that unpleasantly smart-tongued Sanjay Devi would say, was the rub. Other than in a rage, he really wasn't up to taking on Cartup-Kreutzler. Not head on, at least, nor at office politics. Cartup-Kreutzler had filled the ornate, crenelated military magnificence of HQ with his sycophants and allies.

Blutin sighed, reached for the telephone on his acreage of gleaming desk, and picked it up. "Miss Burgess. Get me the Judge Advocate General. And when I've done with him, the Surgeon General." They were both what General Cartup-Kreutzler referred scathingly to as "Johnny-come-latelies." Not the "old army" that he and Blutin knew and trusted. General Blutin was not keen to ask them for help. But the alternative was far worse. He might actually have to do something himself.

The two major generals seldom came into the huge Military Headquarters building. They had offices of their own, and seemed to prefer their less grandiose settings. General Blutin had always felt that rather strange in an officer; but then, as General Cartup-Kreutzler had disparagingly said, they weren't "proper officers." Well, right now that was perhaps what he needed.

General DiMillio, the Surgeon General, looked at the thick fitted carpet. "You do yourselves awfully well over here at HQ," he drawled.

Blutin started to draw breath for a furious retort, and then remembered that he was seeking allies. "The job's got its perks, but"—he pointed to the pile of newspaper clippings he'd assembled—"it's got its problems too. I asked you to come here today to discuss them. I need your help, gentlemen."

The Judge Advocate General, General John Needford, was a tall, ominously silent and very black man. He made General Blutin sweat and feel aware of just how tight his tailored uniform had become. Needford didn't say anything, just walked over to the desk and looked at the clippings.

The doctor snapped first. "I'm a busy man, General Blutin. Tell us what this is about so that I can say 'no,' and I can get back to my work."

General Blutin sucked his teeth. "Well. It's about this affair with Major Fitzhugh . . ."

The Judge Advocate General narrowed his eyes. "You do realize that attempting to influence the course of justice could invalidate the whole case, General Blutin. Anyway, I'll have no part in railroading this man. I said as much to General Cartup-Kreutzler. This retrial is something I intend to see is as fair and legal as possible."

"And I'll stand by the steps my medical personnel took. Fitzhugh shouldn't be in jail."

"Good! Good! Then we agree on this!" Blutin said with relief, sitting down.

The two generals stared at him.

"You mean . . . that's what you wanted us for?" asked the Surgeon General suspiciously. "You want us to support this Fitzhugh?"

"Well," said General Blutin, uneasily, "not support in so many words, but . . ." He rushed his fences. "Look, Cartup-Kreutzler is all set for a personal vendetta on this man. I . . . I think it would be better if we . . . er . . . let sleeping dogs lie. Got out of it as quietly as possible. The man is very popular. I don't want to cause any further trouble, but, well, General Cartup-Kreutzler and his brother-in-law are set on it."

The Surgeon General blinked at him. "Then why don't you tell him to back off?"

"Er. He doesn't listen to me very well," said General Blutin, hoping that he didn't sound as feeble as he felt.

The Judge Advocate General raised his head and pursed his lips thoughtfully. "Ah. Now I understand. You want us—Nick and I—to organize a palace *coup*."

"Well, I, er . . . wouldn't have put it that way myself. But, well, they seem to be being very foolish about this. And . . . um . . ."

The Surgeon General began to laugh, softly. "If even you can see that, General, what do you think that the rest of the world thinks of it? I came here ready to fight. I didn't think I'd come here to rescue you, General. But it sounds like you need it."

*Even you* indeed. That stung. But before he allowed it to goad him, the Judge Advocate General spoke again. "Well, I don't think it's a laughing matter. But seriously, General Blutin, just what do you think we can do? The command structure at the top end is solid with General

Cartup-Kreutzler's loyalists. And the army is not exactly designed to be a democracy anyway."

There was an uncomfortable silence. General Blutin realized that they were actually waiting for an answer. An answer he didn't really have. "Well," he said awkwardly, "this Fitzhugh affair. We seem agreed that, well, General Cartup-Kreutzler is damaging the image of the General Staff with his public pursuit of it. Can't it be dropped? Tossed out?"

The Judge Advocate General shook his head. "No. And I would not be prepared to collude in any such process. The best we can do is to see that he gets a reasonably fair trial this time around. I've looked at the charges. Some of them won't stand. I suspect that if General Cartup-Kreutzler had stayed with a few basic charges, they'd have stuck like glue. But someone has gotten quite imaginative with these charges. There were shenanigans in that first trial. I've put Ogata onto it and he'll root it out. This time I can recommend a good defense team, and a good military judge. But when it comes to prosecution, well, that's a mixed bag." He smiled wryly. "My officers are all ex-civilian professionals. Not all lawyers enjoy a good reputation."

"Do any?" asked the medical man, returning the wry smile. "I've been thinking, General. Your problem is essentially not that Cartup-Kreutzler directly disobeys you, is it? He—and his staff—just find ways of not quite doing what you wanted."

General Blutin nodded, gloomily. "I've tried to assume the reins in the last while. It's been hopeless. There is always a reason why things have not been done. And things are always going to happen. They just never do.

Everything gets referred back to Cartup-Kreutzler."

The doctor nodded thoughtfully. "But, if I am correct, the final appointment of new staff to the General Staff is signed by you?"

"Two signatures. Lieutenant General Cartup-Kreutzler's and mine."

The Attorney General shook his head. "Not according to the standing regulations. Any promotion to the level of staff officer must be recommended by an officer of the General Staff, and approved by you. Or by the elected head of the board of Shareholders. It certainly doesn't need Cartup-Kreutzler."

"Oh. It's just always been done like that," said General Blutin.

"Which naturally means it is right," said the Judge Advocate General sardonically. "Anyway, what's your idea, Nick? I think I know where you're going, but as I think your field of expertise is renal and colonic medicine, I want to make sure that hasn't influenced your judgment. Medical personnel are usually no use in legal matters. They usually try to 'help' the accused."

The doctor laughed. "We're a helping profession. And everything ends up with the kidneys or the colon, sooner or later. There's a glass ceiling in the army's General Staff. There is hardly anyone on it who hasn't had at least twenty years prewar service. If you want to change things, General, you will need to move a few new officers up. Officers with actual combat experience on the front lines. I think I can recommend a few. And they can recommend a few more. Even my grumpy legal colleague could probably recommend a few more, if he wanted to."

The Judge Advocate General scratched his chin. "I wish

I had some spare staff. We're hopelessly understaffed. That's why we agreed to allow regimental court-martials, which in retrospect, was a big mistake. But I suppose we'll have to deal with this. So. Actually, what you need is an attempt to crush the medical, legal and indeed the Quartermaster General's little kingdoms."

The other two stared at him. "The Mongols tried it in China," he said by way of explanation.

That didn't clarify anything, thought General Blutin. However, he managed to keep quiet for long enough to let the Surgeon General be the one who said: "What?"

The Judge Advocate General gave a half-smile. "The study of history would benefit both of you. By putting officers from, if you pardon my saying so, the least efficient part of the army into those parts that run well, they'll either have to shape up or be shipped out by us. And that creates any number of vacancies here. People answerable to you, and not part of the power politics of this place, but also with a great deal of executive power."

His smile became grim. "And, it gives you a reason for having called us in here. You were trying to instruct us on the Fitzhugh case, but we were singularly recalcitrant. So now you want some reliable men from HQ transferred into our units. I should imagine General Cartup-Kreutzler will be so delighted that he'll forgive you for having a meeting with us without inviting him. And just send any new recommendations from him for new staff officers over to the JAG for background checks or a medical evaluation. I think we can guarantee that they'll take a long time. We'll come up with a few recommendations, in reply to that general memo to all departments that you are going to issue. Those, I think, will proceed swiftly."

*     *     *

In another part of the same building, Major Tana Gainor shook her head calmly at the furious brothers-in-law. "No, General. There is nothing I can do about that. He will go for retrial. And I'm not about to return your money, Talbot. I did what I was paid to do. In fact, if you want me to do it again—and you will need me to—it is going to cost you more."

Talbot Cartup snorted angrily. "Don't forget that I've got you pinned."

Tana smiled seraphically. "And, needless to say, if I go down, or have an unforeseen accident—so do you. So let's forget the histrionics and get down to business details, gentlemen. The law is always for sale, to the highest bidder."

"No," Needford said firmly into the telephone, tilting the chair back from the desk in his office. "There's not a chance of that, Len."

After listening to the response, the Judge Advocate General shook his head. "That may be the lamest insult I've ever gotten from you. Stick to physics, Dr. Liepsich. There is not a cold chance in hell that Cartup and his crowd will suddenly be seized by intelligence. I can guarantee you that at this very minute they are digging themselves deeper into the pit."

He waited a few more seconds. "And that one was even lamer. Look, Len, they won't be able to resist. Not with the shiny new shovel I just handed to them."

# Chapter 20

∽

*Under the rooftops, with the rafterlines hung
with a black mass of bats.*

Bats hung and chittered. Bronstein found it wonderful to
have so many others all around again, like some huge,
enveloping cloak. Bats were just not designed to be solitary creatures. Even with three of them, Bronstein had
always felt exposed. Now, in the warm, crowded hang-
ings of the belfry, she felt security in the togetherness of
it all. And yet—she felt even more alone, because of what
the three of them had seen and had to prove to batdom.
It was time to put aside the petty bickering of the myriad
factions and unite against the true foe. Could the bats do
that? And where did they start?

A bat leaned his head towards her and spoke

confidentially, with the gossip's delighted tone of scandal. "You know what I've heard from a friend of mine who was actually part of the attack on that scorpiary? She said there was a dead Korozhet there."

The whole idea sent a frisson of horror through Bronstein's neurons. A horror that she knew was artificial, but nonetheless left her uncomfortable. But she had to start somewhere. "We call them Crotchets. Yes. I saw it, too."

"Crotchets? Surely that's not after being respectful?" asked the other bat doubtfully.

"Indade. Who said bats had to be respectful to Crotchets? We have respect for our elected leaders, our bats, not some Crotchet." It was mere semantics, she knew. But the software in the chip had no programming for alternate names. The K . . . Crotchet language was quite unlike English, she now knew. Each word only had one meaning.

The bat wrinkled her forehead. "I must admit that it is right that you are. I have no feeling of natural respectfulness for a Crotchet. Nasty things, actually."

" 'Tis not right that respect should be imposed. It must be earned," said Bronstein. It was an idea that would ring a chord with any bat.

The bat nodded. "Did this . . . Crotchet die in the course o' furthering our struggle against the oppressors?"

"The Crotchet was a traitor. Death was too good for him," snarled Bronstein.

Another bat fluttered up and squeezed into the chittering huddle. Bats will always squeeze up to someone. They'll usually complain about it. This one whispered in Bronstein's ear. "Easter uprising."

Bronstein fluttered off to report to the Provisional Revolutionary Army Council of the Battacus League. She caught a glimpse of Eamon, going the other way. Doubtless off to a meeting of the Battybund Liberation Army. He was quite high in the Battybund, she'd been told. Given the way bats thought, his password had probably also been "Easter Uprising."

She had a few new ideas to put forward. About a bank, for starters—and not a bloodbank, either.

Later that evening when the conspirators had had a great conspire, and Michaela Bronstein had fed a number of new ideas into her faction, she realized it wouldn't all be plain sailing.

"I take your point, Bronstein, that the Vats too labor under enslavement. And it would be right comradely to lend our aid in freeing them. But a bank? It's very bourgeoisie for a revolutionary movement. And would they not be after calling us bloodsuckers?"

"And does banking not require capital?" demanded another dubiously.

This was something that had worried Bronstein, too. But she hadn't realized just how serious it could be. Before she could speak, this thoughtful conspirator continued, "Would that not make us . . . Capitalists?" She shuddered at the thought.

On the more positive side, Bronstein was not in the least surprised to have the rumor she'd started herself repeated to her by three different bats. It had become slightly garbled, but basically the K . . . unthinkable, had been taken over by evil aliens called "Crotchets" that looked just like the good Korozhet. The evil aliens were in league with the entrenched exploiters, apparently. Now there was a surprise.

# Chapter 21

●

*INB head office, a rather run-down and
light-industrial part of GBS City.*

Chip was intensely grateful that Nym wasn't with him.
Chip's first experience of a sports car, albeit what the
reporter referred to disparagingly as a "kit-car," was a delicious shock. He'd only been on a Vat omnibus, or a
troop-transport truck, or in the sealed-and-not-meant-to-
carry-passengers back of Chez Henri-Pierre's van before.
Oh, and at the wheel of the vineyard tractor that had taken
them nearly all the way to the brood-heart.

Chip hoped that this vehicle differed from that one in
two important respects. Firstly, that it had brakes. Secondly, that it had a qualified driver.

He was sure Nym wouldn't have noticed the

comfortable seats. He was certain Nym would have sworn that the racing shift and small walnut steering wheel meant it was built for him to drive. They sped away from the court.

"Phew!" exclaimed the reporter. "I thought someone would hook onto what I was getting away with. But they're all too busy mobbing Van Klomp. He's the flavor of the moment with HBC, although I hear there is some general at headquarters ready to murder him. No one has managed to get their hands on Fitzhugh yet, so Van Klomp is the best, so far."

All of this was as confusing as fog to Chip. He knew, by now, that Fitzhugh was the intelligence major who had orchestrated the army's move into the scorpiary. Fitzhugh had apparently seen the explosions that Chip and his motley crew had created on satellite images. He'd put two and two together, and taken things into his own hands to take advantage of the situation. It was just as well he had, Chip supposed, or they'd have had to fight their way out again. "It's a beautiful car," he said.

"She is a beaut, isn't she?" said the owner proudly. "Even if she's just a kit-car crib, the engine gives me 470 kilowatts at 5200 rpm. She's a twelve-cylinder twin turbo."

"Er. Fascinating."

The driver grinned and looked at his passenger. Chip restrained himself from telling the guy to watch the road. After all, he'd once gotten the tractor to nearly thirty miles an hour, on a steep downhill. This guy could presumably drive. "Doesn't mean much to you, does it?"

"Er. No. But I know a rat who would commit mayhem to listen to you, and kill to drive this thing."

"A rat!" exclaimed Fuentes. "Drive? Those critters can't

handle mechanical stuff, can they? Anyway, they're far too small."

Chip found himself a bit stung on the rat's behalf. "Well, technically speaking, Nym did drive the tractor. And he adores mechanical things. He figures that he loves them, and would do anything for them, so they must love him and be prepared to do anything for him."

"You make this animal sound as if he were almost human," said the driver with amusement. "Drove a tractor! The mind boggles."

"Mister," said Chip, his hackles beginning to rise. Shareholder arrogance! "You've got to get one thing straight. As far as I'm concerned the rats and bats aren't animals. Not if you mean 'animals' like a side of pork. A side of pork doesn't think and reason and . . . and talk. I bet you've never spent ten minutes talking to your pork chop. Try it with a rat or a bat. They're . . . they're just like people."

The reporter grinned. "I did an interview with a lady you'd get on well with. The colony's Chief Scientist. Real little old battleaxe. She said we'd created two new intelligent species, and we'd have to make space in our society for them. It was on a late night nature slot. She kept quoting Shakespeare at me."

"So do the rats," said Chip.

"Might make a story," said the reporter, thoughtfully.

Chip began to realize that this man saw the whole world as simply a place for news stories.

The first stars were out when they turned into a parking lot at a small, rather dingy downtown building. By that time of night, this part of town—mostly offices and light industry—was almost deserted except for the building's parking lot, which was close to being full.

"Welcome to Independent News Broadcasting," said Fuentes grandiosely. He smiled wryly. "Bit of a dump, really. The area is going downhill fast. We've had to put a fence and guard on the car-park, because the cars were getting trashed at night."

They drove up to the boom. "That's odd. He's supposed to be on the gate. Do you mind opening the boom for me?

Chip got out, and walked over to the boom. As he got there, he tripped over someone in the dark.

The guard was still breathing, at least. Well, he groaned.

War-honed reflexes cut in. Chip looked for foes. And found two. Like all infantrymen, Chip had IR sensitive implanted lenses. The men lurking in the deeper darkness between the vehicles were less invisible than they'd hoped to be.

"Mister Fuentes," said Chip evenly, not taking his eyes off the lurkers. "Drive off and use that phone to call the cops. Do it!"

The reporter was unfortunately not a veteran. He said "What?" and then "Why?"

"Go! Call the cops," snapped Chip.

Fuentes reacted at last. He stalled the car. One of the two shadows stood up with a gun in his hand. "Don't think of starting it again," he said. "Just keep dead quiet and get out slowly." Behind him, the second man also stood up. He only had a pry bar in his hand.

"Help!" yelled the reporter.

Things happened very fast then. There was a shot and the shattering of glass. Chip was already moving. Briefly.

His slowshield froze for an instant, absorbing the bullet impact. A door and several windows were flung open. The two men were now running straight towards Chip.

Chip Connolly didn't think, he just reacted. If you lived through your first week in the trenches you had to react fast. The man with the pry bar had overtaken his companion. He swung, viciously. Only Chip wasn't there. All that was in the way was Chip's Solingen, returned by Sergeant Ngui. You weren't supposed to take side arms with you on pass—but Chip hadn't gone back to Camp after Ngui had returned it to him. This knife wasn't the trash they issued as a trench-knife to the infantry. It was stolen from Chip's old place of employment, the Chez Henri-Pierre. It was a monomolecular-edged chef's knife, a piece of late twenty-first-century engineering from old Earth. Nothing produced on Harmony and Reason came anywhere near.

It was a very, very, very sharp knife, in the hands of a combat veteran who had formerly been a sous-chef. Not a combination to argue with, as the now screaming attacker found out the hard way. The pry bar fell as he clutched an arm slashed to the bone from hand to shoulder.

Leave a Maggot-warrior alive, and you are dead. The scorps took no prisoners. Chip moved in for the kill, without any conscious thought.

Fortunately, his victim wasn't a Magh'. The aliens didn't know what "run away" meant. This man did. He fled like an antelope, screaming at the top of his lungs.

"You bastard!" yelled his companion, taking a pistol marksman's stance and firing again.

The slowshield had been one of the two main "gifts" from the Korozhet, along with the soft-cyber implant. It had changed war from mass, long-range combat, to hand-to-hand fighting, which Magh' mostly did better than people. The slowshield Chip wore was standard issue to all troops. It was implanted just above the breastbone, and powered in the "reception state" by the wearer's own bioelectric field. It hardened, using the kinetic energy of any object coming into the passive exclusion zone that was moving faster than 22.8 miles per hour.

That included bullets. A bullet is a low-mass, high-velocity item. It doesn't activate a slowshield for long. Not long enough for the horrified shooter to realize that he ought to give up trying to reload, and run, too.

Long enough for Chip to stop operating on automatic and think, which undoubtedly saved the gunman's life. It would have been awkward for Chip if the fellow hadn't been so terrified, as Chip had absolutely no idea how to take a prisoner. "Drop it," he said, holding the knife to the man's gizzard. "Drop the gun or I'll gut you like a herring."

And then people bundling out of the building seized the gunman. In the distance a siren wailed.

Chip turned and ran back to the little sports car. Fuentes was still there, his face bloody, the windscreen shattered.

The reporter blinked, and wiped at the blood on his forehead. He looked at it, unbelievingly. "My God! Where the hell was my cameraman?"

There were already some cameramen spilling out of the building. It was a news-broadcasting studio, after all.

Chip knew the discomfort of being the only person who knew nobody else, except for the injured Fuentes.

The place seemed to be under the control of one small woman. She had the type of unlined face and dark hair that made guessing her age very difficult. She gave orders, which people jumped to despite calling her by her first name. Chip, who had been brought into the building, was trying to fade into the background, when she came bustling up, stuck out a hand and said: "Lynne Stark, soldier. I gather we owe you thanks for the life of at least one of my staff. You can put the knife away now."

"He'd better not, Lynne," said another man. "They'll want it for DNA analysis."

Chip looked at the Solingen steel. There was a little blood on it. He very nearly wiped it, by sheer instinct. "Will they take my knife away? It's . . ." he prevaricated. "Part of my issue-kit. I'll be in trouble if I go back without it. Besides, it's kept me alive."

"And from what I can gather from Fuentes, through quite a lot. The police are here already. They've taken the gunman into custody, but not before we got some camera-shots for the program." She beamed at the thought, and then looked carefully at Chip. "You're a Vat, aren't you?"

Chip felt himself redden. Not many Shareholders were that open about the class-divide in HAR society. "Yep. What's wrong with that?"

"Wrong with it?" she wrinkled her forehead. "Why, nothing. It's what's right with it! You, soldier, are just what the doctor ordered—or my advertisers, rather. You've saved at least two lives tonight and caught one of the bastards in the bargain. According to Fuentes, you're an exclusive to dream of. Come into my office, so we can talk business." She glanced at the knife. "I've got some paper towels there, to clean that thing. The hell with the DNA."

She put an arm around him and led him through the hall. "The police will eventually get around to talking to you. You just leave it to me."

Chip found himself wondering, not for the first time, why someone always seemed to insist on changing the rules just when he had almost come to terms with the confusion that was the world as he knew it. "What's all this about?" he asked warily.

He'd been escorted to a rather spartan office by now, and she'd let go of him to get some paper towels from a roll beside a basin. "Here. And sit down. Coffee? Something stronger?"

Now Chip was so suspicious that he was positively bristling. He did not sit down. "Look, lady. What's all this about? Like you said, I'm a Vat and—"

"And so are about seventy percent of our viewership. Or were before HBC handed us the bulk of their market share too. We've been getting good feedback on interviews with ordinary soldiers." She gave a wry smile. "But the officers tend to feel that it's them that we should be talking to. Now, if I'm following what Fuentes said correctly, you're the story our Vat-viewers want. Fortunately, it turns out that Fitzhugh volunteered to train with the Vats. He's possibly the most popular Shareholder on HAR. It appears Van Klomp's surprisingly popular, too."

"He's my new C.O.," said Chip, "And one of the few Shareholders I've ever liked, anyway."

Stark grinned. "Well, nobody really dislikes Van Klomp. We all just wish he had a volume control. But I need a Vat."

"Why?" demanded Chip, his patience wearing thin and suspicion getting the better of him. "Is there some dirty work to do? Or do you just plan to screw someone? Because I'm not available."

She laughed. "Even if I didn't owe you, and want you, I like you. I'm in the media. It's dirty work by the nature of its existence. And honey, I'm gay. You're safe. But I am electing myself your agent, because otherwise you would get screwed. Financially anyway. You do realize that an exclusive to that story of yours is worth big bucks?"

He gaped at her. "What?"

She sat down. "You might as well sit down too. I can see I've got a lot of explaining to do."

Fifteen minutes later Chip was feeling downright stunned. He was swimming against a tide of concepts that hadn't ever crossed his mind: Firstly, that Vats, with twenty times the population of Shareholders, were an economic force at all. They were confined to the lower part of the job-market, true enough; underpaid and indebted—most likely for life—to the Company. But, as Lynne Stark pointed out, they still earned and spent. And when you added it up, they spent as much or more than the Shareholders. Ad spending on this market-sector had been low, but it was rising. INB was trying to build a greater Vat viewership without losing their share of the Shareholder market.

"Then you're out of luck, lady," said Chip. "Most Vats— like me—worked with their hands and eyes. If I looked at a TV screen and not at my work, I'd have cut my fingers off. We listened to the radio, if anything. Besides, the bosses don't like TV at work, and for Vats there's not a lot of free time. We work long hours. " He pulled a wry face. "And what free time we do have tends to get spent on important stuff. Watching a game, if you watch TV, or getting drunk as cheaply as possible. There isn't a big interest in newscasts."

"Wasn't," she corrected him. "But so many Vats are being absorbed into the army that suddenly news about the war is big news. I want your story. We'll sell it on to Interweb. And maybe one of the radio programs. That's a good point, that. Now. Let's get Editorial in here and hear this story."

Two hours, and a lot of coffee later . . .

"My God. Trust the army! And then they arrested you!" the producer said. He shook his head. "I don't know whether to laugh or cry."

Lynne Stark sat up in her chair and reached for the telephone. Then she paused. "The stuff about the Korozhet needs to be confirmed. I need to talk to someone, privately. All of you out of here. And get someone to sew those stripes onto the lance corporal, before the camera shots. I think it's pretty poor recognition, but maybe Van Klomp has his reasons. He's been one of the good guys so far. Start working up the story—except for the Korozhet angle. And let's see if we can arrange a few rat and bat interviews. And we'll need pictures of that wine farm from before the war, and satellite shots. See if you can scare up the guys who were on satellite tracking that night. Might make a nice human interest angle."

When she came into the studio, ten minutes later, she was looking very grim. "We're playing this close to our chests. Unless we've got Virginia Shaw's testimony too, the Korozhet stuff will blow the whole story out the water. So, for right now, we're going with the straight story without it. Tomorrow, Chip, the crew will go along with you to see Shaw. She hasn't been seen since she was taken from the media at Divisional headquarters. Part of the breakfast show will be dedicated to you saying you're worried."

"You mean the Korozhet can just go ahead . . . go on with this . . . charade?" asked the producer, incredulously.

Stark shook her head so hard that the straight dark hair flew out in a black halo. "Not a chance. But they're very popular. They've been lionized as the colony's saviors and our greatest friends. And they're very involved with the upper echelon of the New Fabians. Talbot Cartup has his own advisor, for example. And we have the word of one grunt against that?"

She sighed, slumping back into her chair and giving Chip a brooding look. "I believe you, myself. It fits a pattern of evidence that has been developing already. But most people wouldn't. And the people in power, and the Korozhet themselves, have every reason to want you dead. On top of that, you must remember the soft-cyber chips in the heads of all those thousands of bats and rats. The Korozhet have their own army, potentially. I assume if a rat or a bat can kill a Magh' warrior, then humans are dead easy, right?"

"Right," agreed Chip, "At least, if they don't know how to handle it. But . . ."

Stark waved him to silence. "So, when the Korozhet story breaks, it's got to be fast and the colony has to be in a position to act against them. Right now, it isn't. Right now, their ship, probably well armed, is sitting less than five thousand yards from the core of our colony's technical and scientific support. Let's assume that they're not going to leave too much intact if they do get attacked by a mob. And right now the army is not going to take part in any attack."

"So, are we just going to do nothing?" demanded the producer. From his very aggrieved tone of voice, Chip thought he might resign in a huff.

Stark patted him reassuringly. "We'll start preparing the ground, Charlie. Let people begin to reach their own conclusions. We'll be collecting evidence. When this goes down, believe me, we'll be ready."

By the icy glare when she said it, Chip concluded that she'd have made a really mean sergeant major. She turned to Chip. "The other bad news is that the man you captured has escaped. A captain from the Special Branch came and took him away, and he escaped in transit. Very convenient," she said dryly.

The Specials were every Vat's nightmare. Even though he had been shot at, Connolly was glad the fellow got away. He'd been nothing more than a thief, anyway.

"And you know what else?" continued Stark, grimly. "The cops found the thug that you cut. He'd gotten himself to a hospital. And then he'd had a visit from someone else. They cut his throat, while he lay in the ward. He had no ID, no papers of any sort. The bastards in Specials do a great job, don't they? Want any bet on the evidence 'getting lost' before the case ever goes anywhere?"

The very mention of the Special Branch, the plainclothes arm of the HAR's police, had been enough to give Chip the creeps. Although they were officially part of the government, in practice Special Branch was the instrument of the Shareholders Council—which meant Talbot Cartup, who held the Council's portfolio for Security.

The Special Branch were specialists, all right: masters at torture and the disappearances of uppity Vats. Vat political organizations were banned, and a good thing to stay away from unless you wanted to go "missing." But Chip hadn't realized that they also turned their attention to Shareholders.

It made him feel two things: Firstly, a surprising degree of solidarity with these odd Shareholders. Secondly, a strong desire to get the hell out of here. He was a Vat and a grunt, and both of those learned very quickly to avoid trouble. This stank of it. On the other hand, he had a feeling that he was neck-deep in smelly stuff already.

He began to add things together. "So, you mean that those two who attacked the car-guard and Mr. Fuentes were Specials?" He knew the answer. He just wanted to hear someone else say it.

"Not to mention also being stupid enough to attack you." Stark shrugged. "We may never prove it. But the gunman's picture was on the nine o' clock news. We'll see if we get any feedback from that. And now," she said with a singularly naughty smile, "to slightly more cheery matters. This is your agent speaking. I got you a nice deal, soldier. INB has bought your story for fifty thousand dollars. The first previews and teasers are going out in half an hour with the first feature around eleven P.M. And you can spare yourself from feeling sorry for that shark Lynne Stark being taken to the cleaners, because she just sold the print story and some in-depth interviews to Interweb for thirty-eight thousand dollars, and the radio rights for a further three thousand dollars. Even after the New Fabians take their cut, you can afford to take me to dinner. At the Chez Henri-Pierre. I've booked."

# Chapter 22

ɔ

*Evening in Shaw House, Virginia's rooms.*

Dr. Thom smiled urbanely at her. "Ah, Miss Virginia. And how are you?"

Virginia, who had been having a whispered conversation with Fluff on the subject of escape not two minutes before, managed to smile back. "Fine. Happy to be home. A bit tired still. I'm craving something. Maybe coffee?"

She could almost see the cogs ticking over in his mind. "Well, we can't give you too much, you know. It interferes with your later sleep-quality. But a little more would do no harm."

She knew perfectly well it wasn't coffee he was thinking about. She couldn't wait to get out of his nauseating company. "Was there anything else, Doctor?"

"There was a call today from someone who called himself 'Chip.' Do you know anyone by that name?"

There was a crash from the bathroom.

"*Wha*—?" Thom snatched the door open. Ginny grabbed the chair and lifted it, ready to bring down on his head if he caught Fluff. In a way, she was grateful for the interruption he'd provided. If Dr. Thom hadn't been distracted at that moment . . . he'd have seen her face.

Chip! Chip was trying to phone her! In her isolation she had begun to doubt, suffered the uncertainty of any young woman about her first love. She wanted to dance.

"Weird. There's no sign of anyone, but this glass has smashed onto the floor." He looked up at her. "It's all right, Miss Virginia. There is no one here."

Shakily, she lowered the chair. "I must have left it on the edge of the bath! I'm sorry. It's . . . it's the kidnapping, Doctor. I have nightmares about it. You brought it back, mentioning Chip."

She put on her hauteur, copied from memories of her mother. "He was the little Vat soldier who rescued me. What did he want?"

"To see you," said Dr. Thom. "Don't worry. We'll tell him you're not well enough."

She yawned. She'd perfected that. It was a nice touch, she felt. Perhaps acting was not her metier, but then, she'd decided that Thom was so vain that he would fool himself that she was falling for his patter and that all his plots worked perfectly. "I suppose I'd better see him. I suppose he'll want money. Vats always do. I'll need some, Doctor."

He looked thoughtful. "All right. I think it will be best if he sees you very briefly. We need to allow the public to see you, at least once."

Ginny's fingernails dug into her palms. But she managed to answer lackadaisically. "If I must." Now she wished even more desperately that he'd go. Where had Fluff hidden? Or had he reached the window in time? And she still wanted to jump and scream and dance with happiness and relief.

# Chapter 23

❧

*The Korozhet ship's waterbath chamber.*

"High-spine." The small Orange Third-instar clacked its spines respectfully.

Yetteth kept his eyes averted from the two Korozhet in the chamber and went on cleaning up the revolting regurgitated undigestible remains of the High-spine's meal. The flaccid furry bag that had been the Korozhet's dinner lay discarded beside her pool. He would have to carry that to the incinerators later. Hopefully he would not pass any adult Nerba slaves on the way. They tended to go insane on seeing the remains of their offspring. They couldn't attack one of the Korozhet, but he had no such protection. And while baby Nerba were soft-furred, big-eyed and harmless, the Nerba adults' hide was as tough as hull-metal, and their horns were immense.

"Approach, Kerit. What is it?"

"High-spine, you recall that we found out the name and unit of the human soldier who interfered with the plans of Agent Srattit and played a role in her death. Our monitoring and surveillance group have picked up the details from their newscasts. He is repeating his story. It includes the fact that Agent Srattit was responsible for the kidnap of this prestigious human, Virginia Shaw."

The High-spine rattled with irritation. "The human called General Fredricks said this human was dead. We had asked them that he be sent to us."

"It appears they were mistaken, High-spine. An administrative error, it seems."

"And the humans do not kill those who make mistakes. A foolish Underphyle, like most such. Pass the information onto General Cartup-Kreutzler . . . no. Bring me a communicator."

"At once, High-spine."

Yetteth continued to clean up the mess from the floorplates. Some human had irritated the Overphyle badly. He wished he could understand human. Some of the human slaves had been mind-wiped before being implanted, but some had not. If the Overphyle wanted to question them, they left their memories intact. One of those in his bunk-room still had her memories. Perhaps it would be worth the risk.

Jampad and rats, on the loose in an alien city.

Darleth had realized, very rapidly, that the new rat with the tail-stump was the kind who organized. Since Ariel had joined her band they had moved, rapidly, from being an idea in a Jampad mind, with two ratty followers, to being a band of some sixty rats. They had maps, bus routes, even some strange forms of arms. There were rules, "turf," and the human means of financial exchange. What they called "money." Darleth didn't understand it too well. You'd think anyone with a printing press could make it by the bucket. It seemed to have no value in energy terms either. It burned, but not well or very hotly. Nonetheless, Ariel was collecting the stuff, with which she traded, very successfully, with a human contact.

It was this human contact that also had given them their name. "The Ratafia." Darleth liked it. It was the name of a beautiful mountain district at home. The rats liked it, too. And while the other rats regarded the Ratafia as organized banditry, in Darleth's talks with Ariel she came to realize that Ariel did not.

The rat was preparing a loyal army, even if their loyalty was won with drink and loot.

That suited Darleth perfectly. She needed an army—to defend her, and maybe, somehow, to strike at the Korozhet. If only she could get around the soft-cyber bias. If only she could organize the slave-revolt they feared so.

In the meantime, the rats had proved invaluable in obtaining suitable food. There was little enough of it in the city, it seemed. She had only smelled out a few eating places, and one shop that stocked it. And those raids were getting tougher on all of them.

Ariel said it was called "Fresh Seafood."

It could be bought too, it seemed. But Darleth knew that the rats wouldn't enjoy that nearly as much.

And happy skirmishers were good skirmishers.

# Chapter 24

❧

*Military Police Central Pre-trial
Confinement Facility.*

A place of grayness and bars, which do not a prison make.
Not to Ariel, anyway.

On thinking about it, Ariel was as pleased with the new
situation as anything could have made her except having
Fitz out of jail. She'd learned a lot during her time spent
with Fitz among humans. She knew and understood far
more about how human society worked than any other
rat on HAR, although the other rats provided a great deal
of information about being streetwise.

Not that that was entirely relevant any more. She had
a number of humans on her payroll, now. Meilin seemed
to be involved in some form of Vat organization with a

number of cells. They'd been useful contacts and sale points, once Meilin had set it up. And she had a very good human clerk doing the administration. The army hadn't prosecuted Johnny Simms for helping Fitz, because that would have meant admitting that half the charges against Fitz were garbage. They'd just left Simms be. So now she had a corporal inside Military HQ, and an expert forger to boot, if she needed one. Simms was as loyal to Fitz as she was, even if—hopefully—he wasn't in love with Fitz. Simms had a wife and a newborn child, so Ariel thought she probably didn't have any competition there.

You never could tell, though. Humans were odd.

And Ol' Bluefur-bigteeth was a wonderful stalking horse. No rat would cheerfully take orders from another rat, but Ol' Bluefur seemed different.

She'd been in to see Fitz today. Really, human defenses were feeble to a rat of intellect, as well as a little litheness. Capra had been there to see him too, along with a frightening looking man called Ogata. Ariel kept her head down, out of sight in her usual hiding place, and listened. She felt she could bully Mike Capra, if need be. This other man might be a lot harder.

"Right, Charge I, assault on a commissioned officer. It's the intent to do grievous bodily harm part that weakens their case. They've got plenty of witnesses to say you actually did it."

"Actually," said Fitz, "it was those witnesses that stopped me making it worthwhile. Charlesworth has killed more troops than any other commander on the front."

"While that is probably true," commented Ogata dryly, "and it would be useful if we could prove it, I don't suggest you mention the temptation to homicide to the judge."

"I did the research," said Fitz curtly. "It's in my files at Military Headquarters. And I'm only prepared to tell the truth, Lieutenant Colonel."

Ariel made a note to get Johnny Simms to deliver the file to Capra. He was less alarming than this Ogata man.

"And I will be asking the questions," said Ogata, "so I will choose what to ask you to tell the truth about. Now. Mutiny. Once again, they've overreached. The business about the 'intent to have massacred, to cause loss of life to soldiers of the Army of Harmony and Reason' will make this difficult to stick. Capra has collected the statistics to back us up on this. Injury and loss of life on the sectors of line you commanded as a lieutenant and a captain were very light, they show."

Fitz nodded. "The lowest on the front, simply because the Magh' didn't attack successfully defended positions. It was something I tried desperately to get HQ to apply, without success. But when I was serving on the front line—until that final advance when divisional head-quarters refused to send us reinforcements—we did very well. Even then . . . we lost less men than most sectors lose in ordinary day-to-day combat. And the death and casualty tolls for the taking of Delta 355 must have been exceptionally light."

"There'll always be the idiot that says one combat casu-alty is too many—if they didn't want you to take that action," said Ogata. "But the lieutenant is working on those figures also."

"It's a question of locating records that aren't fully into the system yet," said Capra. "And of locating the witnesses. But I have a list of people from Van Klomp to contact as long as my arm." The lieutenant winced. "Did you *have* to fight with quite so many soldiers close at hand? Most officers don't. And that new Corporal of Van Klomp's— Connolly's his name, the one who rescued Virginia Shaw—will be invaluable for both the spying and mutiny charges. I've been acting for him on charges just about as ludicrous as these. He'll make a good, credible witness, and prove that there was no 'prior plan' for you to have betrayed to anyone."

"As for the 'flight' charges," chimed in Ogata, "we've got hold of the MP that Captain Van Klomp's men kidnapped and brought to you. You were injured in combat, but on hearing they wanted to arrest you, you asked that they be brought to you. That charge we should be able to at least fight on those grounds."

"I don't think I should—"

"It's a minor charge, Fitz," pointed out Capra. "You *were* planning to hand yourself over, after all. And Van Klomp stuck his neck out to give you some defense. The MP captain says you were a model prisoner, and that he regrets having had to arrest you. We might even have to get him to tone down the hero worship a bit. You're causing the high command more headaches, and you are more likely to get them to reform from jail, than you were prowling around their corridors. They're not immune to public opinion, which is going to be solidly behind you. And fixing some of the mess at HQ was your aim, wasn't it, Fitz?"

"I suppose so, if you put it like that," conceded Fitz.

"I do," said Capra, with mock sententiousness. "I'm a lawyer. It's my job to put the best appearance on daft deeds. Now, this business of 'attempting to disrupt a secret plan.' We can—with Lance Corporal Connolly on the stand—prove that there *was* no secret plan. This was a target of opportunity, a huge one, that through negligence General Cartup-Kreutzler was prepared to let pass until rank and file soldiers went ahead on their own and took advantage of. We've got supporting evidence from the guards at his gatehouse, and their major, and the arresting MPs. Getting Daisy onto the stand might be worthwhile, too. It'll destroy his reputation with the public in military terms, anyway."

"That's his private life," said Fitz, rigidity creeping into his tone. "I don't think it's right to get into that."

"If I might point out to you, Fitzhugh," said Ogata sarcastically, "this man has attempted to have you killed on several occasions now. I am something of a student of military history. I would estimate that he could be held responsible for the deaths of thousands of men, through sheer incompetence. It would seem to me that charges of 'aiding the enemy' are those that he will eventually face himself, for his cooperation with the Korozhet. His only interest is his own skin. I think it unnecessary that you have to try to preserve his reputation, for him. Decide where you stand, Major."

Fitz sighed. "I was brought up to believe that a person was entitled to a private life, Lieutenant Colonel. Any person."

"We'll try and keep away from specifics, Fitz," said Capra. "The press will be terribly sad. They love a good scandal. There's been at least one editorial every day on this. Yesterday, they had an article from the Vat sergeant who was with you when you got the GBS Cross. We might use him as witness for this spying and aiding the enemy charge."

"SmallMac? He deserved that medal as much as I did."

"And the lieutenant who served under you then, Cavanagh?" asked Ogata, showing he had also done his research.

"Last I heard he was also a major now. Good kid."

There was a rustle of papers. "I have him as assigned to the sixth division," said Capra. "He's still on strength. We're trying to contact Major Cavanagh."

"It's the spying charges that are the best structured," admitted Ogata. "The witness, Mervyn Paype, and those photographs are their crown jewels. And General Visse's secretary . . . We're looking into both."

"They're complete frauds!" snapped Fitz. "Anyway, Shaw and Cartup-Kreutzler both discussed the plans with their Korozhet advisors. That's a direct line to the Magh'."

"If we can establish that, we will," said Ogata, grimly.

Inside the leg of the prisoners' overalls, Ariel felt terribly discomforted by all this. She didn't share—to put it mildly—the confidence of the lawyers in the legal system of Harmony and Reason.

And why should she? From a rat's-eye point of view, that legal system was a complete joke.

## Chapter 25

☊

*Inside the Office of the Colony's Chief Scientist,
in the remaining frontal section of what was once a
mile-long sub-lightspeed spaceship. It is here that
the technical heart of the colony still beats, using
equipment brought from Earth. This is adjacent to
HARIT, the colony's leading technical university.*

"Dr. Wei, understand this clearly," said Sanjay Devi. "You did not see Dr. Evans killed. You have amnesia about the entire incident."

The small, plump oriental man shook his head, stubbornly. "She was murdered. I saw it happen. The Korozhet killed her, Dr. Sanjay, and nothing you can say will stop me telling everyone I can. You would have to kill me first."

"You damn fool!" snapped Liepsich. "That's exactly what they're planning to do. We're trying to keep you alive."

The biologist blinked, and shook his head. "This is a free country," he said, stubbornly. "It's not right that her murderers should get away with this."

"At the moment," said Liepsich slowly, "the Korozhet blame the murder on your hairy four-armed 'guest,' which they call a Jampad, and claim that it has projective telepathic capabilities. I don't necessarily believe that, but how can we be sure?"

Wei snorted angrily. "Why would a projective telepath be unable to give us a clue to what it wanted to eat? Look, Dr. Liepsich. Dr. Devi. My work is dietary requirements. I've watched literally hundreds of animals 'selecting' foods. We brought everything we thought an arboreal brachiating creature could fancy—from meat to fruits, bark, nuts. I know. Wrong planet, wrong biology. But without being too intrusive, we had established that it was a carbon-based kilotherm, with a hemoglobin based circulatory system. The proteins from the wound dressing we examined were familiar, at least to some extent. Compared to the Magh', or even the Korozhet, that thing was our first cousin. We had to be cautious not to offend a sentient alien by treating it like a lab animal. We thought that we might get some feedback. As a joke I put some prawns from lab three in there. I've seen animals react to food stimuli. When it saw those, I knew we'd found something which is similar to whatever it eats. Its dentition, Mari-Lou said, confirmed it was like our piscivores. And now you're telling me that a creature which is a good enough projective telepath to fake that scene in the passage couldn't even tell us what it needed to eat!"

"We don't doubt you," said Sanjay Devi. "Or at least, I don't. Nonetheless, the official story is going to be allowed to stand." She glared at the Chinese scientist. "I am still the colony's Chief Scientist, Wei. It's a shipboard rank they decided to perpetuate to keep me quiet and sweet. As such, in time of war, I have formal authority over all scientific personnel in this colony. If need be, I'll pack you off to a moribund research station in the arctic regions, with a year's fuel and dry rations. Today, if need be. We're trying to deal with this situation. Having you yelling your head off about Mari-Lou Evans being murdered by the Korozhet would complicate things immensely."

"You mean you're going to let them get away with this?" he demanded, incredulously.

Liepsich heaved himself up from his chair. "I've been patient and polite for long enough, Wei. If I hadn't seen your IQ scores, I'd think you were a moron. Now I wonder if that gas left you brain damaged. Haven't you heard a word Sanjay said? If you open your big yap we're all dead and so is research into—" He ground his teeth. "Look, Wei. Let's say you want to neutralize a powerful acid, and all you have is a bucket of water. Do you pour water into the acid or acid into the water?"

Wei was equally aggressive now. "Don't speak to me like that!"

"Answer his question, please, Dr. Wei," said Sanjay pacifically. "You know what Liepsich is like. Impossible. But clever."

Wei grimaced. Liepsich's rudeness was legendary. So was his ability as a scientist. "Acid into water, of course," he said sourly. "Every first-year undergraduate knows that."

Dr. Liepsich put his hands on his hips. "You, and I, and everyone here are water. You, at the moment, are wanting to jump into the acid. And we are trying to persuade you, by brute force if need be, that that will get you killed and the rest of us burned with acid. We've got to bring the acid out and slowly, gradually, add it to the water. And we need more water. That's what I've been working on for nearly two years now. That's why I didn't even raise more than a token squall when the Korozhet loaded up all my newly acquired Magh' equipment. Because there is a time to squall. And a time to sit tight."

"You gave them all your new material?" asked Wei, incredulous despite the circumstances. Liepsich had a reputation for clinging, limpetlike, to the smallest scraps of research material.

Liepsich nodded gloomily. "Everything we had in the lab."

Wei shook his head. "Everything?"

"Everything they could find," said Liepsich, with saintly earnestness. "They said it was booby-trapped. They would have to explode the traps. But they did promise to return what was left afterwards. Oddly enough, I haven't seen so much as a scrap."

Dr. Wei bit his lip. "It's still not the honorable and right thing to do, acting as if they had done nothing."

"As one of Mari-Lou's closest friends, and a fellow thespian for many years, I know that is what she would have wanted you to do, Dr. Wei," said Sanjay. "We are all just players, of a kind. And the play is the thing . . ."

Her brown eyes were suddenly brimming with tears.

# Chapter 26

☙

*A neo-classical fronted restaurant, complete with
white pillars and a vine-draped pergola, the air
redolent with fine cuisine and money.*

Chip found the experience of walking up to the front
entrance of Chez Henri-Pierre very strange. As part of
the kitchen staff he'd never approached the building from
that side. The white pillars and the trellised pergola of
vines on either side of the porte-cochere were not for
Vats like him. Vats came in through the security system at
the back, which Henri-Pierre had no interest in making
pretty.

Chip had told Lynne Stark that it was a poor idea. Even
the sudden addition of more money than Chip had ever
seen in his life before to his credit balance wasn't going
to change Henri-Pierre's attitude to Vats. And besides,

there were ten places that Chip would rather waste his money than on his old employer.

But the owner of INB had pushed aside his objections. "Firstly, this goes on expense account. You're not actually paying for it. 'Soldier-Hero revisits his civilian life.' It'll be a great human interest story. We've got Maxine Lefeur from Interweb coming along to take the stills."

"Have you got an axe?"

She looked wryly at him. "That's quite a comment about the two-hundred-dollar fillet steaks. Or are you planning to kill Henri-Pierre?"

"No. It's just for the pine tree across the road," said Chip. "You'll need a battering-ram to get Henri-Pierre to let a Vat in the front door."

She laughed. "Henri-Pierre just loves celebrities visiting his restaurant. Any celebrity. And as of seven o' clock this evening, when the news about your trial really hit the screens, you just became one. The call and e-mail trickle also started about then. While we were interviewing you, the news that we were doing so went onto the air. The trickle became a stream. Since then Henry has leaked some teasers through, with old background shots from the satellite pictures. The stream has turned into a flood. The station has never had this number of calls and e-mails before. People want the real story. And it turns out that there are huge numbers of people who are very unhappy about MIA's being listed as 'dead.' "

Chip shook his head. "Ms. Stark, that's not fair. You're playing with people's hopes. I'm afraid that MIA might just as well mean 'dead.' Staying alive in the Magh' scorpiaries is nearly impossible."

"Chip. We're saying that. But before you and your rat

and bat buddies proved differently, there was no such thing as 'nearly.' And there was Virginia Shaw and that alien, don't forget. Perhaps prisoners do get taken."

Chip frowned. "I never thought about that alien. He showed us how to make the Magh' gesture of submission. That might be a useful thing for troops to know. Mind you, he said he was there to be live food for the larvae, to teach them how to kill. I guess maybe there's not a lot of point in it."

She shuddered. "There weren't any humans held there?"

"If there were, they got buried. The larvae must have gone to somewhere close to the egg-racks, because that was where the Jampad was prisoner. The bats rigged explosive booby traps all over that area, and the Magh' triggered them."

Lynne Stark's eyes narrowed. "I'll pass this on to a contact of mine. It could be worth digging around there. You know what sort of story it would make if we found people, or," she said slowly, "their remains."

Chip made a face. "It'd be tricky. The whole tower is designed not to be dug through. It's a double wall structure filled with fine loose stuff between the walls."

"It sounds like it calls for mining engineers." She disappeared to make yet another call.

Unfortunately, she'd come back, still intent on dinner.

So here he was, in the pressed new uniform they'd gotten him for his court-martial, with the new stripes and beret badge. As an "other ranker," he didn't have a dress-uniform anyway. He walked uneasily toward the brass handles of the front door of Chez Henri-Pierre.

"Good evening." The maître d'hotel was new since Chip's time. He had, however, already perfected the art of looking down his nose at dubious guests. "You have a reservation?" he asked, in a cultivated French accent.

The "Sir" was conspicuously absent in the question. *"Mais oui, certainement,"* replied Lynne Stark casually.

The maître d' Hotel looked distinctly alarmed. "In the name of Stark, Gaston," she said, with just a hint of a malicious smile. "This is Lance Corporal Charles Connolly, our newest war hero. Maxine, if you can just get a picture of Gaston here escorting the corporal to our table?"

The *commis* who had just finished laying the table was too young to be conscripted yet. But she had already done some months in the kitchen as a dishwasher when Chip had been called up. She took one look at him, and cascaded the remainder of her cutlery onto the floor.

"Chef!"

In Henri-Pierre's hierarchy-ridden kitchen, a sous-chef was, to a mere *plongeur*, someone of vast elevation. Chip, having survived the egalitarian winnowing of the Magh'— who didn't care what rank they killed—found it mildly amusing to think that he'd once considered himself vaguely important because of it. He'd always known that his promotion to sous-chef had come about because the war had already claimed those Henri-Pierre would rather have had. He supposed that that was why this waif was now elevated from scrub to junior waiter.

"Hello, Claire," he said pleasantly, as she frantically tried to pick up the spoons under Gaston's angry glare.

She blushed and picked up spoons even more hastily, then scurried away to the kitchen. Chip had no doubt at all she would soon be telling this delicious titbit to her fellow kitchen slaves. Perhaps a few of them would remember him.

The turnover of Vat apprentices in this place had always been a little frightening. Even by the standards set by HAR Shareholders, Henri-Pierre had been a savage class bigot. On the one hand, training as a *Chef de partie* in his restaurant was one of the few places a Vat could hope to earn a decent wage, eventually. You usually got enough to eat, too. On the other hand, the work and the hours were worse than almost anywhere else, not to mention Henri-Pierre's brutal discipline.

Chip sighed. With any luck, the news wouldn't spread to Henri-Pierre. He didn't always see every diner, after all. If Henri-Pierre found out he was here as a guest . . . there'd be hell to pay. With the snobbery of any really excellent and successful chef, Henri-Pierre simply didn't give a damn about public opinion. A Vat war hero, so far as he'd be concerned, was just another stinking Vat. As such, not fit to be served at one of his tables.

Needless to say, the boss' attitudes infected the top help also. The waiter who brought the menu was steely in his ignoring of just who the person in military uniform was. Chip recognized him too, but couldn't remember his name. The restaurant's front-end staff wasn't generally friendly with the kitchen staff.

"May I recommend Chef Henri-Pierre's speciality of day? It is *du brochettes escalopes de Chevreuil au Agresto*, with *pommes Dauphinois*. And the chef has asked me to commend his *Baba au Kirch*."

The young photographer looked faintly alarmed. Chip was seized by an irresistible temptation. "It's a house speciality," he said. "Bull-nuts thrust onto splinters of old pine-plank with lumpy pignut gravy and poor-man's mashed potatoes made to stretch with boiled turnip." That would teach the waiter to pretend that he didn't know Chip from Adam.

The waiter gasped. "You are pleased to jest!" Chip remembered that the fellow had always been one of Henri-Pierre's little crawlers—which was probably why Henri-Pierre had gotten a deferment for him and not for Chip. "It is nothing of the sort. Medallions of venison fillet skewered on rosemary twigs, served with a verjuice-flavored creamy nut puree scented with pignoli or pine-nuts. And while *pommes Dauphinois* is indeed flavored with white turnip, it is certainly not 'poor-man's mashed potato.' It was a favorite of the dauphin."

"I read about him in Mark Twain's *Huckleberry Finn,*" said Lynne Stark. "And I am dying to hear the corporal's explanation of *Baba aux Kirsch* or this *Flognarde aux poire.*"

"Well," drawled Chip, his temper being pushed to a thin edge by a long and mentally exhausting day, the surreal familiarity of the restaurant, and the irritation caused by this slimy draft-dodging waiter, "*poire* refers to a pair." He gestured. "Of arthritic arms I think. And in mixed company I can't exactly explain what a *Flognarde* is. But the result is a *Baba aux Kirsch.*"

Lynne showed just a hint of dimple in her cheek. "I think I'll pass on that dessert, and on asking you what *Coq à la Bière* or *œufs a la neige* are. What do you recommend, as an ex-chef?"

"The seafood was always the best. But it was usually hellish expensive." Chip found himself enjoying the discussion of a subject the patrons usually treated like the subject of gonorrhea. He'd also noticed the peculiar absence of seafood on the menu.

"Corporal, after what you've been through, you choose what you'd like. For myself, I think I'll venture on the chef's speciality."

"And for you, mam'zelle?" asked the waiter of the lady from Interweb. She plainly hadn't had to deal with many French menus before. Both the language and the lack of prices obviously perturbed her. "Er. Something small?"

"What about the quail?" said Chip cheerfully. "Then you can really get to understand the meaning of the word 'small.'"

"I've never eaten quail," she said doubtfully.

"Neither have most of the people who've ordered it," explained Chip. "But they have a lot of fun picking hopefully at it. Here. It is called *Cailles en Crapadine*."

"I think I'll just have fish," she said hastily. She pointed to the top item.

"Ah. *Poisson à l'ancienne*. An inspired choice, mam'zelle," said the waiter, obviously relieved to find his way back away from Chip's comments. "And for you, sir?" he asked, hastily, perhaps working out how Chip could translate *Poisson à l'ancienne*.

"I haven't found steak, egg and chips on the menu," said Chip, looking at the waiter. "But I haven't eaten shellfish since I worked here. A *civet de langouste*."

The waiter stuck his finger inside his collar. "Er. We are having a problem with shellfish, sir. The war, you know."

"Spiny lobster come from the north coast," said Chip, mildly irritated. He'd even been there once as an apprentice, as some of the labor needed for oyster-sorting on the trip. The place, with its wild rocky coast studded with pine-clad promontories thrusting into the blue gulf, was something he'd never forgotten. "Nowhere near the front."

"Uh. Yes, sir. But transport and supplies have been difficult."

Whatever the problem was, it wasn't just that. Not by the waiter's expression. The man looked like the fairy on top of the Christmas tree, after Santa had told him where to put that tree. Excessively uncomfortable.

Chip felt vaguely guilty. There were always problems in a kitchen, and in one run by an autocrat like Henri-Pierre, the problem was likely to be blamed on some poor Vat and retribution was likely to be nasty. He knew that Henri-Pierre would have had a blue fit about that *Eminceur* he'd relieved the restaurant of. No matter that the place had owed him the better part of a month's salary, which, as was he was already in boot camp on the last day of the month, Henri-Pierre had taken pleasure in not paying him. That knife had saved his life countless times, and he owed Henri-Pierre that much.

"Er, Chef Connolly." Ah. The man had suddenly remembered who he was. "Considering that you have honored us by coming back here, I am sure that I could arrange that steak you wanted."

"That would do me nicely, waiter. Just fillet steak. No pretty peas arranged in a spiral, no flowers made of carrot matchsticks. No towers of toast and paté, or even crisp-fried green mango. Just good quality steak. Big enough to fill my plate," concluded Chip evilly, knowing that several hungry diners all around him would be going green as they ate their sauce-dribbled filigree slices of something expensive.

"Uh, yes, Chef. And to start?"

Chip was now beginning to thoroughly enjoy himself. "Gin rather than soup, I think. As a mere soldier, you don't have pretend that it's a martini, or put an olive in it and quintuple the price." Being crass was quite delightful, really—even if was a bit petty and he didn't really like gin.

The waiter began to retreat as quickly as possible without turning and running. "I will send the *sommelier*," he said.

"You do that," said Chip cheerfully. He'd already decided. They'd have some of the Clos Verde Directors Reserve Cabernet '03. Between the Magh' destruction and the rats and bats blowing the remains sky-high, that was a vineyard that wouldn't be offering any wine for sale again for a long time. And he'd like to commemorate a memorable meal with his friends. He wished that he could bring them here. Now that would be a party! Especially fat Fal chugging wine out of the bottle. Even if they weren't human he'd rather have them for company than most of the people here.

"There's an odd atmosphere here tonight," said Lynne Stark, commenting on something that Chip had wondered about. He'd been unsure of whether it was just that he was hearing things from the wrong side of the kitchen wall, but the normal polite muted buzz of conversation had changed. It was more like the sound of disturbed bees.

"I wouldn't know," said Maxine, the young woman from Interweb. "This place is rather beyond my purse strings."

"I've been here for a few business dinners."

"Excuse me." The *sommelier* had arrived. He had an ice bucket, tulip-shaped glasses, and a bottle of Piper-Krug, an estate now vanished under the Magh' tide but that had always been the Chez Henri-Pierre most expensive. "Mr. Somerville over there has asked me to bring this to you, Corporal, as a small gesture of his appreciation of what you've done for the colony. He asked if you'd drink a toast to the memory of his late son, Captain John Somerville. He died in the Harrisburg assault."

That brought back the harsh reality of it all. Vats died in droves. But many of the Shareholder families had lost sons and daughters, too, although the ultra-wealthy were usually able to protect their children to some extent. The system was as corrupt as could be. Working here, Chip had sort of forgotten that the bulk of the Shareholders were only "stinking rich" if compared to Vats. Back on Earth, they'd just have been considered "middle class."

Chip nodded. "Please tell him I'd be most honored to do so. To him, and the all the soldiers who've died in this war. And give him my thanks for the bottle."

Champagne, as far as Chip had had experience with it, was a menace to work with in such things as champagne sorbet. The purpose of the bubbles was to come out too soon and make the intended light confection into something the chef would clout you around the ear about. The idea of paying extra to drink bubbles in your wine had always seemed rather pointless to him.

Now, however, well into the second glassful on an empty stomach, he realized that the purpose of the bubbles was not just to make you sneeze but to allow the stuff to creep up lightly onto you. The day, and even the evening, were becoming more amusing as the champagne went down. His table companions were laughing at Chip's description of Colonel Brown's face when Chip had told him how delighted he was to be back, when an enormous platter was brought to their table, carried by two chefs.

The two chefs beamed and bowed. They'd both been apprentices when he'd left, and had been part of the farewell that had given him a terrible hangover for his first day as a boot.

"Good evening, Chef. Welcome back. The kitchen staff have decided that the gin you requested would be better cushioned with this small token of our esteem. We've been listening to the story on the radio."

The platter contained a selection of hot and cold hors d'oeuvres. Chip was expert enough to realize that to put it together in this length of time, most of the kitchen staff must have abandoned cooking for anyone else. He was touched . . .

And rightly terrified. "Maurice. Janice. Before I even say 'thank you,' I want to know where Henri-Pierre is. He'll be furious if he finds out about this."

The petite Janice smiled wickedly. "He's sitting guard over five kilos of tiger prawns in the chill-room. With a shotgun. He thinks that we don't know that he's in there. He's turning blue from the cold, but his prawns are still intact."

"What! Why?"

Maurice shrugged. "Somebody has been stealing shellfish from him—just prawns, lobster, and crayfish—on an industrial scale. And some wine. They don't seem so fussy about the wine. But only the best shellfish stocks vanish. Henri-Pierre is having fits. Blaming everyone. Screaming and swearing."

"Nothing to the fit he'll have when he discovers you've been neglecting customers," said Chip. "I'm . . . well, flabbergasted, guys. But . . ."

"He can only fire us. Or get us called-up, like you," said the hyper-careful Janice, who never took a chance on anything. "And you have proved to us that conscription is survivable. And the kitchen staff . . . We are all so proud of you, Chef."

"I need you standing with them, Chip," said the photographer.

Even at this point, everything could all still have been all right if several of the other diners had not started to cheer. It was certainly not a universal reaction. Others in the crowded restaurant looked very irritated.

Then, with a cymbal clash of the kitchen swing-doors, in strode Chef Henri-Pierre. Most unusually, for the average chef, he had a shotgun slung hunter-style over his shoulder and he had Gaston and Dominic in tow.

He stormed over to the table. His way was blocked by the two young chefs and a huge platter of hors d'oeuvres. The two tried to flee in opposite directions—but, without dropping the platter, could not.

"*Connolly! You Vat-scum!*" shrieked the Frenchman. "What are you doing 'ere in my restaurant? 'Ow dare you come in 'ere?" He tore the platter of hors d'oeuvres from the slackened hold of the two chefs and raised it to eye-level. "And this! You—you—"

He flung the entire platter at Chip.

Even if Chip hadn't been expecting it, most of it would still have missed. Henri-Pierre's poor aim was infamous. As it was, Chip pushed the table over in a cascade of silver and crystal. A few things, including the platter itself and the tray of oysters, hit it. The rest . . .

Chip saw a salmon and avocado mousse describe a

beautiful arc and transform the haughty Mrs. Coutts with a wonderfully face-improving pink and green face-pack. The oyster tray had hit the edge of the upturned table. Oysters and their ice exploded across the room like shrapnel. An oyster splatted down into someone's beautifully bi-colored tarragon-scented tomato and wild mushroom soup.

Chip saw that the two chefs, neither of whom were large, were wrestling with Henri-Pierre and his shotgun. Henri-Pierre was trying to bring the shotgun to bear on Chip.

A waiter, in his haste to get away, ran back toward the kitchen. He forgot the cardinal table-service rule. Never run with skewers . . .

The air was full of screaming. The shotgun boomed, fortunately only hitting the ceiling next to the three-hundred-piece chandelier. The vast concoction of crystal and lights began to peel down slowly from the molded ceiling.

Chip knew he that would be okay with his slowshield, but this madman with a pump-action shotgun was going to kill someone. And Chef Henri-Pierre, 6'8" in his cotton socks and built like a Sumo wrestler, had thrown off the two chefs. He was bringing the shotgun up.

Chip looked for a weapon.

And found a dessert trolley. As Henri-Pierre thrust the shotgun at him he thrust back with two-thirds of an entire Opéra cake. Layers of cake, coffee butter cream and thick chocolate granache went up into the barrel. Lynne Stark had also helped herself to the dessert trolley. She flung a conical glassful of Calvados Saboyon into the chef's face. While Henri-Pierre was wiping his eyes, Chip grabbed the man who had terrorized him as a Vat-apprentice.

"Let go the shotgun, Chef!" he yelled in his ear. "It's got cake up the barrel and will explode if you shoot!"

It was a lost cause. Henri-Pierre was beyond hearing, and he had the sort of temper that was well-nigh impossible to control at the best of times. The spluttering chef continued to struggle to bring the shotgun up to Chip's head, while holding him with a hamlike hand. Chip was struggling to keep the barrel down, but Henri-Pierre was stronger, bigger and heavier than Chip.

Someone hit the shotgun hand, hard, with a full bottle of champagne, just as Chip used the full weight of his combat boots and all the leg-strength he could muster to kick Henri-Pierre in the crotch.

With a yowl the huge chef doubled up, dropping both the shotgun and Chip. Chip kicked the weapon under a table.

And then the chandelier fell, light bulbs exploding and crystal flying, with the sound of police sirens in the background. Chip saw that Gaston and a phalanx of waiters were trying to reach their table, and that Henri-Pierre had staggered to his feet again and had snatched up a ham-slicer.

"Time to run!" said Chip, hauling at Lynne Stark who was flinging yet another gateau at the chef. With the other hand he grabbed the Interweb photographer who—

Was busy taking pictures! Photographs while Henri-Pierre was in a rage and had a knife. Insane. In this particular man's hand, a pump-action shotgun was a lot less dangerous. Chip detested Henri-Pierre, but he'd be the first to admit he'd learned his knife-work from him and that Henri-Pierre was a maestro with a blade.

He kicked the dessert trolley into Henri-Pierre's path. Chip didn't even wait to see the results. He just dragged his companions into flight. The right direction was "away."

Their table, alas, was far from the doors or even a window. Too far.

"Into the kitchen!" yelled Chip.

They fled through the swing doors, bundling through the kitchen staff who were crowding in to see what was happening, past banks of gas-plates and ovens . . .

Into the scullery. Chip lost his footing and fell, pulling down the others he was dragging. The floor was wet, and he'd stood on, crushed and slithered a number of $42-each fresh tiger prawn.

He scrambled up. "Help me haul this table against the latch. And come on! We've still got to get out of the securit . . ."

He caught sight of someone—or something, rather—at the far door.

Blue-furred and familiar.

Another one of those aliens. He'd met one of them in the fight for the scorpiary. A "Jampad," if he remembered the name right. The creature had said that it was the only one of its kind on this world. So what was this one doing here?

He heard someone else say: "Pooh-Bah, I importune you! We can only carry a bottle for each of us. Methinks this case will be the death of you and I. The boss is too busy with his loot to assist."

"But I cannot take eight bottles," complained another ratty voice.

"Whoreson! Just take one, all of yourselves will have to share it," snapped the first.

"What's up?" demanded Lynne Stark, seeing him freeze.

"Rats. Come on. Leave that. Let's run." If rats were here and looting, they'd have left open a way out. That was how rats worked.

They didn't see the rats, or the Blue-fur, but the security gate was open. Chip neatly closed it behind him.

"And now where?" he asked. "Besides a bit further away?"

"My car. The office to get that camera downloaded. And then the police station to lay charges," said Lynne Stark decisively. "I apologize, Connolly. You were right about his reaction. I didn't think anybody could be that bigoted-crazy."

"I don't see the point in a visit to the police. They're more likely to arrest *me*," said Chip bitterly.

"While I understand where you're coming from, let's get some charges in before your ex-boss does."

"Uh, Lynne. Why do you have that in your hand?" asked the photographer.

The INB boss looked at the tall conical glass, miraculously unbroken and mostly full. "I forgot. I'd grabbed it to throw, when we did a runner. Why did you decide to run just then? Not that it wasn't a good thing. The fracas was getting wild. I think your partisans in the crowd were outnumbered but they were doing a sterling job."

"Partisans?" asked Chip.

"Oh, there were some of the diners for you, and others who thought that the chef would be doing the world a favor by shooting an upstart Vat. There was quite a foodfight going on. Now what is this, anyway? I wouldn't normally think about it for pudding but it seems to be what we've got." She pointed at the conical glass.

"*Au diplomate á l'anglaise*. Basically what you would call a trifle, if you weren't being charged forty-five dollars for it."

"Trifle," Lynne Stark said wryly. "I should have guessed. Why couldn't it have been double chocolate mousse? Oh well, come on. Let's go to the office. We can do the station at Wesdene precinct from there. The Mayfair one near here will be full of irate diners."

She smiled mischievously. "Well, Maxine. Those photographs should be worth a mint to Interweb. Remember we got you this story. And we agreed to share pics."

"For the human-interest story, yes. Not for the celebrity foodfight and famous-chef-goes-mad story," said the young Interweb reporter. "And you promised us dinner."

Lynne's smile widened into a grin. "All I can offer you is this unconsidered trifle I picked up, and a teaspoon from the office. But later, when we've done what must be done, we'll send for some take-out chow. I have already ruined one perfectly good frock tonight. With our Chip around, the next dinner would probably be worse."

# Chapter 27

*A mock Tudor mansion in the wealthy*
*northern suburbs.*

General Cartup-Kreutzler was still dealing with a chilly
atmosphere at home. At the office, he wore the trousers.
Maria, however, made sure that he did not have any such
delusions at home. It was *her* family's money, and he'd
better not forget it. And she'd had to come and get him
out of jail when Major Fitzhugh had ruined his little tête-
à-tête with his secretary, Daisy.

That wasn't something that she was planning to let him
forget, ever. However, what she was really bitter about
was that he'd broken one of her Queen Anne chairs in his
attempt to escape from their country getaway.

Since that scandalous affair, she'd let him know that
he'd better be here for his meals of cold shoulder and hot

tongue every night, if he didn't want to be paying her alimony. And he had very little money of his own, anyway.

The telephone rang. He ignored it.

She handed him the phone. "I hope you don't think I'm your secretary," she said arctically.

He labored under no such delusions. His secretaries always had good figures, and a high degree of compliance. Also, they tended to be thirty years younger than Maria. Who had dared to call him at home? It wasn't Maria's brother Talbot. Maria hadn't belittled him for half an hour, and no one else would call. "General Cartup-Kreutzler here," he snapped.

The breathy voice on the other end of the line was immediately recognizable. The general stiffened. The army was in a poor position to offend the Korozhet. They supplied the soft-cybers and the slowshields. Without those, the soldiers would be totally unable to slow the relentless Magh' advance.

Two minutes later, he had INB News on the TV and was just in time to catch a full repeat of the story about the snotty little Vat trooper that had given Fitzhugh his break. As he watched, the fury in him grew. Without this Vat, he would never have ended up in this invidious, defensive position.

General Cartup-Kreutzler wanted Major Fitzhugh crucified and boiled in hot oil. But, in the meantime, this Vat would do.

He picked up the phone again and set some of his staff onto chasing up Colonel Rastapolous. "Try the Paradiso. He's usually there."

Ten minutes later he had his legal advisor on the phone.

"Get to my office. And sober up. I need some charges drawn up."

That meant going in to work, but that was better than staying at home, anyway.

The colonel was fairly far gone into inebriation, despite his boss' instructions. The general looked at him in disgust. The fool was turning into a lush. "Go and drink some coffee," he ordered. "Not Irish coffee, either."

While he waited for Rastapolous to pull himself together, Cartup-Kreutzler telephoned Talbot. He was mildly pleased to think that, judging by the out-of-breath state of his brother-in-law, he'd probably managed to ruin Talbot's evening. "I had a call from the senior Korozhet advisor. You know they asked us to locate the private who was involved in the death of Virginia Shaw's tutor?"

His brother-in-law successfully irritated him with his reply. "Yes. Thom called me earlier. The soldier tried to call Shaw today. We have arranged to allow a meeting, and then he'll be quietly removed from the scene at the Shaw house and delivered to the Korozhet. No one will even know where he disappeared to."

"Leave your little pastime and watch the news on INB. The media will be going there with him, so he can't just disappear. He's been telling his story, and there are any number of things he can be charged with. But that legal fool of mine is drunk again. To be realistic, he'll have to serve the charges in the morning."

"Hmmm. Let me think about it," said Talbot. "It might be easier just to get my men to kill him tonight. Mind you, the Korozhet have asked that he be handed over to them. They suspect him of murdering that tutor of Shaw's. Look, I'll take some advice from a friend of mine; she's astute about these things. If need be we can always get Thom to delay things. In the meanwhile go and push Rastapolous' head under a cold tap. I suspect the best answer might be to arrest him and to take it from there."

"He's being made out to be a hero by the media, Talbot," cautioned the general. "Arresting him could create more complications that we don't need."

There was a silence. Then: "The army has a DNA match for this soldier on file?"

"He's a Vat, Talbot. Of course. If we had enough time we could clone him."

"I think we've got him then, Henry. Thom examined Virginia Shaw. Somebody had been screwing the dummy. He's got some interesting DNA material out of that examination. Odds are that matches that soldier. Public support for rapists is slim."

Now, *that* was an interesting idea. "But surely she'd have complained. Had him arrested. It must have been consensual, Talbot."

"Almost certainly," said his brother-in-law. "She was very affectionate towards him when they first got back. But then, she *won't* be testifying, Henry. Any attempt to subpoena her, we'll meet with medical excuses, and I can deal adequately with providing fake depositions."

"It could work." Cartup-Kreutzler paused. Sometimes his brother-in-law worried him. He could be so inventive and yet so blind. "Do you realize where this could have led, Talbot? We could have handed thirty-four percent of the Company to a damned Vat."

There was a pause from Talbot now. Then he said,

dismissively: "Don't be ridiculous, Henry. He's nothing but some Vat-scum."

"I'm not being ridiculous. Remember what you told me about her. She's brain damaged, Talbot. Your Thom said she had a mental age of about seven after that horse-riding accident. Damage to her speech centers, if I remember rightly. She couldn't speak properly. Is there any sign of that now? No. That's because Shaw had her implanted with one of these animal-control devices we use on military animals. She's a little robot, and doesn't really know how a Shareholder should behave. And she is heir to both her parents' shares in the HAR colony. You know perfectly well that Shaw married Gina Roussel to get control over her fourteen percent of the stock." For once General Cartup-Kreutzler felt that he had his brother-in-law on the back foot.

"A good thing we parted them!" exclaimed Talbot. "To think that I said someone was welcome to screw the dummy."

"If I were you, I'd look carefully at who else might think of doing so," said the general slowly. He'd married a midden for the muck, so the idea might just occur to someone else. "That Thom, for instance. How far do you trust him, Talbot?"

"Not at all," said Talbot. "But I've got the black on him, Henry. He was the kingpin in the methyldeoxymeth-amphetamine ring. That's why I inveigled him into taking up the post as Shaw's personal physician."

"You think that's enough to hold him back from thirty-four percent of the shares, Talbot?"

Talbot snorted like an irritable pig. "Next thing you'll say I should marry her myself."

"It might not be a bad idea, actually. The alliance of two powerful Shareholder houses and all that sort of thing. Think about it."

# Chapter 28

*Scenes various, but mostly Shaw House.*

## VAT PROVOKES RIOT IN TOP RESTAURANT!

*Henri-Pierre L'escargot, the renowned Chef of the*
*famous Chez Henri-Pierre . . .*

"But that's not what happened!" Chip looked at the
paper in disgust. "They've got it all wrong. I never even
said anything to him, never mind trying to force my way
in. It's all lies. Mucking Shareholders!"

Lynne Stark smiled. "I put that one on top for that
reason. The others all have varying but greater degrees
of accuracy—the ones that got feed from Interweb, got
pictures, witness statements, and the facts more-or-less

straight. And believe me, a picture is worth a lot of words. More than a thousand, in the case of the HAR *Times*," she said dryly. "They got their story from a still incandescent Henri-Pierre, and never bothered to check it. I've got some of my staff collecting statements right now."

Stark's expression resembled that of a very well-fed and self-satisfied shark. "Heh. At the very least, they'll have to print a retraction. And HAR law states that it has to be the same print-size, column length and in the same position. Great front page they'll have! I suppose that old fart Laverty thought he was on safe ground with a bit of Vat-bashing."

She studied the headline for a moment. "What an idiot. Even using the term 'Vat' in print was a mistake. The official term is 'cloned citizen.' Under the circumstances, 'Vat' is clear evidence of news bias."

Now she was practically licking her chops. "Vats don't take people to court, but I do."

"I've seen enough of courts," said Chip warily. "I don't mind if I never see another."

"I don't think you will. He'll settle. Now, are you ready for your visit, lover boy?"

Chip blushed. He was wearing one of her dressing gowns. But both of them knew it was merely because his uniform was in the dryer. Lynne Stark hadn't slept alone that night. But she hadn't slept with him, either.

He knew exactly what she was referring to. "It's not like that," he said hastily.

She raised an eyebrow at him. "Really. But yet you told Maxine, when she invited you home, that you were already spoken for, as it were. And that you didn't break your promises. You did it very nicely, I thought, with just the right amount of regret."

"Do you always listen to other people's conversations?" asked Chip sourly.

She nodded. "If at all possible, yes. I sell news, remember."

Chip pointed to the newspapers. "Why don't you just make it up like most of these do?"

"I lack the imagination for fiction," she said, without even a hint of a smile.

General Cartup-Kreutzler took a long pull at the Bloody Mary he habitually had for breakfast. He'd better call in and see if that idiot Rastapolous had actually managed anything coherent in the way of charges against the Vat. He reached for the paper, which, naturally, was the HAR Times. The headlines delighted him.

He reached for the telephone. They could add a few extra charges to the list.

Having led his men in their ten-mile run, Van Klomp had showered, breakfasted and sat down at his desk for his least favorite part of the day, paperwork, when his telephone rang. "Seen the morning papers, Bobby?" asked the voice on the other end.

The cheerful tone in the voice of Lieutenant Mike Capra on the other end did not make Van Klomp feel at ease. He knew the attorney too well. "Not yet," he said grimly. "What's up? Fitz?"

"No," said Capra. "Just your latest protégé got himself into a fight with his ex-boss last night. The papers are carrying three different versions of the event. And before that, the boy got himself into a shooting match with some supposed 'car-thieves.' That was on the nine o'clock news."

"I'd better get the papers, then. Or is there a decent report on Interweb?"

"One of the best," said Capra with a laugh. "The picture of your new corporal about to shove a sticky chocolate cake into the chef's pump-action shotgun is priceless."

"Hell's teeth! Is he in jail again?"

"Not yet, anyway," said Capra cheerfully. "But he's going to see Shaw this morning."

"She should be pleased to see him. I didn't think she'd let him get away."

"There are some odd stories coming out of that lot, Bobby. Old friends of the Shaws have been turned away from the gates when they tried to see her. And Shaw's attorney wound up dead under mysterious circumstances three days ago. This is deep water your new corporal is swimming into, with leaky water wings."

"Not a hell of a lot you and I can do about it, my friend. The kid is determined to go and see her. If I tried to stop him, he'd be like Fitz. Do it anyway."

"This boy of yours may get himself chewed up in the process, though."

"They might find that he's a tough mouthful to swallow. Chocolate cake against a shotgun, you say?" Van Klomp laughed. "I'll put my money on my new lance corporal. That kid has brass balls, Mike—and don't forget he survived longer in the trenches than just about any front line soldier I can think of. And they want to get physical with *him?* Those drunken thugs in Special Branch? Fucking cretins."

"I hope you're right."

"You watch."

*          *          *

Once more in his BDUs, with the new stripes on his shoulders and hat-badge on his beret, Chip walked up to the security officers at the gate with two cameras trailing him.

The security officers looked like they came from a rent-a-thug company, and not one in the high-end part of the business. "What do you want, soldier?" asked the one with the nose suitable for following down broken and winding trails.

"My name is Connolly. I was one of the soldiers who rescued Ms. Shaw. She said she wanted us to visit her, when we got free." It was true enough. She had said that—to the others, along with a promise of better brandy and all the sauerkraut the bats could eat. "I called yesterday and someone said she would be informed."

The broken-nosed guard nodded. "We've been told that she will be expecting you at ten-thirty. You. Not them," he said, scowling at the news crew.

Ten-thirty. A neat two hour wait. And then he'd see her. The cameras had obviously been ready for confrontation at the gate, never mind their exclusion. You could read disappointment in their posture.

In an apartment near the middle of the City, Tana Gainor carefully put on her makeup, and then applied her mauve lipstick. The lipstick was her one deliberate conceit. She knew she had as little need of it as for the rest of her makeup, to attract the attention of men. But it was non-military. The very fact that she could get away with such scorn for the military pleased her. It gave her a little fillip of satisfaction. For some people, going into the army had been a question of duty to their fellow humans. For others, a question of conscription. For Tana Gainor it had been an opportunity, both for profit and power.

She had always loved both. She'd realized very quickly that the alien invaders made the army vastly important, and presented an unprecedented opportunity for acquiring her two favorite things. She continued to run her civilian empire. The trade in various recreational chemicals remained commercially successful, although she'd distanced herself from the actual selling these days. She'd never had the actual need to do so: other than for the profit, but there was the pleasure of entrapment. Knowing they'd be back. Knowing that you'd gulled yet another one. And knowing that it would bring both power and profit.

Tana examined herself in the mirror, then applied a dab of expensive perfume behind her ears and to her wrists. She was not overly fond of the smell herself, but it did appear to appeal to men.

Satisfied that appearance, scent and hair were all perfect, Tana left the vanity table, slipped her mobile into her purse and let herself out of the door. She left behind the snoring man sprawled on the bed, without as much as a backward glance. Lewis was wealthy and useful, as he had criminal associates in the "used car" trade, which had hitherto fallen outside of her usual net. He was both amazingly stupid and a clumsy and physically inadequate lover. Someday she would tell him so. It would be amusing.

She'd just seated herself in her expensive car—having a vehicle that spelled money was one of the reasons she'd spent her evening in the way she had—when the mobile rang.

It was Thom. "I've told you," she snapped. "Don't call me on this number. Call me at work. And call on the main line, not your mobile." She hung up.

Thom was an idiot. He was bound to be caught, sooner or later. She wanted no provable links to him. If calls were routed through the military switchboard, the best record the billing company would have of that call would be that her manufacturer had called military headquarters. A brief once-off call could be explained as a wrong number. It was a source of irritation that Talbot Cartup had provided Dr. Thom with her mobile number, but then he was almost certainly not aware of how careful Tana had been lately. For all his power Talbot Cartup remained an idiot. Another one.

A few minutes later, seated at her desk, checking stock values in the morning paper, Dr. Thom called and told her of Chip Connolly's impending arrest.

Tana flipped over the paper looked at the headlines. She smiled to herself, and began doing some homework on this Vat, before the telephone call she knew she'd be getting from Talbot Cartup, soon enough. She'd already mentally assigned two of her associates. Depardue and Tesco. She derived some satisfaction in making two of her lovers work together. Admittedly, Tesco was more loyal to money than to her, but still.

Two hours after being turned away, Chip walked back to the gate. He was frisked, given a metal detector search and taken to a waiting vehicle. The coffee and donut he'd had with the film crew sat uneasily in his stomach. Part of his mind said that he was being a fool. She was just behaving exactly as Shareholders did. Use and cast away.

Another part of his mind said that he could live with that, but he needed to be sure she was all right. She had trusted him, and he wasn't going to let her down if something was wrong.

They pulled up at a side door. The servants' entrance, naturally. Chip was led by two guards through a pantry section, into carpeted halls, and upwards to a small loungelike room. "Small," at least, by the standards of this mansion.

Virginia stood waiting. She wasn't dressed in a torn dusty skirt and a ripped blouse anymore. She looked instead as if she'd just stepped off a fashion-catwalk.

When he'd gotten over that momentary shock, he realized that something was seriously wrong. The tension in her stance, the way her shoulders were pulled forward. Was she that scared of meeting him again?

The escort hadn't bothered to leave. "Good morning, Mr. Connolly," she said, as if she was greeting one of her maids. She looked at the escort. "You may go. I do think we can trust this soldier with my virtue."

Chip tried not to swallow his tongue. Like that, was it?

"Dr. Thom said we were to stay, miss."

She shrugged. Chip had been very close to dying with Virginia Shaw. You got to know someone's movements and gestures very well, very quickly, under those conditions. That was Virginia nearly exploding, not being casual. "It doesn't really matter. It's not as if this soldier and I have ever wished to be private with each other. And how is that dear little bat Phylla, Connolly. Doing well? Did she recover from her injuries?"

Chip wished that he was a better actor. Or that he had an hour to sit down somewhere and think about all this before he had to reply. Phylla was dead. She'd died rescuing Virginia and her traitorous Korozhet tutor. And she'd been definitely and incontrovertibly a *rat*.

Something about all this smelt a lot worse than the bats, after they'd been eating sauerkraut. The best he could manage cold was: "Uh. Fine."

"And that darling little rat, what was her name?"

"You mean, um, Behan." Behan had been a bat, and was definitely in the great belfry in the sky. He'd had an argument with a mist-wall of alcohol and a lit Molotov cocktail. "She's fine, too."

"That's the one," said Virginia, altering Behan's species and sex in one fell swoop. "Anyway, Mr. Connolly. Do sit down. I must thank you again for rescuing me. I'm afraid I'm still so tired. Quite dopy, too."

They were talking some kind of code. That much he was quite sure of now. He hadn't even begun to figure out just what it meant.

"Dr. Thom said I must keep this brief," Virginia continued. "I'm under his orders now, you know. He's helping me such a lot, just like my dear Prof did."

Chip needed to sit down after that. "Prof" was what she'd called the Korozhet that had kidnapped her. Things were starting to make sense to him, finally.

So: she was a captive, and, if he understood the code right, being doped by this Dr. Thom. He'd be the medical type who had whisked her away when they returned from the front.

"Er." He sought desperately for a topic. Seeing her again, even dressed like this and obviously in dire trouble, still made him want to fold her in his arms. That, and the circumstances, seemed to have robbed his tongue of anything to say. "How's Fluff?"

"He's run off somewhere," said Virginia, waving her hand vaguely at the window. "I believe he's around, but I haven't seen him for ages. You know he's not very loyal to me."

Well, that was true enough. Fluff wasn't "very loyal" to Virginia. The correct way of putting it was "fanatically loyal." And if he read the handwave correctly, the galago was probably listening at the window. They were several stories up, but that would make no difference to the small primate.

And if that wasn't Virginia's foot touching his leg, then there was a dog under the table. He squeezed it between his own legs and was rewarded with a brief, fulminating look before she gazed off into the distance again.

His heart was beating like a drum, pounding in his ears. He was barely was aware of the door opening behind him. "Good morning, Miss Virginia," said someone behind him.

If Chip hadn't been looking intently at her, he might not have noticed the sudden tightening of the muscles in her neck. "Dr. Thom. What brings you here?" she asked, with a smile. "As you see, I have a visitor. The soldier who rescued me."

Chip got to his feet, looking carefully at the two men who had come in. One—a little alarmed-looking man with a camera—he dismissed from his attention, concentrating on the doctor. He assumed he was the doctor, anyway, from the stethoscope hanging around his neck.

Thom was one of those men whose hair looked like it ought to be on the top end of one of the sculptures in Webb Park, and not attached to a live person. It shouldn't be blond, either. His moustache was a work of art, too.

He was easily one and a half times Chip's size, and he walked with a curiously catlike gait. He probably thought it made him look dangerous and sexy.

Thom went over to stand proprietarily behind Virginia. "Of course, Miss Virginia. I told you about him. But it is really time Miss Shaw was allowed to go back to rest." He made no attempt to greet Chip. "If you don't mind, Miss Virginia, Walters is here to get a few pictures for the press release."

The nervous little man snapped frantically. Unlike the photographs Chip had been in lately, nobody made any attempt to pose them together.

"You have a medical problem, Ginny?" asked Chip coolly, measuring things up. "I could deal with it, if you like."

"You and those rats and bats could deal with anything. But not now, Mr. Connolly. You must come and see me again soon."

Chip was pretty sure he got that piece of code, even without catching a glimpse of Fluff shaking his head at the window. "As you like, ma'am."

She reached into her purse. A gun? No, he was getting too paranoid. It was a large bundle of notes, neatly tied up with a piece of ribbon. "The reward I promised you," Virginia said, tossing it carelessly to him.

For a moment, old reflexes surged to the fore. Chip felt himself nearly exploding with in fury. *As if he wanted her stinking Shareholder money—!*

Then he caught the flicker of desperate appeal in her eyes, and sanity returned. Thinking quickly, Chip lowered his head to hide the snarl and turned the tense set of his shoulders into something approximating a servile bow.

"Thank you kindly, ma'am. So generous of you."

"No, it is only fair," said the doctor jovially. "The workman is worthy of his hire, eh, Miss Shaw?"

"Quite," said Virginia. "Now. If you'll excuse me, Mr. Connolly, I must go back to rest. It is almost time for my medication. Dr. Thom, I'm sure you'll see me to my room."

"Of course," he said, offering his arm to help her to her feet. "Stett, Purvis, see the lance corporal to the gate."

Walking down through the passages to the servants' entrance, Chip had time to think. This was going to be as tough to crack as the scorpiary. How could he get the rats and bats together? Did he trust Van Klomp? Instinct said "no." He was an officer and a Shareholder, after all. But it would make life a lot simpler if he could.

"So, Vat-boy," said the one guard, giving his elbow a crushing squeeze. "I'm sure you're going to make a generous split of that nice pile of loot you just got."

That snapped Chip out of his brown study. "Do you want to lose that hand?" he asked, in an even tone that would have made more intelligent men back off.

To be a goon, however, a man doesn't need to be very intelligent. The guard laughed. "You think that uniform makes you tough, Vat? Don't kid yourself."

Chip had noticed the firearm in the shoulder holster. "Have you ever seen what happens to someone who isn't wearing a slowshield when they've got a limb inside someone's slowshield and it hardens?" he asked, conversationally. "Couple of stupes like you tried it on a few conscripts for fun. Cut off the one's hand and the other's face."

Chip twisted his arm free and pulled the guard in close.

"Want to try? Right now the shield will cut you in half if I move fast enough. Want to chance it, asshole?"

Fury and frustration with Ginny's predicament made Chip irrational with anger at this shakedown. He didn't want Ginny's money, but he wasn't going to give it to her jailers either.

"It was just a friendly joke!" squawked the guard. "Hey, Purvis, tell him to let go of me!"

Chip shoved the man away. "Unfriendly extortion, more likely. Take my advice and find a new line of work, punk. In the trenches, you wouldn't last a day."

They'd arrived at the door. Chip got into the waiting vehicle without looking too closely at the occupants.

"Lance Corporal Charles Connolly, number 21011232334000. You are under arrest," said one of the five MPs.

# Chapter 29

ୠ

Divers and sundry charges and specifications.

*CHARGE I: Violation of the Military Code, Article 73 (desertion)*

SPECIFICATION 1: In that Private Charles Harvey Ignatius Portabello Connolly, Army of Harmony and Reason, I Corps, Company C, did at or near sector Delta 355, in the presence of the enemy, quit his place of duty for the purpose of plundering and pillaging.

SPECIFICATION 2: In that Private Charles Harvey Ignatius Portabello Connolly, Army of Harmony and Reason, I Corps, Company C, did at or near Sector Delta 355, in the presence of the enemy, fail to afford all practicable relief and assistance to Lieutenant Martin Rosetski, Sergeant Jessica Dermot and Private Jeremiah Mackenzie, in that he failed to excavate and rescue the said Lieutenant Martin Rosetski, Sergeant Jessica Dermot and Private

Jeremiah Mackenzie after they were trapped underground as the result of enemy action.

SPECIFICATION 3: In that Private Charles Harvey Ignatius Portabello Connolly, Army of Harmony and Reason, I Corps, Company C, did at or near Sector Delta 355, in the presence of the enemy, endanger the safety of I Corps, Company C headquarters, by abandoning his post in the trench lines.

*SPECIFICATION 4: In that Private Charles Harvey Ignatius Portabello Connolly, Army of Harmony and Reason, I Corps, Company C, did, at or near Sector Delta 355, in the presence of the enemy, cast away his issued trench knife and bang-stick, military property.*

CHARGE II: Violation of the Military Code, Article 109 (destruction of property)

SPECIFICATION: In that Private Charles Harvey Ignatius Portabello Connolly, Army of Harmony and Reason, I Corps, Company C, did at or near sector Delta 355, willfully and wrongfully destroy a farm tractor, of a value of greater than 500 credits, the property of Shareholder Emil Couteau, by exploding it.

CHARGE III: Violation of the Military Code, Article 111 (reckless endangerment)

SPECIFICATION: In that Private Charles Harvey Ignatius Portabello Connolly, Army of Harmony and Reason, I Corps, Company C, did at or near sector Delta 355, physically control a motor vehicle, to wit, a farm tractor, in a reckless and wanton manner, thereby endangering the life of an allied alien life form of the Korozhet species.

CHARGE IV: Violation of the Military Code, Article 120 (rape)

SPECIFICATION: In that Private Charles Harvey Ignatius Portabello Connolly, Army of Harmony and Reason, I Corps, Company C, did at or near sector Delta 355, sexually assault Virginia Shaw.

CHARGE V: Violation of the Military Code, Article 121 (theft)

SPECIFICATION 1: In that Charles Harvey Ignatius Portabello Connolly, Army of Harmony and Reason, I Corps, Company C, did at or near George Bernard Shaw City, steal a knife, the property of Shareholder Henri-Pierre Escargot.

SPECIFICATION 2: In that Private Charles Harvey Ignatius Portabello Connolly, Army of Harmony and Reason, I Corps, Company C, did at or near sector Delta 355, steal a farm tractor, various tools, diesel fuel and brandy, of a total value of over 500 credits, the property of Shareholder Emil Couteau.

CHARGE VI: Violation of the Military Code, Article 130 (breaking and entering)

SPECIFICATION: In that Private Charles Harvey Ignatius Portabello Connolly, Army of Harmony and Reason, I Corps, Company C, did at or near sector Delta 355, unlawfully enter the storehouse, distillery, and machine shop of Shareholder Emil Couteau, with the intent to commit a criminal offense, to wit, larceny.

CHARGE VII: Violation of the Military Code, Article 134 (incitement to mutiny)

SPECIFICATION 1: In that Private Charles Harvey Ignatius Portabello Connolly, Army of Harmony and Reason, I Corps, Company C, did at or near sector Delta 355, abuse military animals by plying them with intoxicating liquors until they agreed to support him in his criminal actions, which was contrary to good order and discipline in the Army of Harmony and Reason.

CHARGE VIII: Violation of the Military Code, Article 324 (driving without a license)

SPECIFICATION: In that Private Charles Harvey Ignatius Portabello Connolly, Army of Harmony and Reason, I Corps, Company C, was, at or near sector Delta 355, derelict in the performance of his duties by driving on a public road without a driver's license, in violation of Harmony and Reason Planetary Traffic Safety Code, Section 3246-12.

They took his bootlaces, web-belt, wallet . . . and all the money that Ginny had given him. They put it into a locker and gave him the key. He was sure that the key would be terribly useful.

# Chapter 30

♋

*Shaw House, Virginia's bedroom.*

There was a more than slightly suspicious glint in Dr. Thom's eye as he walked her back upstairs to her room. But Ginny was finding it nearly impossible not to jump in the air and dance down the passage. Two notes down in the wad of hundred dollar notes was her letter to Chip, explaining the situation. Further down the bound stack of money, on a further three pieces of stolen notepaper, were the security details of Shaw House and the fences. Ginny had also taken the liberty of keeping a thousand dollars—she might need bribes—and this was just about the first actual money she'd ever had in her hands. All her life someone else had always paid for everything. It gave her an odd feeling of independence to really have some money of her own that she could hold.

That, and seeing Chip again, made pretending to be doped very hard. She'd endured it before. Now, impatience set in. It was difficult even to concentrate on reading, while she waited. The worst was the lack of news. She sat watching the numbers change on the bedside clock radio. How did the seconds and minutes take so long to pass? The not knowing would kill her. She wished desperately for a phone call—a wild dream, that—or even a TV or a newspaper. Surely Chip could give the information to the press, and get her freed? She'd stopped her ears as best as possible with cotton wool, but she knew that she would just have to resist the Korozhet commands. She was already steeling herself for it.

Then it occurred to her: what she was watching the seconds on was a digital clock . . . radio.

She'd never used it as a radio before. Actually, with a wallscreen TV, she'd never bothered to listen to the radio at all. Before her kidnapping and the murder of her parents, the news had never interested her much. And TV drama had had little attraction for her, compared to good book. As for an alarm—the maids woke you with coffee at the appointed time. The device had been little more than something that had taken her fancy before her implant, and had remained in her room.

After stepping out of her room to make sure that there was no one around, she took the cotton wool from her ears and started to fiddle with the radio. She was rewarded by a blast of music. Hastily, she yanked the plug from the socket, clicked the wall-screen TV on, and wondered how she could have been so stupid as to forget that her room was bugged.

She sat for some twenty minutes staring at the mind-less froth on the TV, before going to look carefully at the clock radio. There was a small dial marked "volume." With it turned close to the minimum, she plugged it in and listened. It was music. She fiddled the dials and heard voices. It was a talk show. Never had such a thing sounded so sweet.

Ginny took up her station in bed with a clock radio between her ear and the bed, and a pillow on the other ear, and soap opera on the TV. Ginny hoped that the lis-teners liked the soapy.

News was something few people missed, until they were denied access to it. Ginny listened eagerly. And then in horror.

" . . . ilitary police today arrested accused rapist Lance Corporal Charles Connolly only minutes after the soldier had attempted to extort money from his alleged victim, Virginia Shaw, the daughter of our late Chairman. Ms. Shaw has been in seclusion since her terrible ordeal but, according to witnesses, felt that she had to confront her attacker and overcome her fear. Dr. Fred Thom, Ms. Shaw's personal physician, described her as 'very dis-traught, but very courageous.' Ms. Shaw granted a private exclusive telephonic interview to HARBS news."

Virginia listened to a voice, not wildly unlike her own, explain how she wanted to move on from being a victim to being a survivor.

"Ms. Shaw has requested, on medical grounds which have been supported by her personal physician, Dr. Thom, that she be spared having to meet her attacker again. According to her Solicitor, John Lo Lee, if leave is granted she will only have to lodge suitable depositions with the court, as there is strong evidence against the accused already . . ."

Before this, Virginia had needed to get out of her home/prison for her own sake and for the good of the cause she hoped to support. Now, she needed to get out of here for Chip. And not all the guards in the universe were going to stop her.

He'd been arrested minutes after he'd seen her. She'd bet he had not even had a chance to read the first love letter she'd ever written. She'd struggled with that letter. It was something she didn't want anyone else to read, ever, but that she'd realized that Chip might have to use to convince people.

She could only hope that no one had gone through that bundle of notes after she'd given it to him.

Now she had to come up with an escape plan.

Twenty minutes later she was once again in her bathroom, water running, discussing it all with Fluff. "I need one as a weapon, Fluff. And I will need a strategy once I get out, to stop them just arresting me. The trouble is, other than the rats and the bats, and Chip, I don't know who I can trust. And I've got to get out of here to save him. They execute people in the military for rape, Fluff."

The little galago looked distinctly worried. "*Señorita* . . . it is true that I can get the key to the garden equipment shed, but the chainsaw she is too heavy for me to carry to you. No, we will have to try the guile. Escape. Then together we will go out to rescue *Señor* Chip. He is a gallant soldier, even if he has usurped me from your affections," he said loftily.

"Oh, Fluff! It's not like that!" protested Virginia,

hugging him. "Besides, you have so many girlfriends there among the rats . . ."

He stepped back onto the bath edge, pacing it as if it were a catwalk. "It is only natural, I am so macho, that all the women they should adore and desire me," said Don Juan el Magnifico de Gigantico de Immaculata Conception y Major de Todos Saavedra Quixote de la Mancha. Fluff loved to strut his stuff, "But, *mi* Virginia, that is merely a physical thing. The love of my heart, she is always for you!" His wide eyes were dewy with earnestness, his delicate mobile ears downcast.

"I bet you say that to all of them," she teased. "Anyway, I love you too, Fluff, even if I can't compete with all your groupies. But we can't just leave Chip to his fate. I must try."

"Indeed, *señorita*, but I believe that we can get out without fighting. We shall hide in a vehicle leaving here." He wrinkled his entire face with distaste. "It is in the truck of the garbage we must go, *si*. With all the fish heads, tin cans, plastic bags and the old cabbage leaves." He seemed to take particular affront at the cabbage leaves.

The idea startled her. "It could work . . . But I'm still going to get myself a chainsaw. I saw the gardeners using a really lovely little one on the hedges. I'll smuggle it up here somehow."

Maybe the average young girl didn't speak of chainsaws in the same way, but Virginia felt that that was their loss. As fashion accessories they had the edge on nearly anything else, when it came to getting you a lot of attention. And respect.

The galago blinked his big eyes. "*Si*. I suppose if the truck it is too difficult to get into, it is something for the defense of your virtue when you do not have me with you. I will go to watch for the truck."

*Shaw House, the Webb Salon, decanter of
rare Earth sherry on the table.*

Talbot shook his head. "I don't care what you say, Dr. Thom. I smell a rat here." He tapped the recording. "She'd been sleeping with him. In this she treats him rather like a bad smell she's possibly met somewhere before. She sounds like a YMCA secretary talking to a stumblebum, not a young girl talking to her first lover—even if he is a Vat."

"Well, there were two of our best men in earshot, Talbot," said the Doctor. "It could just have been that she was embarrassed."

"Mighty cool for embarrassment. I have to wonder about those drugs of yours and that computer chip in her head. It wouldn't be affected, would it?"

The doctor looked surprised. "I hadn't thought of that, to be honest. The addiction would be the same. But her clarity of thought should be reasonable, depending on just how much it does for her."

The head of the colony's security stood up. "We want to be suspicious and alert here. She might be planning a break. I think I want security tightened, Thom. And have you caught that monkey of hers, yet?"

"We assume that it's run off onto the golf course or into the parkland. I've had poison bait put out for it. Some acacia-gum that it is apparently very partial to. But no luck so far."

"Well, get some people from the zoo. No. On second thoughts, don't. They might not be that keen on killing it. And it can also talk, eh?"

Thom nodded. "Yes, it has one of these Korozhet chips in its head, too."

"I'll get you a couple of big-game hunting guides, then," said Talbot. "They've got experience at keeping their mouths shut about canned hunts. Pay them enough and they will kill this creature and keep quiet about it. I'm getting rid of loose ends. And right now they seem to be fraying as I go."

He slammed a meaty fist into his palm. "The military courts were very cooperative, thanks to Tana, so I thought this was a reasonable way to deal with this idiot lance corporal. Then my brother-in-law could, with a suitable military lack of fuss and secrecy, have Connolly handed to the Korozhet. They want him, and what they want they will get, from me anyway. But now I hear that blasted Fitzhugh is up for retrial, about which those uppity Vats and the gutter-press are making a royal fuss, and my dear brother-in-law says he can't pull Connolly out of the Military Justice system, and it's even going to be tricky to get him quietly out of military prison, even if he gets a death penalty. And your precious Tana, having assured me that Fitzhugh was stitched . . . now, she's not only failed at that, but says all she can do is affect the defense and the prosecuting counsel. Her pet judge is suspended pending investigation. So: I need to take steps here."

"Well, it's all in perfect control at this end," said Dr. Thom. "And I'll bet you Tana screwed the money out of you, before the Fitzhugh thing fell apart."

"She did," said Talbot irritably. "Now, you assured me

this drug of yours would make the Shaw girl complaisant. I think it's time we put that to the test. We've got a Council of Shareholders meeting coming up, and a number of issues on the war-funding are going to the vote. I need those votes of hers. I also want to strengthen the hand of Special Branch further. And we need to get rid of this ridiculous 'court-order to wire-tap' regulation. Have you got her to sign those proxy voting forms yet?"

The doctor looked startled. "You said not to."

Cartup smiled inwardly. Always make it the help's fault. It kept them unsettled and unsure of themselves. "When I want your back-answers, I'll ask for them, Thom. Get them signed now. If she makes no resistance to that, I might just take you up on something else you said she'd do for me, when she was full of your pills."

"W . . . what?"

"Lie on her back and let me screw her," he said, enjoying the look on the doctor's face.

Thom said nothing. He just took the proxy voting forms from the drawer and walked off to find his charge.

A few minutes later he was back. "She signed the forms. She didn't even seem concerned," he said.

"Good. Because we're going to test her compliance a lot further. My idiot brother-in-law pointed out the obvious to me. We'll arrange a photo-shoot for tomorrow afternoon. She'll be accepting my ring. I think we'll have to wait a few weeks for the marriage. And maybe a month before the funeral."

The doctor dropped the proxy forms. "What!?"

"Pick those up, Thom. It seems by far the easiest way of avoiding having to get proxies in the future." He stood up. "I'll pass this recording onto my staff. They can probably cobble something incriminating out of it. In the meanwhile I suggest you restrict her movement to that room. One of my men reports that he saw her trying doors on the mezzanine level."

# Chapter 31

ᏋᏋ

*The environment surrounding a small galago. Mostly
darkness, thugs and the bouquet of fresh seafood.*

"Fluff, they've stopped me going off this floor. Thank
goodness I got the chainsaw as far as the bushes under
my window first. Now if you can get that garden line up
to the bathroom, I'm sure I can haul it up."

"*Si, señorita*. The line is ready. She is attached to the
strong line of fishing, which is already attached to the
window catch. You will just have to haul it up. You are
sure you cannot climb down the same way?"

Virginia shook her head. "I know it is a rope to you,
and as easy as falling off a log, but I'm too big. I can't
climb down that string, Fluff. I don't think I could climb
down four stories anyway. But we need to do something.
I can't just leave Chip to be punished dreadfully for

something he didn't do—and that creep made me sign those proxy forms. Those forms will allow Talbot Cartup to use my votes at the HAR Company Shareholders meeting!"

She still seethed every time she thought about it. "I don't know what he's planning to do with them, but it won't be anything good. I'm going to haul that chainsaw up and see if I can cut my way out of here, tonight."

Fluff shook his head agitatedly. "There are a lot of guards, *mi* Virginia. They have guns."

"That's *their* problem," she snarled, the fury at being helpless for so long boiling up. "They have a disadvantage. They need to keep me alive. If I die, the shares get spread out through a whole slew of second and third cousins. I don't have that to worry about. I'll kill anyone who gets in my way."

Fluff was still dubious. "Even if, as you say, they do not wish to kill you, they can shoot you in the arm or the leg. How could we flee then?" He took a deep breath. "No. Better it is by far that I go to our comrades, and bring them to your aid."

"But Fluff. You can't go on your own!"

Fluff took a deep breath. "*Señorita*. Indeed, I will go. Of course I will go! But . . . It is not at all certain I am where I have to go? It makes no matter. Let it not be said that Don Juan el Magnifico de Gigantico de Immaculata Conception y Major de Todos Saavedra Quixote de la Mancha would not go to the help of his comrades-in-arms! Only . . . is it possible that I could have my second-best waistcoat from your cupboard? I would feel better if I was smartly dressed."

The blue and silver waistcoat did make the seven-inch-tall caballero stand taller. It also made him stand out.

"Er, Fluff, it does make you so much easier to see," said Virginia, after a suitable amount of admiration. Fluff adored admiration.

The galago held out his little black-palmed hands. "Virginia, if it is that I am going to die, I would not be looking scruffy." He spun on his toes, doing a perfect swirl of his soft-fluffed tail. "Anyway, I do not plan to travel out in the garbage-truck after all. They are searching. They stick the long sharp rods into the garbage."

"Then how? I mean, there are detectors on the fence, if you tried to jump over. And if you hit it . . ." She shuddered. "That's five thousand volts, Fluff."

"I shall go out in the parcel of the security guard. They are stealing from the kitchen, with the help of the cook. She is leaving the box with the food in it, just outside the scullery door. The guard with the nose that is broken and the one with the ears of the bigness," he said, supremely unselfconscious about his own huge ears. "One of them collects it and takes it out of the gate with them. They search everything, but no one searches them."

Virginia discovered that the little piece of petty thievery took place just after dusk each day, when the day-shift changed over with the night-staff. The security guards didn't go out every night, but those two Fluff had watched for a week now. One or the other went out every night. It would give Fluff the hours of darkness to escape and find the rats or bats. Well, at least to start doing so. Galagos were nocturnal, and in the dark Fluff at least had some advantages to make up for his size.

It had seemed like such a good idea until he had actually closed the box lid on himself. Now, Fluff wondered if he had not traded in his biggest single advantage, which was not his delicate, sensitive ears, or his big eyes, or his soft fur, fine waistcoat and good looks, but his ability to leap thirty-five feet. Inside a cardboard box, containing several pounds of virtually unobtainable wartime luxuries, his leaping was a little curtailed. If someone put their hand into the box, there was nowhere to jump to. Besides . . . the box smelled of seafood. He was not fond of the smell. It was also cramped and cold.

The box was picked up. The other disadvantage Fluff now saw—or didn't see, rather—was that he had no idea where he was. He wanted to escape before he found himself in confined quarters, like a car or a house. But not too soon, either. He wanted to be well away from Shaw House.

He comforted himself with the knowledge that the thief could hardly admit that he'd carried Fluff through security with his stolen goods. The staff assumed that he was somewhere out on the golf course, hiding. Let them go on thinking that.

On the other hand, the thief could just kill him. Fluff had no delusions that, trapped inside something where he could not get away, that could not happen.

"You skiving out again, Kurt?" demanded a voice.

They must be at the gate.

"Yeah, I've got nice bit of crumpet in town. I got to keep her in service or next time I go there I'm likely to find some other bastard's ass in my way."

"And that box is candy just to keep her sweet?"

"Hold your lip, Stett, if you know what's good for you. It's just some kitchen scraps."

"Ha. Let's see what kind of scraps the kitchen is throwing out these days. Come on, let's have a look."

Fluff tensed. Why tonight of all nights? "I'll cut you in for a twenty, Stett. You make trouble and you're a dead man walking."

The threat obviously didn't worry Stett, by his bored tone. "Make that fifty, Kurt. It's a good racket you and Ridell have going. It's worth fifty."

"I don' get that much."

"Fifty, Kurt."

Fluff barely restrained himself from yelling: "Give it to him!"

There was a rustle. "Bloodsucker," muttered Kurt.

"Have a great evening with your crumpet, Kurt. Give her one for me."

The security man said nothing, but the box began to sway again as he moved off.

Some long minutes later, someone else spoke. "You 'ave got it?"

"Yep. But it's gonna cost extra. That blood-sucking bastard Stett is onto me. He wanted fifty just to get it outa the gates."

"We 'ave agreed on a price. 'Ow you get it out is your problem."

"There are other restaurants."

"Not that will buy things like this."

"Well, gimme the money then," Kurt said irritably. "But it'll serve you right if I just stop supplying. You see where you can get this stuff then."

"I do not think that you will stop. Not while you can make money at it," said the accented voice, wryly. " 'ere. Put it in the van. You 'ave everything I asked for?"

"Down to the two kilos of Stavanger bay prawns. You name it, cookie orders it, you get it."

"Here is the list for tomorrow. I must get capers. The growers 'ave lost their farms with the war. But Shaw will 'ave some in the pantries."

"I can't guarantee stuff like that. It'll cost extra."

"For that and the *sauce aux capres* for the coalfish, I will pay extra. Not for other things. Now, I must get moving. The curfew is soon."

As Fluff, stiff and cramped, struggled to open the box and flee into the night, the door slammed. By the time he had gotten out of the box, the vehicle was moving. Fluff didn't mind too much, as it was pitch dark and experience told him he could find places to hide in any car, as small as he was. And surely the farther he got from the Shaw Mansion, the better.

He soon discovered that he was in error on at least one count. The vehicle he was being transported in was designed to be a perfect galago prison, with no place to hide. It was obviously some kind of delivery van, and he and the cardboard box were in the back. There wasn't even a door handle.

Fluff had an awkward choice. Wait for the doors to open and bolt, or climb back into the fishy smelling box. He had no idea how long the trip would last, or where the buyer was going.

"We need a couple of things, Miss Virginia," said Dr. Thom.

He had a syringe in his hand. Ginny desperately wished for two things herself. One, that she was closer to her bed. And, secondly, that she could be sure the little chainsaw under it would pull first time. But she kept her cool, with some difficulty. With Fluff gone, and Chip a prisoner, she felt very much alone. "What is it, dear Doctor?"

"Oh, I just need to take some blood from you. Just some standard checks on your medication absorption."

"You're late with my tablets," she said sulkily, hiding her panic. "I don't see why I should help you. I need them."

"And you shall have them, Miss Virginia. Just as soon as I have some cooperation," he said, showing just a hint of the iron fist hidden inside that apparently solicitous care.

"Oh, all right. But I need them. I actually need more." She let him take her arm and put a blood-pressure cuff on it.

"Oh I think we can increase the dose slightly when I get these absorption results back."

"And when will that be?"

"Usually about two days, Miss Virginia. Now the other matter is that Talbot Cartup is coming to have some pictures taken with you. You might want to dress smartly for the occasion."

"I don't like him," she said sulkily. "He's old and smelly."

The sleek muscular doctor looked at her as he withdrew the needle, the syringe now full of dark red blood. "Well, you could marry me instead, you know. But don't say anything to Talbot. Just go along with him . . . or I might forget your pills. Or cut down on them."

It was a good thing, Virginia reflected later, that she'd been too stunned to speak.


Fluff had opted for hiding in the box again. By the noises out there, they'd entered GBS City. Fluff knew it wasn't his most courageous decision, but it was the easiest.

Maybe . . . Maybe this person would set the box down before opening it. Fluff kept the lid open and stretched and rubbed his limbs. He'd pull the lid closed at the last minute when the vehicle stopped. He wasn't going to be cold, stiff and not ready for action, this time.

The vehicle slowed and stopped. The engine was switched off. Fluff hastily pulled the lid closed, and lay still.

The doors opened and someone picked up the box, carried it for a distance, and put it down. "I will convey the prawns to the new safe in the chill-room. See that the rest is put away."

Fingers inserted themselves into the box. And then there was pandemonium.

Leaping out, Fluff had the advantage on nearly every-one else in the room. It had been dark inside the box. It was now dark out here. Galagos are nocturnal, arboreal creatures. Swinging from tree limb to tree limb was quite as easy as leaping from outstretched human limb to limb as they blundered about in the shriek-filled darkness.

This place was plainly a very large kitchen. Fluff was quite capable of seeing that he had company in his arbor-human adventures. Four rats were scurrying for the doorway, with the Starvanger-bay prawns that had just recently been in the kitchen of Shaw House. Fluff decided to head after the disappearing rats. He'd wanted to find rats, anyway.

A flailing hand made contact with his tail, and he was obliged to bite somebody. Then, as he reached the door, another leaper bounced off the far wall like a cannonball, and actually overtook him. The fluorescent lights flick-ered as if someone had reached the main switch.

There was just time to catch a glimpse of blue fur before the other leaper cleared the southern outside wall. A shotgun boomed. Fluff, in panic, leaped clear over the other wall. He found himself in the middle of a road, trapped in oncoming traffic. At the last moment, he somehow unfroze from the sight of the headlights on the oncoming hooting monstrosity. He leapt straight up and let it pass under him, before hitting the road again, jumping as he touched down. He dodged another vehicle and bounded across the roadway and up a stone-pine on the far side.

He wasn't staying there, either. There was a wonderfully convenient avenue of the trees. Fluff decided that he'd look for the rats later. Right now what he wanted was to be elsewhere. Fast.

# Chapter 32

◯⟋

*Pre-trial Confinement, Military Police Headquarters. A gray cell, 7' x 5' x 7' in its dimensions, complete with prison bed and chamberpot.*

The defense attorney who was assigned to Chip this time resembled Lieutenant Capra the way a cardboard-cutout of an elephant resembles an elephant. From a distance, at the right angle, the two were indistinguishable. Lieutenant Depardue had the uniform, the JAG flashes, the pips. He was roughly the same height and build, and presumably was also an attorney.

That was where the similarity ended.

"You might as well plead guilty, Lance Corporal. I went along to take the deposition from Ms. Shaw. The evidence is damning. You might possibly get some leniency if you plead guilty." Distastefully, the lieutenant leaned back, as if afraid that the mere presence of a Vat-accused might corrupt him.

"Most of these charges, Lieutenant, are the biggest lot of crap I ever came across," said Chip bluntly.

The lieutenant shrugged. "You can try telling that to the judge, Lance Corporal. We've got a pre-trial session with him this afternoon. I strongly advise you to say that you've decided to plead guilty."

Chip had no particular hopes of that session, or of the judge, improving anything.

But it seemed that he had underestimated both.

When the judge got to "you have the right to request a different military lawyer represent you," Chip saw the light at the end of the tunnel. It could have been an oncoming train, but when the judge told him that if the person he requested was reasonably available he could have him, Chip hoped that maybe, just for once, Shareholder justice would work in his favor. When he was told that he'd no longer be entitled to keep the assigned lawyer if he chose another, he was very grateful indeed. Another ten minutes with the son of a bitch and they'd have been able to add murder to the charge sheet, as they probably wouldn't accept Justifiable Shareholdericide as a plea.

The judge instructed that Capra be contacted.

Sitting back inside a cell, Chip was pleased to hear a familiar voice. Any familiar voice. After what he'd been through in the last while, he was in bad need of comforting. The familiar voice was raised in more than a little irritation, though.

"Don't piss around with me, soldier!" snapped Lieutenant Capra. "You can't deny me access. And you can't sit in on meetings between me and my client, either. Provide me with any more excuses and I'll see you ornamenting your own cells."

"General Cartup-Kreutzler's orders, sir."

"The Military Code's orders, soldier. I know which I'd be wiser to obey. If you like I'll return with an order from a military judge."

"You'll have to do that, sir," said the MP.

"I will. Post haste. And an instruction to free him from pre-trial custody."

Within what seemed like a half a lifetime, Lieutenant Capra did return. "They won't let me spring you. It seems you're a dangerous man, Connolly. Apparently a threat to the virtue of all Shareholders' daughters on HAR. But at least they can't stop me talking to you. Now, let's look at these charges together . . ."

Capra flipped through the pages with quick and expert fingers. Practically every page caused him to snort with sarcasm. "Several of them will fail the straight-faced attorney test in a kangaroo court, let alone under the eye of Judge McCairn. God knows what sort of idiot they got to pencil-whip these through the JAG pre-trial appraisal. But let's talk them through. The most serious one is Charge IV. Rapists get short shrift. What I want to know, first off, is have they got any grounds for this at all?"

Chip felt the lieutenant's eyes boring into him. He got the feeling that a wrong answer here, and he might as well put the noose around his own neck. Fortunately, he didn't have any doubts. "No, sir, there isn't. What this is all about, sir, is that Virginia Shaw is in big trouble. Bigger than I am. I've got to get out of here, and if they don't want to let me out, I'll break out of here."

"I didn't hear you say that last part, Connolly. Don't even think about it. This is being 'fast forwarded' through the system, considering the political ramifications. You'll either be for the high-jump or a free man in two weeks, at most."

"Sir, I don't know if Virginia has got two weeks. She . . . she managed to tell me when I went there, that she is being held prisoner by some doctor. She's being doped."

Capra raised his eyes to heaven. "Look, Connolly. Let's just stick to the matter in hand. I don't know, off-hand, whether you're crazy or doped yourself."

"Lieutenant. Last time they said I was crazy, I proved to be telling the absolute damn truth. If you don't believe me, insist she comes in to court to testify. Just see where you get to. You said yourself that you tried last time. You don't know any f . . . anything about Ginny. You just think she's Miss La-di-dah Virginia Shaw. She's not. Why don't you listen to me? Why don't you get hold of the rats and bats who were with us? Ask them."

"Why don't you stop getting quite so excitable, and talk to me. Then I'll listen. And I *am* going to have subpoenas issued for the military animals involved in this case, and Ms. Shaw as well. Because it's a rape case she's entitled to not actually face the accused attacker. But she will have to testify to the entire panel."

Chip counted to ten, slowly. He'd found that this had always worked when trying to deal with culinary disasters. This skeptical officer was the best hope he had, right now. He took a deep breath. "Sir. I'll do my best. I'll tell you everything I can and you can make up your own mind. But I have just one request. Will you tell Senior Bombardier Bat Michaela Bronstein that Ginny said Phylla was a bat and asked how she was doing?"

"Why do I suspect this a bad idea, Connolly? You're not trying to get me to influence a witness, are you?"

"No Sir. Phylla was a rat, and she's dead. When Ginny said that to me I realized that she was trying to tell me something. Bronstein will, too. And I will bet that they won't allow Ginny out, into your court."

"Whoever this mysterious 'they' is, they can't exactly stop her, Connolly. Now . . . Charge one, specification one . . ."

An hour and a half later the lieutenant left Chip, with a list of the rats and bats involved, and a thick sheaf of notes.

He left Chip to his thoughts.

Maybe Capra would have been less satisfied if he'd known that his client was already planning his escape, and the murder of a certain doctor. The only thing that was stopping Chip from taking out a few MPs and making an escape immediately was the certain knowledge that when Bronstein heard about "the bat Phylla," she and the bats and the rats would probably be off to Shaw House.

Mike Capra took a long pull at the beer that Van Klomp had put in front of him. "I'm supposed to be working on Fitz's case. Ogata has me running around like an errand boy. He won't trust the MP investigators. And now the JAG himself and you suddenly push me onto this Vat-kid's case. I can't, Van Klomp. I can't give my best to both cases. I'm going to step aside. Get you someone else."

Van Klomp blew the froth off the top of his quart. "*Kak stories, boeta*. You can fool half the courts on HAR, but I can tell when you're trying to shoot me a line. I've seen those charges against my new lance-jack. Most of them you could tear apart in your sleep. Anyway, this soldier is a fairly vital piece of your defense for Fitzy. They'll stretch Connolly's neck for rape and then you've lost him. There is something else going on here. Tell me."

"I suppose I should be grateful that you aren't a judge," said Capra, ironically.

"There wouldn't be a *bleddy* case backlog if I were," said Van Klomp forcefully. "Now stop drinking my beer for long enough to tell me what it is that's getting to you."

"You're right. A lot of the charges are a joke. A few of the kid's deeds are technically crimes, but prosecuting him for them is ridiculous. The only worrying one is the rape charge."

"That's a load of bull," Van Klomp interrupted. "I *saw* them together, Mike—so did several of my troopers. If anyone was raping anyone, she should be charged. Couldn't keep her hands off him. I didn't notice any complaints from that soldier, mind you, but he certainly wasn't forcing anyone."

"If you'd let me finish. Connolly claims it was consensual, and he is certain she'd testify to that. He's also certain she won't be allowed to testify. He's got a real conspiracy theory syndrome. He even half had me believing him. I suppose he's been through a lot. But it's this bit about her having a soft-cyber implant that got to me."

Van Klomp's eyes narrowed. "Soft-cyber. You mean like the little implants they put into the rats and bats. Or something different?"

"One and the same. He insists it's true, and has been kept a secret. That she was brain damaged as a kid due to a horse-riding accident and her parents used their influence to have her implanted to fix it. I don't know if he's just flipped his marbles, or . . . Well, he said I should ask the rats and bats, cold, without any possibility of collusion."

"That sounds fair enough," said Van Klomp, wiping his moustache. "So what about it if he's right?"

The young lawyer pinched his lips together. "Then it *is* rape, Van Klomp. She is of unsound mind, and he knew it."

Van Klomp traced a pattern in the condensation off his beers on his scarred tabletop. "You've never really had much to do with Fitzy's rat, have you?"

"That pet of his? No."

Van Klomp grinned, showing off his big tombstone teeth. "Take my advice, *boeta*. Don't *ever* say 'pet' to either Fitz or Ariel. Especially not to Fitz. He'll damn near kill you. He's in love with that rat. And she's just a chip of integrated circuits in a rat's brain. But she's a person, too. I know her and I don't have any doubt about it at all. A big improvement on his former fiancée Candy, that's for sure. You remember Fitzy's dear Candy, don't you? You had no trouble considering her human even though she had no brains outside her fanny. Ariel is a lot more human."

Capra shook his head. "Not as far as the law is concerned."

"Then the law is wrong and needs to be changed. What's bothering you, Mike? The letter of the law or the personal morality of the whole thing?"

"The latter, I guess."

Van Klomp stood up, drained his beer, and squeezed the lieutenant's shoulder with a ham-sized hand. "You'll ruin the bad reputation lawyers have spent generations of hard work acquiring. Now, finish your beer and bugger off, Mike. I've got a session on the assault courses starting at o-four-hundred tomorrow. I need to go across to talk to Dr. Liepsich. I'm with Fitz's conclusions about our dear friends the Korozhet. My advice to you is to talk to these rats and bats as soon as possible. You'll stop worrying about it after dealing with them for ten minutes. You watch. Otherwise, go with your heart, *boeta*. Turn my new lance corporal over to someone else. But if you don't . . . well, I think you should stop calling him 'kid.' Don't you ever forget that he's a front-line veteran. You might have a nice degree on your wall, and seven or eight years on him, but he's older in experience than either of us. And he could probably kill me in about ten seconds, let alone you."

Mike drained his beer. Van Klomp had an uncomfortable habit of putting his finger on things. Mike had gotten the idea that when the young Vat had said that he was going to escape, he wasn't just talking big. And listening to the story, he'd gotten the feeling sometimes that Connolly was talking down to him. He resented the Vat's attitude, without thinking about it. Now he realized that Connolly hadn't meant it either. He'd just been there and survived. He knew the man that he was talking to hadn't. The gulf between the initiated and someone who hadn't been there was a vast one. And if Van Klomp considered him dangerous . . . he really was.

"I suppose you'll be right, as usual," he said sourly. "I've already arranged for the rats and bats in question to be brought up to the Military Animal unit at HARIT. I've read of them being used as useful witnesses in a couple of cases. Their testimony should get about the same valuation as a mechanical recording device."

Van Klomp laughed. "You're in for some rude shocks, *boeta*. You should go and talk this over with Fitzy. He'll straighten you out a bit on this, and on Vats, too. He learned a thing or two doing boot camp with them."

# Chapter 33

☞

*Offices, animal holding pens, HARIT Animal
Breeding and Development section.*

By eleven o'clock of the next day, Lieutenant Mike Capra
was beginning to appreciate the truth of what Van Klomp
had said. He was beginning to envy Van Klomp on the
assault courses. The only saving grace that he could see
was that the prosecuting attorney was probably going to
go mad and bite his own balls off after a few minutes of
cross-examination.

"Look," he said, patiently. "You've got to tell the truth.
You know what will happen if you lie under oath?"

The paunchy rat who called himself Falstaff scratched
his long snout. "Methinks our side will win."

Mike Capra put his head in his hands. "Whatever you

301

do, don't say that to the judge. You're supposed to tell the truth, and nothing but the truth, and not to point out that you've chosen sides in the case."

" 'Tis said this law is the insane root that takes reason prisoner," said the rat, grumpily. "What is the point in this testimony if not to win?"

"Bartholemew Boarpig!" said the one who called herself Doll Tearsheet. She had been investigating the office, as they spoke. "I think we should just spring Chip and go to fetch Ginny. There's no drink in this place."

"And have you any vittles?" demanded a very large rat.

"Er. No. Why?" asked Capra.

The one who called himself "Nym" pointed. "The auncient Pistol hath started to gnaw upon your briefcase. We have not had food for an age. Some three hours and a half."

Mike snatched the case away. "I should be done in another half an hour. You'll just have to wait."

"I deduce that this is an antinomy," said the rat wearing spectacles. "Doc," he was known as. "Out of what we now know are the needs of rat nature, your demise will show its naturalness and its necessity."

Mike Capra blinked. Seven years of training became as nothing. "What?"

The smallest rat explained. "Methinks Pararattus means that if you don't feed us, we'll have to eat you. He is a philosopher. They speak like that in order to confuse their prey."

The philosopher nodded. "Indeed, Melene. He must feed us, or become a synthesis of proteins and sugars. For we cannot hold back our bestial natures with this thin envelope of civility much longer, legal human. Or you will shortly be considering the matter *a posteriori*, as it were."

"Fillup me with a three-man beetle!" said Pistol, eyeing him hungrily. "You mean that it is legal to eat him?"

Belatedly it occurred to Mike that he'd read somewhere that the "rats" were really mostly shrews in their genetic endowment—and that shrews had phenomenal metabolic rates. Although these creatures were small, they were, after all, trained to kill Magh', who in turn killed humans with apparent ease, to judge by the casualty figures from the front.

"Ah." He cleared his throat again. "Lawyers are poisonous. And they taste terrible. Jurisprudence taints the meat. Ask anyone," he said hastily, opening his briefcase and hauling out his lunch. Better to be hungry for lunch than to be lunch for the hungry. Wasn't there a story about the rats having been trapped in a bunker for a few days and having eaten everyone in it?

As they devoured his tuna sandwich, he reflected that at least the other creatures couldn't be as bad.

If anything, the bats were worse.

"Would it be at all possible to obtain a wig for Connolly?" demanded the plump bat in a morbid tone, when asked if they could provide testimony on the deaths of any of those in the bunker with Connolly.

"A wig? Look, there is no point in disguising him."

"Oh, 'tis not for a disguise. It is for the song immortalisin' his unjust execution," said O'Niel. "Something like 'Charlie Connolly goes to die . . . *tah tah tum tah-tum* . . . and around the noose the golden ringlets clung.' I'm still workin' on it, but it sounds much better than 'black spiky hair' clung."

"Look. Most of these charges are bereft of substance. Some of them we can get the judge to dismiss out of hand. Charge V, specification 1, for starters. In terms of Special Gazette item 17, that one is right out. With the witnesses I have and based on what I know so far, Connolly should get off. They're not going to hang him. The whole point of this exercise is justice."

"Indade? Justice is unfit? In need o' exercise, is it?"

"The entrenched exploiters will pervert the ends o' justice to send him to the gulags," said the biggest of the bats, fiddling with the straps of his pack. "So if you'll just be telling us where the imperialist swine are keeping our comrade, we can blow them all to smithereens."

With a start Mike Capra realized that, unless he was much mistaken, the pack was full of bat-limpet mines. Those weren't supposed to be taken out of the operational area. The regulations on the matter were exceedingly strict, which . . . didn't seem to mean a damn thing to the bats, did it?

He was still looking at the evidence of intended mayhem, when the third bat swatted her wing over the satchel. "Now, Eamon. You said you'd follow my lead in the strategy here. 'Tis merely his lunch, Lieutenant. Sauerkraut sandwiches, which I have told him not to bring out in public. You won't be needing those right now, Eamon. What we were wishful of knowing was whether you'd had any word from Ginny. Virginia Shaw, I believe you call her?"

"You're Bronstein, right?" he asked. "Lance Corporal Connolly requested that I tell you that Virginia had asked how a bat called Phylla was doing."

The bat thrust her fangy face at him. "*What?* We may

be needing those sandwiches after all, Eamon. Something is wrong with Ginny. Talk, Lieutenant."

Mike Capra realized with a start that he no longer thought of these creatures as some kind of recording device, or glorified parrots. If Shaw was on a par with these, despite what the law said, it wasn't rape. He was, however, feeling that he was not about to be pushed around by them for the second time that day.

"Look," he said irritably. "You'd better give me those . . . sandwiches. I'll have them safely locked away. Between Lance Corporal Connolly, those rats and you lot, you've all exhibited a total and flagrant disrespect for the law. Now, let me make this clear. You will conduct yourselves appropriately. You will stay inside the bounds of the law."

His speech seemed to have had no effect at all. "We need to find a human called Van Klomp," said Bronstein. "He seems to have some brains in his head. No, Eamon. You can't rip his jugular open. The lieutenant can't help being stupid. We agreed, remember? A common front, even with humans against the Crotchets, the evil traitorous spiny rogues."

The big bat—and he *was* big and those fangs were long, white and very sharp—made a sarcastic sound, halfway between a snort and a raspberry. "It's a fool you're being, Michaela Bronstein! These officers are all these 'Shareholders'—exploiters, the lot of them—and they're in league with the Crotchets, damn their alien souls to hellfire. They're in traitorous league with them, I tell you, all except Ginny. And she is one of us. Now we will have to kill him."

Mike Capra suddenly realized three things.

First, that the big bat wasn't joking at all. If he'd been

a rat, he might have been. With rats, it was hard to tell. But the bats—this one, especially—seemed a dead-earnest sort.

Second, that the interview room at the university's old research facility was a long way from any assistance.

Third, that the three animals in there were actually very capable of killing him. There was no braggadocio about it. No threats. They were just being matter-of-fact.

He did some very rapid reassessment. He was in a profession where being able to talk and think fast had always gotten him out of trouble. Now he had a feeling he needed it as never before. He also had a belated understanding that he'd stumbled into something far bigger than just a court-case about one Vat. He wasn't too sure, just yet, where he stood. But staying alive to find out seemed a good first step.

"Look," he said, raising his hands pacifically. "I can't go anywhere. And I think you've got the wrong end of the stick about several things. Bobby Van Klomp is an old friend of mine. I was going to ask him to keep those . . . sandwiches of yours." If he could get these lunatic creatures to Van Klomp, he would gladly make all of this his problem.

"We'll listen. Briefly," said Bronstein, in a fashion that would have done any hanging judge proud.

"Firstly, let me say I'll be very glad to take you to see Van Klomp. He's out on an assault training course right now. Secondly, I have got Lance Corporal Connolly out of jail once already. Killing me . . . Killing anyone, will not help him. Thirdly, if I'm understanding you correctly, I think I've quite by accident found myself as the middle person between a number of people who should all be talking to each other. Do you know who Major Conrad Fitzhugh is?"

"Is he not the fellow who was involved in the attack on the scorpiary we captured?" said O'Niel.

"Yes. And despite that—or because of that, rather—he has been kangaroo-courted and sentenced to death. The case is under review and there will be a retrial, because the JAG is not an unfair organization and we don't take kindly to this abuse." He raised a hand to forestall the interruption. "I am part of his defense team. He asked me to speak to Bobby Van Klomp because he believes that the aliens—who claim to be our friends—have betrayed us."

The plump bat nodded. " 'Tis right that he is, indade. We all witnessed the black-hearted spalpeen of a Crotchet betray us. The divvils are in league with the Magh'."

"O'Niel. Will you be watching your mouth," said the big bat dangerously.

"Och, the divvil fly away with your caution, Eamon. How far did you get with the Battybund, eh? I'll bet no further than I got with the Red Wings. Or Michaela got with her Battacus League. It's new allies we need. I'll have the throat out of this one, if he betrays us."

He looked inquiringly at Lieutenant Capra. "You haven't a drink anywhere about you, do you? All this talking is dry business, which is why I normally leave it to these two gasbags."

"I have not been near the sauerkraut for two weeks!" protested Eamon.

Mike Capra could see a wedge between them to be extended here. But he was also, despite his reluctance to get involved, becoming curious. "Are we both referring to the same thing here? When you say 'Crotchet' do you mean . . ."

"We mean that the evil devils have put a bias into the soft-cyber," interrupted Bronstein. "We cannot say or even think evil of the . . . the other aliens, whose name starts with a 'K.' They are good and wonderful and must be obeyed. But the Crotchets . . . they are wicked beyond even the despised humans. The Crotchets—as we call them and may thus think ill of them—have enslaved our very minds and wills. So. For that cause we'll stand wing to shoulder with humans. After that . . ."

Mike Capra had a quick mind. And by now he'd put a number of pieces of several disparate puzzles into place—and found that all of them were beginning to interlock. He took a deep breath. "There is someone I think you need to talk to. You can talk to Van Klomp first, if you like. But I am sure he'd bring you to Liepsich. I know he was planning to talk him last night about your 'Crotchets.' Liepsich needs to know what you've just told me. He needs to know it as soon as possible. And I think I am beginning to see where your lance corporal and Virginia Shaw fit into this. I thought he might be a valuable witness for the defense of Major Fitzhugh. I'm now beginning to wonder which is the more important case."

He pointed to the telephone. "I want to call Dr. Liepsich. He's here at the university. He's humanity's expert on alien hardware. Will you trust me?"

"Och. Why not?" said O'Niel. "Is it not he that Van Klomp said he'd be sendin' the stuff from the brood-heart chamber to, Bronstein?"

"That was the name, yes. But if he calls someone else . . . I have no knowledge of these telephone-devices," she said, suspiciously.

The big bat shrugged. "Be easy, Michaela. I'll rig a bat-mine on a hair-trigger to his legs. If he betrays us, well, as the rats would be putting it, the next bang he has will be his last one. And these humans attach near as much importance to their private parts as those lecherous rats."

So a few minutes later Mike Capra was on the telephone.

Sitting very still indeed.

"I don't *care*. This is a matter of vital importance, to do with alien equipment. Yes. I'll hang on."

He put his hand over the mouthpiece. "I must warn you. Dr. Liepsich is the colony's resident genius. Unfortunately, he was too busy learning everything else to ever manage to learn manners. He's supposed to be the rudest man on Harmony and Reason. I've used him for expert testimony a couple of times. He is *the* expert, but it is hardly worth it, usually. He insults the judges. That's not wise."

"And now? What the hell are you wasting my time with now, you fleabag lawyer?" bellowed someone on the telephone. "Not another one of your moronic courts full of microcephalic idiots. I won't do it, Capra. I'm busy."

There was only one effective way to deal with Liepsich. That was to catch his interest. You could do that by swapping insults with him, but very few people could manage that. Or you could offer him bait. "I've got information about Korozhet technology."

There was a silence. "Little pitchers," said Liepsich in an entirely different voice. "And why should I care? Goodbye." The line went dead.

"What happened there?" asked a curious Michaela.

" 'Tis a fine grasp of the invective he has," said O'Niel, admiringly.

Mike steepled his fingers. "Unless I am much mistaken he said someone might be listening in. 'Little pitchers have big ears.' I think he'll come across here within ten minutes. It was an internal call and his secretary will tell him that. He'll find us. In the meanwhile, I think you need to tell me everything you can. You might as well start with when you were trapped in the bunker with Connolly."

He'd only had five minutes worth of their misadventures before an out-of-breath Liepsich arrived. His first act was to set a pager on the table.

"If that beeps we've got to run like hell," he panted. "It means the Korozhet are coming. I've got students on lookout duty. The Korozhet are monitoring communications, you idiot. Now what have you got for me?"

"The soft-cyber units fitted into the rats and bats we use for most of our soldiers have an inbuilt bias in favor of the Korozhet."

Liepsich raised his eyes to heaven. "Look, why don't you go and do some divorce cases and traffic violations, Capra? And leave the thinking to those who can. I've suspected that for eighteen months. We've *known* it for nearly six weeks."

Mike Capra felt his jaw fall open. The fact that it was mirrored by the bats did not make him feel any better.

Eamon was the first to catch his jaw. "Indade," he said dangerously. "And you've no fear to coming into a belfry of Crotchet-controlled beasts."

"According to my . . . friend, you should be unaware of it," said the scientist, hiking his jeans up. "Now, get up and let me sit down, Capra. I'm too old and fat for running around. This is actually interesting. The guys working on the source code say it should be impossible for rats or bats to be told. That the information triggers an if/not loop."

Mike sat tight. "I can't get up for fear of blowing my balls off. And unlike you, I still have some use for them. I've got a bat-mine with a hair-trigger on my lap to ensure my good behavior. I hope they put one on yours, too."

The scientist sat on the table instead. The table groaned. "That's a remarkably good idea, Capra. A few of my lady-students would be in favor of making it a permanent arrangement for you. Now, tell me just how you implanted creatures have managed to circumvent some of the basic programming in your software?"

"Indade. 'Tis by employing what Doc calls 'the natural sophistry of the English language.' We can think of them as 'Crotchets' who are evil. Crotchets are similar to, but not quite equal to the Korozhet who we know must always be good."

"I'm glad the originator of your language downloads isn't around to hear that," said Liepsich dryly. "She's become quite overinflated enough with her own cleverness. So the fuzziness of the English language is the key, is it? Just the news a respectable empiricist needs to hear. The worthless poets proved right, in the end."

"But there is also Doc who can speak of it directly. He uses paper."

"Paper?"

"Plato's forms. I wouldn't mind filling in some myself."

A small smile cracked the scientist's visage. "And where is this 'Doc'—this unsung genius who has found a purpose for either paperwork or philosophy, both of which I had previously considered completely useless."

"He's over in the rat section," said Mike Capra, almost standing up to go and fetch him before he remembered what was attached to him.

"You'd better disconnect that thing," said the scientist, pointing to Capra's lap. "He has no concentration span, and he nearly forgot it and disturbed *my* concentration. I know we should see blowing his nuts off as evolution in action, but still. He's supposed to be one of the finest minds in the legal profession, which probably makes him almost good enough for Physics 101. That's a rare thing in the law. I suppose we should preserve it, more as a curiosity than anything else."

"You're slipping, Dr. Liepsich. That could almost be a compliment," said Mike Capra.

"It was," said the physicist. "Why don't one of you unwire him, one of you go and fetch this rat-philosopher, and the third one tell me just how you came to undo this programming? We've been struggling to work out how to do that in theory. Maybe we can get some closer clues, especially from the one and only experience to run directly counter to it." He picked up the phone. "I need one of my programmers to sit in. It'll make her day anyway, seeing lover-boy Capra like this, so don't be in too much of a hurry to undo that circuit."

"There is another one who managed to override the Crotchet installed bias," said Bronstein. "She actually managed to refuse a direct order. A direct order spoken in Korozhet. We could not do that."

"And is she around, too?" asked Liepsich.

"No," replied the bat. "We fear Virginia is in dire

trouble. The message we have from her suggests she needs rescue."

The scientist's eyes narrowed. "Virginia Shaw?"

Bronstein nodded.

"Leave that mine on his testicles," said Liepsich, irritably. "An explosion down there might stir his brains into activity. Nothing else would. How long have you been sitting on this group, Capra? Van Klomp said last night he'd arrange for them to come to me. The big Dutchman seemed to find it funny, as usual. You idiot! I've been wanting to get my hands on these for about two weeks."

Mike Capra had the satisfaction of seeing his captors looking nearly as puzzled as he felt. And he could tell that the abrasive Liepsich had shifted to genuine irritation instead of conversational abuse. "Why?" he asked cautiously.

"Because these are the nearest I have to firsthand witnesses of the Magh's—or the Magh's borrowed technology—at work. The biologists, especially the animal behavior section and xenobiologists, are just about eating their own socks with eagerness. We need more insight into these . . . Crotchets, and the Magh'."

"If you've known about this for six weeks and suspected it for so long—why have you not told the world?"

"Because, Capra, we're a fraction less stupid than we look. We have a general public besotted with the Korozhet, we have an army reliant on them, we have not one but two armies of rats and bats who cannot help but be loyal to the . . . Crotchets, and we have a large, undoubtedly heavily armed ship full of enemies sitting right here in our midst. Right next to most of our unprotected key targets. We've lost one scientist already when the . . . Crotchets came to kill the blue-furred alien. We know they're monitoring our communications. We know that they're transmitting a narrow beam to someone or somewhere inside Magh' territory. Moving openly right now would be about the stupidest thing we could do."

"Methinks that not all these humans are as slack-witted as we had thought," said Nym, from the windowsill. "You'll forgive us listening in, but we rats have no liking for surprises."

"Nym!" said Bronstein. "Are you all there?"

"No, just myself and my companion of the unbounded stomach, Falstaff. The rest hath gone a-foraging."

Fal poked his nose around the corner. "Aye, and we fain wish to know why you keep such poor table. And what this is about Ginny?"

Mike Capra had used the interruption to gather his scattered wits. "You knew Virginia Shaw had an implant?" he asked Dr. Liepsich.

Liepsich shrugged. "We found out recently. Her behavior has some interesting corollaries. We had suspected that there might be more flexibility when an implant was inserted into creatures with a higher level of cerebral function. I'd like to do some research there too—but access has been explicitly denied."

"She's been issued a subpoena," offered Capra. "She'll be at this case. The one that I am trying to interview these witnesses for."

"I see. And when is this happening?"

"Two days time. It has been set forward under major political pressure apparently. Ridiculously, I thought. I was going to open my arguments with an insistence on a postponement so that proper investigation could take place."

Mike looked at his lap, at the rats and bats. "Now, I am of the opinion: the sooner the better."

"Maybe we should leave that gadget attached to you," grunted Liepsich. "It seems to improve the blood circulation to your brain, anyway."

# Chapter 34

℀

*The inner-city of George Bernard Shaw City.*
*Mostly from an elevation.*

Moving from tree to tree, Fluff concluded that he was in favor of this "arbor day" and "greening the inner-city" he had once heard Virginia's father give a sententious speech on. It was a lot less boring a subject when people with torches and spotlights were trying to find you. And he was not at all sure that these were the right people to give Virginia's letter and the details of the security perimeter of Shaw House to. As with the money that Virginia had put in the waistcoat pocket, he felt the weight of these responsibilities. Either that weight or the lack of trees was hampering his ability to get away. Or it could have been exhaustion.

At last he was obliged to settle for buildings instead of trees. These were more abundant, if less leafy.

However, at least he could now choose his direction. The trees had kept him going down certain streets, which the police in their cars had known better than he did. He soon realized that the buildings, while not offering as much cover, allowed him to go where cars could not.

At length, he was sure that he'd shaken them off. He clung to the side of one of the higher buildings, looking down at the distant view. All he needed now was a suitably svelte maiden to hold in one paw and he could be like that tragic hero he had admired so much. He stood on the seventeenth floor window ledge, and did a bit of chest beating anyway.

Someone whistled, wolfishly.

Fluff nearly plunged to his death.

"Hello handsome," said the rattess who was supporting the ornamental light on the cornice. Unless Fluff's eyes deceived him, she was wearing what looked like black fishnet stockings. "If you hath the money, I hath the time."

Fluff was looking for the rats. He hadn't expected to find them just here. Or quite so easily. Suspicion prickled. "Alas. I am entirely out of money. And candy and even strong drink."

" 'Tis sad," she said sympathetically, arching her tail. "But a girl like me has got to make ends meet. As frequently as possible, but not for free. So what's your name, sailor?"

"*Señorita*," he bowed. "You may call me—" He suddenly remembered he was a mission of secrecy and gravity. "Ah . . . Kong."

"Well, Kong," she said admiringly, with just a trace of

regret. "I was looking for someone called 'Fluff.' He looks rather like you but wears red. The boss wants to see him. You haven't seen him anywhere, have you? And isn't he a bit better resourced than you are?"

"Ah. And who is this boss of yours, *señorita*?"

"Ol' Bluefur-bigteeth. He's the big cheese of the Ratafia."

According to the Cervantes in his download, "Ratafia" was a drink of some sort. And the bluefur sounded rather like the alien Fluff had seen in the chaos of his escape from that box.

"Why?" he asked warily. "A party of the cheese and wine? I thank you but not tonight. I am also called Fluff, it is true. But it is something of a headache I am having."

She chuckled. "Honey, misery acquaints rats with strange bedfellows. I doth not ask Ol' Bluefur-bigteeth why he wants you. And he doth not ask me why I pursue my vocation. I just know word is out to find you. Go on up. Tell him Sally Lunn sent you. In case there be a reward."

So, as there seemed no obvious way out, Fluff continued to climb. Fortunately the building was in the Nuevo-Art Deco style, which meant that there were many handholds. Fluff had a feeling that this *Grand Brie* was not going to be pleased with him for interfering in the banditry.

Actually, Ol' Bluefur-bigteeth *was* pleased to see him again. Well, once he had established that the waistcoat was detachable and that despite this one being blue, Fluff was the same creature that the alien had last encountered in the scorpiary.

Fluff had no trouble in enlisting his help for Virginia. Not when he explained—in Korozhet—that the evil enemy of both of them was behind her kidnapping.

"What do you mean 'the evil enemy of both of you'?" demanded Bluefur's assistant, the severed-tailed rat named Ariel.

"Well, *señorita*. It is this thing which she is called 'the Crotchet.' It is very like the good Korozhet. But it is an evil thing which would enslave us, by falsehoods and the lies in the soft-cyber."

Ariel blinked. "I can think of that idea. So, you were with Virginia Shaw, were you? Suppose you tell us the whole story, especially about these 'Crotchets.' I could probably talk to Van Klomp about your precious girl-friend."

The galago shook his head, furiously. "No. Virginia she say only to trust the rats or the bats who were with Chip. Especially Bronstein or Melene."

"As it happens, I know those rats and bats are sup-posed to be brought up here to testify in a case for Capra. I presume this is the case this 'Chip' is in, no?"

"*Si, señorita*. I need to tell them. I have the maps . . ."

"We'll put out the word," said Ariel. "Now. Tell me your story about the . . . Crotchets. Start from the begin-ning."

# Chapter 35

☞

"The pot is coming to a boil nicely, then," commented Sanjay Devi, looking out from her balcony at the magnificent view of the city it provided. Although, as always these days, her eyes were fixed on the one thing that marred that view—the pumpkin-shaped Korozhet ship that was almost as big as the remains of the old slowship which had founded the colony.

"Pumpkin soup," she said wryly. "Who would have thought a small dash of brash young lawyer would have been such a key ingredient in the recipe?"

"Not me, that's for sure," grumbled Liepsich. "Adding lawyer to a recipe is like pouring salt on ice cream." His eyes shifted sideways. "I'll grant the occasional exception. On occasion."

General Needford just looked bored. "Why is it that

physicists think their piddly little particles are the most complex things in existence? From a legal standpoint, they're as boring as an introductory class in torts. So are physicists trying to make wisecracks."

His own eyes, even darker than Sanjay's, were also fixed on the Korozhet ship. "We may not be able to meet again in person. Not till it's over. So. Does all seem well to you? Well enough, at least."

Liepsich shrugged. "We're losing control, you know."

"Of course," said Sanjay. "That's the solution. If you weren't crippled by those physicist's blinders, you'd understand that. The general was asking if there were any *problems.*"

She'd seen enough of that hated ship. Coming to the end, she didn't want to waste more precious time on it. Devi turned away and moved toward the open glass door leading into her house. "There are some, I think. Probably small ones, but who knows? I'll make us some tea."

Liepsich went back to grumbling. "I'd rather have coffee."

"I know. I'll make us tea. You wouldn't like my coffee anyway."

"I know," Liepsich grumbled.

# Chapter 36

ᔕ

*Pre-trial Confinement, Officers subsection,*
*Military Police Headquarters. A gray cell, 7' x 5' x 7'*
*in its dimensions, complete with prison bed and*
*chamberpot. With striped blanket on the bed (item*
*FW304, officer issue).*

"The idea that is worrying me most is that the soft-cyber units inside rat and bat heads have an inbuilt bias. I'm pretty sure you're right about it, too," said Fitz. "Ariel just slides away from that point. She won't concede that the Korozhet might be double-crossing us. And believe me, Mike, she's not stupid."

"Well, Liepsich says that it's a cast-iron certainty. He's also sure that there are some key programming phrases that trigger this behavior. With these rats and bats from my other case for him to investigate, he seems to be getting somewhere. That case is keeping me busy enough."

The attorney sighed. "Either Cartup-Kreutzler's SJA is a clever idiot, or he's doing this deliberately. There are holes you can drive a bus through in both of your cases, but they're superficially sound. Anyway. I came to MP headquarters to check out a few things, and seeing as the detention facility was close I just stopped by to check on you. The media are having a frenzy out there. To top it all, they've lost several miles of Sector Delta 355. The war correspondents and the ground commanders have made things white hot for Military HQ. There are open calls for you to come and take control of the sector. The front-line troops are apparently in a ferment about it. It was your action that got the war correspondents right down to the front line, and that's causing Military HQ headaches by the bucket. Now, I've got to go to Connolly. His case is making waves among the Vats, in a way that probably has the Special Branch ready to murder both of us."

"Be careful, Mike," warned Fitzhugh. "Most Shareholders think of Special Branch as a bunch of swaggering clowns, because they don't have much contact with them. And there's plenty of truth to that. Sometimes, the incompetence of Special Branch is mindboggling, not to mention the level of alcoholism in their ranks. But you ask any Vat—I have—and you'll get a very different picture of Special Branch. They're a bunch of thugs, Mike—brutal as all hell, when they think they can get away with it. Those bastards do commit murder, literally. Hell, they tried to kill *me*."

"I know. I defended you, remember? But right now I

am altering my route home because I don't want to run into Lynne Stark and her reporter-commandos. They're thick as pea soup out there."

He was unsuccessful at avoiding the pea soup. Lynne Stark was waiting in ambush, in person. "Most of what I would like to say is sub-judiciae," he said, holding up his hands.

"I know. But I actually want to talk to you, off the record," said the head of INB. "Corporal Connolly saved the life of one of my staff. I've checked you out. He couldn't do much better. We're trying to wage a media war for him, obviously. We're waging a legal war already with the HAR *Times* on his behalf. They were ready to back down most humbly and expensively, when this lot blew up. Now, despite the fact that he has not a hope in hell of winning, Laverty of the *Times* has decided to stick to his guns. The charges pressed by myself, Connolly and Maxine are going through the process. Several other diners have also pressed charges against the chef. Henri-Pierre Escargot will be lucky to stay out of jail. He's out on bail at the moment and his lawyers are desperately seeking a deal. Any kind of deal. Advise us: What's going to help Connolly most?"

Mike Capra paused. "I'll have to think about that, Ms. Stark. And take some advice. Maybe I need to talk to your lawyers about this. Who are they?"

"Fish and Johnstone."

Mike had to grin. "Only the stickiest, Ms. Stark. Treacle and wallpaper glue. You do know I used to work for the same partnership Jim was with before he went off on his own?"

"Who do you think told me you were over-clever and too honest for your own good? Now, the other matter is this Korozhet thing—especially this business of 'advisors.' We've been collating evidence for a massive exposé. We've got a fair amount already. I can push this forward if you like. I'd prefer not to, but if it's going to help inform opinion so you don't have to fight uphill, well, say the word."

Mike looked suspiciously at her. "Have you been talking to Liepsich?"

The woman smiled impishly. "No. But I will be. Thanks for the steer, Lieutenant."

*Pre-trial Confinement, NCO section
Military Police Headquarters.
A grey cell, 7' x 5' x 7', complete with prison bed and
chamberpot. With gray unstriped blanket on the
bed (item G465, NCO issue).*

"Well, the good news is that we're a couple of specifications down, including the knife you're alleged to have stolen from your chef. The JAG advised them to withdraw that one. And the charges of assault on your chef . . . heh. It appears that the prosecution decided that the picture of a large chocolate cake being shoved into a pump-action shotgun might not secure a conviction. But—"

Lieutenant Capra drew a deep breath. He wasn't looking forward to what he had to say next. His attitude toward this Vat NCO had changed a great deal in the last few days. Anyone who could do what he had done with that bunch of unmanageable and reprobate animals deserved respect. Mike knew full well that he couldn't have gotten them to tie shoelaces, much less wreak havoc on the Magh'.

"You were right, Lance Corporal. I've received a couriered letter from Shaw's solicitors about the subpoena I had issued. It included a medical report from Drs. Thom and Neubacher. They say Virginia Shaw is medically unfit to attend the trial, and that duly authenticated depositions have already been taken from her by the prosecution."

There was a lot more to the letter, basically telling Mike that he could whistle Dixie in front a high court judge before he'd get as much as an interview with her. But there was no point in telling the boy that. "I've demanded copies of the depositions."

He took another deep breath. "Look. If we can validate the fact that Ms. Shaw has an implant—and there were rumors about why she wasn't seen with her parents until about a year ago—we can get the court to disregard her evidence. The mental competency of a witness . . ."

"Forget it," said the soldier curtly. "You even mention the subject and I'll tell the judge to change my plea to guilty. And I mean it. I'll not have Virginia mocked as brain damaged. Have you got that?" The stocky man's hands were pulled into fists. And the forearm and neck muscles bulged. "I'd rather they hanged me. Virginia has had enough of that from her parents. No one is ever going to do that to her again."

"Forget I ever mentioned it." It was very plain how this Vat felt about the colony's leading Shareholder. Mike wasn't looking forward to the moment when Connolly discovered that his precious Virginia was going to get married. Well, maybe the boy accepted that. Shareholders and Vats didn't mix.

Connolly walked away, plainly getting control over himself. He picked up a paper from his bed, sat down and waved it at Mike. "One of the MPs brought me a paper this morning. Seen the front page of the HAR *Times*?"

So he knew already. Yet now his voice was calm. "Take a look at it, Lieutenant."

Capra got up and walked over. The picture of Virginia Shaw putting on a flashy diamond whilst Talbot Cartup watched avuncularly was quite a conversation stopper.

"She really looks sick, doesn't she?" said Chip sarcastically.

But Mike's eyes were immediately drawn to something else in the photo. Capra hadn't become a success in his profession without an eye for detail. "That's the wrong hand."

"It is?" Chip stared. "I guess it is, now that you mention it. Wrong finger, too. Most people wouldn't notice."

"Talbot Cartup didn't. But I bet you a fair number of women do."

"Have you told Bronstein?"

Mike Capra had the feeling he was wading deeper than he wanted to be, here.

"Uh. Yes. She said to tell you not to worry." He didn't say that that statement worried *him*. A great deal, in fact.

But it appeared to relieve Connolly's mind. He sat back and relaxed. He no longer even seemed particularly interested in the case, but Capra pressed on.

"Look. Because they are using depositions and not witnesses in person, they can't impose the death penalty. Not on that charge, anyway. And there is appeal. They can't deny you an appeal, and they can't pretend that she's sick forever."

Connolly shook his head. "You really don't understand, do you? Once she's married to this galoot, Virginia is going to die. Well before any appeal."

But he seemed relaxed about that also. Except . . .

There was just a hint of coiled spring in the way he moved. Almost as if he somehow knew that action was coming, and he was ready for it. And he seemed to regard the court-martial proceedings as irrelevant. Before his last case, the man had been a mass of nerves. Now, it was as if the possibility of being sent down for life in prison was just another minor slippery stepping stone on the way to crossing a much bigger river.

Capra thought it over and decided that, in the end, he was a lawyer. Connolly's lawyer.

See no evil, hear no evil, speak no evil. Nope, Your Honor, I didn't notice a single thing that might have led me to suspect that my client . . .

Mike decided to leave that thought unfinished. Some part of him almost shuddered, considering the possibilities. And another part of him finally realized just how utterly decrepit was the regime which the Shareholder system had wound up putting in power on Harmony and Reason. Only arrogant cretins would think that you could control a man like this just by putting him in a cell. Not if he linked up with his rats and bats, for sure. Together, they'd destroyed an entire Magh' scorpiary.

# Chapter 37

☊

*A candy store in downtown George Bernard Shaw City.*

"We have two nights," said Bronstein, "to find and free Virginia. And at this stage, we have not the least idea where to start and it is a large city. Do we ask these humans?"

"Pararattus and I have spoken of this," said Melene. "Alack. We think 'Tis not wise to allow the human Capra into our confidence. Aye, he will defend Chip, but he is not flexible enough to do things our way. Methinks we shall have to go scouting tonight in this city."

"Begorra. 'Tis a big place compared to boot camp," said O'Niel warily. "I suppose you would be after us flying around it?"

"That," said Eamon, "is what less fat bats do, normally."

Nym nodded. "We rats will go out a-scouting too. There

are many scents on the breezes. We'll smell her out, belike."

Bronstein pinched her black lips together and considered. "Tonight we will all go scouting. If that fails, on the morrow we'll have to risk asking Capra, Liepsich—or Van Klomp if he comes to visit. I'd prefer Van Klomp. I am disposed to trust him."

"Liepsich too. He has a way with words," said O'Niel.

"But I know not what he speaks of, sometimes," admitted Melene. "Even Doc doth get confused."

So that night the bats and rats evaded the mechanisms that were intended to keep them in the holding quarters at HARIT—which were adequate for dumb beasts but not intelligent or talkative ones—and set out into the city.

" 'Tis a looting rat's Land of Milk and Honey," said Melene, looking in awe at the contents of the exclusive sweetshop.

"Say rather a land of chocolate and liquor," countered Doll. "Look, Melene. Candied violets!"

"Arrant thieves!" said a voice from above them.

Melene and Doll froze, and looked cautiously upward. Some seven rats looked down from an upper shelf. For the first time, they regretted parting company with the others. But they bared their fangs nonetheless. This was surely worth fighting for.

The strange rats bounded down, showing that they too were ready to fight.

"Hold!" snapped a supercilious rat from the rear. "You know the boss said no fighting."

"Spoilsport," muttered one of the rats. "And two pretty maids they are too. Couldn't you turn a blind eye, Pooh-Bah?"

"Oh, I could, if you insulted me with a sufficiently large bribe, but unfortunately the Lord High Archbishop is incorruptible. Come, you two rat-girls. Leave the merchandise and let's go and see the boss."

Outnumbered as they were, Melene and Doll decided to go along with the escorting rats. But Doll clung to her expensively gilded box of comfits. The rats were plainly familiar with their route, and they were not in the least perturbed by the elevator ride. Doll and Melene, on the other hand, found sitting on the roof of a human-transporting box in its dark shaft quite awe inspiring. To think of all the laborious steps avoided!

They got off just short of what was the absolute top. They had to climb the last few yards.

The room had once been a rooftop elevator mechanism housing and general junk store. It now had become what could only be described as an oddly shaped nest, elevated on a pile of boxes in one corner. There was a neatly arrayed supply of loot of all sorts, many varieties of bottles among them. The place smelled rather strongly of seafood. A small, slightly plump but heavily scarred and tailless rat was busy arranging the bottles. Something about her said: *don't mess with me.*

The Jampad leaned over the edge of its nest and surveyed them.

Melene twitched her nose. "You smell like the one we met in the Magh' scorpiary. Are you?" she asked in Korozhet.

It shook its head. "Yes." Then turned to Pooh-Bah. "These are the ones we sought. Ariel will take them to the little one."

The tailless rat looked at the two of them, wrinkling

her lip into a ratty grin. "Methinks the sooner you take him away the better. Come." She pointed at Pooh-Bah. "And where is the boss's cut, Pooh-Bah? Cozening rogue."

The rat sighed, wrinkled his nose regretfully, and began taking things out of his pouches.

"I'll see to it later," she said. "I'll take these two down to Kong first."

Nervously, the two rattesses followed Ariel out of a rat-hole and out along the roof to a fire escape and down to an empty apartment.

Well. Empty of humans, anyway. It was plainly a rat house of ill-repute. Doll beamed. "Homely," she said.

"Methinks you should come and meet the gigolo."

"We'd love to," said Melene. "But we have to find Virgi—oh!"

For there was Fluff, sitting on a divan. Beside a rattess, unless Melene was much mistaken, wearing fishnet tights.

"Oooh! 'Tis absolutely stunning he looks in blue, eh Mel?" Doll winked lustily at the galago.

"Ah, *señorita!*" exclaimed Fluff, leaping to his feet and strutting about. "My life, she has been a desert without your saucy badinage to succor me."

Doll looked vaguely puzzled. "I gave you a saucy bandage to suck? Nay, it must have been one of the other girls, sweetling. I have some crystallized violets, tho'. 'Tis both candy and flowers at the same time. A great saving in effort."

"Methinks you should keep your paws off him and your tail tucked up tight," said the strange rattess in the fishnet tights. "He's mine as long as his money lasts."

# Chapter 38

ತಿ

*Military Court C, George Bernard Shaw City.*

Chip thought the trial counsel looked like a weasel. The kind of weasel other weasels distrusted. He wasn't the only one who thought so. One of the noncoms had asked to be excused from the court panel, claiming she could not be unbiased. "From the minute I saw his shifty eyes I knew he was as guilty as sin!"

"Sit down, Sergeant," said Judge McCairn. "That's the prosecuting attorney."

According to Lieutenant Capra, they were lucky there. "McCairn's one of the best. He's an amateur thespian. We all went to see him once in one of those operettas— not something you'd have gotten me to dead, otherwise. He made a fine Model Major General. I believe he was

Polonius in another play before the war. He might understand the rats better than most people. He's got a sense of humor, too, even if he doesn't let it show in court. But for heaven's sake don't make jokes about his name."

Well, that might be true, not that Chip had any faith in Shareholders of any stripe. But the trial counsel, Captain Tesco, was another matter. He was out to crush any stray Vat. And he had plenty of wind, too.

"Today," he said loftily, "the prosecution will present you with evidence that will show incontrovertibly and beyond any reasonable doubt that Private Charles Connolly did betray his uniform and the core values that we of the Army of Harmony and Reason hold dear. Not only did Private Connolly desert his station, and engage in debauched acts of drunken looting with military animals, he also abandoned his fellow soldiers to a slow and cruel death. We will present to you with hard DNA evidence that the Private Connolly did engage in rape. We have satellite evidence and expert testimony showing him destroying the property of citizens, engaging in theft— even driving without a license! We have depositions from no less than the daughter of our dear late Chairman of how the accused endangered lives, broke the military laws of civilized warfare, behaved treacherously and misled and intoxicated military animals. Ms. Virginia Shaw's testimony can be compared to that of Caesar's wife. And is it not said that Caesar's wife is above suspicion?"

"The correct quotation is 'Caesar's wife *must* be above suspicion,' Captain," said the judge dryly. "That is hardly the same thing as a presumption that she is. And considering the context of that quotation, I hardly think it is germane to this issue. Continue."

"Ah. Well, we have the braggadocio testimony of the former private himself admitting much of this to the media." He turned to the panel: "The State of Harmony and Reason wants you to examine the evidence carefully, especially the witness depositions of Ms. Virginia Shaw. At the end, I am certain that you will be able to find, beyond any reasonable doubt, that the accused is guilty of all the offenses he has been charged with."

The trial counsel's case rested principally on what Captain Tesco considered incontrovertible facts. He'd tried plenty of Vat conscripts and gotten them convicted with far less. The idea of using animals as witnesses was quite abhorrent to him. He had suitable depositions from the only other human witness, which backed him up all the way.

It was something of an irritation to have that young pipsqueak cross-examine at all, in fact, especially because he soon proved better at it than Tesco had expected. The satellite monitoring technician was a case in point. Henry M'Batha had been a reluctant if truthful prosecution witness, and Tesco had been satisfied with his testimony.

Then Mike Capra stood up.

"Mr. M'Batha. Tell me: Just how accurate is satellite positioning? I have been told that we lost geostationary satellites when the initial Magh' landings took place."

"It did damage precision, Sir. But the picture-to-map detail is accurate to within ten yards."

"Ah. Mr. M'Batha, I took the liberty of getting the details of the A34 roadway from the central planning offices. The road in question was four yards wide. So: Is it possible that the vehicle you were tracking was not on the road?"

The man smiled broadly. "You're quite correct, sir. I was mistaken. I can't in fact swear that it was on the road. It could have been next to it."

Mike Capra raised his chin, pursed his lips. "I would like the panel to note that, contrary to what was stated by Captain Tesco, there is reasonable doubt that the accused was driving on a public roadway."

And then the wine farm owner. "So, Mr. Couteau. You had in fact abandoned the property to the advancing Magh'?"

"Yeah. The army told us we had twelve hours to get out, that they might need the place. We'd been moving stuff out from before, but the harvest was late and had slowed things up."

"I see," said Capra. "So what was still there, was in fact abandoned?"

"It was still my stuff," protested Couteau. "My house! Those vandals blew it up!"

Capra looked down at a paper in his paper. "I see that you put in a claim some two months ago—before this incident—to the war office. I also consulted your insurers, Bevan and Daughty. They informed me that you had claimed a loss of some one hundred thousand bottles from your cellar, and ten thousand gallons of brandy. It is a curious fact that, according to the deposition from Ms. Virginia Shaw, there were three pot-stills and one large stainless-steel vat. I have talked to the manufacturers of the stainless vat supplied to you. Oddly, the largest was just seven hundred gallons. I believe, Mister Couteau, that your insurers wish to talk to you after you leave here. Subsequent to my enquiry, they're also following up the number of bottles you ordered, too, as well as your cellar size."

As Capra spoke, the former wine-farm owner had gone from ruddy-faced bombast to pale, sweaty and nervous. "I . . . I might have been mistaken about the amount. It's been a very traumatic period."

Capra raised his eyebrows. "I would hardly say this was the testimony of a man who had established anything beyond a reasonable doubt."

"Objection!"

"Sustained."

It might be struck from the record, but it wasn't struck from the Court panel's minds, no matter what the judge might instruct.

"Mr. Couteau, it seems to me that as you have lodged a claim for redress with the army, and it would seem that you have received a substantial check from your insurers, that were the property to be recovered it would either have belonged to the army or your insurers? So I simply don't see your interest in this case at all."

By the time the former wine-farmer had left the witness stand, it seemed likely to Chip that he'd be heading for the nearest volunteer enlistment point before the army or the insurers caught up with him.

Then the poised Doctor Thom came to the stand. Chip felt his muscles tense up, and forced himself to relax. Even if he caught and killed the doctor now, it wouldn't do Ginny any good.

"Dr. Thom, you have testified here that you examined

Ms. Shaw after what you have described as 'her ordeal.'"

"A terrible thing to have happen to a young girl reared in delicate circumstances," said the doctor.

"Indeed. It would be," agreed Capra. "Now tell me, Dr. Thom. You say here you examined Ms. Shaw on the night that she returned to Shaw House. Whereupon you discovered, as you put it, that she had been 'violated'?"

"That is correct, yes. A terrible—"

"Quite. Dr. Thom. You've already expatiated at some length on the horror. You very efficiently took seminal fluid sample for DNA analysis at the time."

"Yes." The doctor nodded. "It was my duty to do so as a physician."

Capra raised his eyebrows. "But you seem to have forgotten the other duties incumbent on you as a physician, attending to an alleged rape victim. Firstly, under HAR law, that you must report the matter to law enforcement authorities as soon as possible; and secondly, that the victim must with all possible speed be conveyed to a district surgeon for examination."

Thom smiled. "I *am* a district surgeon and the matter was reported to Major General Visse."

Lieutenant Capra raised his eyebrows. "Yes, Dr. Thom. You are *today* a district surgeon and have filled in the case reports as such. Unfortunately, you weren't a district surgeon at the time that you did the examinations. Your registration is only four days old, Dr. Thom. How convenient."

"Objection!"

"Denied. Continue, Lieutenant Capra."

Capra did. "You registered—after reporting the crime. You then falsified the medical reports."

"I did not! Those reports were compiled from my notes!"

"You dated and signed those reports as of ten days before you became entitled to even have the requisite forms, Dr. Thom. That makes them fraudulent and of no legal standing whatever," said Capra, relentlessly.

"I acted in the best interest of my patient!"

"No, you did not. Not, at least, in the manner prescribed by the Harmony and Reason Medical and Dental Council. You reported the matter—not to the police as the law prescribes, and not immediately—but some two weeks after the offense to a senior military officer. Why, Dr. Thom? Why didn't you follow the prescribed route set up to protect rape victims? Is it because this rape never happened?"

But the doctor had regained his composure. "You are insulting the reputation of a gently-bred young lady, Lieutenant. I acted as I did because of the extreme sensitivities of this case. You're not just talking of some Vat-slut here, Lieutenant. This is Virginia Shaw we are talking about."

The judge cleared his throat. "The law makes no exceptions, Dr. Thom. Virginia Shaw is as entitled to its protection as any other woman. Whether she's a 'Vat-slut' or not, to use your term—a term which has no legal standing, incidentally."

The doctor stiffened. "You have her deposition. You have semen samples. Are you suggesting that we let this Vat-scumbag get away with it because I made a few technical mistakes? On a technicality!" His voice was rising in anger.

"No, Dr. Thom," said Capra pleasantly. "I am simply proving that as a witness your testimony is worthless; that you break the law habitually; and that you are a liar."

"Objection!"

"Overruled. It would appear to me, Captain Tesco, that you have prepared this case very poorly. I instruct you to withdraw those District Surgeon certified medical reports from the evidence. If you like, the doctor may enter his original medical reports. But they are of no legal standing."

They came to the depositions made by Virginia Shaw.

"I must point out to the panel that while depositions are normally taken in the presence of representatives of both the defense and the prosecution, these were taken prior to my becoming defense attorney for the accused. I did apply to have them retaken, but permission was refused on medical grounds. I applied to the JAG to have these depositions set aside, but this has been refused also. We will be presenting evidence that indicates that the testator may have been mistaken. I call your attention to two matters stated in these depositions that have already been proven false. To wit: that the stainless steel vat at the Clos Verde contained ten thousand gallons, and that Ms. Shaw was examined by a registered district surgeon. In fact, these depositions are riddled with inconsistencies. It remains the opinion of the defense that the matter should be revisited."

"You demolished that lying creep of a doctor."

"Only on the face of it. The point is, Connolly, whether we like it or not, he has got a believable point. We are talking about Virginia Shaw. You might get off that charge on a technicality. But most of the panel still believes you guilty on the basis of those depositions. That doesn't help the rest of your case, even if they're not supposed to let it weigh with them."

Chip shrugged. "Do your best."

Then it was the defense's turn.

Lieutenant Capra addressed the panel. "Much of our witness testimony must come from various military animals. Their testimony has been considered to be as good as that of a mechanical recording device, because the nature of the soft-cyber device does not allow them to forget—or to create false memories as we humans can. These are facts for which I will be producing expert testimony. Please remember, their ability to communicate is limited. The rats tend to use the language of the Bard, and the bats are rather Irish. They are quite prone to misunderstanding and are literal rather than figurative in their usage of language. I will attempt to keep their testimony simple and clear for this reason. I hope my learned colleague, Captain Tesco, will do the same."

A flicker of a professional poker-player's glance and Mike Capra was sure that he had set that hook well. And he could say later—in all innocence—that he had warned him!

The bat perched on the witness stand and peered balefully at the panel and at the packed court-room.

"Senior BombardierBat Bronstein, could you tell us at what time that day you and the other bats, rats and Private Connolly dug your way out of the collapsed bunker?"

"To be sure. It was at fourteen hundred hours, fifty-one minutes and thirty-seconds that I personally left the bunker." Bronstein looked thoughtful. "I estimate that

Connolly was between ten and fifteen seconds behind me."

"Objection, Your Honor. It is impossible for an animal to tell the time like that. It doesn't even own a watch."

"Your Honor, if I can explain," said Mike Capra smoothly. "The bats are bombardiers and sappers. Dealing with high explosive and timers naturally requires great precision. To that end, the soft-cyber device implanted in bats has an active electronic clock, which, according to the deposition of expert testimony I have entered as item three of evidence for the defense, is accurate to within the same limits as a cesium clock. The deposition is from Dr. Liepsich, of HARIT, the acknowledged expert on Korozhet devices. The bats' memory, as I pointed out, is electronic in nature and thus more reliable, if less flexible, than ours. I am sure Senior Bombardier Bronstein would happily give you a demonstration of her timekeeping skills."

"Indade. The court sitting today began three minutes and seventeen seconds late," said Bronstein obligingly, "due to the captain's late arrival at ten hundred hours, twenty-nine minutes and thirty-two seconds, the point at which he arrived at the doorway of the court and was reprimanded by Judge—"

Tesco held up his hands hastily. "I withdraw my objection."

Mike acknowledged that with a nod of his head. "I would like the panel to note that it is recorded in dispatches from Sector Delta 355 that the line was lost to the enemy and a general retreat of all survivors sounded at approximately eleven hundred hours. In other words, Private Connolly, far from abandoning his post, stayed at his post. Specification three of charge one, therefore cannot stand. Now, Senior Bombardier Bronstein, in your own words tell us about the situation when the Magh' burst through the wall of your bunker. Try to be specific about numbers and time."

Bronstein was. She testified in a very clipped fashion, as Mike had instructed.

"So. When Private Connolly rescued the rat known as Phylla from the cave-in—considering that he had a weapon in one hand, could he have held onto any other weapon and rescued the rat?"

Bronstein shrugged. "Not without extra limbs."

"And how many seconds had the then private to choose whether to try and recover his bangstick or to save a valuable military animal?"

Bronstein blinked at him. "About a quarter of a second. Approximately. Difficult to be more precise."

Mike Capra nodded. "In the heat of a combat situation the then private made a value judgment. He lost a piece of military equipment in the process of saving a military animal. I think he made a very good call. If we have to reduce this to financial issues, an issue bangstick costs the Army $5.75. Cloning, rearing and the implant costs for a Military Animal Class 1, otherwise known as a 'rat,' are approximately $480."

They moved on, and so did the day. Cross-examination of Bronstein proved that even if you had to put up with a fake Irish accent, soft-cyber chips were better recorders of events than humans. "Yon clerk has recorded what was said. Would you be having me recite it back to you?" And she did, until the judge asked her to stop.

She glowered at the trial counsel. "You would not be after questioning my memory again, or I will trink your blud."

Tesco looked at Bronstein, who was licking her long fangs with a very red tongue. "Your Honor, the witness is threatening me!"

"Merely making a joke at your expense, Captain," said the judge dryly. "Military bats are not vampires. Senior BombardierBat, refrain from doing so."

"It's ink he has in his veins anyway," said Bronstein, with a batwing shrug. But the cross-examination was very sparse after that.

Next on the stand was Fat Fal. He bounded up and perched on the very edge of the witness box and winked at the crowded courtroom.

Wisely, Capra kept his questioning to simple confirmation of the details of Bronstein's testimony.

Foolishly, Captain Tesco decided his time had come to demolish a witness. A fat rat was surely no opposition. "I suspect that we can discount the evidence of this witness, as he is drunk."

Fal looked down his long nose at the trial counsel. "Suspicion always haunts the guilty mind," he said, sniffing. "You reek. Canst still stand with that much bad sack in you?"

"*Henry IV*," said Judge McCairn, with—amazingly—a straight face. "As the Bard would have said 'Hoist by your own petard,' Captain Tesco? Proceed."

The flushed Tesco stuck to his guns. "I mean what I say, sir. I saw the rat in question drinking before it came up to the stand."

"On a point of information, Your Honor," said Capra. "Rats are issued a grog ration by the army. There is, as a result, a high level of alcohol dependency among them, but this does not appear to affect the soft-cyber in any way. And, sir, as they are considered to be military animals, there is in fact no regulation that says that they cannot be drunk or drink on duty or at any time. But the truth is, a drunk could not survive Magh' attacks. Rat Falstaff here has survived a year of those. He may drink—as many of us, including myself, and my learned colleague, do. In his case, unlike ours, it does not have a direct effect on his memory. This is a scientifically provable fact."

"I see," said the judge, making a note. "Have you any further questions, Captain? Or have you forgotten them . . . under the influence?"

"Very funny, Your Honor," said Tesco perfunctorily. "Ha ha ha. Now we have established that the then Private Connolly encouraged you to drink the looted brandy—"

"Nay," interrupted Fal. "Hath the wrong of it, as usual. He tried to stop us drinking, said it would make us go blind."

"Do you expect anyone to accept such a story?" asked Tesco sarcastically. "How did he try to persuade you, rat? Tell us."

Falstaff looked at the captain, focusing on his glasses. "Show me your hands, sirrah!" he barked in a parade ground-squeak.

Startled out of thinking, Tesco held them out, before pulling them back hastily.

"Ha!" exclaimed Fal with satisfaction. " 'Tis as I thought. Methinks I see hair sprouting there. That and blindness are caused by hoisting your own petard, and not drink, as any rat doth know, and as we explained to Chip. And why, methinks you could be living proof thereof."

When the court had at last been stilled and order restored, the now livid trial attorney continued. "You're a joker, are you, rat?"

"Aye," agreed Fal. "I am not only witty myself but the cause of wit that is in other rats."

"*Henry IV* again," murmured the judge.

Tesco threw the judge a murderous glance, and then turned his attention back to the rat. "But you're not going to evade the question. The then Private Connolly encouraged you . . ."

"Aye, Chip's a valorous whoreson, though you'd not think it to look at him. He's mingy with vittles tho'. Rationed the food to make it last."

Captain Tesco pounced: "So you admit he plied you with drink."

Fal shook his head. "Thou art ever the carping costermonger. Nay. Thrice nay. He even snatched the bottle away from the Auncient Pistol, when we had cracked a bottle of the wine we found."

"Ah. So he drank it himself, did he?"

"Nay. He spilled on the ground." The rat hauled up his belt. "The waste was very great," he said mournfully. "He said if we drank before we'd found food, we'd belike to eat him and the bats. 'Tis true."

"Cannibalism!" Tesco waved his arms theatrically. "What kind of witness is a self-admitted cannibal!?"

The judge cleared his throat. "Actually, Captain Tesco, cannibalism is devouring your own species. I do not believe rats are part of the human species."

Fat Fal spluttered indignantly. "Certainly not!"

"On a point of information, Your Honor," said Lieutenant Capra, "there is considerable evidence, including the well-reported and unpleasant Mactra bunker incident, to indicate that the rat is simply speaking the truth. The rats have to eat roughly every four hours. They're voracious and have a phenomenally high metabolic rate. It is clear that Connolly acted in the best interest of the military animals in question. It is also clear that the then private attempted to behave in a provident manner, conserving food by rationing the rats."

"Objection, Your Honor," snapped Tesco. "The creatures were feasting on food and drink stolen from Mr. Couteau!"

"It has already been established, Captain," said the judge, "that Mr. Couteau was no longer the owner of the food or the wine. Since he had lodged claims for his property, it was now owned by the army. The then private simply issued army rations to military animals. To be fair, he could scarcely have filled in a requisition form, and waited hopefully, without being accused of negligence for their welfare. It appears from the rat Falstaff's testimony that he attempted to do so prudently. I suggest you move on, or at least speak on the basis of accurate fact."

Having had his train of thought repeatedly derailed, Tesco went on to attempt the picking apart of a specific incident. "You claim that the accused attempted to persuade Ms. Shaw not to accompany you. When he went, had you not gone and had she, if she had wanted to and were able, and if there were no restraints on her to go, would Ms. Shaw not have been brought forcibly, meaning along with the Korozhet that you state was carried, netted to the tractor?"

"Objection!" boomed Capra. "That question should be taken out and shot, Your Honor. It's a traitor to the English language."

"Indeed. Rephrase it please, Captain Tesco."

The trial attorney did. At length. It was something he did well.

Falstaff scratched the base of his tail. "He draweth out the thread of his verbosity finer than the staple of his argument, doth he not?"

"Answer the question, rat!" demanded Tesco.

"Happily," said Falstaff. "If I could but make sense of it. It seems a thing full of sound and fury, signifying nothing. Mayhap 'tis too many beans in your diet. Doc hath the same problem."

By the time the attorney had got a "No" out of Fal—which was not the answer he'd wanted—he looked in dire need of a drink. That bought him to his next line of attack.

"The truth of the matter is you are not an unbiased witness. You took a willing part in the then Private Connolly's illegal activities and were wounded in the ensuing fracas."

Fal drew himself up. "What base calumny is this proceeding from the heat of the oppressed brain, you Bartholomew Boarpig?" he bellowed, indignation coming out with every syllable. "To thus impute my fracas was injured in open court! I'll have you know I was wounded in the cheek."

He turned around and waved his broad furry tail-end at the crowd. "See!"

                    °        °        °

Doll's coming to the stand next did nothing for Tesco's equilibrium, either.

"Would you say that you're sexually active, rat?"

Doll looked injured. "You perfumed milliner! Did'st think I'd just lie there?"

It only went downhill from there.

When questioned about Chip and Virginia's relationship, the prosecutor decided to press her. "I'm afraid I think you're lying, rat," he sneered.

Doll sneered right back at him. "Thou'rt a soldier? And afeared? Fie, my lord, fie. Hie him hence, and off with his head, Judge. A soldier that hath admitted his cowardice in open court before witnesses. For shame."

"Answer the question, rat," insisted Tesco, refusing—this time—to be drawn.

Doll looked at him with pure scorn. "I'll answer no questions from such an arrant coward. Get me an honorable inquisitor, sirrah. One who is not afeared."

"It was a manner of speaking, rat," said the judge. "Answer the questions put to you. You are under oath."

Doll looked thoughtful and then began counting on her stubby fingers. "Nay. I deny it. I have been under Falstaff, and on top of him, and under Nym, and Doc, and even Pistol, and Lennox and Ross, aye and Seyton too in the enlisted rats pub . . ."

"I mean you are sworn to tell the truth," interrupted the judge, before she could start counting on her toes.

Doll nodded. "Indeed. But it is yon scraggly swasher, whose pois'nous lies out-venom all the worms of the Nile. Why do you not make him be mounted by this Oath? It might screw some sense into him."

The judge looked distinctly tempted. So far both Tesco's

case preparation, and the charges, obviously hadn't impressed him much. "While the idea has merit, rat, that is why we remind the panel that their decisions must be fair, impartial and open-minded. They are instructed that it is the facts and not their opinion of the trial or defense counsels that must weigh with them."

Doll nodded. Pointed a stubby forefinger at the panel. "Didst hear him, all of you? The judge said you can ignore"—she jerked a disdainful dab of the tail at the trial counsel—"yon Bartholomew Boarpig's wild canting."

"Objection!"

"Sustained. Witness, confine yourself to answering questions, please. Rat, I did not say the panel should ignore the trial counsel."

Doll considered this. "No. You said, as I did, that they canst ignore him, not that they must. Now, what is your question?"

But Captain Tesco, that past master of circumlocutionary speech, that had battered many a witness into involuntary confusion in his favor, had met his match. He'd lost his thread. By the time the day's testimony was over, he was plainly exhausted. And he'd yet to break Connolly's story.

Court was finally adjourned. The next day Chip knew it would be his turn. He wished that he had an implanted memory to rely on. Or even Shakespearean English.

## Chapter 39

☞

*Milk-floats, Palladian mansions and golf courses:*
*Places which are the stuff of dreams with the*
*right company and superglue.*

" 'Tis a tough crib to crack," said Nym, peering at Fluff's hand-drawn detail of Shaw House's defenses.

"But can we do it?" asked the galago, anxiously. "Virginia, she is very worried about Chip. And me, I fear for her safety."

"Oh, with a few bat-mines 'tis possible. But it is getting there . . ."

Pooh-Bah smiled rattily. "In my role as Minister of War, I can advise. For a small fee."

Wordlessly, Fluff handed over some of Virginia's money.

Pooh-Bah grinned and tucked it into one of the eight pouches on his belt. One for each persona, apparently. "Humans have good systems to piggyback on. Deliveries to Shaw House take place every day. I am of the opinion you should use one of the early morning ones."

"Ah. The delivery of the milk! She is there at about six-thirty in the morning. I had considered it and the truck of the garbage as a way to get out. But gate guards they inspect. They have the detectors of the bodyheat. And one of the guards goes along with the driver to the kitchen. It is why I came out with the box with the guard."

"The heat detectors are intended to detect humans," said Ariel. " 'Tis possible you might set it off, I suppose."

"Ahem. You might care to insult the great scientist with a small bribe," said Pooh-Bah.

When the rat had stashed some more of Virginia's money in another of his belt pouches he said: "Not inside the insulated chill-chamber of the milk-float."

"They'll look there, surely?" asked Eamon.

The supercilious rat raised his eyebrows. "For people, aye. But for bats and rats? Nay." Pooh-Bah pointed to the map. "We have checked with the local Ratafia. The float stops here, to off-load two pints of milk and an orange juice. 'Tis a mere matter of taking a lift with the number twenty-nine omnibus that goes to deliver the Vat-servants." He pointed elsewhere. "A quarter of a mile, alack," he said with an expression of sorrow at the mention of such a vast distance.

Even Fat Fal blinked at him. " 'Tis not far. What are the minefields between these places like?"

"Ah. One forgets. I hath become accustomed to the

city life," said Pooh-Bah. "No mines. Dogs. Aye, and cats, even. But they are usually easily deterred with a shock-stick, obtainable for a small fee from the Minister of Procurement."

He held out a ratty paw. On accepting the money, he added: "What my colleagues the Ministers of Procurement and War and the Chief Factotum have perhaps omitted to mention, and it falls to my duty to do so as a man of God, is that most dogs will run away if you shout at them in human. 'Tis effective, if not quiet. Shock-sticks are best for cats on the hunt though."

"Right—so we go by this omnibus thing to here, and thence from there on foot, and thence from there into the milk-float, within which we secrete ourselves."

"Methinks there's no possibility of there being a beer-float instead?" asked Pistol gloomily. "If word of this leaks out . . . Our reputations, Iago, our reputations!" He sighed leakily. "Ah, well. If it must be done, best 'twere done swiftly. Press on, MacEamon."

"Then, once the milk-float is within the fence, we emerge, kill the guards, blow the place to glory and—"

"Forget the killing," said Ariel. " 'Tis not Maggots you fight here. Humans become relentless, even if you kill some misbegotten knave. The rats have thrived here in the city in secrecy. You bats must adapt yourselves."

Eamon looked at her in disgust and assumed his folded-wing posture of what he thought was dignity, and everyone else thought was constipation. "Not kill these vile oppressors! What will you be after having us do? Pat them? Kiss them on the cheek?"

"Well, we hath learned not to kill them too obviously," conceded Ariel. "You could get Falstaff to sit upon them, for example. Or . . ." She pulled a tube out of a pouch. "Use this. Carefully."

A method of mayhem he did not know! Eamon was fascinated. "Indade? Do you hit them with it? What is it?"

"Cynoacrylate," said Ariel. "The humans call it Super-Glue. 'Tis a wonderful substance, even tho' a girl-rat must have a care with it." She went on to explain just how useful it could be to creatures the size of small cats, that could move silently in the darkness.

"*Señorita*, this glue, she is good. But these guards, they have the guns," said Fluff. "They are not at all afraid to shoot."

"Hmm. Well, indade, let's give them something to shoot at. You can get some ammunition?"

Pooh-Bah held out a paw. Bronstein glared at it, and licked her fangs, pointedly.

"The Attorney General hath informed the Procurator General that this will be provided on a pro-bono basis. Though why you couldn't settle for fireworks which are not such a weary way to the shops . . ."

"Fireworks would do nicely, indade."

"There's a Chinese shop on the ground floor of this building. 'Tis a place of great variety. Although," said Pooh-Bah with a grimace, clutching himself, "the stuff called Pyongtong is to be avoided."

The last remark required explanation, which provoked a great many interested and thoughtful looks from the rats. When they went down to relieve Mr. Wen Pei of some of his fireworks, a number of small tins of this numbing substance were added to the loot. Rather to their surprise, Pooh-Bah insisted on them leaving some of

Ginny's money on the counter. "Never leave droppings on your own doorstep. Wen thinks 'tis ancestral spirits a-visiting his shop."

The bats might be satisfied with the planning so far, but the rats felt that it left one important detail unsettled: How they got out. That was how rats tended to think. It was as near to forethought as most of them would ever come, admitted Doc.

Fluff had an answer. He pointed at the river shown on the map next to the Shaw estate. "This bridge. She is on pontoons. You can blow that up and they cannot follow us. Then we shall go out through the fence . . ."

"What are 'pontoons'? Some form o' trousers?"

"No, she is wooden planks on the big floats. It is what is called 'an hysterical relic' from the original settlement days before the real bridges. Virginia's papa he was proud of it. Virginia she liked to go and bounce on the thing. It rocks."

"Begorra, why can we not take a boat to where this river comes out?" demanded O'Niel. O'Niel had been cheerfully philosophical about the fact that they could not fly over the fence to Shaw House, or fly around until the movement-sensor-projectile launcher units had been disabled. Flying was not his thing anyway, if he could avoid it. But the information that he'd have to cover a quarter of a mile, carrying his share of the fireworks and bat-mines, had not gone down well.

"Indade. You'll all understand that 'tis not that I find any indignity in the use of a milk-float, but the divvil fly away with all this hard flyin' when a bat can float all the way." He pointed to the map. "See, here is the military's courthouse on this river. The one from Ginny's house joins it. If we could take a boat, instead o' flying . . ."

"There are detectors both above and below the water," said the galago.

Bronstein looked at him with narrowed eyes. "To be sure. But there won't be on the way out, will there be, now? Not after we've dealt with the control room."

The milk-float trundled up to the gate, its headlights casting twin pools of glowing mist in front of it. When it stopped and the driver got out to drop off two pints of half-and-half and one whole-cell orange juice, the rats and bats moved in, along with several large containers of, apparently, tutti-frutti ice cream. The rats had bandoliers of stolen Super-Glue.

"Ecod, 'tis cold in here," complained Pistol, as they trundled off toward Shaw House. "Canst we not make a fire?"

"It calls for hot and rebellious liquors in my blood," said Falstaff, cheerfully. "Anyone bring any grog?"

"Nay. But what about a pint of full-cream?" offered O'Niel, a milky moustache adorning his black face.

Falstaff and Pistol shuddered and cowered back.

The vehicle slowed. The rats slipped in behind the yogurt. The bats hung themselves behind the cooling coil. Someone opened the central chill box and gave a perfunctory glance inside. "No bombs today, Milky?" A hand came in and pulled out a pack of yogurt.

"Don't steal that. I've got to account for it!"

"Got to check it for explosives."

"It's not right."

"Tough. Off you go. Henry, go with him."

"It's not my turn, Captain."

"Tough."

The little milk-float trundled onward. They could hear the wheels crunching on the gravel of the long drive. Eventually it stopped. The bats, rats and Fluff tensed.

"Help me carry this crate," said the one voice.

"Not a chance, Milky. I don't get much chance to sit on my butt. It's your job."

"Blast you, you lazy son of a bitch! Ow!"

"Now," said Bronstein, peering cautiously from under the chill-chamber lid. "Go. Go. Go."

Nym and Falstaff lifted the lid, properly. The milk-man was backing away and holding his face with one hand, while balancing a crate against his side. "You didn't have to hit me," he complained. It was still misty and half-dark out there, and the imposing bulk of Shaw House loomed above them.

The young security guard was turning back to the seat of the milk-float, strutting a bit. "Shut up and get on with it." Fortunately, the trainee-bully had chosen to turn so that he did not see the struggling rats or the galago.

He didn't see O'Niel flutter above him and drop an open pint carton of strawberry yogurt onto his head either. The milkman did. Openmouthed, he dropped his crate. And then reached down and grabbed several cartons to fling at the livid yogurt-faced security officer who was chasing him with a nightstick. The rats and Fluff had ample time to move themselves and the two ice-cream boxes of fireworks across to the flowerbeds and in behind a convenient azalea.

The rats and bats split off to their various tasks. The bats concentrated on laying out an independence day's display of fireworks and trip wires just ready to be hooked up. Because it was Eamon's baby, they found a potting shed with suitable nails, wire and other implements: enough to start a new war in the bat's hands. But he barely had sufficient time for setting a few, when they got the low-pitched whistle.

The telephones were out. So was the flight detector on this side of the building. Super-Glue had been added to the workings of all the downstairs doors, bar the kitchen one which they intended to leave by. All of this was done before the cook had poured a bucket of soapy water over the milkman and the security guard.

Fluff and the rats set off up the ivy, the bats fluttering close by. The ivy wouldn't have supported a child-burglar, but even under the stress produced by Fal's waistline the climbing plant stayed attached to the wall.

They didn't head for Ginny's window. Instead, Fluff led them to the room that served as the security monitoring center. It only had one occupant at six-thirty on a winter morning. He was playing a computer game instead of watching the screens.

It was a good game. He didn't even hear the rats and bats enter. The first he knew of the attack was a wire around his neck, a rag in his mouth, a bat fluttering in front of his face with bared fangs.

"If you would be going on with living, be keeping dead still," said Bronstein evenly.

He should have listened. Instead he lunged for her in a clumsy half-dive. It might possibly have been a graceful dive, if Melene hadn't already tied his bootlaces to the chairlegs, and Doc his neck to the backrest height adjustor.

He fell hard, nearly crushing Bronstein. She had her

teeth through his nose, and it was only his fall that saved his jugular veins from her claws.

Bronstein let go and fluttered clear. "Stupid bedamned primate." The others were on him now . . . including Fluff, who had seized a set of brass knuckles from the desktop and was two-handedly belaboring the back of the guard's head with them. The man's initial instinctive fight reaction was gone. Now he was a terrified fetal ball, still with a turpentine scented rag from the garden shed in his mouth.

"Stop hitting him and bind him fast, Fluff," said Pistol. "Here. He hath handcuffs. Come. Let us drag him to yon radiator."

Eamon, Bronstein and Doc took up station at the door in case someone had heard. It was bolted. And, fortunately, there were castors on the chair which they were able to roll him onto, and the radiator was close. Melene had hit on Super-Glue as the ultimate restraint. Glueing his testicles to the floor was singularly effective.

O'Niel was already placing a strategic bat-mine on Shaw House's central electrical trip switches. Using a pair of insulated pliers, Nym was effectively disabling all the electronic surveillance equipment, all the alarms, and switching off the electric fence controls.

Someone kicked the door. "Hey, Stett, open up. I've got the coffee."

Fluff, and the rats and bats left, quietly, by the window. A dazed and bloody-nosed Stett watched them leave.

To Fluff and the bats the climb to Ginny's window was a cakewalk. To Fluff, that was because he was a galago. To the bats, it was because they could fly.

To the rats, it was one overhang too many.

"Methinks we'll go around," said Falstaff. "I sweat to death and lard the lean earth as it is."

So the rats took a nearby window, and Fluff and the bats went on. They looked in at the skylight window and there was a sleeper in the bed. The bathroom window was closed.

So Fluff broke it. He rather liked those brass knuckles.

Then he nearly fell four stories. There was Virginia. Up. Dressed in her most outdoor clothes, with a bandanna around her blond hair. It was more of a rag than a bandanna, now. It had once been white, with a red splotch on it. Now it was dirty-white and peppered with old bloodstains. She'd worn it through the Magh' tunnels. This was her equivalent of dressing for action. That and the chainsaw.

"*Mi* Virginia!" he said shakily, leaping to hug her. "Who is that in the bed?"

"A few pillows, Fluff," she said, grinning so widely it looked as if her ears were in danger. "And Bronstein! Eamon! O'Niel!" Then she hastily put her finger to her lips.

"The listening post she is down," said Fluff from her shoulder. "But how did you know we were coming, Virginia?"

She reached up and stroked him, gently. "I didn't, Fluff. I . . . I thought you might be dead. And the blood tests come back this morning. I had to try now. I was going to try for a hostage and the golf cart. I didn't know if it would have worked, but I had to try. Oh, it's so good to see you all!" Behind her glasses a small tear blinked and there was a crack in her voice.

"Enough talking already," said Eamon gruffly. "Let's move out. Be starting that infernal machine."

"The noise?"

"There'll be a-plenty in a minute or two, anyway," said O'Niel. "Once they get into the control room."

Ginny pulled the chainsaw. Shaw House equipment was, naturally, the best—and well-maintained to boot. It growled cheerfully to life. Dead on cue, there was a small bang and the lights went out. Eamon fluttered up to the window, and O'Niel out of it.

"I can't go that way!" said Ginny hastily.

"Be easy," said Eamon with an evil batgrin of mayhem-delight. "I've just activated the fireworks-mine with the remote. And O'Niel is going to set the trip-wire hookups. Sure, it is a pity not to watch, but we have other business. The first thing they'll do, is come for you. They'll not be expecting us to be in here with you."

That, thought Virginia, was true. And it was the best thing that had happened—except possibly seeing Chip— since she'd been trapped in here. The last two days, wholly alone, had been horrid. Now . . . well, she felt stronger already.

Someone was fiddling with the outer door-lock already. "Miss Shaw?" It was Jailor Juliet.

"Yes," said Virginia.

"What's that noise?" demanded the woman, suspiciously.

"The mini-generator for when the power goes off," replied Ginny, proud of the prevarication.

"Stay put, Miss Virginia. We're under attack."

"I think there is someone in my bathroom," she said, with a good nervous quaver.

"Keep down! I'm coming in!"

The lock clicked open. Juliet, a torch in one hand and a workmanlike automatic in the other, stepped cautiously into the curtained room.

A torch is a useful thing. Only it doesn't help much when a bat puts its wings over your eyes. The bats had been bred with Magh' killing in mind. Their canines were more than an inch long, sharp as a needle with a cutting inner edge, and capable of penetrating Magh's exoskeletons. The gun dropped from a nerveless slashed hand and fell to the floor. The woman screamed and ran, flailing wildly and shrieking.

Outside in the garden, the air was full of screaming also. It sounded like a war out there. Ginny scooped up the gun, put it into her pocket, and then followed the bats into the dim corridor.

"All right, Ms. Shaw. Hold it right there," said a guard, shining his torch at her. For a moment Ginny froze. Then she gunned the chainsaw and began walking forward.

"Stop right there or I'll shoot!" warned the guard.

"I'm too valuable for to you shoot me," said Virginia calmly. "Drop it or I'll cut you in half."

"I'm not kidding, Ms. Shaw! You can't get out of here—there are thirty of us. I'll shoot you in the leg if you take another—*agh!*"

The firearm went off. The bat dropped like a stone. Furiously, Ginny ran at the guard. Clutching at his Eamon-ripped throat, the man fled.

Ginny dropped to her knees next to the fallen Bronstein . . . Who sat up.

"Indade, they've never heard of slowshields. Come on, Ginny. Let's go."

"But not so fast," panted O'Niel, rejoining them. " 'Tis a powerful amount o' flying you ask for a bat of my rotundity, Eamon."

"How goes it out there?"

"Two groups of them are shooting at each other," said O'Niel cheerfully, as they hastened down the wide staircase to the mezzanine. "T'ose screaming rockets are great!"

And there, in the gray predawn, at the foot of the stairs, Ginny came face-to-face with her nemesis. Smiling at her was Dr. Thom and some five of the security detail. He had a syringe in his hand, and a little Korozhet-made device pinned on his chest.

"Well, well, Miss Virginia. What have we here?"

Ginny gunned the chainsaw. But, quite involuntarily, she took a step backwards.

"What? Running away? We can't have that, Miss Virginia," he said with a toothy smile. He clicked the button on the Korozhet device. "Come to me, now," came the command.

Virginia had been steeling herself to resist the Korozhet-spoken orders ever since she had realized what had been done to her. Now, suddenly, she realized that she didn't have to. She squeezed the chainsaw trigger hard and obeyed at a run.

Too late, the doctor realized just what he'd said . . . and what was heading toward him. Obediently.

His martial-arts training took over. The kick might have disarmed Virginia if Melene hadn't quietly Super-Glued one shoe to the floor. She was still busy with the other one. His foot came up in a wild arc, instead of a carefully controlled one. And hit the chainsaw blade, instead of the arm he'd been aiming for.

His expensive calf-leather loafers proved exactly why lumberjacks wear safety boots. He fell with an awkward snap, screaming.

The chainsaw followed him down. The tip came closer to his chest as he tried to squirm into the marble floor.

He whimpered in pain and terror.

She lowered the blade, slowly.

And tore away the piece of Korozhet circuitry he had pinned to his lapel.

Only then did Ginny have eyes for the rest of the scene. The rats coming up from behind as silently as only they could had wreaked havoc on a party who had waited, eyes focused on a chainsaw coming down the staircase towards them. Super-Glued boots all round hadn't made for great mobility against highly mobile enemies. Several of them would be needing the doctor when he'd finished attending to himself. They were all down, torn boots and broken ankles bearing ample testimony to the quality of the Super-Glue. The guard who had been standing next to Dr. Thom was the only one who wasn't worried any more. The syringe intended for Ginny still quivered in his shoulder. Empty.

She swung the chainsaw over them. They stayed down. Thom had plainly told them to keep their weapons in their holsters, and now Nym and Doc were busy confiscating guns. Falstaff had found someone's hip-flask and was standing on the unfortunate's chest, drinking from it.

"Right. You four rogues in buckram," said Doll, nastily. "Drop your breeks and smalls. Or Ginny will treat you as the auctioneer and land agent treated the ladybird—she will rend you asunder."

They left them, glued by their hands and butts to the cold marble. Doc even took the time to put a pressure bandage on Thom's foot.

Ginny had to intervene to stop them glueing all the mouths shut. But a piece of Doc's surgical tape was adequate enough. Eamon set up—with the assistance of a little glue, some fishing line and two firearms—a neat trip-wire arrangement on the stairs. Melene glued a few doors, just on general principle.

" 'Tis the kitchen we seek, Ginny," explained Bronstein. "We planned to leave that way, and then head for the pontoon bridge."

"It's back there. Where Melene is glueing doors."

"Whoreson! Is there any other way out? We glued doors all around, except that."

"The garages. Did you glue those, too?"

"Nay," said Nym, brightly. "We could take a vehicle!"

"You can't drive," snapped Bronstein, hastily.

"I can drive a golf cart," volunteered Ginny brightly. "If we sabotaged the others . . ."

Bronstein nodded. "Right. Move out to it." And then to Ginny as they legged it down the passage, "What's a golf cart?"

"Er. Well, you said you came in the milk-float? Like that, but smaller. An electric motor, and can do about fifteen miles an hour. We can go across the golf course to the pontoon bridge. I know the way. They don't."

°          °          °

The large underground garage was still full of her father's collection of vehicles. It was dark here except for the light seeping from a small row of high windows—which Ginny knew were at ground level outside. Fortunately, Ginny knew exactly where the little candy-striped golf cart was parked.

"Right," she said. "Pull the keys from the ignitions of the cars and squeeze some Super-Glue into the works. There are spare keys, but they're in the safe-room."

She settled herself onto the familiar seat of the golf cart, put the chainsaw beside her, then reached down and snatched up Nym, who was stunned by such magnificence.

"Can I drive? Please? Just a few yards?" pleaded the big rat, wringing his paws earnestly. "Methinks 'tis the vehicle of which the stuff of my dreams are made of."

"If we get out of here and to Chip, you can have it. For your very own. Until then I drive," said Ginny firmly. Nym appeared to find that an almost paralyzing vision. He sat on the bench seat making no moves towards his usual mechanical fiddling, except for occasional small and ecstatic *Brmm! Brmm!* noises.

The other rats piled on. The bats clung to the awning and they set off up the ramp to the doors. Ginny was glad that the golf cart had lights.

She pressed the garage-door remote.

Nothing happened.

Belatedly it occurred to her: There was no power. And a golf cart—even a candy-striped one—wasn't going to bust through the doors.

"What's wrong?" demanded Doc

"They're electric doors."

Eamon, O'Niel and Bronstein were already looking. At least they weren't hampered by darkness. "There's a space here between the frame and door. Three mines will do the job, indade!" said Eamon expertly.

There were voices coming down the passage, as the bats worked hurriedly and Ginny tried to roll the little cart back down the ramp.

"Heads!" said O'Niel.

The explosions echoed through the garage, and a sheered bolt whanged through the darkness. Hanging drunkenly, the door was now open. Well, there was a gap, anyway. Too small for a car, but just about possible for a golf cart. Ginny eased forward, and, with one wheel virtually over the edge of the ramp, scraped out into the dark.

"Careful with my paintwork!" said Nym crossly.

Outside there was serious gunfire. There was also thick mist. Someone had plainly just triggered one of the tripmines and piles of Wen Pei's fireworks stock had gone into action.

There was no need for lights any more, though. Ginny turned straight off the driveway and drove through a flowerbed. It was her flowerbed. She'd drive through them if she liked. She headed away from the gunfire, away from the gates. But Cartup's security had been just behind them in the garage, and would be following. It wasn't the longest head start in the world.

On the other hand, most of the security staff didn't ever go out for a round of golf. There was some interesting rough, and sand and water features on the route she had planned.

The golf cart was at least quiet. And the misty morning

provided some cover. But she did wish that it wasn't candy striped.

Behind them, she could hear some of the searchers. And barking. Someone had let the Dobermans loose.

Ginny couldn't help laughing. The idea was to let the dogs loose if you weren't running around the premises. Some of Cartup's security service were going to get bitten.

They rode on. Ginny had the advantage of knowing just where she was going: to the pontoon bridge.

With the little cart firmly parked on the bridge, Ginny got off it and took the chainsaw to the thick polyprop ropes. She cut the downstream two first, studiously ignoring the yelling, the baying of the dogs chasing security guards, shots, and the sound of a motor vehicle getting closer. The pursuit would hear the chainsaw, but there was no help for that. She cut the first upstream rope. The lurch, when it parted, was nearly enough to heave her into the river.

Then the final rope, and the small raft spiraled free and began drifting gently and silently down the river. Ginny knew that the river wasn't particularly deep or fast, and was rather full of golf balls. She hit the kill-switch on the chainsaw and looked back. She could dimly make out the lights of the vehicle. It must be heading for the bridge.

A gust of breeze brought the voices to her.

"She's cut the bridge. You bastards will have to swim across. At least there won't be any dogs on that side."

And then they drifted out of earshot and out through the pillars that marked the edge of Shaw House land.

Freedom was sweet, even when they bumped across a rock, and Ginny realized that she had a raft full of non-swimming rats—on a vessel she had no way of steering, heading down the Tiber River toward the distant sea.

The good ship *Pontoons-and-candy-striped-golf-cart* bobbed onward. The breeze stirred the mist. She could feel the early morning sunlight during the thinner patches. Virginia knew that the sun would burn off cloud layer soon enough. It would be another of Harmony and Reason's bright blue-sun days in an hour or so.

"What's the time?" asked Ginny.

"07:15:32," replied Bronstein. "And the court is in session from 08:30 this morning."

"Aye. I didst hear the lieutenant complaining bitterly about it," said Pistol. "Well. When's breakfast?"

"Begorra," said O'Niel, sitting back. "When we get ashore. Unless it is Friday. If it is, there is bound to be fish for the having in all this weary ocean."

Well. It was an ocean by bat standards, anyway. And by the standards of a woman who needed to get ashore and find her way to a courthouse. And possibly to feed the rats before they ate her. "Why don't one of you bats fly up and see if you can see where we are." She picked up the chainsaw and pull-started it. "We can spare a plank or two for paddles."

Eamon launched himself into the air. He came down a few moments later.

"The city is over yonder," he pointed with a wing-tip. "It is a tedious way yet. But you'll see it soon enough. The mist is breaking up."

About ten minutes later the mist did clear. It wasn't an encouraging sight. The Tiber was navigable. That had been one of the reasons they'd built the city here. But Virginia had never examined the river with an eye to sailing a raft down it. How was she going to get her transport off it? The river had high berms on either bank. They might have to walk, if they could get ashore. With a sigh, Virginia started paddling. At least, with the mist gone, it wouldn't be quite as easy for river-steamers to run them down. But paddling the raft across two hundred yards of current with a piece of plank was going to be no fun.

And then she saw the fishing boat. The occupant was rubbing his eyes disbelievingly. She waved at him, and paddled towards him. "Ahoy!" yelled Nym.

The fisherman picked up a bottle. Looked at it. Looked at them again. And deliberately tossed the bottle overboard.

When they'd dried Falstaff off as best as they could, they arranged a tow, and also purchased some fish to feed the rats.

# Chapter 40

◌

*Military Court C, George Bernard Shaw City,*
*Judge McCairn presiding.*

"As a captive it is your duty to attempt to escape. Not inflict a cowardly attack while masquerading as prisoners. Not to head further into the scorpiary," said Captain Tesco.

Chip looked at him long and steadily. "Well?" demanded the TC. "Explain that."

"Can I ask you a question, Captain?" said Chip.

"No. I ask the questions. You answer them!" snapped the TC.

"This is not the Spanish inquisition, Captain," said the judge. "It may be something that the lance corporal requires clarified. You may ask, Lance Corporal."

"Thank you, Your Honor." Chip turned on the trial

counsel. "Do you know just how many soldiers have been trapped and then escaped from behind a Magh' force field, before we did it?"

"That's an unreasonable and irrelevant question."

"It seems perfectly reasonable to me," said the judge. "The answer is none, Captain Tesco. If we do not include the lance corporal."

Chip acknowledged this with a nod. "That's what I was trying to say, sir. During this war there must have been many thousands of soldiers trapped behind the force field when the Magh' advanced. But the only human soldier to escape traveled in what Captain Tesco here says was the wrong direction. Based on the fact that, of the fourteen of us who started, eleven of us got out, I'd say that that makes my direction the right one and his direction the wrong one."

"But you were not, in fact trying to escape. You didn't expect to escape by going that way," snarled the prosecution relentlessly.

"No, sir," said Chip, beginning to get irritated. "We expected to get killed. No one had ever escaped, remember. But we weren't prisoners, is the point. I wasn't captured until the very last stage, after which the only real part I took in the fighting was to try and protect a civilian. Although you seem to have forgotten about it, Captain, it was our duty, as you put it, to encounter and engage the enemy. What you meant was why didn't we commit suicide by taking on the Magh' in head-on encounters where they outnumbered us thousands to one, instead of fighting them from ambush and in hit-and-run attacks? That would have saved you the effort of this trial. Well, sir, we did 'encounter and engage' the enemy. We beat them, Captain Tesco. We beat more Maggots than the whole of your high command ever has. One soldier, one mucking Vat private, one civilian, a cute little monkey and a bunch of rats and bats, thinking creatures that the army uses as cannon fodder, proved that we could do what you couldn't. That's what this joke of trial is all about. You've got to shut this Vat up before the whole lot of you brass get showed up as total incompetents."

"Have you quite finished?" asked the judge dryly.

"Yes," said Chip, in a militant tone that said *I could go on for another half-an-hour.*

"Well, let me make something clear too, Lance Corporal. No trial I preside over will ever be a joke. The bulk of these charges are enough to make me angry, never mind you. I will make you my personal promise that the JAG will be conducting official enquiries into how these charges got through to trial in the first place. However, the process of the courts must be respected. I will have no more such outbursts, Lance Corporal. The only evidence of substance which remains is that of the depositions of Virginia Shaw. Rape is a serious charge, no matter how incompetently handled. Rape—"

There was a scream of wood being devoured.

Chainsaw in hand, Virginia Shaw kicked the now lockless door open and stepped into the crowded courtroom. The sun was behind her, a flight of bats above and the rats running a phalanx of interference around her. She had a dirty-white red-and-brown stained bandana holding back her hair, and a small galago on her shoulder. On the witness stand, the rats had looked amusing. Now, stalking around her, lips rolled back, red-tipped fangs exposed, they looked deadly instead.

"Rape never happened!" she said, loudly and clearly.

It was very plain—by the horrified expression on his face—that the trial counsel knew just who had burst into the courtroom. "What is the meaning of this interruption? Sergeant at Arms—"

His voice was lost in the mechanical yowl, as she gunned the chainsaw. It was remarkably effective as a crowd silencer. Her glasses gleamed through the blue smoke as she spoke. "My name is Virginia Mary Shaw. I am the woman that Chip Connolly is accused of raping. You will hear my testimony. Statements—which are complete forgeries—have been entered in my name, to try to convict an innocent man. I will correct this situation."

The judge's gavel banging proved ineffectual this time. It took the mechanical scream of the chainsaw again, and Fluff, standing on Virginia's head, roaring in his best sergeant major voice: "*ALLAYOU SHUDDUP!*"

In the gathering hush the judge said: "I see that the emotional and physical frailty that Drs. Thom and Neubacher attested would make it impossible for you to attend this trial . . . seems a trifle overstated. It is always preferable to have live testimony before the trier of the fact. I accept that you are a relevant witness to this case, and will allow you to testify. But I must ask you to put that tool aside before you are sworn in. And I am going to order this court cleared."

Virginia walked toward the front of the court. "Judge, I have been kidnapped and held a prisoner in my own home, by people who have used and abused my name and my votes. People that I believe intended to murder me. I'm only free because of this 'tool' as you put it. I'm not going to put it down. And, although I would like the people in this court to keep quiet enough to hear me, I want every one of them to remain. I want this heard by as many people as possible. Secrecy and isolation enabled them to capture me, and abuse my name. I won't allow that to happen again. If you won't let them stay, and won't listen to me with my chainsaw in my hand, I'll walk out and tell my story to the news people on the courtroom steps."

"Choose, Bezonian," said Fal cheerfully.

The judge was plainly unused to this in his own courtroom. On the other hand . . .

She was Virginia Shaw. Chip could almost see the cogs turning in his mind. If he insisted on procedure, it wasn't going to do him or the military justice system any kind of good.

"Can we approach this a little more reasonably, Ms. Shaw? I'll agree that the court should not be cleared. I appreciate that you've obviously been through a lot. But I really can't allow something that can be construed as a weapon in my court."

Virginia set her chin, mulishly.

Chip cleared his throat. "Can I suggest something, Judge? Seeing as I am the one on trial and I'd like Ginny to testify."

The judge nodded. "That seems reasonable. What do you suggest, Lance Corporal?"

"Would you accept a bodyguard, Ginny? And have your chainsaw back just as soon as you get to that door?"

She smiled devastatingly at him. "If you're that bodyguard, and you keep the chainsaw."

He shook his head, even before the judge could speak. "Can't do that properly, Ginny. Besides, I'm manacled.

But myself I'd trust Van Klomp and a bunch of his paratroopers. They're *my* unit," he said proudly.

She considered it. "If I can have the rats and bats as well, then we have a deal."

The judge nodded. "Very well. It's irregular, but so are the circumstances. If the lieutenant colonel is willing, of course."

Van Klomp stood up. "I'd be pleased, no, actually, I'd be honored, sir. Private O'Hara, Corporal Abbas and Sergeant Jacobovitz from the Airborne are here to testify for the defense. Will we do, Ms. Shaw?"

The trial counsel finally found his tongue. "Objection. Your Honor, this is most irregular! The court should be adjourned. There are no grounds—"

"Objection overruled," growled the judge. "Your conduct in obtaining those depositions has to have been most irregular, Captain."

"Uh, they were taken by my assistant trial counsel. I'll certainly be investigating the matter. But I am sure that it is all a perfectly logical and innocent mistake. We had affidavits from a well-respected doctor . . ."

"The matter will be investigated by the JAG," said the judge grimly. "Be sure of it, Captain. Now, let us proceed with swearing in the witness."

Swearing in proceeded. The paratroopers assumed wary, watchful stances around the witness box. The bats found light-fittings to cling to. The rats took up relaxed positions around the witness box. Something about that relaxation made it clear to everyone that they could become very active, very fast.

Mike Capra stood up. "Ms. Shaw. Have you at any time

made any depositions, any written statements, any prior testimony as to the conduct of the then Private Charles Connolly during the period in question?"

"I have not," said Ginny, clearly and calmly. "I have, in fact, not ever made such statements. Any depositions you have been shown can only be forgeries. And I'd like to place on record that Charles Connolly behaved toward me like a hero and a gentleman throughout."

"Thank you, Ms. Shaw. Your Honor, may I move that those depositions and the contents thereof be removed from the roll of evidence, and that the panel be instructed to disregard their contents."

"You may indeed," said the judge. "However, I further instruct that they should be handed to the military police to be held as evidence."

"Your Honor, I must protest," said Captain Tesco. "This is clearly a case of Stockholm Syndrome, where she has begun to identify with her captors. She has again fallen under the evil influence of these creatures of her former captor. The earlier depositions were taken with the support, and help, of expert and experienced psychiatric doctors."

The judge nodded. "That's one possibility. It must of course be tested."

"And of course the threatening influence of the military animals must be removed," said the Tesco, seeing he was onto a winning line.

"*What* psychiatric doctors?" demanded Virginia. "Name them. Name one, and say when they were supposed to have been seeing me?"

"I'm afraid I cannot remember the names and details," said the trial counsel airily. "However, these will be established for the court and the people in question subpoenaed."

"Your Honor," said Mike Capra, "Captain Tesco can hardly make the assertion that Ms. Shaw's earlier testimony was taken with the assistance of these expert psychiatric doctors without him having an inkling of who they were, or when they saw her. I cannot see how any court could be expected to believe that."

"I was reliably informed that this was the case. By a source very close to the Shaw family," added Tesco, radiating confidence and pride in equal quantities. "And I am not the one being cross-examined, Your Honor."

Virginia snorted. "Well, tell me who your reliable informant was, then. They don't exist, outside of your imagination."

Tesco drew himself up and said in a pitying tone: "I'm afraid the information is confidential, and cannot be revealed in an open court. I will happily do so in the judge's chambers. One has to feel very sorry for Ms. Shaw. However, as the historical case of Patricia Hearst shows, with professional help—"

Capra smiled nastily. "Your Honor, since Captain Tesco says that he has no objection to telling you who his source of information was, privately, he could surely have no objection to writing the name down and giving it to you, here and now. Then I will ask my client one short question. I will then place the next step in your hands."

The judge steepled his fingers and looked thoughtful. "Captain Tesco does have a point that the psychological fitness of a witness to testify must be established and that Stockholm Syndrome is a possibility I cannot discount in this case. However, I cannot see any harm in your request.

Write this name on a piece of paper and hand it to me, Captain."

Tesco bridled. "Your Honor, I must protest against any further questioning of this witness until the psychological evaluation has taken place."

Capra rose smoothly to the challenge. "Your Honor, this question will have nothing to do with Lance Corporal Connolly, and will relate to the possibility of Ms. Virginia Shaw suffering from Stockholm Syndrome."

"Very well. Let me have that name, Captain Tesco."

Tesco scribbled irritably, and the sheet of paper was handed to the judge.

Mike Capra turned to Ginny. "Ms. Shaw. Your engagement to Talbot Cartup and pictures of you putting on your ring have been in the media. I notice that you aren't wearing it today. Is the engagement still on?"

"Objection!" said Tesco furiously, as Virginia shook her head. "Your Honor, this is a general court-martial, not an interview for a gossip column!" he protested.

The judge looked at the piece of paper in front of him. "Objection overruled. Unless the witness feels that we are intruding into her private life?"

Virginia smiled at him. "I have never been engaged to Talbot Cartup and I would certainly never voluntarily contemplate marrying the person who kept me prisoner and who intended to murder me once he had forced me into marriage, so that he could have my shares." She pointed at Chip. "If he'll have me, that is the man I want to marry."

Neither the judge's gavel, nor Fluff's and Van Klomp's bellow, could still this riot. It might have been more than the chainsaw could have dealt with.

It was however quelled by Ginny raising her hands . . . maybe she wanted to speak. The courtroom hushed to listen.

The prosecutor counsel was quicker. "Your honor. I didn't want to shame Ms. Shaw in court, but I must tell you that the witness is a drug addict and thus subject to delusions. It's not her fault. A dependency caused by her traumatic experiences . . ."

Virginia laughed. It was such a strange and cheerful sound in the tension that even Tesco stopped talking.

"Your Honor, I'm prepared to take a blood test right now to prove him wrong. However, I suspect that the toilet bowl in my bathroom is hopelessly addicted to the pills they've been trying to feed me. And that statement is an admission of guilt from that man. He must be in cahoots with Thom and Cartup or he could not have known about the pills."

"Your Honor," said Capra, stepping into the breech. "I am willing to bet large sums that the name on the sheet of paper Captain Tesco gave to you . . . is the name of the man who is charged with the colony's Security portfolio. Talbot Cartup has now been accused by the key witness in the prosecution's case, of kidnapping and of fraud. I would like to move that this court case be adjourned. The JAG will have to appoint a new trial counsel, as Captain Tesco appears to have compromised himself. This will allow for Ms. Virginia Shaw to be examined by independent psychologists, and, as she has indicated she is willing to do so, to take any drug tests the court may deem necessary."

The judge rubbed his chin thoughtfully, then nodded. "We will have a recess of half an hour. And I will see both of you in my chambers. Now."

"Er. Yes, sir. If I might just answer a call of nature first," said the now sweat-streaked Tesco.

The judge nodded again. "Very well. Five minutes, gentlemen. In my chambers."

The judge's chambers were austere. The only glimpse of any other aspect of the man was a small picture of his wife and children. And on the wall, an equally small and obviously amateur watercolor of a river, willows, and some not very convincing swans.

Lieutenant Capra arrived before his opposite number. The judge looked at him in frosty approval. "Well, at least you're on time, Capra."

Lieutenant Mike Capra had the wisdom and grace to say: "This time, Your Honor." Then for want of anything else to say until the TA got there, he said "Nice picture, sir."

"It's dreadful. But I painted it. It's the Avon River in England. I made a pilgrimage there, just before the ship left Earth." He raised an eyebrow. "I suspect any other military judge would not have enjoyed the Shakespearean rats. I know that I was assigned this case out of roster sequence at Judge Advocate General Needford's instruction. I have been wondering why. I dislike being manipulated."

"Sorry I'm a bit late, sir." Tesco had arrived.

The judge looked sternly at him. "Not, I suspect, as sorry as you're going to be. Your conduct in this case has not been exemplary, Captain. You've done the JAG's reputation no kind of good with it. There are some very hard questions that are going to be asked at the inquiry that will follow. Now . . ."

                    °              °              °

Eventually, after some thirty-two minutes, Mike began to smell a rat. And it wasn't one of the ones guarding Virginia Shaw, either. Tesco was doing what he knew how to do best: arguing technical points, when he didn't have a toe to stand on, let alone a leg. And he was doing it at length, despite the fact that he was raising the judge's blood pressure. Something was wrong with this situation.

He cleared his throat. "Your Honor," he tapped his watch. "I don't want to interrupt but—"

Someone was pounding on the door. They didn't wait for it to be answered. The court sergeant at arms nearly fell into the room. "Your honor . . . The prisoner . . . he's gone," he gasped.

"What?!" exclaimed the judge. "But he was under guard. Manacled."

"The awaiting-trial room . . . Someone shot the guards. Close up, with silenced weapons. They botched the one. The sergeant is still alive."

The judge stood up and handed the phone to Capra. "Contact the MPs immediately. My orders. I want roadblocks. I want whatever force they can muster. I'm going to see the wounded man and then I'll want that line to talk to the Judge Advocate General."

"Sir," said Capra, dialing, grateful he knew the number.

"You'll accompany me, Tesco," snapped the judge, striding out, and leaving the TC to scurry after.

The judge was back, grim-faced, a few minutes later. "A good thing that one of those rats is a medic." He shook his head. "I get the feeling that humanity has underestimated, and grossly undervalued, what we've created there. Sorry. This is a bad business, Capra."

"Yes, sir. I just don't understand why he had to escape. He was basically off the hook. I was convinced that he was innocent."

"He hasn't escaped and I am also convinced he was innocent." The judge sat down heavily. "He's been kidnapped, Capra."

"By whom, sir?"

"By people claiming to be members of the Special Branch. There's a writ of habeas corpus that we found in the cell, which was dropped in the struggle. It was signed by the Special Branch Chief Director and High Court Judge Jurgen, who is known to have ties with Talbot Cartup. And a syringe. I think we can be fairly sure that Connolly didn't go voluntarily."

"What! But I told the MPs . . ."

"I'll correct the information. You'd better get out while I talk to the Judge Advocate General. We're neck-deep in filthy water. Politics. See if you can hold that young woman for five minutes, while I organize an MP escort to Special Branch headquarters. They're not going to get away with this."

So Mike went back to the courtroom. Something was niggling at him, besides the fear that he'd have to face Virginia and her chainsaw. On the way there he put his finger on it.

Tesco. The opportune call of nature and the delaying behavior in the judge's rooms. He'd bet the weasel had indeed been making a call and that it wasn't to nature, unless Talbot Cartup had changed his name.

He found Van Klomp doing a better job of calming Virginia than he could have done. Van Klomp was doing it by mobile telephone. The airborne were being told to be in their helicopters, with their bangsticks, within fifteen minutes. Van Klomp was giving very precise orders about Special Branch headquarters. When he got off the 'phone, Mike said: "You'd better talk to Judge McCairn, Bobby. He's heading the same way with a bunch of MPs."

"Bugger his Moeras Paddas. That boykie is one of *ours*, and they don't do this to us." Van Klomp was as angry as Mike had ever seen him.

"Calm down and listen to me. McCairn won't take this either, and neither will General Needford. Believe me. But they could use backup. You go in first and you'll be the next one I defend against a court-martial. Now. Give me two minutes and I'll see if we can make it legal." He walked back to the judge's chambers, and with a cautious knock entered.

Judge McCairn was bellowing on the telephone. "What do you mean you've got no manpower and it'll take you half an hour? You'll meet us at the Special Branch headquarters in twenty minutes."

He slammed the phone down. "Idiots! I asked them for sufficient men to take that building by force if need be. And that fool major tells me he's got barely twenty men immediately available. The earlier call of yours disrupted things, I'm afraid. I need manpower!"

"Ahem. Sir, how would Lieutenant Colonel Van Klomp's paratroopers do, sir? They can chopper in there inside twenty minutes."

Judge McCairn smiled savagely. "Yes. That'll do nicely. Tell him to organize. I'll get onto General Needford and tell him what I've instructed. And you'd better come along.

I may need a defense attorney myself. They don't do this in *my* court!"

Capra left at a run. He found Van Klomp pushing his way like an icebreaker through the reporters, with Virginia in his wake. "Wait for the judge. You've got cover!" he yelled.

Judge McCairn wasn't far behind. All of them crammed into the jeep: Ginny—white-faced and clutching her chainsaw—rats, bats, Fluff, three large paratroopers, Judge McCairn and Mike Capra.

A pack of reporters followed.

"General Needford will be there, in person," said the judge grimly to Van Klomp. "We want our prisoner back, Colonel. We want those who attacked and murdered our court staff. You're hereby instructed to place them under arrest. You are authorized to use whatever force is necessary to do so."

They arrived at Special Branch headquarters, to find three of the paratroopers' choppers already circling. Van Klomp got out and began waving his arms at them. One set down on the roof. A truck with some fifteen MPs screeched up. The MPs looked warily upward, and clutched at their whitebanded hats. The down-blast from the choppers was ferocious. Almost as ferocious as the camouflage-painted men rappelling out.

"Back up!" bellowed the judge to the MP captain.

A staff-car drew up, and a tall, very black and impassive-faced general got out with a set of papers in his hand. "Search warrant," he said to the saluting judge and parachute lieutenant colonel and MP captain.

He didn't say it to Virginia Shaw, as she was already stalking her way up the stairs to the door of the Special

Branch headquarters, gunning her chainsaw. The rats and bats were running cover around her. On her shoulder, Fluff beat his chest and brandished his brass knuckles. Fortunately, in sequence, not simultaneously.

"Sergeant Major!" bellowed Van Klomp. "Get in there before she does. Assist and accompany the MPs. Apprehend and take into custody anyone who offers resistance."

The camouflage-painted men stormed the doorway in a solid phalanx. Van Klomp chuckled. "I'd forgotten that we had that drill on today. I hope they frighten the shit out of the Specials. Do them good for a change. Come on, Your Honors." He pointed to the search warrant. "The job isn't finished until the paperwork is done."

They went through the door most Vats described as *the one way road*. You might go in there, but you never came out.

"Just what is the meaning of this?" the bulky and aggressive plain-suited man demanded. "Is this a coup d'etat or something?"

"Who are you, sir?" asked the MP captain.

"I'm Chief Director Asmal. Who the hell are you? And what are you doing here?"

The MP captain handed him the search warrant. The man looked at it, tore it in half and tossed it to the floor. "Get yourself and your men out of here this instant, Captain. You have no authority to be here! This is a *civilian* police unit."

John Needford had come in behind the MPs, without the man noticing him. "Pick up that document, Asmal," he said, in the kind of quiet, powerful voice that always gets listened to. "I am Judge Advocate General Needford.

I signed that document. It is cosigned by Supreme Court Judge Stephens. It's a legal document. Are you presuming to argue the law with me?"

Chief Director Asmal's bombast took a dent. "But the military can't do this. The police—"

"Your ignorance of the law—if that's what it is—is appalling for someone in a position of authority," said Needford icily. "In terms of Special gazette proclamation 734 of 16 June 029, while Harmony and Reason is at war, the Military Police may act in a civilian capacity if and when the need arises, and must act in any case where there is a conflict between civilian and military personnel. Now, we have come here to fetch one Lance Corporal Charles Connolly, who was illegally removed from military custody by your personnel. In addition, military personnel have been killed by your people in our military court. On the basis of reasonable evidence against personnel from this department, I requested a search warrant."

Judge McCairn stepped forward. "We have several witnesses, and we have a document—which would have no legal standing, but does have your signature on it—which was found at the scene of the crime."

Chief Director Asmal shrugged. "You've got nothing legitimate to complain of, that cannot be addressed through normal channels. We're authorized to take whatever steps we see necessary to preserve the security and integrity of this colony. I'm going to call Lieutenant General Cartup-Kreutzler now, and you lot will be out of here before I count to ten."

Suddenly, he leapt about two feet—into McCairn's arms, squealing in terror.

He had a slight excuse. A sudden loud chainsaw shriek at your back will do that to you.

The judge shoved him away, into the wall. Chief Director Asmal suddenly found himself facing a very angry young woman with a chainsaw. "You'll tell me, right now, where Chip is." She twitched the trigger. It chewed a piece of his expensive suit.

All the bombast evaporated. "He . . . he's not here. Talbot said he had to be taken straight to the ship."

"What ship?" she snapped.

"The Korozhet ship. They wanted him. We . . . we've got the extradition papers. It's duly authorized by Council."

Van Klomp pulled her back. Or Asmal would have been half the man he'd been.

Even the huge Van Klomp couldn't hold her for long, though, Ginny was so utterly furious. The mob of news reporters outside were thus treated to the spectacle—faithfully captured on many cameras and camcorders—of Special Branch's Chief Director racing out of his own headquarters with a young woman in hot pursuit with a chainsaw. Unfortunately, the chainsaw finally spluttered and ran out of fuel before she caught up with him, or the news ratings that night would have been even more spectacular than they were.

As it was, in Vat households, viewership was estimated at ninety-seven percent. Even out of fuel, and wielded by a slender woman, a chainsaw makes an amazingly effective bludgeon—and Chief Director Asmal may well have been the single most hated man on Harmony and Reason.

It was also noted by statisticians, a year or so later, that an astonishing number of girls were coming into the universe with the name of "Virginia." Odd really, since that had never been a popular name on the planet before. Certainly not among Vats.

# Chapter 41

"That's it, then," Devi said softly. Her eyes moved to the door opening onto the balcony. Through the glass, she could see the city and the two great ships that loomed over the skyline. "It's over."

"I'd hardly say it's 'over,' Sanjay," came Liepsich's voice over the telephone.

Devi shook her head, even though the physicist couldn't see the gesture. "To be sure. But our part in it is over. We were never the solution, you know. Only the ones who could create a soluble problem. Which we did. Isolated the poison into an organ that could be surgically removed, if you will. The surgery itself will be done by others."

There was a barking laugh in the receiver. "Van Klomp bears a lot more resemblance to a battle axe than a scalpel."

"All the better."

"Don't forget that Talbot's still on the loose."

"I'll handle Talbot."

As much as she'd tried, she hadn't been able to keep the steely purpose out of her voice. She could hear Liepsich's sudden intake of breath on the other end.

"What difference does it make, Len?" she asked gently. "I feel quite well, I assure you."

*"If you'd stayed back on Earth . . ."*

"I wouldn't have been able to help create a new world. Three of them, in fact—don't forget my other children." The last clause was a command, not a reminder. "You can't live forever, anyway."

Silence, for a moment. Then, even more gently than she'd spoken: *"I care for you deeply, Sanjay."*

"I know. Give my love to John, would you? Add an insult if you can think of a suitable one. And now, goodbye. Killing swine requires a sharp blade."

She hung up the phone, slowly but firmly.

# Chapter 42

☙

*An office at HARIT animal-holding facility.*

In the hours that followed the raid on the Special Branch, Mike Capra learned just what command competency meant. It meant someone like Van Klomp. Van Klomp arranged to send a detachment of soldiers and police to Shaw House. The result of that was the capture of Dr. Thom and a large amount of incriminating evidence—not to mention jackhammer damage to some of the tiles of Shaw House. Van Klomp also got his factotum-and-woman-of-all-trades Meilin in to comfort Virginia.

And, by the looks of it, to plot with her. A snatch of conversation which Mike overheard and rather wished he hadn't mentioned the Vat Liberation Organization. The VLO was a banned group. It had been described some months back on television by Talbot Cartup, wearing his Security portfolio hat on behalf of the Shareholders Council, as a dangerous and subversive organization.

Van Klomp had also gotten Ginny Shaw to lean on her father's family connection with General Blutin, getting him to authorize a paratrooper guard for Virginia.

Then Van Klomp had organized a meeting of all those involved . . . or as he'd said, all those that he could get to admit to it.

Mike cleared his throat and began to address what he was privately calling *the convocation of conspirators*.

"Right. To bring you all up to speed: As far as we have been able to work out, the fat was never really in the fire until Virginia got loose. We've checked on his call record, and Tesco did phone Talbot Cartup to tell him that Virginia Shaw had showed up at the court and blown the case out of the water. He also told Cartup that she had repudiated the engagement and announced her intent to marry Connolly. Up to that point, we think, sending Connolly to the Korozhet was something Cartup had intended to do when convenient. By using Ginny's proxies the matter had been voted on some two days ago, but Cartup wanted to do it quietly, with minimum publicity. But at the point that Ginny acquired bodyguards he didn't control and was talking loudly to all and sundry as well as the media . . . well, the only coin around was Connolly."

Capra cleared his throat. "Connolly was supposed to have escaped from custody, murdering people in the process."

There was a little uproar in the room. "Yes, that's right," said Mike harshly. "The killing of the guards was planned and premeditated, not just something that happened because Special Branch screwed up the operation."

Van Klomp murmured something to one of his paratrooper sub-officers. Capra decided to ignore the part of it he overheard. If he wasn't mistaken, the colonel in command of HAR's elite paratrooper unit had just planned and premeditated the destruction of Special Branch. If true, that was in shocking violation of a multitude of laws, but . . .

*Good riddance*, thought Mike to himself, and plowed on.

"It all makes sense, if you look at it from Cartup's point of view. Virginia had just painted Connolly as a hero. Having him 'escape' and commit murder in the process would make a lot of the rest of her story less believable. They'd also have a valuable hostage to ensure your good behavior, Ms. Shaw. According to Asmal, who has been singing like a bird, Tesco was supposed to take you aside and tell you to shut up or get Connolly back in pieces. Unfortunately for them, the snatch didn't go according to plan. When Tesco saw that one of the MPs was still alive and that the document that the Special Branch police had used to talk their way in had been found, he did a runner."

"There is a warrant out for his arrest," said the Judge Advocate General, grimly. "And for the arrest of Lieutenant Depardue. I take exception to this kind of corruption in our ranks. I'm going to stamp it out. I'm fairly sure that Major Tana Gainor was at the bottom of all this, but until they are arrested I can't proceed against her. But we'll find them."

"Only, like Talbot Cartup, they haven't yet been found," said Van Klomp.

"I don't really care much about these things," said Ginny curtly. "I just want to know what's being done to get Chip back."

Mike pulled a face. "We're pursuing all the channels, Ms. Shaw. The extradition to the K . . . Crotchets was definitely extra-legal. But the Crotchets are not being cooperative. They're sitting behind their force shield and not talking to us. As you know, there have been massive protests about this on the streets. Survey data shows that some fifty-seven percent of all Shareholders and ninety-three percent of all Vats disapprove of the Korozhet conduct. They're losing public trust."

"Which was something we weren't sure how to turn around," said Lynne Stark. "And Corporal Connolly wanted that side of his story told. I held it back."

"It is still worrying me to see opposition to them so 'in their face' just yet," said Liepsich, with a scowl. "Yes, we're a long way into the soft-cyber programming code. We've got the hang of their electronic self-destruct booby traps. And we've devised an effective way of switching the slowshields on and off at will. We think we've understood, finally, just how the force field is made. But we are no wiser when it comes to cracking it. So: we have a problem. Armed enemies sitting in the middle of our city. There are two potential enemy armies out there—the rats and the bats."

"Nay. Never!" said Fal righteously

"Well, hardly ever," amended Doll, scratching where no lady should in public.

Ginny had been listening to everything with increasing agitation. Now, she got up and started pacing around.

"I've been talking to a lot of people. I've made some arrangements. I have pushed very hard for a Shareholder's meeting. I want to put it to the vote: Either the Crotchets give Chip back, or we declare war on them. Destroy their ship if need be, and take him by force. If I can't get the backing from the Council of Shareholders, I'll go it alone."

"You'll need more than votes to get inside that ship," said Liepsich dryly.

"Which is what I want from *you*," she said, pointing at the scientist.

"And what will you give me in return?" asked Liepsich.

Ginny had a feeling she was being tested. "What do you need?"

"You. Or rather cooperation from you and your softcyber," said Liepsich. "What you may not know is that the mop-up team Van Klomp and Judge McCairn organized for your house turned up a lot of interesting materiel. And some interesting people, too. Most of them ran, but some couldn't. Some are still attached to marble slabs. Remind me not to insult you too badly, Shaw. The MPs also brought me this." He held up the mangled remains of the badge that once elicited her cooperation. It was cut and battered.

"You broke the speaker-circuit. But the rest is in good shape. And to my code-cracker's delight, it's got what he thinks are command strings. And it is definitely a Crotchet-made device."

Ginny nodded. "You'll have my cooperation, if I have yours, sir. Although I will bring my Super-Glue along."

"Done," said Liepsich, "and my first act is going to be to fit you with a slowshield. Because someone is bound to want to shoot you soon, at this rate."

"Then I won't be able to use my chainsaw. And I prefer going on the offensive."

"No. You won't be able to use it—not unless I fit you with one of my switchable ones. Which is what I plan to do.

"Now, what about the rest of you?" demanded Liepsich. "What are you going to do?"

"Interviews with Ginny and you, indicating that Crotchet and Magh' hardware are one and the same," said Lynne Stark.

"I'll do it, but not yet," said Liepsich.

"Further moves with the officer 'reconstruction.' I know it sounds trivial," said the Judge Advocate General. "But it cuts right into the heart of the military system. Of course, JAG investigators will continue to look into Connolly's case. I know it is not of immediate importance to you, Ms. Shaw, but dropping all the charges against him before you go to face the board of Shareholders will be ammunition. And I also want those who corrupted justice in my unit. I want them badly. We'll also have to look at the other cases involving these people, notably that of Major Fitzhugh. The level of public anger at the army about all this is threatening to knock the Council off its pedestal. It also gives us the possible opportunity of reorganizing control of the army, which we may just need, soon. If we are to fight the Magh' and the Korozhet simultaneously, that is."

Capra nodded. "In the meanwhile, Fitz's retrial will go forward, sir?"

The JAG nodded.

Capra pointed to the military animals. "We'll want some of you rats and bats to testify. And perhaps, if you could lend me your services to investigate something. There are two witnesses, particularly this man, Mervyn Paype. His testimony in that first mock trial was damning. We need to deal with him . . ."

"Indade!" said O'Niel, with a fiendish flash of long white teeth in his black crinkled face. "To be sure. You can leave it to us. The traitorous rogue will be dealt with afore ye can say 'abracadaver.' "

Mike cringed, knowing his boss was listening. "I must ask you to be circumspect."

Fal clutched himself. "Surely that's not necessary. That would be the unkindest cut of all."

"Not that! I meant . . . careful. Do things correctly."

Fal clutched even tighter. "I should think so!" he said. " 'Tis not a place to be taking short cuts." He turned on the relaxed-looking Nym. " 'Tis most at ease you are, about such a threat. Or," he sneered, "is it only the private parts of that poxy golf cart that you care about?"

Nym shook his head disparagingly. "Alack, if only your wits were as wide as your waist, Fal. It's merely the official term for short-arm inspection."

Fal looked even more puzzled "Why? 'Tis not as if we're going to slip the cozening coxcomb the muddy conger."

Melene snickered. "No, something a little harder, sharper and longer. Soon he'll be a greenery-yallery . . . foot-in-the-grave young man."

"Besides," said Doc, thoughtfully, "if we're going to kill him, it wouldn't make any difference if Pistol or Fal gave him the clap first."

Mike Capra put his head in his hands. He could almost sympathize with that son of a bitch of a prosecuting attorney. "Listen. You can't go and kill the witness."

The assembled bats and rats looked at him in some puzzlement. "Why not?" asked Melene, finally.

"Because . . ." The young attorney realized that he'd have to bring this down to their level. Morality, and the fairness of law, meant little to these creatures. They had no experience of either. "Because if the witness turns up dead, it's as good as an admission of guilt by Fitz. I've got to establish that the man is lying. All I want you to do is to try and find out some background for me. But he has to be able to get into the witness stand for us to establish that he's a liar."

Eamon crinkled his forehead further with the effort of thinking about that. "Well. I suppose we cannot be kneecapping him either, then. If he has to stand, that is. We could break his elbows, mind."

"Methinks we could circumspect him!" said Pistol cheerfully, rubbing his paws in anticipation.

"You can't intimidate or maim the witness either!" begged Mike.

Fal shook his head in disgust. "Methinks we'll have to resort to slipping him the conger, after all. No wonder you were insisting on us having a short-arm inspection."

General Needford held his head in hands. His shoulders were shaking slightly. "I foresee that the law," he said unsteadily, "is going to get a lot more complicated. I think I will withdraw as much as possible from this case and leave things to Lieutenant Capra and my friend Ogata."

# Chapter 43

*Places of confinement: initially a clean, neat room*
*with a couple of comfortable issue chairs. Part of the*
*room is barred off.*

Chip Connolly had been sipping a cup of tea that one of the MPs had made for him. He was beginning to relax completely for the first time since he'd been to Shaw House. Ginny was free, and had a chainsaw in her hands, and she had the rats and bats to guard her.

Then he looked up at the suits that had come into the back room, and realized that his troubles might only just be starting.

There were four MPs, and, as the case had gone on they'd become increasingly easygoing with their prisoner. By now it was apparent that they, at least, had acquitted him.

"Excuse me, but only military police personnel are allowed back here," said the sergeant firmly.

The leader of the suits reached into an inner pocket and took out his badge. "Special Branch," he said. "We've come to collect the prisoner."

The sergeant blinked. "He's a military prisoner. You can't do that."

The lead suit pulled out another piece of paper. "Here is my authorization. Signed by Chief Director Asmal and Judge Jurgens. You can't stop us."

The sergeant took the piece of paper and examined it. "I'd need to talk to Judge McCairn fir—"

"Sarge!" yelled Chip. "Guns!" He flung the tea, hitting the second suit in the eyes just as the man raised his weapon and fired. The gun had a silencer and made scarcely any noise. The sergeant crumpled, still clutching the piece of paper.

Then everything happened very fast. Chip tried to retreat, and fell over his forgotten manacles. Then he felt the needle, as he wrestled with one of them. He managed a head-butt and felt a nose crunch. Flaccidity seemed to invade his limbs. He still heard the lead suit say, "Quick. Grab him and let's run. Someone might have heard that shout."

The rest was blackness.

When Chip awoke, the first thing he was aware of was the reek of naphthalene. He tensed. He knew that smell all too well. Korozhet . . .

Immediately his mind was filled with warm, fuzzy-nice images. Korozhet were good. Korozhet were kind. Korozhet could do no wrong.

He tried to sit up and failed; opened his eyes, reluctantly. He was in a small, tall room, metal-walled and racked to the roof with what appeared to be shelves. Metal shelves, about eighteen inches apart, populated by aliens. He was lying on the floor, and a blue-furred alien and a naked woman were leaning over him. This had to be a nightmare. The naked woman was not Virginia.

He groaned. Then, realized that he too was stark naked.

"Do you understand English?" the woman asked, in an odd high-pitched voice.

He nodded, his mouth still too dry to allow him to speak. "Well, at least they didn't mindscrub you. We're taking a chance, but Yetteth says that they don't hear so high. You'll feel better presently when the implant gets a proper nerve interface. It takes a while."

" 'ater," he managed.

"There's a wall-nipple," she pointed. "And try to pitch your voice higher."

Chip struggled to his knees, and to the metal nipple. He sucked at it and was rewarded by some vile-tasting water. It was still very welcome.

He blinked at the Jampad. He couldn't speak Korozhet—although he knew they were wonderful masters and theirs was the best language in existence—but he'd love to ask the alien just how it had gotten here. Lieutenant Capra had told him that Liepsich had said that it had gotten away from the wonderful Korozhet's assassination team. Of course, the good masters would never kill anything that wasn't evil. Capra must have been mistaken. Or he, Connolly, must have misheard. The blue-furred creature must have come to its senses and come here, because surely this was the place of the masters . . .

He wrinkled his forehead with the effort of thinking. Capra had said that the Crotchets had tried to kill the Jampad . . . what was it doing here? Jampad hated the Crotchets' guts.

Then it struck him, thinking back to the rats, rats, and Virginia. *Crotchets. Think "Crotchets," Chip.*

The rats and bats seemed to be able to think ill of "Crotchets." Chip found, with a little effort, that he could, too. And found he could make a horrible kind of sense of where he was. And now, unlike earlier when he'd thought of the Korozhet, the benign and wonderful creatures, he could hate and fear the Crotchets. Whatever had happened to him since the Specials had snatched him, had also included him getting a soft-cyber chip implanted in his head.

To think that he'd once mocked "head plastic"! He wondered what download they'd put into his memory. Would he speak Shakespearean English? Or start saying "indade"? Or speaking in the Cervantes-style? Then he realized that none of these were true. He'd only had one language added: Korozhet. And he would be able to think no ill of them. And he would have to obey them. He'd seen how Ginny had struggled merely to *speak* against them.

"How did they catch you?" he squeaked, in what he realized was passable Korozhet.

"They came to our farm one night," said the woman. "Snatched the whole family. I don't think any of the others are alive any more." There was terrible pain in her voice. "But at least I can still remember them, unlike Marie. They took everything from her. Even her name. I named her after my little girl. My daughter died too."

Chip peered at her. And realized, with horror, that he had seen this face before in a newspaper. She'd not been gaunt and lined in those pictures. And . . . it had been before the war. Before the Crotchets, or the Magh' had arrived. The disappearance had been blamed on the farm-help.

"They hung the Vat-kid," he said quietly. "Everyone had thought that he was mad, insisting that the family he worked for had been snatched by aliens. They blamed him."

"Andre?" she said incredulously. "He wouldn't hurt a fly! He couldn't even kill chickens on the farm."

"And I," said the Jampad in an appallingly mangled English accent, "Soldier of the Kishran water skirmisher was. Our tunnels collapse was. Magh' me captured. You other Jampad met have?" There was a desperate yearning that transcended the alien-ness of the thing.

Chip nodded. "Yes. One. I thought you were him. Ginny said that he was a pilot in a Jampad starship."

"Starship? My people starships have not?" The alien was nodding his head, furiously.

"They did, according to Darleth. He said he was shot down. They killed the rest of the crew, but we freed him from the Magh'."

"And . . . he was killed. Here. Masters . . . speak it."

Chip shook his head. "He got away, we think."

The creature rocked and keened softly. At first Chip thought he was distraught. "What's wrong?" he asked.

"I think it is a sort of prayer," said the woman. "He does it sometimes. Tell me about . . . Home. Please. I have heard whispers from other humans that there is a war going on out there."

Imagine not even knowing that! Well, if he was right, she'd been captured long before the war. Before the . . . Crotchets were supposed to have arrived, in desperate haste, to warn humanity on Harmony and Reason of the approaching Magh' slowship peril. They'd claimed they'd damaged their engines in the race, so they could not move. Ha. "Yeah. We just took a Magh' scorpiary. And I just found out that the Crotchets are behind it."

"Crotchets?"

"You know. Fellows like beach balls with a lot of pricks on the outside. They look a lot like our beloved and wonderful Korozhet, but they're different. You can think how bad Crotchets are."

The woman blinked. "Crotchets," she said experimentally.

And then with more vehemence "Crotchets!" She sighed. "Why didn't I think of that? It's . . . it's so obvious."

Chip understood now, how difficult it would be to think of this piece of lawyerly double-talk. But knowing it before the chip was inserted had made all the difference. "It works. A fair number of"—she would never have heard about intelligent rats and bats—"other implanted ones do it out there."

She sighed again. "It does, indeed. But they will find out now, when they question you. You won't be able not to tell them. That's why they haven't mindscrubbed you."

"I need to get away from the . . . Crotchets." Somehow he knew that it would be terribly evil to even think of escaping the beloved Korozhet.

"The only way to do that is to die. You will be incinerated, and your ash dumped."

"If that's what I have to do, that's what I'll do," said

Chip, grimly. If there was no way out he'd kill himself before he talked and gave Ginny and the rats and bats away. But how?

A siren rang out. "Come. Or no food get," said the Jampad.

"I think not." Chip shook his head. "I'm not hungry yet. Actually I feel as sick as a horse. And I suppose they'll take me for questioning when I am up. How long can I pretend to be unconscious, before they come looking?"

The woman shrugged. "You never can tell. They'll leave a body in here until we lug it out, or it rots. When we go out to eat they'll assign us to tasks. They have visual and auditory pickups in here, though. We think that they're not always active."

Chip sighed. It was so much to absorb and his head hurt terribly. "Which is my shelf?"

"Marie's old shelf," said the woman with pain in her voice and pointed.

Unsteadily, Chip got to his feet and managed to climb into it. The effort was of such an order that he did not have to fake unconsciousness.

# Chapter 44

♋

*A universe centered around Virginia. Animal*
*Holding Pens, Grecian-style HAR council chambers,*
*and Webb Fields Auditorium.*

"Talk, argument. And more talk!" said Ginny furiously.
"That's all they're doing. Chip could rot before they actually do anything. Well, I want action. And if they don't
provide it I'll organize it myself. I want an army. And if
I've got one thing out of this, it's access to some money,
even if the money that the MPs confiscated from Chip is
still securely locked up. So: I want you to organize a meeting with the Ratafia for me. I'm going to get me an army."

" 'Tis easy enough to organize," said Melene. "This
afternoon?"

Ginny scowled even more fiercely. "This afternoon I

have two things I can't avoid: Firstly I've promised Meilin I would come and speak at her Vat rally in support of Chip. And before that, I have a session with the Council of Shareholders. I want Talbot Cartup stripped of any possibility of using power. I've got some new lawyers, and they say that Chip's extradition was illegal, but the best speed for their legal steps is another three days. So: I want to go to the Council and get a new motion passed stating that the extradition is illegal and that the K . . . Crotchets must return him. Immediately and unharmed. I wanted them to state 'or face war' but the people I have talked to say I'll be opposed in setting any terms or conditions."

She thumped her fist. "If there are no terms and conditions, they'll weasel and squirm for years. But I'll try their way first. Otherwise—tonight, I'm hiring."

" 'Tis a huge ship," said Melene, doubtfully. They could see the silvery pumpkin-shape of it from here.

"And it was a vast scorpiary," said Ginny, determinedly.

Nym nodded. "I'm seeing if I can fit some armor to my golf cart. I've got a line on a used V-eight engine, instead of the electric one, and one of the techs at the university is helping me with a frame to support it. I'm with you. But the money would come in handy for accessories. Methinks chrome has a vile price."

She hugged him. "I've got a credit card, now. Let's go shopping, Nym."

"Well, you can buy me some more grog," said Fal. "Otherwise I might be too sober to go."

"A few pints o' full cream and some o' t'at strawberry yogurt might be nice," said O'Niel. "I'd never encountered it before, but I was liking it foine."

"O'Niel! Milk!" said Pistol in tones of horror. "If I were to govern, I would make it a felony to drink even small beer. Now, I'd not be going on this daft expedition, except that I've remembered Connolly still owes me several dozen hogsheads of whiskey. I'd fain get that, and I'll not see it, if he's dead."

"I'll get them for you, if you get him back for me, Pistol," she promised.

"Nay. 'Tis Connolly's debt. You can owe me another hogshead or two," said Pistol cheerfully. " 'Tis my intent to drown in them, but I'll have a ladder put so I can get out to leak afore I go."

"Mercenary bunch," said Bronstein. "Capitalists! Still . . . um . . . Ginny. You wouldn't care to become a major shareholder in something else would you? The Bats' Bank? We won't be bloodsuckers! 'Tis just a way of Vats winning free of Shareholders, by liberating them o' the iniquity of compound interest."

Ginny raised an eyebrow at Bronstein. "I'll talk it over with Chip. You know he's got rather strong feelings about Shareholders."

"Uh, we were thinking of a cooperative. You know . . ." Then Bronstein realized what Ginny had said. "Er. To be sure. We'd better get him loose, then. Not that you have to coerce us, Ginny. We're supporters anyway."

"I know," said Ginny, quietly. "But you don't know how much it means to me to have you with me."

The Council meeting gave Virginia her first sure insight into the fact that Talbot Cartup might be on the run, but he wasn't beaten yet.

"I'm afraid," said the Chairman, "that until probate is

granted we cannot allow you to exercise your vote in this Chamber. As a Shareholder in your own right, you may of course petition the Chair to address the house when the open session is declared."

Her new legal advisor got to his feet. "Mister Chairman. I'd like you to explain to the Council how, if this is the case, you accepted proxy forms allowing Talbot Cartup to exercise Ms. Shaw's vote?"

"Ah. We were not aware at the time that there were some legal challenges to the disposition of Aloysius and Gina Shaw's estates," said the Chairman smoothly. "And as Virginia Shaw is still under twenty-one, her votes cannot be exercised without her trustees' consent."

The attorney cocked his head and pursed his lips. "So, in other words," he said grimly, "not only were the proxies obtained under duress, but the Council failed to get the permission of those trustees, thus rendering this vote for extradition null and void. An illegal exercise."

"Er, yes," admitted the Chairman. "Done in ignorance of the facts, unfortunately. It is a rather an embarrassing situation. But we have on the agenda a motion to ask for Connolly's return."

" 'Embarrassing' is the wrong word, Chair," said her counsel, grimly. " 'Actionable' is the correct one. And 'ask' is the wrong word too. 'Demand' is the correct one there. But Ms. Shaw should at least be allowed to speak. To tell us how she would exercise her vote."

Eventually, in the open session they were able to raise the matter of the conspicuously absent head of the Security portfolio. Her new attorney spoke first.

"We've hired private investigators. We're running parallel investigations with the police for the cases in which the Special Branch are implicated. We've had nothing but complete cooperation so far from the Internal Affairs Department of the National Police."

He didn't add *amazingly enough*, nor did he explain that Van Klomp's paratroopers were launching what amounted to a systematic campaign of intimidation against the police—and were being eagerly assisted by hundreds of Vat soldiers who had been stationed in GBS City. That campaign had—so far—stopped short of homicide against the regular police. Eighteen such policemen had been admitted to the hospitals suffering from various traumas, true, but most of them were no worse than some bruises or bloody noses.

The army's campaign against Special Branch, on the other hand, showed no such limits. Special Branch had murdered military personnel and the army was responding in kind. Any Special Branch detectives who fell into the hands of Van Klomp's soldiers received multiple fractures at a bare minimum. Eleven Special Branch detectives had been "shot dead while resisting arrest." So far as anyone could tell, the paratroopers' definition of "resisting arrest" ranged somewhere between *he didn't get his hands up fast enough* to *he looked at me cross-eyed*.

"The corruption and level of misconduct on the part of Special Branch we've uncovered so far is utterly appalling. Among other things, we've discovered that almost all the staff on Shaw House premises are Special Branch operatives. They denied it, of course, but a number of them even had their ID badges with them. It seems they thought they were above prosecution."

A senior council member rose to reply. "While I

appreciate that you have had problems with a few renegade elements of the Special Branch, who were misled by Dr. Thom, it is simply impossible to take these steps. Why, if the Special Branch was disbanded—"

"*If* it was disbanded?" snorted Ginny angrily. "In case you've been living on another planet, Special Branch is being held responsible by the army for murdering army personnel. The question is not 'if' Special Branch will be disbanded. The question now is simply whether there will be enough of the thugs left alive to disband at all. The paratroopers are in a pure fury."

The senior council member gaped at her. "But . . . but we might all be murdered in our beds! These Vats are getting out of control!"

Ginny stood up. She'd been totally terrified of speaking in public at first. But, if she didn't, Chip would be doomed. As it was, all she could do was speak, until probate was passed and the shares became legally hers. Funny, how they'd been happy to accept her proxies, but not her actual vote. Well. She'd just have to use her voice as well as possible.

"This colony, fellow Shareholders, was set up to escape tyranny and repression. To build a new utopia, for all the people of Harmony and Reason. Not just some of us. The right to free association and public assembly is set out in our constitution. That right does *not* just apply to Shareholders. We have no need or right to have a repressive organization, with basically unlimited license and no controls, here on Harmony and Reason. If, and this is a very big 'if,' the Special Branch is not simply disbanded as it should be—as I intend to demand that it be—then the Council must move and move swiftly to take proper, accountable control over them."

The Chairman was at his most icy. He knew he had little to lose. He was a well-known Cartup family loyalist. When she wielded her votes, he was going to be out of that position. "We already have someone who is responsible for the Special Branch, that you want removed. Talbot Cartup is only implicated by your accusation, Ms. Shaw. A man is innocent until proven guilty."

She looked down her nose at him. "Not that Special Branch has ever respected that legal axiom. But leave that aside. Firstly, if you suspect a man with bloody hands of axe-murder, you take his axe away and put him in custody while he awaits trial. If he is given bail, there are strict conditions set to stop him committing another crime. The trial will establish his innocence or guilt—but you don't leave him on the loose with his axe, Mr. Chairman. And secondly, by giving all responsibility for the Security portfolio to one individual—without any checks and balances on that power—we, as the Council, must accept the blame for that individual's actions. We need to set up those checks and balances. We also need to at least suspend Talbot Cartup from that post, until the courts decide on his innocence or guilt."

"Those seem fair calls to me, Mr. Chairman," said one of the younger councilors. "Shall we put that to that to the vote?"

The two motions passed . . . by the slimmest of margins. But when it came to direct action against the Korozhet, unless they returned Charles Connolly, Ginny had less luck. The Council refused to do more than issue another amorphous, weak-worded request, without time limits or the intimation of threat.

•    •    •

Afterwards, still seething with fury, Ginny spoke to Bronstein.

"Look, Bronstein. I've changed my mind. You've got a deal right now. But I need your support. This is the deal I am offering . . ."

Virginia looked out onto a sea of faces. Meilin's VLO was far larger than the Special Branch had reported . . . or the public's curiosity about the guest speaker was larger than anyone had guessed. There was a whole stadium full of Vats. Many of them were women with young children, the men and unmarried women being off at the war-front. They hadn't cheered when she'd stood up to speak. But they hadn't booed her yet, either.

Virginia cleared her throat, and flung straight into it. "I'm here because one brave soldier made me realize that Vats are not second-class citizens." A ripple of surprise ran through the crowd.

"I am here to tell you I am going to stand by you and for you." They liked that, but didn't trust it. Well, she wouldn't have, either. But if the Special Branch could play dirty, so could she. "And here's my first—and unconditional—demand. *Abolish the Special Branch.* Destroy it, root and stem."

They cheered wildly, then. She had them.

"It is the system that has to change. You can change a system in two ways. Either you can smash it, in which case a lot of people are going to get killed. Our people as well as their people. Or you can take it over, and nobody has get hurt. Nobody but the Special Branch." She smiled at the crowd. "They've always said 'anyone can become a

Shareholder, just as soon as their debts are paid.' Only . . . the longer it takes the deeper in debt you get. Twenty-two percent per annum, compounded, interest on interest. The Shareholders get rich and you get poorer."

Now the crowd booed. She held up her hands for silence, and they were still.

"I intend to break this. Completely. No Shareholder child is expected to pay for his or her upbringing. But to do this legally, without bloodshed, I will need votes. And to get that I need Shareholders to support me. And we need to do it without fighting on the streets, except in self-defense, because if we fight they can repress us. As soon as I have legal control over my fortune—and I own one-third of all the shares in the colony—it is going to be given to the Bat Credit Cooperative."

A sea of tonsils stared at her from the open mouths on the stands.

"To explain, I am going to hand this microphone over to one of the organizers. Michaela Bronstein."

The stunned crowd watched a bat on the podium tap the microphone with a wing-claw.

"Indade, we're planning to break the stranglehold of Shareholders. We don't wish to make money out of this project. We bats have no interest in money. Ask those Vats who have fought beside us on the front lines. All we want in exchange is freedom for the uplifted creatures. We want you to vote for us to be recognized as sentients. As well as the rats." Bronstein shrugged her batwings. "I can talk and think. But any human can legally kill me as they would sheep. We will support you, but we want your support in return. We need to stand wing to shoulder against those who oppress us. We've fought as comrades in arms in the trenches. Will you stand with us here?"

The clapping was hesitant at first. Then, as Virginia held out her arm, and Bronstein flew onto it, the clapping became a wall of sound. Virginia raised her arms and hushed them.

" 'Tis a vile underarm bouquet you have," said Fal, with a snigger from his perch just inside the podium.

Somehow, that made the rest easy. "And when we have those votes, we'll move on three things. Firstly, we want to move to a 'one person one vote' system, instead of the votes being weighted by shares. Secondly, we want a debt cancellation for the rearing of clones. Thirdly, we want recognition of full sentient rights for the uplifted creatures."

She waited for hush again. "We are going to do all this because we can. Because when we start to organize there is no force that can stop us. We are going to free Chip Connolly. We are going to drive the Magh' and . . . their allies off Harmony and Reason. We are going to build a free society of equals. We are going to do this—"

She stood in the dramatic position she'd assumed, frozen.

Literally.

The bullet that interdicted the slowshield Liepsich had fitted saw to that.

# Chapter 45

♋

*Mostly in the nest area of the head of the Ratafia.*

After the sort of day she'd had, Ginny thought, nothing should faze her. The paratroopers had killed the would-be assassin. That was perhaps unfortunate, since it might have been better to capture him and make him talk. But . . .

The paratroopers were more concerned with completely, thoroughly and utterly terrifying the police—especially Special Branch. They'd practically blown the assassin into shreds.

Afterward, Ginny and Bronstein had calmed the crowd. That had taken some doing. If she had been killed, a riot would indeed have occurred—which, clearly, was what Special Branch had intended.

Surely no more could happen today?

This phone call had knocked her back in her tracks. Not even being shot at had done that. They hadn't yet been able to find Talbot Cartup. But he'd found her.

He didn't beat about the bush. "I've got access to Connolly, Shaw. If you want him that badly, I'll arrange it. But the price is going to be very high."

Virginia sat down, hard. "All right. I'll pay. What do you want and when?"

"Oh, not money, Shaw. I have plenty of that. A number of other things. The first one is for you to drop all the charges against me. The second one is to stop your rabble-rousing among the Vats—I don't need any extra trouble from them. The third one is that a motion will be put forward in the Shareholders Council to reaffirm the Council's confidence in Special Branch and with me as the holder of the colony's Security portfolio. You'll vote for that."

"I can't. Not until probate is granted on the will. Council objected."

"Hmm." There came a heavy chuckle. "I *have* made things rather difficult for myself, haven't I?"

There was a brief pause. Then: "Well, I gather you are a convincing speaker. You'll make another speech saying that in the light of new evidence you want me back heading the portfolio. You can arrange the checks and balances . . . I'll provide you with names of suitable candidates."

"Very well."

"And then I will want a number of shares as a deed of gift. I'll leave you with one percent of the stock. More generous than a dummy deserves, and I'll keep silent about your uplift status. That would cost you all of them."

"You can have anything you want," said Virginia. "But first I want proof that Chip is fine. When he is free and well, you will have all the things you want."

"You'll just have to trust me, Shaw. He's fine."

"Cartup, I have no reason to ever trust you. You provide me with proof. Let me talk to him, and I'll start doing things. Until then, Talbot Cartup, we're hunting you. And trust *me* on this: if Chip Connolly doesn't get back safely, I'm going to cut you in half, personally, with a chainsaw."

For five minutes after she put the phone down she sat there, shaking.

Melene came in to the room. She took one look at Ginny, and handed her a small bottle from her rat-pack, without a word said.

Ginny drank from it, glass clattering against her teeth. She stood up. "Take me to the Ratafia. Take me now. I need to start fighting and I need people who won't just talk."

"Is simple the problem, as I see it," said Darleth. "Openly attack the Korozhet, the rats cannot. At the idea, even you wince. Even if we could, the weaponry on the ship is fierce. Force fields they have. When in place these are, the Korozhet only can use the heavy laser. What they do is to raise these for very little time, and then launch missiles from the targeting spines on the top of the ship. There are two force fields—like airlock, not one like Magh'. Many thousands of the people, the Jampad, with heavy lasers we force our way in. And then the ship was exploded, with most of the slaves and attackers killed, when the Korozhet fled in their lifecraft."

"I don't think we can take them on frontally—even if the soft-cyber would let us. But we can raid . . ." said Meilin.

Virginia had been less than surprised to see the Vat organizer there. Too many ends in this tied together. Somebody, somewhere, was pulling strings, she'd slowly come to realize. She had no idea who it was, although it was clearly someone who—for whatever reasons of their own—seemed determined to shatter the existing political setup on Harmony and Reason.

At the moment, that was good enough. One day she'd track them down. Right now she had other priorities.

The Jampad nodded. Virginia had learned that meant *no*. "To gain entry means the double-front portal. No other ingress have the Korozhet ships. The last reports from our attackers before the ship was destroyed they said there was a force field inside the entry port. We believe, but not know, that the inner portal is a fire chamber that is triggered if anything other than Korozhet or an implanted slave goes into it."

Ginny frowned thoughtfully. "They must bring things in. I mean we've been paying them for the soft-cyber and slowshield units. We could hide in that."

The Jampad nodded furiously. "It is irradiated. Only through the double portal do live things pass. And, from what my people could establish, only implanted victims or Korozhet themselves."

Ginny sighed. "So what you are saying is that we can't attack them."

The Jampad shook his head. "We can. The Korozhet, my people attacked, and their client species very successfully when they come out of the ship. Their slaves they use as soldiers, and some, like the Nerba, are very good. But while inside the ship they are hidden, they can only be attacked with great force. I prepare for the guerrilla fight."

Ariel wrinkled her ratty snout. "Methinks I'll talk to Fitz, Ginny. Strategy and tactics are his thing. I'm going there later tonight and he goes to court tomorrow. He needs something else to think about."

"I'm sure he has enough on his mind," said Ginny, wanly.

Ariel patted her hand. "He has a very wide mind. It encompasses everything from chocolate to war."

Virginia sighed. "I'm still due to see Liepsich tonight. I'm not sure when he sleeps. I'll talk to him about the problem. But I still want to hire the Ratafia. I want Talbot Cartup found. He's trying to blackmail me with Chip's freedom. If I could trust him, I'd gladly give all he asks. But if I catch him before the police do . . . I'll get real cooperation. Even if I have to get Fat Fal to 'circumspect' him."

"Methinks the rats will be a bit worried," said Gobbo doubtfully, "with this move into formal employment."

Meilin laughed. "You'll have to shift from burglary to other enterprises soon anyway. The humans are going to catch on. And once they do that, it could just become easier to work than steal."

"Steal! Steal?" said Gobbo. "A fico for the phrase. Convey, the wise call it."

"Call it what you like, they'll stop your conveying too. But there is work you can do."

"I know," agreed Gobbo. "But work . . . it hath such an ill ring to it."

"Regard it as I do," said Pooh-Bah. "As something one of the other seven do while I am not around."

# Chapter 46

∞

*The office of Dr. Len Liepsich.*
*A place in which you might find anything*
*from a book on Egyptology to a treatise on the*
*molecular structure of fullerene complexes.*
*And last month's lunch, with green fur on it.*
*And an espresso machine, too well used.*

It was approaching midnight and the physicist was showing no signs of slowing down. The only real clue to just
how little sleep he'd had in the last few days was that his
eyes looked like roadmaps. And he was talking a little too
fast. Virginia suspected there was something other than the
ever-present cup of coffee affecting his mind. She ran the
information she'd gotten from Darleth about the Crotchet's
defense system over his hairy ears. You could tell he was
interested because he scarcely bothered to insult her.

"For a blonde, you provide rare insights. And not just of a view of vacuum by peering into your ears. We'd figured the missiles. We've got some plans in place to try to deal with that. We'd figured heavy laser fire. There is some stuff still mounted on the slowship. I've got somebody organizing those. What we hadn't got is this business of double force fields."

"I'm fascinated by what you've figured out," she said dryly. Liepsich grinned. She continued. "What I am interested in, is what do we need to do to get in there?"

He scratched his stubbly chin. "You know, there is always more than one way to skin a cat, especially if you know a lot about cats. Now, I figure that there are two ways—at least—that we can get at the ship. Their fields must be down for missile launch, as you said. We can hit them just then. It's a small window, but a window. That's the best solution a military man will evolve."

She'd learned to read Liepsich's elliptical utterances by now. "So what would a thinking man do?"

He grinned again. "Why don't you sign up for physics? You have too good a brain for politics. All that needs is a big mouth and the ability to lie with a straight face. You've got the mouth for it, but I'm not sure how well you lie."

Ginny was not distracted. "Answer my question, Dr. Liepsich. I might even sign up for a physics degree. Later. If you can prove to me that you're not too dim to teach it."

He gave her a thumbs-up. "Twin thrusts. The soft-cybers. The Jampad made it pretty clear that there are slaves inside that ship. The soft-cyber bias stops them rebelling. If you removed that bias, the ship would have an enemy within."

"Except that you can't do that," she said.

He raised his eyebrows. "Says who?"

She hauled him out of the seat he was flopped into. "How? Do it! Do it now." She hated and feared the fact that her mind was not entirely her own. This was indeed a holy grail.

He shrugged, still in her grasp. "We're getting there. We've been working on the source code. The Korozhet obviously hadn't counted on the fact that even if the colony is mostly back in human nineteenth-century technology, not all of the slowship's equipment is. We've been writing a section of what would be called—in old terms—a computer virus, to reprogram the soft-cyber chips. We're getting closer. It's no small job."

"Do it faster."

He looked thoughtfully at her. "Do you realize that if we get it wrong, we scramble the soft-cyber system? Destroy its memory. We can do that right now. To knock out the basic bias and still leave it intact is a lot harder. Now, can I sit down again?"

Virginia let go. She'd forgotten that she was holding him. "That would destroy my memories, right?"

"You? Maybe," he admitted. "Most of them, probably. The chip would be intact, just the programming screwed. A rat would go back to being a rat, but we could reprogram its soft-cyber."

"Except . . . they . . . *we* would lose our memories."

Liepsich nodded. "Yep. But you'd still be alive and you wouldn't be enslaved."

Virginia blinked. Shook her head. "I can't. I can't part with those memories. They . . . they're too precious. Maybe the others . . . I'll ask."

"Except that we can't deal with it on a one-on-one basis. We just don't have the time to do so, or even the equipment."

"But how else do you do it?"

Liepsich grinned nastily. "Use some of that plastic inside your blonde head, Shaw. The Korozhet need some way of relaying orders to all of you at once, obviously."

She looked warily at him. "What?"

"How blonde," he said. "Hadn't you worked out that you're carrying a radio-receiver in your head? It probably constantly says 'breathe in, breathe out,' in your case."

"It's too bad you weren't born a rat, Liepsich. You would have had a little more skill with insults. Although you'd probably still be considered the rats' village idiot. Can't you jam radio signals? And can't we just use radio to affect the prisoners inside their ship? And does this mean that the revolt we tried to foment among the rats and bats is a lost cause? Or will they be able to resist?"

Liepsich smiled. "You really are too able for politics. We've identified the frequencies now, and got jammers set up, we hope. Inevitably the Korozhet will target the jamming devices, but we've got as much redundancy set up as we can. The radio call uses one of the master command phrases—what they used on you to make you obey Dr. Thom. I doubt if mere semantics could help the rats and bats dodge that. So, yes. The revolt that the rats and bats have tried to set up won't work. And that pumpkin-shaped Korozhet ship, unfortunately for my attempts to examine it, is opaque to just about every form of e-m radiation, including radio. It might work if you could get transmitters inside."

"And if your jamming fails?" asked Virginia. "And our

resistance fails? What happens to us?"

Liepsich took a deep breath. "Well. Either we let you go and become the utterly loyal slave-warriors of the Korozhet. Or, if that starts to get close to the breaking point, we'll have to lose Harmony and Reason's best defense against the Magh'."

Virginia knew exactly what he meant. She closed her eyes, briefly. "You said there was another thrust."

"Ah. Just an idea," said the scientist.

"Out with it, Doctor Liepsich! Or I'll get my rats to cut your tongue out. Or better, Super-Glue your lips together so you can't insult anyone."

"You play rough, Shaw. How blonde." He smiled. "Okay. Slowshields explode if they impact a force field. We think that if you managed to make a circle of them you could, theoretically, have a hole in the field. Briefly. If you had enough slowshields you could in theory over-load the entire field. But—and I emphasize the 'but'—the energy discharge would be in the multimegaton level. It would fry things for several miles around and possibly destroy the ship. We just don't know."

# Chapter 47

☙

*Military court Complex, Court B,*
*Judge Silberstohn presiding.*

"Do you know that there are over fifty thousand people on the street out there?" said Lieutenant Capra to his senior counsel, as they did their last pre-trial preparation.

"They're certainly being noisy enough," said Lieutenant Colonel Ogata dourly. "And I assure you, Lieutenant, that's nothing to what it will be like if we lose this case."

"We're not going to lose."

Ogata turned a frosty eye on him. "Nothing is that certain, Capra. If we had a judge like McCairn, maybe. But Judge Silberstohn . . . He doesn't have a sense of humor. Remember that."

"And one of our star witnesses is in Korozhet custody.

I'm not sure using those military animals is a good idea, Colonel. Take my advice, and keep questions to a minimum. You're better off if you stick to Virginia Shaw's testimony. She's a good witness, and she's still got shock value."

"I plan to," said Ogata, "but always remember: that's a military panel. They trust the military and instinctively . . . should I say 'look down' on nonmilitary persons. It's a subconscious attitude in some cases, but it is real. The rats and bats are Military Animals."

"That's something that's sure to be challenged in court soon, sir. They're not 'animals,' or at least not 'dumb animals.' And they don't see the world quite as we do. They're amoral about some things and yet honorable about others."

"Different ethos and mores. And this seems more appropriate to realms of philosophy than last minute pre-trial preparations. It's not relevant," said Ogata, sternly.

"If that's what you think, sir," said Mike Capra, "wait 'til Doc gets up to testify. He can confuse a certified genius. That's why I kept him out of the last trial."

Ogata frowned. "In the brief meeting I had with the rat he seemed relatively coherent, if a bit long-winded."

"Just don't even give him an opportunity to talk philosophy," warned Mike. "And he takes the subject to a wider reach than I would have thought possible."

Ogata looked a little startled. "I suppose it does encompass the spectrum of human thought," he said. "Now, let's get back to the case in question."

An hour later they went into the packed courtroom. The crowd outside was even larger than it had been earlier. With her presentation, Major Tana Gainor demonstrated that she actually had no need to resort to foul means to win her cases. She obviously just preferred certainty to litigation.

"Outside, and here in this courtroom, there are those who clamor for us to follow the popular will, to abandon the law and oblige the crowds. This," she said to the judge and panel, "is not what we stand for. We are not going to pander to the mob."

Mike could tell by the judge's expression that she'd hit exactly the right chord. Well, Tana always did her homework carefully. She always did her dirty work carefully, too. Still there were some surprises awaiting Her Nastyship.

She pointed to Fitz. "We have a man on trial here, a man who is very good at manipulating the masses for his own evil ends. Conrad Fitzhugh has abused the trust that the army and the people of Harmony and Reason have placed in their officers. We will display to you evidence, hard evidence, that can but lead you to one conclusion: This man is a spy, and a traitor who abused his rank to pursue his own goals, the goals of self-enrichment, at the expense of the lives of the men and women of our great armed forces."

She went on in this vein, in a very convincing, indeed, heartfelt style for some time. She didn't actually say much, but that was plainly secondary to her purposes.

Brigadier Charlesworth was an impressive witness. He was a heavily decorated divisional commander. He had been assaulted, with a deadly weapon, in front of equally impressive witnesses.

Ogata stood up to cross-examine. "Please show us the scars, Brigadier."

"What?"

"The scars of this assault with a deadly weapon," said Ogata.

"Objection!"

"Overruled. Continue."

"Did you in fact sustain any flesh wound from this assault?" asked Ogata. "If so, is there any reason that you cannot show the scars to the court? Is it perhaps actually on your buttocks?"

"Objection!"

"Sustained. Will the defense refrain from insulting the witness. He is a distinguished officer."

Ogata turned to the judge. "Your honor, I can only imagine one other place that the witness could be injured that he would be reluctant to show us the scar," he said, without even a hint of a smile. "Therefore it seemed a polite alternative to the other possible question. Less embarrassing for the witness. I would not ask a witness to show his buttocks or any other part of his body that he or she considered private to the court. But in the interests of justice the scars from the wound should be displayed."

The judge nodded. "I take your point, Lieutenant Colonel Ogata. Brigadier. Would you mind?"

"There isn't a scar," said Charlesworth grumpily.

By the look on Tana's face she'd have given him one. "Your Honor," she said, "I am afraid that proves nothing. Major Fitzhugh thrust a deadly weapon into the witness' stomach, with the intent to do grievous bodily harm, if not to kill the brigadier."

"I see," said Ogata. "A thrice-decorated combat veteran, a martial arts expert, would of course have no idea how hard to strike to inflict bodily harm. Is that what you're suggesting? That's ridiculous, Major."

"Are you going to continue your cross-examination of the witness?" asked the judge dryly.

Ogata nodded. "Yes, Your Honor. Tell me, Brigadier, about the preparations for this plan for the attack on Sector Delta 355."

"That's classified material," said Charlesworth. "I cannot divulge war plans."

"Even details of long-completed plans—which, according to you, were entirely disrupted because of Fitzhugh's actions?"

Brigadier Charlesworth nodded. "If it hadn't been for Fitzhugh, we'd have gone considerably further in our advance. He aided the enemy with his actions."

"He did, did he? Well, Brigadier, I put it to you thus. The reason you cannot reveal details is not because these are classified documents. It's because there was no plan. There is no evidence of any preparation at all at Brigade headquarters."

"Objection. This is conjecture."

"On the contrary," said Ogata, icily. "I have an impressive list of some one hundred witnesses who will testify that Brigade headquarters was in fact asleep, bar the guards."

"The planned assault wasn't due for another two days, man!" bellowed Charlesworth.

"I see. Despite the fact that the force field went down at 06h29 of that day, a crucial and deciding factor in this campaign. Are you claiming that Fitzhugh engineered this plan going into effect two days early?"

"Fitzhugh engineered that the force field should go down then. It would have been a much more general collapse, but the weapon was triggered too early. And I can't tell you more because the information is classified."

"How convenient, Brigadier," said Ogata. "It may interest you to know that we have expert testimony on force fields, and the possibility of 'bringing them down' from the outside. We have considerable evidence that the force field was collapsed from within, and that far from interfering with your plans, all that Major Fitzhugh did was to make the Fifth Infantry Corps take action on a target of opportunity, which you'd been ignoring."

"That's nonsense," blustered Charlesworth. "And no one knows more about Magh' equipment than the military. There was certainly no 'target of opportunity.' We respond to those."

"I would like the panel to note that Brigadier Charlesworth has stated under oath that a target of opportunity is responded to. I'll be calling Colonel Abramovitz, of Eastmoreland 2nd Conscript Regiment, and your Communications officer, Lieutenant Mussy, to the stand to prove that this is not in fact the case. Now, Brigadier, I would like to ask you about the operational capability of your command."

"Objection. This has nothing to do with the case," snapped Tana.

Ogata fixed her with his icy stare. She did not wilt, although any lesser mortal might have. "I thought the charge against Major Fitzhugh claimed that he had damaged the military operational capacity of the 4th Division. It therefore seems a sensible question, Your Honor. Entered as evidence we have a statistical analysis of the brigadier's command effectiveness: measures of territory lost, human, and materiel losses. I thought in the interests of legal economy, as the brigadier features as the least successful divisional commander on the front, he could clarify certain matters."

By the time that Ogata had finished with Brigadier Charlesworth his credibility as a witness, and his ability as an officer, were in severe need of reinforcements. But Ogata made sure that when they moved to help, they too became targets. "So, Lieutenant Colonel Nygen. You did not actually go past the old second line of trench defense at Sector Delta 355?"

"I'm a senior officer," answered Nygen. "We don't go into front-line positions."

Ogata looked askance at him. "According to the information available, the new front was approximately thirty-six miles from you. Yet you've testified that Major Fitzhugh 'was endangering the troops' by 'attempting to lead them to their destruction.' You must have remarkable eyesight, Lieutenant Colonel."

"Naturally, I had reports from officers in the field. This is the way the military works, sir, which you rear echelon chaps may not understand. A commander can't be everywhere and see everything. We learn to rely on the chain of command."

"Thank you for informing us, Lieutenant Colonel," said Ogata. "So, please tell me which of your officers told you Fitzhugh was attempting to lead your troops to destruction, and endangering their lives?"

"Lieutenant Colonel Burkoff," replied Nygen.

Ogata raised his eyebrows. "Who just happens to be the only officer who died during this attack. I have spoken to every other officer who participated in this attack. I have a list of witnesses here who are prepared to state that they did not inform you of anything of the kind. I also have Lieutenant Colonel Burkoff's wireless operator as a witness, who will confirm that the lieutenant colonel never contacted you."

"Objection, Your Honor," said Tana. "This is not the issue here. The issue is that risking three thousand men outside of the military chain of command can be considered as an attempt to lead them to their destruction. Anyway, in whom do we trust? Some conscript Vat radio-operator or a well-respected officer?"

The judge shook his head. "We trust in the law, and in dispassionate consideration of the evidence, Trial Counsel. Continue, Lieutenant Colonel Ogata."

"Yes, sir. Lieutenant Colonel Nygen, are you aware that the casualties sustained in the attack, and subsequent capture of Delta 355, are the lowest day-by-day for an entire sector, for the entire course of the war?"

Nygen snorted. "The fact that Major Fitzhugh was lucky has no bearing on the matter."

"Indeed," Ogata agreed with an inclination of his head. "It would not have. But I am going to attempt to prove that the major was *not* lucky. He was effective. He did not betray the soldiers of the Army of Harmony and Reason to any enemy. He merely did what you were supposed to do. Pursue war against the Magh' in the most effective manner possible."

"Objection."

Fitz listened to the stream of objections, testimony and questions. Well, at least this was no kangaroo court. Ogata was also making no attempt to deny the "crimes" that Fitz had committed. Instead he was using Fitz's deeds to expose the simple lack of competence of the officers testifying. Whether they convicted him or not, Fitz knew that he'd finally opened up the army's General Staff like a tin can. And Ogata was taking care to expose the worms in that can to public scrutiny. Fitz wondered just how General Cartup-Kreutzler was enjoying this public demolition.

Strangely enough, his concentration was not entirely on the trial. It was rather on the information that Ariel had brought him in the small hours of the morning. Details of what she called "the Crotchets'" military methods. There had to be ways of defeating those. And, if he read things aright, it was an issue that was going to be current pretty damn soon. If he got out of here, instead of on his way back to death row, that was going to be the next problem that was going to loom large.

When the first of the prosecution's spying charge witnesses got up to testify, Fitz expected things to go backwards. After all, it was as neat a "stitching" as he had ever come across. It was his word against the counterintelligence security agent, and the agent had photographic evidence that would have convinced Fitz had he been one of the panel. Officer Paype gave his evidence with a straight face and great professionalism. He detailed convincingly how Major Conrad Fitzhugh had passed on detailed battle plans and taken large sums of money.

Ogata stood up to cross-examine. "Officer Paype. As a counterintelligence officer of Special Branch, would you describe yourself as a skilled professional?"

"I think that would be a fair description, sir," said the Special Branch operative.

"And this . . . sting operation? Is it something of which you have prior experience?"

"My record speaks for itself, sir. This is fourth one I've testified in, with the court reaching guilty verdicts in all cases. The Special Branch is the elite. We know exactly what we're doing."

"And you would describe everything, including your record keeping, as 'professional'?" asked Ogata.

The witness nodded. "As far as possible, sir. We are engaged in covert activities, so some of our records are restricted. We also can't compromise ongoing surveillance and operatives in place."

"You've been one of these 'operatives in place'?"

"Yes, sir," said Paype. "That's how I entrapped Major Fitzhugh."

"In other words you're skilled at deception?"

"Objection! The defense is attempting to lead the witness." Tana could see where this was going.

Ogata was all innocence. "Your Honor, I am simply attempting to clearly establish the skills of the witness. I think it a fair question. We have established he has successfully deceived a number of people in the past. That means he must be a very skilled liar. I don't see any other possible conclusion. I think we have established that he could possibly have lied his way into Major Fitzhugh's confidence. Is this not a fair conclusion?"

The judge thought about it. Nodded. "It would seem that his profession must require a certain, shall we say, 'flexibility' with the truth. Continue, Lieutenant Colonel Ogata."

"I have no need to, on that issue, Your Honor. I just wished to establish that the prosecution's witness is a professional liar."

"Objection!"

The judge looked thoughtful again.

"May I put it another way, which perhaps my colleague will not object to," said Ogata, calmly. "The witness in question might have the very highest standards of loyalty to the State, but in order to do his job professionally, has to be a very good liar."

The judge nodded. Ogata's sheer imperturbability had that sort of effect.

Ogata turned back to Paype. "So tell us, Officer. How did you manage to be turning over a hundred thousand dollars to Major Fitzhugh, and receiving war plans, on the night for which you claimed Travel and Expenses for operations in Port Durnford? We have logged the pay records as evidence." There was no need to point out that the rats had brought out the Special Branch pay records.

"That's where the exchange took place," said Paype easily. "It proves rather than disproves my point."

Ogata smiled for the first time in the entire case. "Being glib is an advantage to a liar. Sometimes it can trip you up. Are you sure this was the case?"

The smile plainly put the wind up the witness. "I can't reveal operational details," he said, hastily.

"How convenient," said Ogata, still smiling. "And what would you say if I told you that at the time you claim this exchange was happening, Major Fitzhugh was with General Cartup-Kreutzler at Divisional headquarters in Stanford?"

"I said that I can't reveal exact details," said the agent. "But let's say that I wasn't actually in Port Durnford. I was entitled to T&E, but we have to be careful. We can't have some clerk in the pay-office giving away our place of operations."

"I see. So we may assume you were in some place outside town? Possibly close to Stanford on the North Eastern Front?" asked Ogata in a mild tone.

"You wouldn't be far wrong," smirked Paype.

Ogata shook his head regretfully. "It is a great pity, for you, that I am not going to say that Major Fitzhugh was with General Cartup-Kreutzler visiting Divisional Headquarters in Stanford. If I did say that I would be as much of a liar as you are."

After this, using convenient background information which the rats had brought in, Ogata soon had the confident Special Branch man falling nervously over his own feet.

"He'll make the man necrotic yet," said Ariel quietly, from where she'd somehow managed to slip into the wainscoting above him.

"You mean neurotic."

"No, that's what Falstaff did to Visse's secretary."

And thus passed the first day.

Things went rather awry on the next day, when the defense called Doc to the stand to testify that they had created a target of opportunity. Doc and the judge had differing opinions.

"To do so, rat, was against the law!" snapped the judge.

"Judges," explained Doc kindly, "appear to think that the law is an immutable divinity, and that you are the voice of that divinity, to be obeyed. Unfortunately, Judge, history has proved that this is not the case."

"I do not need to be instructed on the subject of law, rodent," said the judge, irritably. "The law is the foundation of our society and must be preserved. Now continue your testimony before I find you in contempt."

Doc, caught up in the throes of a debate, cheerfully pressed on despite the threat. "Actually, metaphorically speaking, law is more like the mortar. It comes after, and to reinforce civilization, not before. And when the people, who are the bricks of our society, need to be reorganized, it's the old mortar that has to go. Justice, however, usually prevails eventually, because justice is actually a flexible and changing concept that is based on current mores, and exists in the eyes of most of the beholders. And I am not a rodent." He bared his sharp teeth. "As ought to be obvious, even to a judge."

Needless to say, this went down like a ton of building rubble into the judge's swimming pool.

He didn't like finding out that a military animal could not be held in contempt, either, as it was not actually a "person," legally speaking—but then, that's how the judge was trying to speak.

# Chapter 48

❧

*Inside the rock beneath the feet of the people.*

"You need to see this, Liepsich," said Lynne Stark. "The HAR *Times* and HBC were things we never counted on. We never made any plans for them. But they've obviously responded to the fact that Cartup is out of the equation and that they need market share. They've jumped onto the anti-Korozhet bandwagon. I'm faxing the front page of the HAR *Times* through to you. It's also on HBC's *Today* broadcast. You'll need to move even faster."

When the fax arrived, Liepsich started swearing. "Damn those idiots to hell. Why the hell couldn't they have waited another twenty-fours?"

❖       ❖       ❖

## KOROZHET MAY HAVE BEEN
## SUPPLYING BOTH SIDES!

*Spectrographic examinations of metal items taken from the captured Magh' scorpiary and the metal parts of slowshields (shown below) are identical. Metallurgist Dr. Jason Fiennes confirms that this is "simply too improbable."*

"The one time in his life Fiennes has to be dead right," muttered Liepsich. "And it had to be today." He picked up the phone. Then put it down again, and left as fast as his falling-down jeans would allow.

HARIT was almost an outgrowth of the old slowship. The ship's hull-metal was still the toughest human-made substance on the planet. The door he entered would have passed for a broom cupboard easily. Indeed, inside were several buckets and a mop.

He used the password to activate the secret door.

"Open Sez Me."

The elevator dropped him into a part of Harmony and Reason that the colony had forgotten. When the ship arrived they'd been justifiably cautious about their Earth-ecology seeded planet. First access had been into the isolation test-chambers below the ship, from whence the portals had dealt with the remote sample vehicles, and later the suited scouts. The test chambers had been built tough. Tough enough to withstand anything the colonists could—or couldn't—think of. Within a month, the initial labs below the ship had been abandoned. Hull-metal and multiple layers of reenforced concrete-plaz lay above. Rock and a

Faraday-cage surrounded it. Liepsich still had to marvel at the idea of having the kind of technology that could build something like this . . . and then abandon it. Harmony and Reason had been close to the Eden that the eco-seeders had promised. There were no inimical land-lifeforms, not even microscopic ones. There was no need for this place, and after that long confined journey onboard the slowship, no desire for anyone to stay here.

The place wasn't abandoned now. When Sanjay Devi had shown it to him, back when the Korozhet had first arrived, only a few key technicians and scientists had come down here. At that stage, the Aladdin cave's entry had been undisguised. They'd started work on hiding it almost immediately. The ship still had treasures—too few to make a difference in the war—but too precious, as Sanjay had said, to give to those idiots to waste. It was down here that the soft-cybers and the slowshields had been researched. It was down here that the first scientists had died of the booby traps. Liepsich still had a piece of the shrapnel in his thigh.

In the last three weeks, a lot of hardware from the captured scorpiary had found its way down here. So had a great deal of the command and control equipment from the ship above. So had a lot of the crew. The crew were the odd-fish in the colony. Granted a single share for their needed technical skills, many of them had stayed with the essential technical tasks that the colony needed them for, in those early years. Some had gone off to try business, or farming. But many had stayed. They were well rewarded and reasonably comfortable—and doing jobs that could only be done with the old Earth-made equipment on the ship.

In the last three weeks they'd mostly been moved down here. It was crowded and busy. It was down here that the "virus" program was being created. In the meantime it was one of the places that no implanted person or animal could be allowed to know existed.

One of the techs saluted him as he got out of the lift. It was getting too damned military down here for his taste.

"Henry." He held up the piece of paper. "You'd better move us to condition orange. The Korozhet are not going to like this. They're not going to like it at all. If they lie their way out we've got some time. If there is no denial within the next couple of hours we've got problems, I reckon."

"Condition orange declared two minutes back," said Henry M'Batha. "We picked it up too."

As Liepsich walked over to the section that held the virus programmers, to see how they were getting on, he sighed. He got the feeling that humanity was riding around in a huge black fog-cloud, that was now turning into a thundercloud . . . with a lot of thunderheads rolling around loose in it. It was quite a question as to whom they would hit. And there was not a lot he could do about it.

Talbot Cartup looked absolutely nothing like his normal self.

Sanjay Devi found that very satisfying.

"Are you sure that these calls can't be traced?" he demanded.

"Trust me, Talbot. I was in charge of setting up the first telephone exchange here. Neither your call to Virginia Shaw nor to your various henchmen can be traced, Macbeth."

"Macbeth?" He looked puzzled. "Oh. The play."

"The Scottish play. Life often resembles it," said Sanjay, going back to her paper-laden desk. "You'll be safe enough here . . . till Birnam Wood to Dunsinane doth come," she said wryly.

"Well, I wish you'd give as much attention to my problems as that rubbish. I've sent a request to my contact on the Korozhet ship, but I haven't got a reply yet."

"Patience. You might try calling them up on that communicator of theirs again. You've been Thane of Glamis as the master of the colony Security. When Shaw died . . . you became Cawdor. Now, offer them enough, and they will make you King."

"You know, sometimes I think you're entirely mad! We don't have a king," he said irritably. Nonetheless, he went to fetch his Korozhet-built communicator.

She looked at him from under lowered brows. "Double, double, toil and trouble." It was a trifle awkward him using a Korozhet instrument, but the room pickups would doubtless still get it. Liepsich's computer enhancement tools back at the ship would take all the feeds and make it an audible recording.

A few minutes later he bustled over, looking far more cheerful. "Maybe you're right. Maybe I should aim for a monarchy. It's a novel idea. It would sort out a few problems."

"So what have you arranged, Talbot?" Sanjay thought that no statement of hers deserved an award for dramatic integrity more. She could only bottle down her disgust by pretending it was a stage performance.

"Tirittit had to take it to their high-spines," said Talbot. "But what they really wanted from Connolly was to

Eric Flint & Dave Freer

interrogate him properly. So, as soon as they've done that, as long as I deal with this anti-Korozhet sentiment, hard, they'll release him. I'll be getting audio-recordings from them tomorrow, reassuring Shaw. I had to give them certain guarantees, something of a more formal alliance and certain . . . what they call 'levies' of Vats, but they've promised to back me up, militarily if need be. The last thing I thought I'd do was come out of this mess stronger. But I've got the votes of—"

He proceeded to list Shareholders that Sanjay had tried for years to establish the names of. "—in my pocket. I've still got control over the Special Branch. We set up a redundancy for this sort of contingency. Special Operations Director Perros is still in place. I'd better contact the others and then Shaw. Damned good thing Perros' men failed to take her out at that Vat meeting. You can be sure I'll reward you well for this, Sanjay."

She raised her eyebrows. "All the perfumes of Arabia will not sweeten it. Call them."

"You could confuse a saint. I meant a portfolio on the new Council. Not perfume," said Cartup.

She stood up. "I don't want to confuse saints. Make your calls, Talbot. I'll use my mobile. I make you one prophecy. You can be sure that no man of woman born will kill you."

"More of your gibberish. I suppose I'm safe then." He picked up the 'phone and began dialing.

Sanjay walked out onto her balcony and drew the glass door closed behind her. She looked out across the city. Hard to believe it had been nothing but scrub once. Now the suburbs and trees looked like they'd always been there. The remains of the great slowship that had brought them here still dominated the skyline, with the huge pumpkin-shape of the Korozhet ship a close second.

She drew a deep breath, ignoring the stabbing pains in her chest, and dialed. She was not in the least surprised that the answerer enquired "And who doth call?" in a haughty tone. She'd always had a soft spot for Pooh-Bah. He'd always struck her as the perfect example of successful socialism in one body.

The little golf cart swayed dangerously around corners. The candy-striped vehicle's steering was being pushed to its limits and microns beyond. Virginia didn't even seem perturbed. "How good is this information?"

"As good as itself," said Gobbo, clinging onto the rail. "And the tears of it are wet."

Virginia had no time right now for Shakespearian sophistry. "How do you know we can trust her?"

"Meilin said she was one of the founders of the VLO. She gave some passwords that no one else would know."

"It just seems insane. Why should he go to someone like that to hide?" asked Virginia, suspiciously.

"And thereby hangs a tail," said Melene. "Methinks she hath cozened a cozening rogue."

"She said something about giving him enough rope. Perhaps she thought he would go into rope-selling, and when he did not, she decided to turn him in."

Pooh-Bah found this quite logical. "Marry, 'tis passing strange to a person like myself, of haughty and exclusive pre-adamite descent, to engage in vulgar trade. But I believe that the Master of the Buckhounds and the Groom of the Back Stairs have invested heavily in a scheme to make inflatable rattesses."

Before there could be any more startling commercial revelations, they arrived at Sanjay Devi's home on the hill that overlooked the town. The rats poured off the golf cart and began moving in. Virginia followed them, and the paratroopers following the golf cart, followed her.

*Dunsinane*

"No answer from Shaw," said Talbot Cartup, pacing.

"She is coming here," said Sanjay, tranquilly.

"What!"

Sanjay looked askance at him. "You do seem to have trouble understanding things, Cartup. Perhaps it is because you're so stupid. But then, I did choose you for your stupidity. And your vanity."

"What?" Talbot stared at her.

She'd never insulted him before. She relished it. And she was playing the role of her lifetime. "I've betrayed you to her," she explained.

Talbot gaped at her. "But . . ."

"It was necessary," said Sanjay. "I selected you as the vilest of weeds when I discovered Shaw was dead. You were a useful weed. You choked all the others out, and brought out and fed the resentment of the Vats with your stupid brutality. Some of the other weeds might have allowed more freedom. But you made sure, for me, that the only way out for them was by destroying the HAR Shareholders' monopoly on power. You did more for the VLO than I could."

"What? How could you?"

"Is that all you can ever say, Cartup? 'What?' " She

cackled. "Cauldron bubble . . . Like the witches did to Macbeth . . . I didn't make you fall, Talbot Cartup. I simply gave you the opportunities to choose your own fate. To imagine that your petty vendettas against Fitzhugh or this Vat-boy Connolly could succeed. To not see my plans with two new intelligences . . . What you have done is to erode the very ground under your feet. You've done what I could not, Talbot Cartup. Your greed has poisoned this sick system enough to bring it down. Now your crimes can take you down with it."

"You bitch," he said, incredulously, "you're neck deep in all the things I've done. You advised me! You hid me. You're an accomplice and I'll take you down with me."

She shrugged. "If I'd kept my hands out of your affairs . . . you'd have crawled off and hidden in legal evasions and poisoned this society for years. I had to make sure you were eliminated. You've known all along that a second Korozhet ship landed with the Magh'. You and Aloysius Shaw both knew from the initial satellite data."

"Shaw was an idiot. He didn't believe it could be true. He said that it would cause unrest to start such rumors."

"I had wondered about that. He was a pompous fool, but not as much of a villain as you. And, in a way, this society needed a true villain, or it would have limped on for generations, oppressing more and more people. You were perfect for my purposes in that way, Cartup. You've colluded with the Korozhet and become wealthy and powerful. But we could never catch you. The evidence was hidden, and you had a powerful team of hiders backing you. So: when this blew up, I gave you houseroom. Recordings of all your conversations have gone out from here to the three people I trust: John Needford, Len

Liepsich, and Lynne Stark. You've been entrapped redhanded. A sting, you might say."

"You bitch." He snatched at his car keys. "You won't get away with this."

She shook her head. "The doors on this house are very secure, Cartup. Old ship doors. At the moment they're set to only be openable from the outside. You haven't got a hope."

He snarled, and dropped the keys for a knife lying on the table. She'd been sharpening it earlier. "I've got you, Devi. That'll do."

She smiled tranquilly. "But not for long, Cartup. I'm dying of cancer. It's quite incurable. I wanted to see Harmony and Reason free of your sort before I went. I wanted to see our dream drawn back from the nightmare that people like you and Aloysius Shaw were prepared to delve into, for the sake of your own power and greed. Go ahead and kill me if you dare. Or are you afraid?"

Outside, vehicles screeched to a halt. "Not of you, you old witch!"

As he stabbed, she whispered: "I hear the wailing of the women, for the Queen is dead."

The words were finished with a bloody froth on her lips. But, like everything in her life that she'd set out to do, Sanjay Devi had succeeded in using the line that had prepared her for that moment.

Talbot Cartup was still standing above Sanjay Devi with a bloody knife in his hand, when rats and bats burst into the room, with Virginia and half a dozen paratroopers behind her. There was a glass door and a balcony behind him.

And, in the end, Sanjay Devi had chosen the right line again. It *wasn't* any man of woman born that killed him. Tripping over a rat, as a bat flew at his face, and falling off the balcony to the rocks below did it.

Two paratroopers were trying to give Sanjay first aid. Another one was calling for an ambulance. She waved the one who was trying to staunch the blood away. "I'm dying, anyway. I want to speak to her."

She beckoned Ginny closer. "I knew he might weasel out of anything but red-handed murder, my dear. I'm dying. I give my children into your care, Virginia Shaw. Take good care of them or my ghost will haunt you. Be sure of it."

"Your children? Who?" Sanjay Devi was a well known Shareholder. She'd never married, and if she'd ever had children they'd been kept a complete secret.

"The uplifted ones, first—the rats and bats I created in my witch's vats. I was the one who persuaded your father to put an implant into you, my dear. Because I saw you as their best chance. My other children are the Vats. I bred them up. I have millions of children, and I wanted a future for them. Not slavery. Either from our culture or . . . the Crotchets. You take over now. I've worked in secret. The time for that is over. Raise the revolution."

The ambulance arrived, but Virginia Shaw had a feeling the medics were too late.

All she could do was nod.


It took the police some time to recover Talbot Cartup's body from the dangerous and slippery rocks below the balcony. The bats had been able to tell them that he was indeed dead and not worth risking life and limb for.

Since then the bats had been locked in deep discussion, while the rats had cheerfully looted some booze.

"We have decided, Virginia. You have here as many rats as are likely to fight, but we need more bats for any raid on such a target. So we need to send Eamon south to raise the standard with our organizations."

"And I might have guessed that both the Red Wing and the Battacus League would steal our password," grumbled Eamon irritably. "We used 'Easter Uprising' first."

"First or last. We need them all," said Bronstein. "And I'd like to go myself, but you're a stronger flier and will not be turned to drink and forget your mission like this wastrel." She pointed a wing at O'Niel, who had just accepted a stoup of Sanjay's single malt from Doc.

"Just because I am sometimes taken with drink, doesn't mean I can't think, Bronstein," said O'Niel. "Not that Eamon is not a better flier, even if Shamus Plekhanov is a better bat with explosives."

"Hmph," said Eamon. "Well, I'd better be going. 'Tis a long fly."

One of the paratroopers had been listening in. "Where to?"

"To divisional headquarters, Sector 3-350," answered Eamon.

"You should take one of the transport planes," said the paratrooper with a wry smile. "You could be there in two hours."

Eamon nodded thoughtfully. "I'll be doing that."

He flapped upward. "I'll return with a mighty bat brigade."

"Is he serious?" asked the paratrooper.

"He's always serious," said O'Niel. "Sensible, no. The airfield is the other way, to be sure. I'd better get after him and tell him."

Fortunately, for short-sprint-flights, O'Niel was quite capable, for a plump bat.

# Chapter 49

॰૭

*In the green and naphthalene reeking ship-halls*
*of the Korozhet slave-ship.*

Chip knew that it was bound to end, sooner or later.
He could stay in here until he starved or the slave super-
visors came to haul him out.

He'd yet to find any way of killing himself in this room.
Besides, the soft-cyber in his head said that would be a
disservice to the masters. So: he waited. When the time
came he would find a way. The slaves were apparently
supervised by low-order young Korozhets, small, short-
spined and very orange. Neuters and males, according to
Yetteth. They were neither very intelligent nor very strong.
They tended to use aliens that the other prisoners called
Nerba as brute force. Your mind would let you resist

Nerba. Your body was ill-advised to. They looked like armored bipedal water buffalo, with too many joined limbs and long mobile tails which split into a two-fingered "hand."

There was no way of telling night from day here in the vast bowels of the Korozhet ship, but Chip kept count of the food sirens. It was just after the seventh one that a Korozhet supervisor came for him, with two Nerba to carry him if need be. "Come," ordered the Korozhet. "Medium-spine Natt is to interrogate you."

He got up from the sleeping shelf to walk. A lash of some kind snaked across his naked back. "Walk lower. It is not fitting that you stand taller than even a First-instar, slave."

He hunched his shoulders and bent his legs and walked as slowly as he thought he could get away with. His eyes darted around looking for a death-chance. He waited too long. The small orange-spined Korozhet clattered his spines with impatience. "Pick him up, Nerba. Do not break his shell. We will go through the power section and save me much ambulating."

Chip found himself carried through a section of the ship where the air smelled distinctly of hot metal, even above the naphthalene reek. Much of the machinery was so alien he could not even begin to recognize it. But one piece he did. The last time he'd seen one, a fountain of sparks had been showering from it.

At a guess that was a force-field generator, near as dammit identical to the one in the brood-heart of the scorpiary.

Chip was eventually tossed down in front of a slightly redder and longer-spined Korozhet, sitting in a shallow waterbath.

Chip was planning to lie as much as he could. He'd just never realized quite what an effort defying the Korozhet and the soft-cyber had been for Ginny.

The medium-spine asked questions. Chip answered. He could hate the Crotchets, but to refuse to answer a direct question—from a Korozhet, in Korozhet—that was near impossible. And he was struggling to think fast enough to come up with evasive answers. At length the medium-spine started to clatter his spines. "Call Third-instar Clattat. This must be heard by him. The slaves rebel!"

The small, orange short-spined one raised his killing spines. Chip desperately wanted to dodge, but felt that would not be serving the master. "We kill any slave who rebels," said the small Korozhet.

"Unfit-to-spawn one! It is not this slave that rebels. It is the others. I have been instructed to hand this one intact to Sixth-instar Tirritit."

So, soon, Chip found himself being questioned by a larger Korozhet. When this one asked if the rats and bats could disobey, Chip had to answer in the affirmative.

"A direct order?"

"Yes"

"How do they do this?" demanded the Korozhet in-quisitor.

Chip struggled to defend his friends. They found cover in the English language. He found refuge in Doc. "It is possible with the use of Plato's forms."

The last two words were English. And that too came to his rescue.

"How does this Platoforms tool work?"

"I do not know. I do not understand it." That was true.

"Is it used by all?"

"No."

"Will it be used by humans on the soft-cyber?"

"It is a human thing. It was done to one rat as an experiment." That was true.

"But there are many of these slaves who broke their conditioning!" said the Second-instar.

Perhaps he could make them afraid? Fluff had tried to stop the Korozhet shooting Virginia by clinging to the laser. "One attacked the weapon of the Korozhet," volunteered Chip.

The resultant clattering of spines and reek of naphthalene was almost overwhelming. The Third-instar Clattat spined away hastily to seek an interview with the High-spine.

"What do we do with this slave?" asked the small orange Korozhet. "Are we to kill him because he rebelled? Any slave that rebels must die."

"Soft-spined sexless it, that will never even become male. He has not rebelled, as I said. Send him back to his quarters. You heard the Third-instar. He is wanted in good condition."

Yetteth was once again on cleaning duties for the High-spines when a Third-instar dared to come clattering in, and interrupted. Yetteth had seen a Fourth-instar killed for less. "Most High-spine. I have news of slave revolts among the implants we have placed among the humans."

That was enough to lower the dart-spines on the Deep-Purple Tenth-instar High-spine.

"Speak. Revolts? How is this possible? There is sometimes a rare malfunction or a slave of great will who overcomes some of the programming. But it is a rare thing. Our statisticians tell us that it is unlikely in low-order uplift minds in a proportion of less than one in twenty million."

"The humans have a device they call a Platosforms which enabled all of the slaves to rebel."

The High-spine clattered her spines. "This is ascertained? I have worrying reports here that the human media are attacking us, too. Accusing us of supplying both the Magh' and themselves."

"But that is correct, High-spine."

"It is not fitting that a putative subject species be aware of this. Besides this tool might somehow be brought into the ship, or affect the slaves on the ship."

Another one of the High-spines clattered. "The lock detectors do not exclude and incinerate implanted slaves. We could have these rebel slaves on our ship."

"We must begin their destruction immediately," said another. "These humans are not worth the risk of farming any further. The rewards have been great, but risk outweighs the reward."

The high-spine clattered her spines. "Agreed. We cannot take these chances. There is no greater danger to the Overphyle than rebellion of slaves. Begin the firing sequences. Contact the spawnship on the tight-beam. Tell them of this and tell them to order the Magh' advance. Send out the call for our slaves who are in the human army. The humans cannot hold the Magh' without their implanted soldier-creatures. And the soldier-creatures will come to us."

"How do we know if they are still loyal?"

"If they come, they are loyal. They outnumber the humans. And they are better killers."

# Chapter 50

❦

*Hell: Because war is that place,*
*no matter where you actually are.*


Down in Aladdin's cave, the movement of the missile aiming spines on the top of the vast roundness of the Korozhet ship was detected.

"Condition red. I say again, Condition red!"

Within a minute . . .

"Missile launch detected. Multiple missiles. Incoming."

All over George Bernard Shaw City, the sirens wailed. Siren systems set up when humans had still thought that this was going to be a conventional war, with missiles and air raids.

Many people had forgotten what they meant. There was chaos, from the streets full of protestors outside the courthouse to the crenelated grandeur of the Military Headquarters. The soup course of the elegant lunch being set on the vast tables caused some inelegant and painful accidents. But that was all. None of the Korozhet missiles would be wasted on useless targets.

The four geological/defense heavy lasers that the slowship had mounted were hooked up to the ship's power plant. They fired. They were energy expensive, never intended for simultaneous power-draw. But as the ship's fusion plant was almost certain to be a target, that made little difference.

Their targets were not the missiles, but their launch spines.

At the same time, not knowing just how the missiles were guided, Aladdin's cave spewed out as wide a range of jamming mechanisms as they could.

Some of it might even have worked. Not, however, for the old human slowship. That and the power plants south of the city were successfully hit. Fortunately, the bunker underneath the slowship had been designed to withstand tactical nuclear warheads. The non-nuclear explosives being used by the Korozhet were powerful, but not powerful enough to penetrate it.

Just as the judge was attempting to take down the rat who was, if not helping Fitz's case, at least giving the judge a novel view of his own unimportance—the alarms started. Then the lights in the windowless courthouse went out, as the ground shook. There was the sound of breaking glass. Fitz had thrown himself down, instinctively. The explosions were large, but not close. The screaming and panic in the courtroom were far louder.

Having been a front-line officer took over.

"*Quiet!*" Fitz's voice was loud, but more like a whip-crack in its force. Only one hysterical screamer remained. "Shut that person up," he instructed.

Someone did.

"Right." Panic kills. If you're in charge you've got to keep your cool or your troops will lose theirs. "This building itself is not under attack," said Fitz. "Is that clear to all of you? This building is not being attacked. There is no cause for panic. Sergeant at Arms?"

"Sir!" said a voice from the darkness.

"Take two MPs and get out there and scout. Ariel," he knew she'd be in here, somewhere, "go with them."

"Sir!" There was relief in that assent. Relief that someone was taking charge.

The door opened. Several people headed after the three towards the rectangle of light.

"Stop right there," snapped Fitz. "The rest of you, stay put. If we get an 'all clear' out there we'll move out. In an orderly fashion. There will be no running. You will all maintain physical contact with someone. Do we have any injured?"

"I'm bleeding," said someone. "Glass I think."

"Right. Move, or help any injured to the light at the door. Doc. Treat them."

As this was happening, the sergeant at arms came back. "Chaos out there, sir. But no shooting. There are some fires. We saw a fire engine go past."

"Right. Sergeant, assist the wounded. Let's get out into the light. If there are any more incoming, all of you, scatter and get down."

He found himself with his arm being held joining the

procession towards the outside. It was only when he got into the lighter passage that he realized that it was the hand of his mauve-lipsticked prosecutor, holding him.

"I should kill you now and save myself a lot of trouble next time," she whispered poisonously.

"Just try it," said Ariel, leaping up onto Fitz's shoulder in one of those prodigious bounds that the rats were capable of. " 'Twill be my pleasure to bite you properly. The street is full of idiotic screaming humans, Fitz. One said the missile trails came from the . . . Crotchet ship. Some of the city is on fire."

Major Tana Gainor let go of Fitz and ran for the doors.

They got out onto the steps and into the light. Several of the wounded were being tended on the steps. It seemed more a case of blood, minor injuries and fear than anything else.

"The phones are down," said one reporter, shaking her instrument.

The sergeant at arms came jogging up. "What do we do now, sir?"

Fitz shrugged. "I'm the prisoner around here, Sergeant. Why don't you ask your judge? I just gave orders in there because somebody had to." The military judge in question was sitting on the steps looking at the milling crowd and the fires burning where the south side power station used to be.

The sergeant at arms tried asking him. Judge Silberstohn, so ready to lay down the law to an obstreperous rat, blinked at him. "I don't know," he said, in a lost, slightly quavering voice.

Lieutenant Colonel Ogata came up, with several of the officers from the panel. "Major, we appear to be having a military emergency. I've spoken to several of the people who were out here when the attack took place. It would seem that the missiles came from the Korozhet ship. I think we can be fairly sure that they've taken out Military Headquarters. They've certainly taken out communications, power and the old slowship. You're the only one of us here with any first-hand combat experience. We need your help, Major. We need it now."

Fitz looked at the scene. "I'd be glad to serve," he said dryly. "However, these leg shackles are an impediment."

Ogata looked down. "Oh. I think we can extend parole, Major. For the duration," he said, with an almost straight face. "I'll put it to the panel to vote on."

They all nodded vigorously, which was just as well as the sergeant at arms was already unlocking the shackles.

"The ayes have it," said Ogata. "Now, Major Fitzhugh. What do you advise?"

Fitz took control. "We need communications and assessment. We'll need drivers, and we'll need reliable observers. We need to scatter civilians and get them away from fire-zones as quickly as possible. Colonel Jones, if you would . . ."

Within twenty minutes they were digging in, in the park across from the courthouse. Sentries and lookouts were posted. Patrols were going out. Couriers and observers were driving set routes to establish what had happened. An aid station had been set up. And the former prisoner had the judge lying down on a blanket in the aid-station. He seemed to be in shock.

The next attack came some twenty minutes later. The missiles went straight up and out, and exploded without hitting any targets. The thousands of plastic cubes that were scattered far and wide were not directly fatal.

"We advise all humans to proceed to the Webb Fields. Your colony is under attack by Jampad. Proceed to the Webb fields for processing into our safe shelters. The Korozhet will protect you. Do not bring weapons or any metal objects as the Jampad weapons detect these. We advise all humans to proceed to Webb . . ."

Endlessly repeating their message, the cubes spread Korozhet poison. And a lot of sheep-minded humans did in fact start heading for the vast Webb sports complex west of the city.

Of course, a lot did not. The first helicopter up had drawn fire from the Korozhet ship. It was a tragic—if direct—way of telling anyone who looked up that the Korozhet ship was not treating human aircraft with any tolerance.

Fitz, with at least five thousand soldiers and civilians taking orders, did his best to counter the Korozhet instructions. But communications were in a shambles. Even radio was jammed. They had a few old wire-based field-telephones from the signals unit working. Everything else had to be done by courier.

Mike Capra was one of the forward observers watching Webb Fields through a pair of binoculars. He was able, later, to reassure the officers of the temporary field command that in fact Military HQ had not been a target.

A little later he was able to report in person: "There were four bus loads and about sixteen staff cars." He looked askance at Conrad Fitzhugh. "And I think I can safely assure you, Fitz, that Major Tana Gainor will not be prosecuting you again. She's quite recognizable, even through binoculars. And she was part of that crowd of top officers who pushed their way through to the front of the queue. The Pricklepusses took them away, into their ship."

"Methinks, the army just got a lot more efficient," said Ariel, contentedly.

"I was about to send a runner back when we had some more action, which I thought maybe I'd better actually come back to tell you about personally. Webb Fields have come under mortar fire. Heavy smoke. The people on the field have been scattering in panic. If it had happened ten minutes earlier, we'd have been digging generals out from under bushes."

"Did the mortars come under any tracking fire? We saw some laser-fire from here."

"Yep. It was just the three mortar rounds. Almost simultaneously. Then the lasers opened up from the ship. I don't think they were H.E. bombs. There was just a lot of heavy smoke."

"We'll have to see if we can get a cordon in place, to see if we can stop any more people going in. And we need a line laid out there. I wish to hell we could get radio comms."

# Chapter 51

♋

*Scenes various across George Bernard Shaw City,
and inside the Korozhet ship.*

"Give us another half an hour," said the pimply programmer. "That's a craphouse full of code. We got rid of the command-phrases that will extract instant obedience. But there may be other things. I think we're there but we're just checking."

"We'll do our best," said M'Batha. "But we've had missile strikes on fifteen of the jamming transmission points. We've only got another three. Pretty soon we'll have to switch off or we'll have nowhere to broadcast the virus from."

The programmer shook his head. "I think we're not going to get there."

"If we don't, we can try the chipwipe one, even if that leaves us with stripped to near useless defense against the Magh'," said Liepsich. "But I reckon there isn't a plan C."

Ginny had headed back to the university animal holding compound after they'd flushed out Talbot Cartup. Fortunately, with the stop at the police station to make her statement, and moving at golf cart speed, they'd still been en route when the Korozhet struck the slowship. Even with its new V8 engine roaring behind them, the armor panels around the cart and the weight of chrome gadgetry that Nym delighted in slowed them down. That was probably just as well, as the rat insisted on driving. Nym's grasp of—not to mention, respect for—the rules of the road approached zero from the wrong side.

That was also the side of the road he liked to drive on. A candy-striped super-powered armored golf cart, accompanied by two Humvees full of paratroopers, was enough to disrupt traffic somewhat. So far no traffic authority had tried to pull them over which, Ginny thought, just proved that you could get away with a lot if you had enough audacity and candy-stripes.

When the missiles struck the slowship, the explosions nearly had Nym drive them into a ditch in his screeching halt. The shockwave swept over them, not quite fast enough to harden slowshields. The paratroopers took up defensive positions around them, spilling out of their vehicles. Since the assassination attempt at the stadium, the paratroopers had been hyper-edgy. One of them tried the radio. All it gave him was a burst of static. All that gave Ginny was hope. Liepsich's jammers must still be working.

"We're going to have to take you back to our base," said Sergeant Jacobovitz. "That's what Colonel Van Klomp said we were to do if there was any serious trouble, ma'am. I think you'd better get into the jeep with us."

"Methinks not," said Nym firmly. "But I will let Ginny drive and use this 'overdrive.' I hath promised I would not use it, but it will engage the full and awesome power of my engine. This noble vehicle is armored. Yours are not."

Ginny had driven the golf cart many times before. She'd never had to do so at sixty miles an hour before. Fortunately, the road was a broad one. Nym's golf-cart battlewagon got to the paratrooper base with no further disasters.

Van Klomp was there, giving orders. The camp itself was cleared. The paratroopers were digging in, out in the assault course area.

"I need you to lock me up," said Ginny calmly.

Van Klomp looked like a man who had had enough surprises for today. This was one too many. "I haven't time for that legal crap, Ms. Shaw. I'll lock you up when it is all over."

"Don't be a fool, Van Klomp!" she snapped. "The Crotchets are trying to take control of our soft-cybers. If you don't lock us up, we'll kill you if the radio-jamming stops."

"Oh. Hell's teeth. Does that mean all the bats and rats on the front will be coming here?"

"If the radio-jamming stops, yes. Unless the rebellion seeds we've planted have grown. But I doubt if that'll be enough to fight such a direct order. It's also possible that

Liepsich might have a counter-program, a sort of virus that will either wipe our memories or, if we're very lucky, wipe the pro-Crotchet bias. They were still working on it."

"Not much hope there," said Van Klomp grimly. "The university copped a direct hit."

"But their jammers are still on. And what else can I do?"

"Nothing. Abbas. Take them and lock them in the cells down at the police station. Steel doors should even hold the rats for a while. And it'll give some protection against incoming. It's a solid building."

So, three minutes later, Virginia was left in a cell full of rats and bats.

And her fears. Was Chip still alive? Regretfully she had to admit to herself that there wasn't much hope. A tear found its way down her cheek. Soon she might not even have those precious memories. If only the jamming could hold.

"High-spine, the radio jamming continues. We are attempting to neutralize it, but our missile-launch portals were heavily damaged by the initial laser-fire from the humans. And every time we have taken one transmitter off, another comes on. However we think we have pinpointed the central transmission source. We believe it is being coordinated from under the remains of their slowship."

"Which implies that it survived a direct hit."

"Yes, High-spine."

"Take a ground-force out, with heavy mining equipment. There must be a reinforced bunker underneath.

Destroy it. In the meanwhile desist wasting munitions."

The High-spine turned her attention to another high-instar. "How goes the human slave capture at this 'Webb fields'?"

"Since the initial batch, few have come, High-spine. We think there is resistance happening. Intimidation." She clattered her spines in disapproval.

The High-spine turned her attention back to those she was sending out to destroy the bunker. "Gather information on this when you go in, Rettitit. Take captives if possible. And Territ. The humans we have: Begin the mindscrub so that we can use them against their species-mates. If they are mindscrubbed, they will not rebel. All of the slaves taken on this world are to be mindscrubbed before implanting now. Begin with the females. The humans' only desirable social trait is that they are supposed to treat females with awe. They will be reluctant to kill them."

Yetteth took his bucket and sidled away. He could do nothing about this war. But he still wanted to know. It was compulsive. And the human Chip would want to know, if he came back alive from the questioning.

George Bernard Shaw City, smoldering and in fear.

"There is a sort of lander type thing just off on the edge of Webb Fields. That isn't force-shielded. They've got several high-walled enclosures there. They've got some of those who obeyed the order to go to them for shelter there. We could attack that," suggested one of Fitz's impromptu "General Staff."

A soldier ran up. "Major, it's Lieutenant Capra on the field-telephone. He says there are two massive vehicles coming out of the Korozhet ship. Some kind of hovercraft. They're heading east, sir. Towards the old slowship."

"There's not much left there. All right, soldiers. If they want something from there, it's our job to stop them. I'll want Alpha company, Sergeant. See they're in the cars in two minutes. And I'll want those 'sappers' and their supply of explosives."

"Fitzhugh! You can't go," protested a colonel, who had been part of the trial panel. "We need you here, man."

Fitz shook his head. "This command center is up and running. This is stuff you can all do as well as I can. Most of you have more experience at it, in fact. With respect, fighting is something I can do better than all of you. Come on, Ariel. Let's roll."

Fifteen minutes later, they were surveying the two alien hovercraft that were slowly coming down the street. The aliens were plainly checking for resistance on their route. The second hovercraft had two captive children on the aft deck. On the foredeck, huge aliens with enormous horns were operating what was plainly some form of scanner. Inside the transparent dome, Fitz could see the prickly forms of their enemy.

He and Ariel crawled back, before they came into range.

"The Benmore building," said Fitz curtly, to the driver of his commandeered vehicle.

They raced along the back-streets. Two minutes later Fitz's "sappers"—a pair of demolition contractors—were setting charges. His troops were doing a hasty door-to-door check for any remaining occupants of the plush apartment block next to the canal.

By the time the two alien hovercraft came in sight, Fitz's makeshift troops were well back. Whatever sort of scanner the aliens were using would have to penetrate three buildings and an earth berm to detect them. One spotter remained on the roof. The rest were in the vehicles ready to race in . . . or away.

They were armed with a mixture of issue bangsticks for the few slowshield-wearing military personnel, and an assortment of firearms and knives and hammers for the rest. Fitz had heard that a hammer had killed the Korozhet in the scorpiary. He wished desperately that he had some more front-line troops, but those were seldom posted back to the capital. He had several maintenance units, two boot-camps' worth of raw recruits, a lot of supply clerks and JAG officers, the medical corps—who had taken over civilian evacuation—a signals unit, and a hundred or so men who had been on pass in the city. He'd used these as stiffening in the units they'd formed with the townspeople.

The new units were as often as not "officered" by Vats. Certainly all the NCOs were Vats. But the class distinction had gone by the board now that they were fighting for their lives.

What he'd really wanted was Van Klomp and his paratroopers. But their camp was abandoned. Van Klomp would be around somewhere. But he hadn't stayed in a known possible target—showing more brains than most of the units, whose officers had kept them sitting on their hands. A sweep through Military HQ had gathered a further five officers—recent appointees, as well as a fairly large supply of clerks. Apparently the General Staff, having received assurances from the Korozhet, had left them behind as there wasn't sufficient transport.

"Count of three," said the observer from the rooftop. His orders were to try and drop it on the lead hovercraft and the nose of the second. The prisoners were probably going to be killed by the Korozhet. They might be killed by the debris, but Fitz still didn't want to risk dropping the building on them. Demolition is not that exact a science.

"NOW!"

Inside the landspeeder the explosions were muffled. The dust ahead was still rising when Fitz and his soldiers got there. Dust was going up, and bits of the luxury apartments were still coming down. They were out of their vehicles and running in, firing small-arms for some form of cover.

The second Korozhet craft was still moving. As they got to the deck, it lurched. One of the privates was cutting the two children loose, as Fitz took down his first Korozhet at close quarters.

Then his muscles spasmed terribly and he felt himself helplessly arc over backwards into the rubble.

He was conscious, able to hear and see, still breathing. And paralyzed. Fitz could see a orange-spined prickleball with what was unmistakably a hand-weapon.

It said something.

Ariel was standing on his chest. She started forward. Just a pace.

Then she bared her teeth.

"NO!" she hissed between those teeth. "Mine. Mine."

So the Korozhet shot her. A brief dart of red light.

Fitz, unable to move, felt her fall. And felt her lifeblood stream onto his chest. The little pawhands clung convulsively onto his shirt-pocket. And then released.

The Korozhet spined down, with one of its horned alien henchmen. The Korozhet spine-suckers plucked up Ariel. The horned alien began to lift Fitz in its clumsy fore-paws. Suddenly the creature jerked, and dropped him face down on the rubble.

Fitz couldn't move. Face down, he couldn't even see. He could hear the shooting, though. It sounded like an entire barrage. He lay there, grieving. He had three last Cointreau-centered liqueur chocolates in that top pocket, that he'd been saving for Ariel.

He was not too sure how much later someone turned him over. He was not sure he cared. Not even when he realized that it was Van Klomp's big ugly face looking down on him.

It was almost two hours later that Fitz began to recover some movement. After that he had a couple of wild, almost epileptic muscle spasms, and found that he could at least begin to sit up. He was weak, and wretched.

Van Klomp came into the aid station.

"*Boeta*, I thought you were dead. I should have known it was too good to be true."

"Ariel's dead, Bobby. She tried to protect me. Stood over my body. And the bastards killed her. I even couldn't move to help her." Fitz knew there was heartbreak in his voice. But Bobby Van Klomp was more than a friend. He was more of a father than his own father had ever been.

"Oh, hell's teeth. I'm sorry, Fitzy. She loved you, that mad rat of yours."

"She loved me enough to stand and defend me, when her soft-cyber was programmed to make her obey the

Korozhet. I think that's why they shot her. But I wish
they'd at least left me her body."

"Fitzy . . . I don't know what to say, boykie. All I can
say is your lot did a hell of a lot better ambush than ·we
had prepared on the other side of the canal. You made
them pay a very high price for her. You got two kids free.
One's got a concussion and the other a broken leg, but
they're alive and free. You killed twenty-seven and
destroyed one of their hovercraft—and you only lost three
of yours."

"Only thanks to your lot getting there. I wish I'd known
where the hell you were."

"I moved my boys into the assault course grounds,
except for the ones in that first chopper those bastards
shot down. They're dug in there. Then we set up a sort of
'combined arms' group—the new recruits without
slowshields and with as much firepower as we could
manage to scavenge, the vets with bangsticks and
explosives—and went and scouted Webb Fields. We
dropped a few smoke-rounds on the crowd, in order to
chase them out of that trap. But then we got our mortars
taken out, and we've been scouting for an opportunity
since."

Fitz's stood up. "Be ready for lots of opportunity. I plan
to kill every single stinking Pricklepuss on this planet
before I'm done. I'll give Ariel a funeral pyre worthy of a
goddess."

Van Klomp smiled crookedly. "I don't think the rats
have 'goddesses,' Fitzy."

"They do now."

# Chapter 52

༄

*The ship of slaves and the new
slave compounds, outside.*

Yetteth had long since lost track of the time that he'd been a prisoner. In all that time he'd never been outside the ship. Very few of the thousands of Korozhet on the ship ever left the vessel, and, from what he could gather, slaves never did.

That made sense, of course. Until the Magh'-clients had finished clearing away the humans and the new world was open for Korozhet settlement—or, at least, until all subterfuge had been abandoned—the Korozhet didn't want the humans seeing their existing slaves of many species, or they might just guess what the Korozhet were up to.

It appeared that all pretense had now been abandoned. Yetteth was one of a group that were ordered to go out to the slave preprocessing station where the humans were being mindwiped. Someone had to move the empty and comatose bodies across to the implant station. It was not an easily mechanized task, and Korozhet did not do manual labor. That was for the lower phyla.

The alien air smelled sweet. After the naphthalene reek of the ship any air would have smelled sweet, but this was really pleasant. A little dry and rather warm, but certainly something to set the scent tendrils tingling. Yetteth fluffed them out slightly, picking up every nuance as the second force field was dropped and they walked across to the preprocessing station.

Yetteth nearly earned himself a nerve-lashing. He stopped . . . His scent tendrils flared, nearly doubling in size.

The breeze brought him a scent he never ever expected to smell again.

One of the People.

Female. And she was within a relatively short swing or swim.

Hastily he walked on, seeing that the overseer was heading back this way on its floater.

The cage was full of humans. They were still clothed, and their eyes were open. But there was nothing behind those empty eyes. Korozhet mindwiping techniques scoured all traces of memory and existing personality from the brain. For all practical purposes, these "people" were newborn babes. Not even that—fetuses, in a nonexistent womb.

With a sigh, he began the work he was ordered to do.

In low gravity like this, carrying a human was an easy thing for a Jampad. He picked up the first one, a female with yellow head-filaments, and carried her across to the implant-station. Then he came back for the next one. And then the next one.

A Korozhet hovertank came hurtling drunkenly across the open field. There was smoke trailing from it. The plex-dome was shattered—and Yetteth knew from his own combat experience that it took a huge force to even damage it. Of the normal crew of fifteen Korozhet with dozens of Nerba to man the paralyzers and do the heavy lifting, there was very little sign.

The hovertank dropped clumsily in front of the pre-processing station. One of the masters got out with a dripping, small, longnosed creature balanced on two spines.

Yetteth dared not wait and watch, much as he wanted to. He carried the next human across. This was another female, with lips of a peculiar color—like the ice fens of his home planet. Odd. He'd never seen another human with that color lips. Perhaps that was an the result of the mindscrub. The effects of the process were sometimes extreme. Some of the mindwiped humans weren't just comatose, they were dead. He remembered the human woman who had died in the slave quarters. Her lips had gone blue.

Inside the preprocessing station he was told to put her onto the work surface.

"Strip the false integuments off her, slave," snapped the inserter.

As he did so, Yetteth saw that the remains of the small creature lay on one side of the workslab. It had been split in half and the soft-cyber implant was being removed from its brain.

The Third-instar who had brought the creature in was still talking, clacking its spines in agitation. " . . . ambush. All of Fourth-instar Cattat's crew were killed. This is one of the rebels . . ."

"I understand that," said the inserter impatiently. "That is why I am removing the implant." The Korozhet pointed a spine at the human female with the odd-colored lips. "I will insert it in this creature, so we can begin an interrogation."

The inserter noticed Yetteth had finished preparing the human female. "Take this filth away." He pointed a spine at the small, stumpy-tailed creature.

Yetteth picked up the small creature's remains. Despite many scars on the body, the fur was still very soft.

Once outside he took a chance, and put it down, gently, in the gathering dark. Nothing that had fought such a fight and managed to inflict such damage on the . . . Crotchets, should be tossed in with the regurgitated remains of Korozhet dinners. He would have burned it with honor, if he could.

Obviously the Third-instar's concern had been relayed to the High-spine, because Yetteth found himself and the other slaves being whipped and sent back to the ship in haste. The cages of humans were left to their own devices as the hovertank and the Korozhet retreated back into their force-fielded ship.

All life can be expressed as a stream of machine-code. This scene is, too.

"I'd like to test it," said the pimply-faced programmer. "There might be a bug."

"No time," said Liepsich. "It works or it doesn't work. And down here we'll have no way of knowing. Kill the jamming. We'll have to go with it."

"The minute we stop they'll send their signal. Anything that has a soft-cyber will turn on humans."

"That's a chance we'll have to take. We'll be transmitting within seconds, I hope."

Pimple-face shrugged. It was a lot of weight on nineteen-year-old shoulders. But the best programmers in the colony were terrifyingly young. "Okay, we're ready to rock-and-roll. I couldn't strip out all of the Korozhet terms without leaving gaping holes in the software. The programs would have crashed. So I've inserted a human 'and/if' replace statement."

"Which human?" said Liepsich, pausing in the very act of hitting the jammer toggle.

"Oh, he's long dead. One these classical music figures from old earth. Did some melodies that are still around."

"Quality lasts," said Liepsich hitting the button. "What was his name?"

"Elvis Presley."

Virginia knew to the microsecond when the jamming transmissions stopped. She'd just been thinking about how incredibly stupid she'd been to let fear drive her into volunteering herself to a cell with rats that were getting hungrier and hungrier, with no sign of more food being delivered, instead of taking her chainsaw and at least having a go at the . . . Crotchets, when it hit.

Suddenly she knew that she had to get back to the ship. Had to! Had to come and defend the beloved masters. They needed her. They needed her now.

A weak part of her mind creeled in revulsion and fear. She had just time to see Nym and Doc neatly engineer a slowshield interdiction which cut into the door-metal . . .

When it all changed.

She no longer had any desire to run to help any master. Only a vague inclination to do a pelvic thrust. For the first time since Chip had been kidnapped she managed to smile.

"Right." She took a deep breath. "I *hate* Korozhet. *I want to kill the Korozhet!*"

Soon they were walking down the road to the paratrooper base—except of course for the bats who flew above, chanting: "Kill Korozhet!"

Well. Fluff stood on her head and hooked his thumbs into his waistcoat pockets. "I speet upon hound dog Korozhet," he said proudly.

There was a solitary sentry at the base. He was the one who had been supposed to bring their next meal.

"I was just bringing it. Honestly. Just the radio started working again. I've been talking to Lieutenant Colonel Van Klomp. We've got contact with the front. With all the army divisions and the other towns! We'll be bringing reinforcements in. We've got a fighting chance at last."

"Get on that radio again," snapped Ginny. "And tell him to get his broad behind over here as fast as possible. Tell him it's Virginia Shaw. And tell him I have an answer. Make it quick!"

Virginia's name still got attention. Less than fifteen minutes later Van Klomp arrived, with a tall, grim-looking scar-faced man. "I thought you were supposed to be in jail," said Van Klomp.

There was just an edge of tenseness in the gruff voice. Hinting that if she was some kind of trap for Korozhet . . . she would be dead very rapidly.

"Suspicious minds," said Virginia with a smile. "You can thank Liepsich that that won't be necessary any more. That's why he isn't jamming the airwaves any more. They've broadcast a virus in the last couple of minutes. I can hate Korozhet now. If I can hate Korozhet, I can kill Korozhet. And Lord almighty, I feel my temperature rising."

"And you couldn't have even said that before," said the scar-faced man. "Well, it came too late for my Ariel."

Van Klomp's eyes narrowed. "So that bastard Liepsich survived the missile attack. I might have guessed. We've been running medical search and rescue around the old ship. We've only found two bodies so far."

"Presumably that's what that party of Korozhet were after," said the tall scar-faced man.

"Yep, Fitz." Van Klomp put his hand on the other man's shoulder. "I know it's no consolation, but that ambush of yours saved millions of other implanted creatures."

"And I want to take that liberation into the heart of that Korozhet ship, and blow it wide open," said Virginia. "And I am the only one who can. At least we are the only ones who can. But I'm prepared to do it. They believe the implanted animals are coming. And Darleth has told us only implants and Korozhet will get in through the portal."

"What?" demanded Van Klomp.

Virginia spelled it out. "Get Liepsich out of his hidey-hole. Get me a transmitter and I'll take it into that ship. If Darleth is right, it's full of implanted slaves."

Fluff leapt to the floor. "*Señorita*, you will not. Only fools weel rush in where wise men fear to tread. I, Don Juan el Magnifico de Gigantico de Immaculata Conception y Major de Todos Saavedra Quixote de la Mancha, will go."

"Oh, we'll come too, Don Fluffy." Doll gave him a lewd wink. "Unless that Sally Lunn hath stalled my variety. She played the strumpet in your bed."

"Wench stealer," muttered Pistol. "Now there are three hogsheads of whiskey that say I should go . . ."

"I'm going," said Ginny with a grim finality. "They took Charles Connolly. And I'm going to get him back."

"And us bats. We're all off to the Korozhet in the Green, baby," caroled O'Niel.

"Ach. O'Niel. If you could sing like you drink and fight t'would make you a fearsome creature," said Bronstein.

"If there are enough of you, and you manage to get rid of that force field—we'll back you up. Hard and fast," said the grim-faced Fitz. "Now what we need is Liepsich."

"Methinks you should try the radio," said Nym. "I'm going to work on my battlewagon."

"Hmph. You lean unwashed artificer. You love that thing even more than good sack," said Fal. "Now that's what I want. Or maybe that Sally Lunn. Not a golf cart."

" 'Tis an ill-favored thing," said Nym with a wry pride. "But mine own. And methinks it could pack a fair amount of explosives and radio transmitters."

"I think," said Melene, consideringly, "that we should pack less of the explosive and more of the Ratafia. We need to contact Darleth."

# Chapter 53

❤

*The Korozhet ship, within its portal,*
*and deep within its noisesome bowels.*

"The one thing the Crotchets fear more than anything else is a slave revolt."

Yetteth's words still echoed in Chip's mind. Perhaps if he'd known that before . . .

Deep down inside, he knew that was self-deception. Even the smallest bending of the truth had been difficult to near impossible. How Ginny had managed to actually directly defy the compulsion in her head was beyond him. But he knew, after what Yetteth had told him, that out there he'd caused a war. He knew that humans had fought back— and apparently successfully. At least, from what he could tell, the Korozhet on the ship seemed in a bit of a panic.

493

He was ready to bet that if she wasn't dead, Virginia Shaw would be among them. Yetteth had seen one dead rebel rat. That could only be one of Chip's comrades. He hadn't been able to work out who it could have been, so he feared for them all.

Now, with the Korozhet ship in uproar, locked down into battle status, Chip was trying to do the unthinkable. Sabotage. It was as awful a thought as rebellion.

A slave would sooner die than do that. Well, he could always do both at once, if need be. Chip Connolly had no particular faith in paradise hereafter. On the other hand, he had a lot of faith in his fellow soldiers, and in Ginny. But with a force field between them there was not a lot they could do.

So he had to remove that obstacle.

How?

At the council of war Darleth took something of the lead. After all, the Jampad had more experience fighting Korozhet than anyone else. Now that her Ratafia was able to fight—and now that her Lieutenant Ariel had been murdered—Darleth was dead keen for direct engagement.

So, surprisingly, were the Ratafia. Ariel had earned herself a great deal of respect. And the Ratafia, as an almost entirely rat organization, had discovered honor. It was a concept that the rats tried their best to rationalize around, needless to say.

"If we let them deal thus with our Capo—why, then there is neither honesty, rathood nor good fellowship in us." Sally Lunn slipped a small dagger into the top of her fishnet stockings. "And a girl like me needs a great deal of rathood. Besides this new computer-virus hath left me feeling all shook up."

Meilin's Vat Liberation Organization, with a cell and communication structure designed to survive all that the Special Branch could throw at it, had stood up to the Korozhet bombing better than the ordinary civil structures. "We've got lines of communication now and we're organizing. But—and this is a 'but'—if those missile launchers on the ship get firing full pace again we'll have problems. Still, we've found another three thousand two hundred troops who were out on pass when this went down. My people are moving them forward, Major Fitzhugh."

Despite being outranked by several officers, Fitz had simply taken over command and Van Klomp was content to let him do so. "Strategy and tactics are his field, Colonel. When you've been organizing logistics—like you have—you are maybe less good at it than he is."

"I accept that. But you've also got field-command experience, Colonel. You ought to do it."

Van Klomp had just shaken his head. "I'm too big, Colonel. Big men like me have simple strategy and tactics in a fight. I wish like hell we had that lance corporal of mine. Connolly. If he was here I'd make Fitz listen to him. He's a small man, but he wins. In the meanwhile we've got Fitzy. So long as we can stop him thinking he's invincible."

Liepsich had come out of his hidey-hole, insulted them all, and gone back into it to prepare as many radio transmitters with preset virus replays as possible.

Nym and a squad of mechanics were working on the golf cart.

"It's not properly speaking a golf cart any more," admitted the sergeant. "The steering, accelerator pedal and the bonnet ornament are still the same. But everything else—from the chassis to the engine, is either reinforced or carrying so much chrome it's more like a half-baked APC. He's very proud of it."

The sergeant jerked an oily thumb at an equally oily Nym. "Its amazing how like one of the boys he is. He drinks beer. And we're teaching him about football. I hadn't realized what the critters were like. I thought they were some sort of trained animals."

"They're more than animals, but they're not the same as people either, Sergeant. Well. Not the same as humans, I should say. I think we're all going to have to start redefining the word 'people.' "

"Yes, Major. But you can get on with rats. Bats are weird."

"It's bats that are what is worrying me right now. According to radio reports, at least twenty thousand are AWOL from the front lines. Amazingly, the rats are standing firm against the Magh', but I have no idea if the bats can do the same. Fortunately, the bats can't possibly fly here in time to make a difference, even if the soft-cyber-virus hasn't sorted it out."

Fitz took a look at Nym lovingly polishing a running board. "Does the rat realize it's not likely that the golf cart is going to survive all this?"

"Oh, he knows, sir. But it's the first car he's ever owned. He's real proud of it."

Two hours later the golf cart drove slowly onto Webb Fields. There were some seventy-two rats in, around and on top of it. And one human. And two bats clinging like windshield wipers to the candy-striped awning. Ginny knew that just one blast of the heavy-lasers would destroy the golf cart and all of them. They trundled forward toward the Korozhet ship.

On cue, a fusillade rang out over their head from the far edge of Webb Field. The lasers on the walls of the huge ship above winked on. Ginny winced.

But the Korozhet fire was being directed at the small-arms fire that was apparently trying to stop the golf cart from reaching the Korozhet ship. Darleth had obviously been correct. The Korozhet could detect soft-cybers. She just hoped that the rigged fusillade had indeed been remote from those rifles. But Fitz and Van Klomp both knew that fire on the ship drew fire.

So, the transformed golf cart that was humanity's—using the term broadly—latest variation on the Trojan Horse, trundled forward. The golf cart bumped into the outer force field . . . And then the little golf cart was moving again. The Korozhet had relaxed the field to let them in.

Nym patted the wheel. "My culminating treasure that pleasures beyond measure. Feel the power!"

"I'd rather feel the long and the short of it," said Fat Fal. "Doll, I know 'tis crowded and time is short but I have some candy I stole . . ."

They bumped again, against the inner force field. This too was raised. The golf cart trundled up to the ramp, right under the bulk of the vast ship.

It began to roll up the ramp. The doors spiraled open—much the same way a camera-iris does, and the way the door into the Magh' brood-chamber had done. A small orange Korozhet appeared.

"Leave the human vehicle," he clacked. He had what Ginny recalled was a laser-pistol in his spines. He was flanked by the armored and horn-headed creatures that Darleth had identified as "Nerba." Stupid but good slaves, she'd said.

They also had some kind of weapon, a heavier riflelike device.

"You have a human," the Korozhet stated, in its own language. The alien's spiny sea-urchin shape had once inspired her with respect and deep affection. Now it was all that she could do not to heave.

Ginny had dismounted. Now she groveled. So did the others—except the two bats. They'd slipped down the far side of the golf-cart.

"Yes, master," said Virginia in Korozhet. "I am one of the implanted ones. We come from the Animal Research College." She gestured to the left, since the bats were working on the right. "There are many attackers coming. We have killed many out there. They are assembled and ready. I can show the master."

She'd moved further to the left and was pointing. The Nerba, and indeed the Korozhet, had followed her.

Gobbo had explained it to her. "Standard thief trick. You always look where someone is pointing." It worked. Even on radially symmetrical aliens.

"You shall show the higher instars," said the Korozhet. "They will direct fire onto them. Come. Strip. Place all the false integuments and other items in the hopper. Slaves do not wear such things."

There was no questioning that you were to be a slave. The programming in soft-cyber probably made it seem all right . . . well, it used to make it seem all right. Now,

Ginny found it a little difficult to take off all her clothes, even though the only observers nearby were either aliens or rats and bats, not one of whom would be in the least bit aroused by her nude body.

But, she managed. They walked forward into the inner chamber of the starship. Obedient to the Korozhet orders, the rats had already off-loaded their gear into the hoppers. That was going to be an explosive hopper, shortly.

Some radio transmitters went in there, too. She hoped that everyone had clicked their timers. Others . . . well, Liepsich had expended precious old Earth resources. The transmitter attached to her glasses didn't even have metal in it. It didn't have much range either. She had another in her hair.

Ginny was terribly self-conscious about her nudity; which, leaving aside anything else, left her feeling very defenseless. The ship had at least two thousand Korozhet in it, by Darleth's estimate, and many thousands of soft-cyber implanted loyal slaves. If the transmitters were discovered, or didn't work, then they faced awful odds and they were weaponless. The Korozhet had laser weapons. The devices the Nerba held were possibly a smaller version of the paralyzer that had apparently been used on Fitzhugh. A very popular weapon with slavers, for obvious reasons. Dead livestock were worthless.

"Put the device on your face into the hopper."

Obediently, she moved towards the hopper. "I cannot see without them, master."

"Keep it, then. We normally eliminate damaged slaves but we need some for putting down these rebels."

The inner iris opened.

"There are many more implanted ones detected.

Thousands come," said a Korozhet inside. "We cannot bring all into the ship. They must be deployed to deal with the humans. These too."

Chip applied something only a Vat would know. If you are carrying a bucket, even an alien bucket, full of something smelly, very few people will assume you have no reason to carry it. Or to take it anywhere.

Even here, a slop bucket was an amazing disguise. The slaves moved pretty well anywhere, anyway. There were always trivial manual tasks to be done, and the ship was in something of an uproar. Thinking careful thoughts about his most distracting subject—Ginny—Chip moved inwards, to the very center of the ship's power plant.

At last he was next to what he was sure was the force-field generator.

There was quite a complex control panel. A Korozhet operator was moving his spikes over it. He had parted with some of the indigestible remains of his last victim onto the floor. Chip humbly began to clean up, studying the works, steeling himself.

If his plan failed, he was going to be killed. If it didn't fail . . . he'd probably be killed anyway. It was no use just switching it off temporarily.

The Korozhet got onto its spikes and ambulated across to some instruments. Chip braced himself. Trying his utmost, he managed to move toward the panel. But he felt like someone stuck in jelly.

Just inside the inner iris, Virginia adjusted her glasses.

Suddenly, Chip could move freely again. He ripped

the cover off the control panel and emptied the bucket's contents onto the works. Then he hit it with the bucket for good measure. The shock arced him backwards.

But it must have done him the world of good. He had absolutely no trouble at all hitting the Korozhet with the five-sided bucket.

He started with the deadly spines, shattering them. Then, almost gleefully, he hammered the alien into a pulp. In fact, he made a dance out of the murderous business, swinging his pelvis with every blow of the bucket.

He also had no trouble picking up the laser gun from the smashed remains of the Korozhet, and, using a broken spine from the dead Third-instar to trigger it, expend a lot of its charge on several of the power cables.

In three shots. *One for the money, two for the show—*

A part of his mind—small part—was a little puzzled that he was still shaking his pelvis while he destroyed the control panel. Maybe it was because he hadn't seen Ginny in so long.

# **Chapter 54**

☙

*In the corridors of the Korozhet ship: alien, metal,*
*and remarkably like corridors anywhere.*

Watching from the vehicles under their earth-coated
tinfoil and stuck-on shrubbery, Fitz had the pre-strike
tension all over again. The waiting was always the worst.
Once you got going and the adrenaline kicked in . . .

Of course, the assault might not happen at all. If the
sacrifice of those rats and bats and the girl and her galago
had been in vain—they'd pull back just as quietly as they
came. Fitz peered at the tiny candy-striped vehicle standing in the ship's lightpool, again. Courage came in all
shapes and sizes. But his task was to win this war. If this
bold stroke failed, they'd reorganize and go on. And on,
if need be.

Liepsich had provided a diffraction meter that indicated force-field states. Fitz watched it with one eye and the ship through the camouflage crack with the other. His driver sat with his finger on the keys. He hoped the vehicle started well from cold. They'd slowly pushed the vehicles forward from where they'd been towed to, with the pushers hiding themselves behind foil and earth shields. No fast moves, hopefully no infrared . . .

Seventy yards to cover. The young reporter he had for a driver claimed his car could do zero to sixty in 4.2 seconds. If that was too slow, the lasers would take them out before they reached safety under the belly of the ship. There might be weapons there, of course. If one of the shields came back on they'd splatter. And then they'd have to stop, and not be hit by the other vehicles. Then there was the question of the doorway. One of the paratroopers behind him had the triggers to the bat-mines that would hopefully be placed on the door's works. After that . . . well.

No one knew. Not even Darleth, sitting behind him.

Why was it getting darker?

"It's a GO!"

Fuentes had been watching the diffraction meter, too. The sports car snarled into life. He floored it. The camouflage leapt away from the car as they hurtled toward the ship. Behind him, someone hit the bat-mine triggers.

It was a skidding halt . . . against candy-striped armor. But the one advantage of the convertible was that it had no roof in the way. The five of them bailed out over the top.

Even at a full sprint, Fitz could not keep up with the blue furred one. Or the shower of bats dropping in with folded wings.

"Begorra! I'd be thinkin' you timed this with military precision," said one huge bat, who nearly knocked him flailing off the ramp. "Come on, up the ramp, primate! Faster! Kill Korozhet!"

The air was almost solid with bats, now. "They're allies!" yelled Fitz, back at his squads, arriving with squealing tires and bumps. "Up!"

But the bat-mines that Bronstein and O'Niel had placed had not been effective enough. The iris door was still closed.

"Shamus Plekhanov!" bellowed the bat. "This needs you."

A bat with two bandoliers flapped out of the mass. "Eamon, now. You'd not be implyin' I'm a better sapper than you?"

"I'm saying that Longfang O'Niel said that you were the best in the Red Wing, and he places his shots better than I do. Besides, it's shaped charges we'll be needing and the Battybund don't use them as much as you do. 'Tis a bit sissy, we think."

The bat snorted, but went to work, motioning them all back.


Meanwhile, inside the ship:

The first reaction that Virginia got to "adjusting" her glasses, was that the huge Nerba guard dropped his weapon.

"Pick up!" snapped the Korozhet.

But the huge horned creature did not pick up the weapon. Instead, it lowered its head and backed off. Ginny noted that the other Nerba was looking at its weapon. The huge creature seemed puzzled, although it was hard to tell.

"I ordered you to pick it up."

Ginny had spent time with the rats. She could see lips sliding back over those red-tipped teeth. Not that those teeth, so deadly against Magh' or humans, would be adequate dealing with spiny-armored Korozhet. The creatures were fragile, true, when struck with heavy blunt objects—but rat-fangs were stilettos, not broadswords.

The creatures had toxic darts and secreted nitrous oxide, too. Back in the hopper, Ginny had a gas mask. It was at least thirty yards away.

The Nerba retreated again, until it was against the wall of the passage. It made an odd mooing sound.

The Korozhet shot it. Casually, it seemed to Ginny. Apparently, that was standard procedure with a disobedient slave.

Then the lights went out, just as the second Nerba lowered its head and charged the Korozhet.

What were obviously smaller emergency lights came on. A sound like a mixture between a rattle and a severe case of gas erupted from speakers.

The Nerba hadn't survived his impact with the Korozhet. But the Korozhet hadn't survived either.

"Get our kit and let's move in!"

The bats were already swooping on the hopper, snatching bat-mines. Ginny grabbed for the chainsaw first. Then clothes. The skirt she just stepped into, and she decided that the blouse buttons could wait. A girl had to dress slightly for success, even if a chainsaw was the finest in fashion accessories.

Behind her she heard a dull thump.

"Bat-mines. Too early, methinks. Let's move out, Ginny."

"Ay, *señorita*. Let's she roll and rock!" Fluff was back on his habitual post on her shoulder.

They headed into the unknown.

But they hadn't got more than five hundred yards into the ship, when the strains of "The Rifles of the BRA" overtook them. Bats flooded overhead in an almost solid stream, singing.

"I think we have air superiority," said Doc.

"If they've all been at the sauerkraut, we'll have wind superiority, too," said Melene, twitching her nose.

"Well, I think their singing needs the right instrumental accompaniment." Ginny gunned her chainsaw.

Fal took a swig from his bottle. "And get to some of these fretful porpentines, before the bats kill them all."

Down in the energy section, with an enemy laser gun and heavy alien bucket, Chip Connolly prepared to go down fighting. Or at least breaking things.

And then he heard it. A far-away sound. And never was bad singing so sweet.

*"Charlie Connolly goes to die on the bridge o' toon today . . ."*

If that wasn't tuneless O'Niel leading that singing, then he was Henri-Pierre's mustachioed mummy. Grinning like a madman, swinging his bucket, Chip advanced towards the noise.

*"Oh I've been a wild rover for many's the year . . . and I've spent all me money on whiskey and beer. . . ."*

Bats swept in, in a triumphal flutter. "Connolly, you inartistic dog! You've ruined O'Niel's song by not being dead," said Bronstein, her claws digging into his shoulder.

Then, panting, Ginny ran in. The chainsaw fell to the floor, as did the bucket.

" 'Tis quick work," said Pistol. "Undressed already, and Ginny half so, you puffed and reckless libertines."

"I've got a chainsaw," said Ginny, picking it up, but keeping one hand on Chip. "No one tells a lady she is undressed while she still has her chainsaw."

"And I have a bucket. No man is undressed with a bucket." Chip brushed away Ginny's tears with a caressing hand. "I don't even have a handkerchief . . ." He touched his temple. "But I do have a soft-cyber implant, Ginny. They made me a slave, and I betrayed all of you. But I did manage to break their force field."

"Begorra!" said O'Niel in a fine imitation of disgust. "Why did I bother to come? No job to do, no drink, no strawberry yogurt—and me fine lyrics are purely ruin't."

"Just burning love," said Pistol. "Thank you very much."

Fitz, Van Klomp and the rest of his force were beginning to feel like spare parts. The bats were going through the ship like a flying tide. Even the various aliens they encountered were too busy trying to kill Korozhet to pay much attention to the newcomers.

Then it started becoming apparent that some of the Korozhet were releasing their nitrous oxide. Sheer speed and unexpectedness, particularly of the bats, had ensured that many of the Korozhet had died first. So had thousands of the slaves turning on the Korozhet—a totally unexpected thing. But, in the upper parts of the great globular ship, there were a few Korozhet who had had enough time to try and fight back. And nitrous oxide had incapacitated enough of their prey in the past.

So, now, human soldiers with gas masks from the local chemical plant finally had a job to do. Part of that job was getting the alien ex-slaves out of the ship. Now that the ship was at least partially disabled, Fitz had sent a radio op back to the entry portal calling hundreds more human soldiers in, along with medical teams. Troops without slowshields—but with shotguns—soon began proving that human buckshot was superior to harpoons.

Fitz met a recognizable alien in the upper passages. It was the blue furred one, Darleth. She'd said that she could hold her breath for up to twenty minutes, as an aquatic species. The Jampad's homeworld was apparently vastly tidal, and thus Jampad needed to be able to both swim and climb with equal facility.

Only this wasn't her. It wasn't the same blue, and it was wider.

"High-spine chamber up here." It pointed with one of its arms. "Have many lasers inside."

The gas got to it finally, and it staggered.

"Abbas. Simmons. Carry it out and get it to the medical teams."

The Jampad had known about the gas. It had made a deliberate decision to tell them about the danger ahead. Fitz had already come to trust one Jampad; he decided to trust another.

They'd worked out how to work the spiral iris doors by now. Opening it slightly, while lying on the floor, Fitz gave the occupants inside a grenade. With the hiss of laser fire coming through the door, his soldiers followed it up with two more. And then another two for luck.

The High-spines inside the chamber would never see

another instar. The paratroopers opened the iris further, and filled the room with buckshot.

After that it was little more than mopping up.

Half an hour later Fitz came out of the ship. Van Klomp was already there, using his loud voice in lieu of translation skills. So far there were just car-lights lighting up the scene, but someone was stringing wire and setting up spotlights. He saw Fitz on the ramp.

"*Ja*, boykie. We're moving them back into town. Away from the ship, with a bat to each squad of ten as a translator." He pointed to the alien forms and oxygen tanks. "Just as soon as the medics say they're okay. You should hear the band-aid mechanics bitch about alien physiology, and trying to stop those dumb big things with the horns from going back into the ship as soon as they can stand. We thought we'd have to shoot them to stop them until one of the teams brought a bunch of cute fluffy puppy things out of the ship. You've never seen such a fuss."

He took a deep breath. "Fitzy, that blue furred fellow. The one Sergeant Abbas says you found and told you there was some sort of ambush waiting. He showed us something."

Conrad Fitzhugh was uneasy. Van Klomp did not speak quietly unless he was deadly earnest. "Tell me, Bobby."

"Ariel's body. He was told to dump it in the incinerator. He didn't. I've got it over behind the aid station."

Tears had already started in Fitz's eyes. But his voice remained steady. "Take me to it, Bobby. I need to see her. I need . . . to pay my last respects. I never got that chance."

Van Klomp put a large hand on Fitz's shoulder. "Better

not, Fitzy. She's been badly mutilated. Her head . . . down to about mid-chest has been split. Yetteth, that's the Jampad-fellow, says they do that to take out the soft-cyber. We'll bury her with honor. But best you remember her as she once was."

Fitz shook his head. "No," he croaked. "I need to see her. To tell her I loved her. No matter what she looks like."

So Van Klomp took him to where he'd laid the little body. And, at Fitz's request, left him to his grief.

Robert Van Klomp walked back over to the ramp, and got back into organizing mode. Someone had to do it, although he noted that Ogata made an even better field officer than he did lawyer. Mike Capra came up to him. "Guess what I just carried out of that ship in an interesting state of undress?"

"What?"

"Major Tana Gainor. The stitcher, in person. She probably thought she could screw her way out of trouble with the Pricklepusses, but this time she got screwed. They've mindwiped her and put an implant into her head. We found her in solitary, in the ship. All the other slaves were in dormitories, but Tana Gainor was in well-sealed solitary. Maybe the Korozhet were brighter than we gave them credit for."

Van Klomp snorted. "Almost a pity that those command-phrases Liepsich said the Korozhet used don't work any more. That's a woman I'd have cheerfully used for cannon fodder."

He shook his head. "Now, I have a problem fit for your lawyerly talents. One of the sergeants has just pointed out that there are that herd of human-sheep out on Webb Fields in those Korozhet enclosures. He's been over and he says there are about fifty in one enclosure that might be dead. They're just lying about whereas there's a clamor coming from the bigger enclosures. Get yourself a squad and head over there. Check it out. Liberate them. And document the bastards. Take names. We know some people were cooperating with these Pricklepusses. I want to know who they were when this is all over."

Someone tapped Fitz tentatively on the shoulder, as he sat on the ground next to the small body resting on Van Klomp's bush jacket.

"Excuse me, Major," said the medic respectfully. "I don't want to bother you, but we've got a woman who has just come round in the aid-station. She seems a bit confused. She's insisting on seeing you. She . . . Ah, well, she threatened to bite us if we didn't get you immediately. It might just be something urgent, sir."

Wordlessly, Fitz covered the small body with his own jacket, and got up to follow the medic. Dawn was beginning to break over George Bernard Shaw City, and already the scene was assuming some kind of normality. Vehicles were coming and going. The aid station now seemed full of humans rather than aliens. Fitz recognized one of the women on a stretcher as General Cartup-Kreutzler's blond and buxom former secretary, Daisy. She stared upward with vacant eyes. He was damned sure she hadn't been part of the assault. "What happened here?" he asked the medic.

"Dunno, sir. They're from the compound on Webb Fields. There are forty-three of them. Physiologically there's nothing we can find wrong. But they're not really responding to stimulus, except in the most basic way."

"In Daisy's case," said Fitz sardonically, "that's just about situation normal. Still, even for her, this is extreme. What are you doing with them?"

"Just stabilizing them. Cleaning them, keeping them warm. They've no more sense than a newborn. Less, if anything. The woman who wanted you is in this ambulance."

Fitz ducked his head and looked in. "Fitzy!" said the woman lying there, sitting up and shedding the sheet that had covered her nudity.

"Major Gainor." Fitz's smile had no humor it in at all. "Talk about the original bad penny. Are you in *that* much of a hurry to resume prosecuting me? You worthless bitch."

She blinked at him. "Doth not love me any more?" she said tragically.

Fitz frowned. "What the hell are you talk—"

Suddenly, from nowhere, an old line of poetry came to him. From something by Keats, if he remembered right.

> *Or like stout Cortez when with eagle eyes*
> *He stared at the Pacific—and all his men*
> *Looked at each other with a wild surmise—*
> *Silent, upon a peak in Darien.*

His eyes flashed to Major Gainor's head. The hair had been shaved away from part of it. There was a small, fresh scar on the scalp.

And Ariel's head had been split open, to remove her soft-cyber implant.

" 'Twas not that I meant to persecute you," insisted the woman on the bed. "Well. Except for the chocolate. If you loved me, you would give me more dark chocolate Cointreau straws."

"Ariel?" he croaked.

The implant-scarred head nodded. " 'Tis an ugly tailless body, true. 'Twill take some getting used to, especially these dullard teeth. But 'tis now mine own, Fitz."

The aid center had seen a lot of strange sights since they'd set up shop at about two that morning.

Aliens of various sizes and shapes.

Bats full of laughing gas and Irish song.

A large rat weeping over his golf cart's scratched paintwork.

A pair of blue-furred creatures having a "who-can-jump-highest" competition while making ear-shattering hooting noises.

But they all agreed afterward that the sight of Major Conrad Fitzhugh swinging a naked woman around in his arms until they both fell down together too dizzy to stand, too happy to care, laughing and crying, was perhaps the oddest.

"Kinky, you ask me," muttered one of the medics. "She's the one who was prosecuting him, you know. The guy's a freaking masochist."

# Epilogue

Endings in books are neat. Endings in real life tend to be more ragged and indeterminate. Nonetheless, this was an ending of sorts. Gradually, within a few days, a semblance of order had been reestablished in GBS City. Van Klomp found he had to impose most of it. Still . . . he had the voice for it.

By the end of the week there was even power in several parts of the city.

Dr. Wei had a Korozhet prisoner to study; though, first, he had to get the Super-Glue off.

The remnant of the army high command that still had its mind was back in Military Headquarters, spending its time constructively trying to think up excuses for its former behavior—which the charitable were calling "utter incompetence" and a distressingly large number of people were calling "treason"—and thus not interfering with actual military affairs.

Virginia and Chip had stopped making love long enough to be abused by Liepsich for causing such damage in the Korozhets' former ship, which the scientist seemed to regard as his personal new toy. And conspire . . . well, argue with the bats.

A certain candy-striped vehicle had been resprayed and given the freedom of a grateful city. Within the week, every other motorist on the streets was deeply regretting that spontaneous gesture.

And . . .

Ogata took himself out to see Conrad Fitzhugh, whom no one had gotten around to returning to court or pre-trial confinement yet. Fitz and Ariel were staying—at Virginia Shaw's insistence—at Shaw House. The place was something of a menagerie these days. The doors were being repaired and replaced and one wing was becoming a bank.

Fortunately, the bats didn't mind flying in windows.

"And how is Ariel fitting into her new residence?" asked Ogata with a smile.

"She's making a lot of changes. Fortunately, she disapproves of mauve lipstick. Any kind of lipstick, in fact. She finds walking without even a vestige of a tail awkward. She made a bonfire out of all of Gainor's high-heeled shoes. And she complains at least once an hour about her useless teeth. Or do you mean where we're living?"

"It seems a good answer to both questions," said Ogata. "You do realize that, despite the Korozhet having put Ariel's soft-cyber chip into Tana's mindwiped brain so that they could question her, as far as the Army is concerned you are now cohabiting—I assume lewdly, yes?—"

Fitz grinned. The grin, on that scarred face, looked as serene and self-satisfied as a shark's. "She's still a rat, sir. In almost everything that matters, anyway. A rat's idea of slow seduction is waiting until she finishes her chocolates. And, as it happens, Ariel wasn't in a slow mood." He cleared his throat. "Neither was I."

Ogata rolled his eyes. "Yes, well. What I thought. So you are now living in sin with the person who is supposed to be prosecuting you. This is, to put it mildly, a conflict of interest. As far as the army is concerned, Ariel is still Major Tana Gainor, and she's AWOL."

"That's the least of your problems," said Fitz. "You're a lawyer, Colonel Ogata. Until it's changed—and even then it won't apply retroactively—the law on Harmony and Reason considers the woman's body that of Tana Moira Gainor. So long as the mind is sound, which this one sure as hell is, and never mind who it belongs to. Legally speaking, Mike Capra tells me, that last is a mystical and meaningless abstraction."

Ogata looked a little taken aback. "That would surely depend on the definition of 'sound.'"

"That might be true. But having acquired a perfectly usable but large and empty mind the person that is Ariel is expanding her Ratshipness into it all. She was a bright rat and Gainor was a smart woman. The combination has made Ariel intimidatingly intelligent. I pity anyone who tries to prove in court that there's anything 'unsound' about her mind. Trust me on this one."

"But her personality . . . uh, that is . . ." Ogata, unusually, seemed to be groping for words.

Fitz shrugged. "From what I can see, it's all Ariel. I admit, it's a bit hard to tell sometimes. Tana Gainor was a predatory person and, well, in a lot of ways that describes Ariel to a T. The rats *are* predators, technically speaking, since their personalities are based mainly on shrew genetic stock. On the other hand, Ariel's as loyal as they come, which God knows Gainor wasn't. She even told me she's willing—though I'd have to make it up to her with plenty of chocolates—to abandon sensible ratly promiscuity for this silly human 'faithful' business."

Fitz's grin seemed fixed in place. "Have you any idea of just how *rich* Tana Gainor was, Colonel Ogata? Ariel was down at the bank finding out, the day after she 'woke up.' Trust a rat to check her loot first. Ill-gotten gains, most of it, I don't doubt for a minute. But there's no proof of that, and—legally, legally—it all now belongs to Ariel."

Ogata's skin color made it difficult for him to turn pale. But he did a pretty fair imitation. "Oh, no," he groaned.

"Oh, yes," countered Fitz. "Have you any idea what the ex-2IC of the Ratafia is planning on doing with all that money? I did get her to swear that she'd wouldn't actually break any laws, although I'm sure she'll interpret that promise with a ratly twist. The bats might be altruistic with Virginia's fortune . . . but I promise my Ariel is not, with her own."

The taller of the two surviving conspirators sprinkled soil on the grave. "Now cracks a noble heart. Good night, sweet princess, and flights of angels sing thee to thy rest."

He dusted off his hands. "I shall miss her. I surely will."

The other conspirator, in a well-practiced gesture, hitched up his pants. "Now that she's not around to hear it . . . Well. So will I. A lot. She was the only one around who could really give me a good match, insult-wise."

General Needford gave Liepsich a level stare. "There are times when you remind me of a five-year-old. I admit, you're precocious."

The scientist smiled. "Not that you aren't so bad yourself. Courage, courage. We'll still need to work together, in the years ahead, even if our conspiracy is now over."

"True. Now that Sanjay's dead, her children will need godparents for a while. But only that, henceforth. We will manipulate them no longer."

"Don't think there's much need to, anyway."

The general shrugged. "Even if there were, I'd insist we forego it. We conspired because we needed to. The need now gone, we must be careful that the habit does not develop its own dynamic. Let Sanjay Devi's final gift to us be her favorite saying: 'All life is an imitation of the Scottish play.' Beware the danger of ambition."

Needford looked every inch the judge, now. Even Liepsich shied away.

"Hey, relax! The thought never crossed my mind. Besides . . ."

Liepsich's laugh was almost a cackle. "Manipulating *that* lot, now that they're out of their cages—much less controlling them—is something only a madman would choose for a hobby."

The quartermaster was practically livid.

"It's all very well getting the cooperation of the miserable creatures. 'Winning their hearts and minds,' all that blather. But what kind of military requisition is a million pairs of rat-sized blue suede shoes?!"

# Acknowledgements

I'd like to express my thanks to several people who helped me greatly during the writing of this book. With trepidation, I wandered into the arena of military law. Major Rich Grove, of the Judge Advocate General's Corps, United States Air Force, provided me with much advice, help and an amazing level of tolerance for stupid questions. Any errors in this area are of course mine and not his. I blame the bad lawyer jokes on him entirely, though. Judith Lasker helped not only with the proofing, but also with the legal side. Gunnar Dahlin did possibly the most meticulous job of proof-reading I've encountered. As I am the world's most inventive speller I'm very grateful. Rog and Cheryl Daetwyler were also most helpful in that regard. Jim Crider gave some much needed help with auto matters. And, as always, my deepest thanks to my coauthor Eric and my wife Barbara. Between the two of them they steer the supercharged golf cart of my writing along.

—Dave Freer

*The following is an excerpt from:*

# ALPHA

## by

## Catherine Asaro

available from Baen Books
September 2006
hardcover

# I

# A Guest in Virginia

Lieutenant General Thomas Wharington had weathered his share of challenges, but nothing like Alpha. She was an android in Air Force custody, female in appearance, apparent age thirty, though no one knew how far her artificial brain had developed. As human as she appeared, she was a machine—a deadly biomechanical construct.

Thomas directed the Office of Computer Operations, a deliberately vague term for the Machine Intelligence Division of the National Information Agency. Founded twenty years ago, in 2012, the NIA concerned itself with the world mesh, formerly known as the Internet. He also headed the Senate Select Committee for Space Research, which those with the proper clearances knew as the Committee for Space Warfare Research and Development. In his youth, he had been a fighter pilot. He had flown an

F-16 jet, later the F-22 Raptor, and now he was spearheading the development of the F-42 for the Air Force. Over the course of his career, he had received the Congressional Medal of Honor, the Distinguished Flying Cross with silver oak leaf cluster, and a Purple Heart. Physically fit and benefiting from medical advances, he looked more than two decades younger than his age of seventy-two.

Alpha was Thomas's primary tie to Charon, the megalomaniacal fanatic who had created her. Before his death, Charon had controlled a shadowy criminal empire. The Pentagon knew he had intended to build an army for rent to the highest bidder—but an army of *what*? Constructs, like Alpha? Something else? Had he set in motion some master plan before his death? No one knew. They had too few details, and Thomas feared they were running out of time.

The secrets remained locked within Alpha.

"I can't do it," Thomas repeated.

"You'll be fine." His daughter handed him a bulging shoulder bag decorated with puppies.

Thomas wasn't the type to quail in a desperate situation, but this morning he was in over his head. They were standing in the entrance foyer of the house that belonged to his daughter, Leila Wharington Harrows, and her husband, Karl. Looking sharp in a gold silk suit, with her blond hair swept up into a roll, Leila normally presented a cool face to the world. Right now, though, her hair was escaping its roll and curling in disarray around her face.

"So where is that husband of yours when you need help?" Thomas asked.

"Dad, don't get mad. Karl is coming home early from his conference." Leila pushed the bag back into his hand. "I'm really sorry. I had a nanny, but she got sick. And I couldn't get out of the trip. The partners say I'm not pulling my weight at the firm." Anger edged her voice. "If we didn't need the money, I'd quit this damn job."

Thomas liked less and less what he had heard about the law firm where she worked. "Leila, if you need money—"

She cut him off before he could offer. "We can manage."

He understood she wanted to do it on her own. But he wished he could ease the strain of her life. He wondered what it said about him, that he felt more comfortable offering money than looking after his granddaughter for a few days.

"Well." He spoke awkwardly. "I guess I can manage."

"You're a gem." Leila smiled, perhaps too brightly, but with warmth. "Jamie would rather stay with her Grandpa anyway. She loves spending time with you."

"The feeling is mutual. I just don't know how I can take care of a three-year-old for a week." He could probably find babysitters while he worked, but what would he do with her when he was home? Three-year-old girls were a mystery to him, even after having been the father of one. That had been thirty years ago, during his days as a pilot, and he had been more comfortable in the cockpit of an F-16 than a nursery.

A door upstairs creaked, and footsteps padded on the stairs. As Thomas looked up, a small girl with large blue eyes and gold curls came into view. She held a big stuffed kitten in her arms.

Thomas smiled. "Hello, Jamie."

His granddaughter's angelic face brightened. She ran down the steps and trotted over to him, holding up her toy. "See my kitty, Grampy? Her name is Soupy."

Thomas felt his face doing that thing again, turning soft. He awkwardly patted her toy. "She's a fine kitty."

Jamie dimpled at him, and he felt as if he was turning into putty. She looked so much like Leila at that age. He sighed and picked her up, kitten and all.

To Leila, he said, "I'll do my best."

The NIA was in Maryland. Even more shadowy than its precursors in the intelligence community, the agency was on almost equal footing with the CIA in the National Security Council. Thomas could have fit two of his previous offices in his present one and had room to spare. Currently, a screen installed on his desk was displaying a report from the Links Division, which analyzed mesh traffic for patterns that might warrant investigation. It seemed an arcane discipline to Thomas, half analysis and half intuition, but Links had a good record of success in tracking criminal activities through the mesh.

Basically, the report advised the NIA to monitor the site for a hardware store. They suspected it sold industrial espionage as well as widgets, specifically, that it employed agents from Charon's black market operations. Their purpose: to spy on an institute whose maintenance department ordered from the store. The Department of Defense had contracts with the institute in the development of artificial intelligence, or AI, one of Charon's specialties.

A buzz came from the comm on Thomas's desk. He tapped its *receive* panel. "Wharington here."

A man's voice came out of the comm. "General, this is Major Edwards. I'm on my way to the base. Would you like to grab a pizza for lunch? It might soften our guest's mood."

"Very well, Major. I'll meet you out front." Thomas knew what "guest" Edwards meant: Alpha, their captive android. For reasons that weren't clear, she would talk only to Thomas, when she talked at all. Questioning an android was an exercise in frustration; she didn't react to known techniques. Yet to Thomas, she seemed human. He couldn't make himself authorize the mech-techs to take her apart and analyze the filaments that constituted her brain. Eventually they might have to resort to such measures, but for now they were trying less drastic forms of interrogation.

He left notes for his appointments with his second in command, Brigadier General Carl Jackson Matheson, or C.J. Thomas could speak with Senator Bartley tomorrow morning and reschedule today's staff meeting for tomorrow afternoon. His housekeeper, Lattie, had agreed to look after Jamie until he came home. He would miss his appointment at the barber, though. He supposed he should be glad he still had a full head of hair. Its grey color seemed to delight Jamie. She surprised him. He had expected to fumble for words around her, but this morning he had greatly enjoyed their breakfast conversation.

Thomas shut down and locked his console and picked up his briefcase. Then he headed out for "lunch." He wished they really were going for pizza. Perhaps they could pick one up on the way, a large pepperoni dripping with cheese and grease. Unfortunately, he would spend the entire meal feeling guilty and recalling his doctor's admonitions on the dangers of his former eating habits. Yes, it could shorten his life if he ate what he wanted, but at least he would die a contented, well-fed man. He had no wish to have another heart attack, and his cholesterol levels were finally normal, but damned if his reformed eating habits weren't a bore.

"Out front," where he was meeting Edwards, was a euphemism for an underground lot with NIA hover cars and trucks. Had Edwards contacted him from within the NIA, he would probably have been more forthcoming about their plans, a visit to the safe house where the Air Force was holding Alpha. But he had called from his car as he drove through suburban Maryland, an area riddled with mech-tech types who loved to ride the wireless waves and explore any signals they could untangle. NIA signals were encrypted, but with all the mesh bandits out there nowadays, no security was certain.

Thomas took an elevator that operated only with a secured code. It listed no floors; the only clues it was doing anything were the hum of the cable and a few flashes of light on its panel. The lights stilled as the hum faded into silence. The silver doors snapped open and Thomas walked into a cavernous garage. Cars and trucks were parked in separate sections, and pillars stood at intervals, supporting a high ceiling. The columns glimmered with holo-displays of innocuous meadows and mountains.

He went to the nearest column and ran his finger across a bar at waist height. The meadow disappeared, replaced by a wash of blue, and a light played across his face, analyzing his retinal patterns. A message appeared on the screen: *Proceed to station four.* At the same time, the display on a distant pillar changed to blue, specifying "station four." He walked over to the new column and waited. The garage was silent, with a tang of motor oil.

An engine growled, and he turned to see a hover car floating down a lane delineated by holo-pillars. The car had a generic look, except for its dark gold color, a bit flashy for the military, but appropriate for a general. Its unexceptional appearance served as camouflage; it was actually a Hover-Shadow 16, the latest model in a line of armored vehicles with "a few extras," including machine guns and an AI brain. The digital paint used on its exterior could mimic any design programmed into the car, and its shape drew on technology used for stealth fighters. Thomas appreciated the Hover-Shadows; riding in one reminded him of his days as a pilot.

The car stopped a few yards away and settled onto the concrete, remarkably quiet given its turbo fans and powerful engines. Robert Edwards got out from the driver's side. A man of medium height with light brown hair, he would blend into any crowd, except for his Air Force uniform. Just to look at him, most people wouldn't guess he had played offensive tackle at the University of Missouri or that he had defied his jock image by majoring in physics. Thomas enjoyed conversing with Edwards, who could go with ease from predicting which teams would make the Super Bowl to discussing galactic formation. He was a steady officer, one of Thomas's handpicked aides.

"Good to see you, Bob," Thomas said.

"Thank you, sir." Edwards opened the back door.

Thomas slid into the car and swung his briefcase onto the seat. Edwards was also trained in escape and evasion, but Thomas didn't expect trouble. Charon had died several weeks ago. However, Thomas's boss, General Chang, continued to take precautions. The "safe house" where they had Alpha was in fact a fully secured installation.

As the car hummed out of the garage, Edwards said, "Would you care for music? I have that Debussy recording you like."

"Thanks, but no. I have to work." Thomas spoke absently as he took a foot-long pencil tube out of his briefcase, then set the case on his lap in a makeshift table. He slid a glimmering roll out of the tube, his laptop film. Then he unrolled the film on his briefcase and went to work.

His files held a wealth of detail. Biomechanical research had diverged into two paths: robots developed for specific purposes, with designs that optimized their performance; and androids intended to follow human appearance and behavior. Collectively, robots and androids were called *formas.* Thomas knew the AI side of the field best; he had majored in computer science at the Air Force Academy and earned a doctorate in AI from MIT. He read widely, especially the work of Kurzweil, McCarthy, Minsky, and more recently, Dalrymple. Groups such as theirs deserved the fame. It aggravated him that a criminal like Charon had achieved more success. Then again, "success" was relative. Charon's work had drawn the attention of the NIA because he had trespassed against the nation's interest, not to mention the bounds of human decency.

Thomas scanned the history of Charon, a man who had begun life as Willy Brand. By the time he was seven, Willy was living on the streets. He might have died there if not for one person: Linden Polk. A scholar and a teacher, Polk was known for his innovations with android skeletons. He was also known for his dedication to outreach for disturbed youth, which was how he met Willy. Wild and unrepentantly criminal, the eight-year-old boy had a life no one doubted would land him in prison. But Polk recognized a rare genius within him. With mentoring, Willy straightened out, went to school, and eventually earned a doctorate in biomechanical engineering, after which he joined Polk's research group.

Willy had always been odd, and he never truly respected the law, but he stayed out of trouble. Then Polk died—and Willy lost his lifeline. His already troubled mind crumbled. In a heartbreaking act of denial, he imaged Polk's brain, built an android, and copied Polk's neural patterns into its matrix. But the project failed. He couldn't bring back his father figure, the one person he had ever loved—and his grief pushed him over the edge into insanity.

Willy reinvented himself as Charon, an enigmatic mogul who set up corporations to develop his bizarre but lucrative ideas. He stayed in the background of his businesses and eventually hid his involvement altogether. He became the wealthiest nonexistent person alive.

Charon wasn't the first fanatic who craved an inhuman army that would obey his commands without question. Unlike his predecessors, however, he had both the financial resources and the intellect to make his obsession into reality. Twisted by loneliness, he also created Alpha: an immortal mercenary with no free will; an AI dedicated to optimizing his financial empire; and a forma sex goddess. Obedience, wealth, and sex: she gave him everything he craved.

Charon also copied himself. His body was dying from a lifetime of misuse, so he became an android. Nor was he satisfied with one version of himself. He committed the ultimate identity theft. When a man named Turner Pascal died in a car accident, Charon imaged Pascal's neural patterns, rebuilt the body with a filament brain, gave it Pascal's patterns—and then downloaded a copy of his own mind into Pascal. It was the perfect disguise; he stole Pascal's face, mind, personality, and body. He considered Pascal inferior and never doubted he could control the mind of his rebuilt man, a hotel bellboy who had barely finished high school.

That arrogance had been Charon's downfall.

Pascal wrested back control of his mind and escaped from Charon. He sought help from Samantha "Sam" Bryton, one of the world's leading AI architects. Sam. She was like a daughter to Thomas. Charon sent Alpha after them, Alpha grabbed Sam and Thomas instead of Sam and Turner, the Air Force sent in operatives—and by the time it was over, Charon was dead.

Thomas gazed out the window. Vehicles moved smoothly through Washington, D.C., which only a few decades ago had earned the dubious honor of being named the city with the worst traffic in the country. Now traffic grids controlled the flow and minimized congestion. Nearly half the vehicles were hover cars, and little trace remained of the smog Thomas remembered from his youth. In the south, across the Potomac, the silver spindles of a new federal center pierced the sky, tall and thin, sparkling in the chill sunlight. Thomas had never realized how much he liked living here until he had come so close to dying as Charon's hostage.

Major Edwards soon crossed the river and entered Virginia. As they reached more rural areas, the traffic petered out. Large houses set back from the road were surrounded by lawns or tangled woods. The landscape gradually buckled into the Appalachian Mountains, with forests of pine, hemlock, wild cherry, poplar, and white oak. In a secluded valley, Edwards stopped at a guard booth on the road. The badges he and Thomas wore sent signals to a console within the booth. In the past, the guard would have leaned out to touch their badges; nowadays they never rolled down the windows. It added an additional layer of protection, but it meant security also required extra identification, from the passengers and from the car. Beetle-bots hummed in the air, ready to accompany them and monitor their progress.

The guard motioned them through, and an invisible barrier hummed as they crossed the perimeter. About half a mile farther along, they came to the safe house amid well-tended lawns and groves of trees. The "house" resembled a hospital, but its old•fashioned architecture also evoked a cathedral. The grounds sloped through scattered pines and trees with yellow, green, and red leaves. Paths bordered by azalea bushes curved around sculptures that swooped in arcs of bronzed metal.

Edwards pulled into a carport shaded by trellises with leafless vines. As he and Thomas walked to the front door, a chill wind blew across them, presaging the winter. The genteel feel of the place made it seem as if they were visiting friends rather than a prisoner who was potentially one of humanity's most dangerous creations.

Two "orderlies" were waiting inside, burly men who had more martial arts than medical training. Each wore a staser on his belt, a stun gun that could knock out a large adult. They accompanied Thomas and Edwards down wide halls with gold carpets and artwork on the walls, and through several security gates. Finally they reached a normal door, except Thomas knew its attractive wood paneling hid a steel portal half a foot thick.

The room beyond was pleasant, with a sofa and armchairs in pale green. Paintings of pastoral scenes graced the ivory walls, and a blue quilt covered the bed. The room had no windows, but plenty of light came from an overhead fixture and lamps with stained glass shades in the corners.

A woman was waiting for them.

She stood across the room with her back to the wall, watching Thomas with the feral wariness of a trapped animal. Six feet tall, with another two inches from her heels, she matched his height. Her black leather pants fit her snugly, and her red blouse did nothing to disguise her well-proportioned figure or the definition of her muscles. Black hair was tousled around her shoulders, and her dark eyes slanted upward. She exuded a sense of coiled energy, as if she might explode any moment. The biomech surgeons claimed her android body had three or four times the strength and speed of a human being. Her internal microfusion reactor supplied energy. It disturbed Thomas for many reasons, not only because Charon's technology surpassed the military's work, but also because she looked so *human*.

So female.

"Good afternoon, Ms. Alpha," Thomas said.

She spoke in a dusky voice. "I am not 'Ms.' anything."

He went farther into the room, but he halted a few

yards away from her, so she wouldn't feel pressured. Edwards and the orderlies stayed. Even knowing Alpha was a weapon, Thomas felt strange that his CO assigned him three guards as protection against one attractive young woman. Her first day here, Alpha had tried to fight her way out. She hadn't come close to succeeding, but she had injured several orderlies.

"I'm not going to talk to your flunkies," Alpha said.

"Then talk to me," Thomas said.

She regarded him impassively. This was the second time he had met with her at the safe house. The first time she had interacted with him more than with anyone else, though she still hadn't said much. He was curious as to why he succeeded even a small amount where others failed. It also disconcerted him, for he had no idea what conclusions she was making about him.

Thomas indicated the sofa. "Would you like to sit?"

"No." She narrowed her gaze. "So you're the boss."

She made it a statement rather than a question. It wasn't completely true; he was director of one of the two divisions that comprised the NIA, but that didn't put him in charge of this safe house. General Chang, the Deputy Director of Defense Intelligence, had assigned that duty elsewhere. But Alpha was programmed to respond to authority, and Thomas *was* overseeing the work with her. If that convinced her to respond, he would use it to full advantage.

He said only, "That's right."

"Where is Charon?"

"Dead." Thomas wanted to offer sympathy. He quashed the urge, knowing it was inappropriate here. He also wasn't certain how a machine would response to compassion. Yet still he felt it.

"He's not dead," Alpha said.

"You saw him die."

She crossed her arms, which could have looked defensive but instead suggested a vulnerability he doubted she had intended. "The android called Turner Pascal carries Charon's mind within his matrix."

"Pascal says he isn't an android."

Alpha waved her hand. "The human Pascal died."

Thomas suspected it would take the Supreme Court to figure out the tangled definitions of humanity posed by Pascal. "Either way, he isn't Charon."

"Charon downloaded his brain into Pascal."

"Pascal deleted it."

She snorted. "If Pascal is human, how would he 'delete' another mind within his own?"

She had a point. "Regardless. He isn't Charon."

"How do you know?"

"Doctor Bryton verified it."

Alpha cocked an eyebrow in a perfect imitation of skepticism. "Samantha Bryton? She would believe anything Pascal told her."

"Why?" he asked, intrigued.

"Love has no judgment." Alpha laughed without humor. "She's infatuated with a forma."

Pascal's relationship with Sam bothered Thomas a great deal, but it wasn't something he would discuss with Alpha. Regardless, he would never have defined Sam's cautious, cynical view of romance as infatuation.

"Pascal thinks he is human," Thomas said.

"He's more than half biomech."

"He isn't the first person to receive biomech prosthetics."

She uncrossed her arms and put one hand on her hip.

"Like his *brain?* He's a frigging AI, Wharington."

He almost smiled. Had Charon programmed her to cuss? It didn't serve any functional purpose. Thomas wanted her to have developed it on her own, for that would mean she could evolve independently of Charon's designs.

"Why does Pascal bother you?" he asked.

Her fist clenched on her hip. "He doesn't conform to specifications."

"You mean he has free will."

"That is an irrelevant comment."

"Why? Because Charon denied you that freedom?"

At the mention of Charon, her face lost all sign of emotion. It chilled him. He was aware of his guards watching, but he refrained from glancing at them or doing anything that might dissuade her from talking. After about a minute or so, though, he gave up trying to wait her out. Silence often provoked humans to speak, but apparently she could stay in whatever state she wanted, for as long as she wanted, with no visible effort or unease.

Thomas broke the standoff by sitting in an armchair across from the sofa, facing her. He settled back, stretched his legs under the coffee table, and considered Alpha.

"If Charon is gone," he asked, "who is your boss?"

She continued to stand with her back to the wall. He tried to see some chink in her expression, some flaw in her too-perfect skin, some indication she felt stress, tension, unease, anger, anything. He found none.

When she didn't respond, he tried another approach. "Alpha, do you want free will?"

"What?" She looked as if he had put an indecipherable command into her system.

"Do you wish to make your own decisions?"

"No."

He had expected her to say yes, *wanted* her to say yes. But he was reacting as he would to a person, and she was a machine designed to lack free will. She was trapped within her programming as thoroughly as she was imprisoned at this safe house, and it bothered him far more than it should.

"If you don't make decisions yourself," he said, "who will?"

"Charon," she said.

"Charon is dead."

Silence.

"If I'm the boss," Thomas said, "you should answer to me."

"You aren't my boss."

"Then who is?"

"Charon."

He felt as if he were caught in a programming loop that kept going around and around the same section of code. "Charon is dead."

She hesitated just a moment, but for an AI it was a long time. Then she said, "You may be a compelling specimen, General, but I wasn't made for you."

Well, hell. Apparently androids could be just as blunt as young people these days when it came to their private lives. He cleared his throat. "I didn't have that in mind." He almost said he had come to debrief her, then decided that wasn't the best choice of words. So instead he added, "I need you to answer some questions."

Her expression turned stony. The effect was almost convincing, but after her total lack of affect a moment before, he didn't believe it. Unexpectedly, though, she didn't refuse to speak.

"What questions?" she asked.

"Charon has a base in Tibet."

She gave him a decidedly unimpressed look. "No. One of his corporations has a research facility in Tibet."

Thomas met her skeptical look with one of his own. "Hidden at the top of the Himalayas? I don't think so."

She stepped toward him. "Charon is a genius. Of course people struggle to understand him. They lack his intelligence."

"Did he program you to say that about him?"

"Yes."

That figured. Charon had been some piece of work. "He had great gifts," Thomas acknowledged. "But his sickness constrained him."

She folded her arms as if she were protecting herself. "People always call the brilliant minds unbalanced."

Thomas wondered if she had heard all this from Charon. Her ideas sounded oddly dated. "Alpha, that's a myth. Geniuses are no more likely to be mentally disturbed than anyone else. Charon was a sociopath and he had paranoid schizophrenia. It probably limited his work by making it harder for him to plan or to judge the feasibility of his projects."

Her lips curved in a deadly smile. "He created me. If that isn't genius, nothing is."

When she looked like that, wild and fierce, her dark hair disarrayed, her eyes burning and untamed, he was tempted to agree. He suppressed the thought, thrown off balance. He had to remember she was a machine.

"Did he program you to say that, too?" Thomas asked.

"No."

He smiled slightly. "What makes you a work of genius?"

Her voice turned husky. "Maybe someday I'll let you find out."

He thought of pretending she had no effect on him, but he didn't try. She could interpret emotional cues, gestures, even changes in posture. It was a tool AIs used in learning to simulate emotions. Unfortunately, it also made them adept at reading people, better even than many humans. If he put on a front, she might figure out he wanted to hide and use that knowledge in their battle of words.

Right now, they were battling with silence. He tried to read her expressions. Sometimes she simulated emotions well, but other times, she either couldn't or wouldn't. To be considered sentient, she would have to pass modern forms of the Turing test, which included the portrayal of emotions. Over the years, the tests had become increasingly demanding, but they all boiled down to one idea: if a person communicated with a hidden machine and a hidden human—and couldn't tell them apart—the machine had intelligence.

Decades ago, people had expected that if a computer bested a human chess master, the machine would qualify as intelligent. Yet when the computer Deep Blue beat Gary Kasparov, the world champion, few people considered it truly intelligent; it simply had, for the time, good enough computational ability. Nowadays mesh systems routinely trounced champions, to the point where human masters were seeking neural implants to provide extra computational power for their own brains. Thomas couldn't imagine what that would do to the game at a competitive level. What defined machine intelligence then?

Older Turing tests had relied on sentences typed at

terminals, with the typists hidden. The most modern test, the visual Turing, required an android to be indistinguishable from a person. Some experts believed human brains were wired to process more emotional input than an EI matrix could handle. They considered the visual test impossible to pass. Although Thomas didn't agree, it didn't surprise him that only a handful of machine intelligences existed. Alpha passed the visual Turing only if her interactions involved tangible subjects. When pushed to more complex questions of emotion, philosophy, or conscience, she shut down.

While Thomas was thinking, Alpha studied him. After a while, she stalked over, sleek and deadly in her black leather. The orderlies stepped closer, but he waved them off, keeping his gaze on Alpha. She halted by the couch, on the other side of the coffee table, as tense as a wildcat ready to attack.

"You can't control me," she said. Her voice made him think of aged whiskey.

"But you have no free will," Thomas said. "And Charon is dead."

"I have orders."

It was the first time she had revealed she might be operating according to a preset plan. "From Charon?"

"That's right." She had gone deadpan again. Every time Charon came up, she ceased showing emotion. Why? In a person, he might have suspected some sort of trauma associated with Charon, but with Alpha he couldn't say. Although she presented an invulnerable front, something about her made him question that impression. It wasn't anything he could pin down, just a gut-level instinct on his part.

"What orders did he give?" Thomas asked.

"Return to him." She sat on the couch, poised on the edge like a wild animal ready to bolt. "If I can't, then protect myself."

"How? And against what?"

"Do you really think I would tell you?"

"With you, I never know," Thomas admitted. She had already said more to him today than she had to everyone else combined.

Unexpectedly, she said, "I like it that way."

"*Can* you like something?" His scientific curiosity jumped in. "Most people think an AI doesn't truly feel emotion."

"Here's an emotion for you." Alpha looked around at the guards and her room. "I don't like being cooped up here."

"Where would you like to be?" Maybe she would bargain.

"Outside."

"Why? Aren't you just simulating unease?"

She smiled with an edge. "You think you're clever, implying my request is illogical. You humans love stories about people outwitting machines by virtue of your purportedly greater creativity, blah, blah, blah. But you see, we read all your books. You couldn't come close to mastering the breadth of human knowledge if you worked on it your entire life, but it takes me only weeks to absorb, process, and analyze the contents of an entire library. I know all the scenarios and supposed solutions humankind has come up with in your ongoing paranoia about the intelligences you've created. You try to outthink us, but ultimately you fail."

Thomas leaned forward. "Yet you miss the most obvious flaw of your analysis."

She raised an eyebrow. "Do tell."

"We are becoming you." He watched her closely. "Do you really believe humanity would settle for being second-class citizens to our own creations? We will incorporate your advantages within ourselves while retaining that which makes us human."

She waved her hand in dismissal. "It's all semantics. Whether you choose to call yourselves formas or human won't alter the facts. Biomech changes you, whether you put it in a robot or your own brain." Her eyes glinted. "Who knows, perhaps it will overwrite what 'makes you human.' Corrupt your oh-so-corruptible selves."

Thomas gave a rueful grimace. "Maybe it will."

She seemed satisfied with his response. "You want to bargain with me. Fine. Take me for a ride outside and I'll tell you what orders Charon left me."

"You know I can't do that. You might escape."

"True. Do it anyway."

Thomas had to give her points for audacity. "Why?"

Her expression went completely flat. "Because you want to know what Charon ordered me to do."

Thomas wondered if she knew the unsettling effect it had on him when she turned off her emotional responses. At times he thought she used her human qualities as a weapon, banking on his difficulty in separating her sexualized appearance from her biomech nature. Yet if she had realized how she affected him, why suppress it? She "lost" her emotions when she spoke about Charon.

"No matter what orders he gave you," Thomas said, "I won't take you out of here."

"Your loss."

He smiled dryly. "Actually, it would be that if you escaped."

To his surprise, she laughed, a low, sensual rumble. "And what a loss that would be. For you."

Good Lord. A laugh like that could make a man lose all sense of reason. "You don't lack for self-confidence." After a pause, he added, "Or at least the simulation of it." He kept forgetting that.

Her smile vanished. "Make no mistake, General. More is at stake than my freedom."

"Such as?"

She met his gaze. "Human ascendancy on this planet."

—end excerpt—

from *Alpha*
available in hardcover,
September 2006, from Baen Books

# 1634: The Galileo Affair
by Eric Flint & Andrew Dennis
0-7434-9919-0 ◆ $7.99
*New York Times* bestseller!

# 1634: The Ram Rebellion
by Eric Flint with Virginia DeMarce
1-4165-2060-0 ◆ $25.00

# Ring of Fire edited by Eric Flint
1-4165-0908-9 ◆ $7.99
Top writers tell tales of Grantville, the town lost in time, including David Weber, Mercedes Lackey, Jane Lindskold, Eric Flint and more.

# Grantville Gazette edited by Eric Flint
1-7434-8860-1 ◆ $6.99

# Grantville Gazette II edited by Eric Flint
1-4165-2051-1 ◆ $25.00
More stories by Eric Flint and others in this best-selling alternate history series.

◆◆◆◆◆◆◆◆◆◆◆◆◆◆◆◆◆◆◆◆◆◆◆◆◆

# THE SF OF ERIC FLINT

## MOTHER OF DEMONS
Humans stranded on an alien world precipitate a revolution.
Also available at the Baen Free Library, www.baen.com.

pb ◆ 0-671-87800-X ◆ $5.99

## BOUNDARY with Ryk E. Spoor
A "funny" fossil is found in the American desert, and solving
the mystery of its origins takes paleontologist Helen Sutter all
the way to Mars. . . .

hc ◆1-4165-0932-1 ◆ $26.00

## THE COURSE OF EMPIRE
### with K.D. Wentworth
Conquered by the Jao twenty years ago, Earth is shackled
under alien tyranny—and threatened by the even more dangerous Ekhat. The humans will fight to the death, but the
battle to free the Earth may destroy it instead!

hc ◆ 0-7434-7154-7 ◆ $22.00
pb ◆ 0-7434-9893-3 ◆ $7.99

## CROWN OF SLAVES with David Weber
A novel set in the *NY Times* best-selling Honor Harrington
universe. Sent on a mission to keep Erewhon from breaking with Manticore, the Star Kingdom's most able agent
and the Queen's niece may not even be able to escape
with their lives. . . .

pb ◆ 0-7434-9899-2 ◆ $7.99